DRAWING
THE
DRAGON

BY APRIL ADAMS

This book is a work of fiction. Names, places, characters and incidents are products of the author's imagination or are used fictitiously. Any resemblance to actual events or locales or persons living or dead is entirely coincidental.

ISBN 978-0-98440033-1-7

This paperback edition January 2013

Designed by Lucia Lento - Drop Dead Design.com
Manufactured in the United States of America

For Jim, who finally understood.
And for Grandpa, who always knew.

ONE

Calyph closed his almond shaped eyes and wondered briefly if all was right with the universe. The thought was fleeting, more like a phantom whisper; such as, *did I eat lunch yesterday?*

His blue eyes opened slowly as he drew in a deep breath and tilted a pointed ear towards one shoulder and then repeated the gesture on the other side, stretching his neck. If actually asked about the state of the universe the elf was sure he could come up with something witty, if not profound. But he was tired as hell and, since no one was asking, he didn't give two shits about the universe.

He rolled his shoulders back, feeling the smooth weave of cloth rub against his skin. After a season of wearing heavy linen, the silky sensation was almost erotic. He had shed his field pack as soon as he came aboard the ship, glad to be relieved of its weight. It felt like he had been wearing it for years, though it could not have been more than a few weeks. But now that he was without it, he felt a bit naked.

He had bought new clothes for his journey with what little money he had. The new belted tunic hung over new pants that were tucked into the tops of his old leather boots. The clothes were comfortable country wear, but now he wished that he had waited. He would prefer to look a little more like the crew he had joined.

The elf's ears poked up out of sandy blond hair that seemed to grow a shade darker every year and his blue eyes held a sharp awkwardness from an adolescence long gone. An innate social discomfort had kept him somewhat isolated for most of his adult years in a vacuum of his own making. Only his surety in his skill kept him from an all-out social phobia.

He was physically exhausted and didn't especially want to be aboard a ship and far from home. He preferred having his feet on solid ground but he was needed and not many elves, or humans for that matter, had his capabilities.

The ship had an odd smell, like wet silver. He knew that in a few hours his sense of smell would become acclimated, and he wouldn't notice it at all. But for now, here it was, hanging in the air and distracting Calyph from the maps he was trying to study. His exhaustion along with the fact that he was less than thrilled to be aboard made him feel pouty, and the fact that a little discomfort could make a grown elf feel pouty, made him feel petty to boot.

"You are distracted because you don't want to be here," the troll by his side rasped without turning its head to look at him. The troll was massive – though more in density than actual size. It was sexless, but Calyph always thought of it as male, possibly due to the gravelly voice. He was heavy and bulky with thick limbs and cumbersome head but was not quite as tall as the elf, which was unusual for a troll. But Calyph was a very tall elf and the troll was very old.

"I most certainly am not," Calyph denied, turning his attention back to the maps before him. He scowled at the expanse in an attempt to prove the troll wrong, as if he could. The troll knew too much. Some people said it knew everything but Calyph knew better. The troll knew a lot, but it certainly didn't know everything. Calyph had been with him long enough to know that it had a hard time trying to fathom human emotion.

The troll was mostly a historian, but it could just as easily divulge anything current. It knew the history of the races, *all the races,* and was willing and able to offer them up in any form or fashion. One only had to ask.

Of course the answers always depended on the questions. For it was not just *what* one asked that determined the answer one would get, but also *how* one asked. The troll was naturally ambivalent about the questions as well as the answers. For him, it was about being correct.

"You are looking at the wall more than you are looking at the maps," the troll stated.

"I am not!" Calyph argued, forcing himself to fix his eyes on the maps while at the same time he felt his mind wander away like a wayward sheep.

The elf listened to the sound of people moving though the silver wet smell of the ship and ran a hand through his hair. He was familiar with many of them but not really comfortable with any of them.

Ready to give up and go get something to eat, the elf opened his mouth to speak when he felt the deck of the ship shift ever so slightly under his boots and his mouth closed with a snap. It wasn't a rock or a shake, not even a tremor, just a slight edging to the side, as if the ship had been gently nudged. It was barely enough for him to detect. But he did. He looked at the troll.

"Did you feel that?" Calyph asked.

The troll turned his massive head to look at the elf, his face impassive, but said nothing. Of course he felt it. He turned his attention back to the maps they had been studying.

"What do you think that was?" Calyph asked.

The troll tipped his head to indicate he was listening but did not turn back.

"The only thing that would move a ship this big," the elf persisted, "is a storm. Or another ship."

The troll's head swiveled around to look at him again, his face as expressionless as it was before, as it had always been. Calyph chewed at his bottom lip. He turned his own head away from the troll, his pointed ears trying to siphon off sounds.

Mostly they were just the usual sounds of a ship, sleepy creaks and groans that were barely detectable, even to his ears. He could hear footsteps in the corridor and voices of the crew, some in the corridor, some close by and others far away and faint. He closed his eyes and he could detect, even fainter, the breath of the sleeping Dragon. His eyes flicked open, blue and curious.

"Is the Dragon expecting any Fledglings?" he asked.

The troll made a low sound, a manufactured combination of a growl and a murmur, a sign that he was considering the question. "It is expecting three," he said after a brief pause, his voice rumbling and clicking. "But not for some time." He turned his large head back to the maps.

The elf blew air out through his teeth in exasperation. He paused for a second, just long enough to make up his mind. He wasn't going to wait for the troll and certainly not argue with him. Any fool knew that arguing with a troll was pointless. He turned and strode from the hold where they had been scanning maps.

The Captain of the ship had changed their course to avoid a threatening storm and Calyph was worried they might get caught on the edge of it anyway. The ship was easily capable to outrun the storm but the Captain had wanted to keep them as close as possible to their original course.

The excited activity in the passageway told him it was most likely the other possibility he had considered – another ship. Calyph considered returning to his cabin to retrieve his field pack then decided against it. He wouldn't need it as long as he was aboard the ship. He hoped.

He poked his head out into a corridor that was quite wide, much wider than a normal ship, and full of crew all hurrying in the same direction. Calyph followed a young, brown-haired human down the passageway and noticed that the troll had decided to follow. The elf ran up the stairway to the next deck without looking back.

He could tell from the hustle and bustle that it wasn't just another ship – it was a Fledgling. He could hear the Dragon sigh as the Fledgling breached, or maybe he just imagined it.

One thing the elf knew for sure was that if that Dragon was not expecting a Fledgling, and one had come early and unexpected, only one person could be responsible - Jordan Blue.

Calyph emerged mid-ship and felt the first whispers of cold air prickle his skin. He turned from the corridor into a wide-open jet fighter bay; the one reserved for the Fledglings, and felt the cold shock him, stealing his breath. The bottomless cold of deep space.

Mid-ship starboard encased the Fledgling Bay of Dragon 787, more commonly called the Opal Dragon. Calyph looked out the gaping maw of the bay door and into the black velvet of the galaxy, pricked with the bright multitude of stars. The cold gnawed at him. Daintily at first, as if just trying to get a taste of him, and then sinking its teeth deep into his flesh with great, hungry bites.

The Dragon was normally quite warm – even when the bay doors were open and everything held snug by a membrane thin field. But when a ship came through that field, it brought with it a wake of bitter cold that would take hours to dispel.

Deep space was an ominous presence, huge and cruel and constant. For Calyph, staring out into the frozen emptiness was like looking into the eye of a God that had long been dead. But even the vast emptiness was little compared to the cold that sucked the soul and body dry. Calyph knew it had killed more pilots than plasma fire.

Maybe the cold isn't a physical thing at all, the elf thought. He stared out into the black, mesmerized by the unfamiliar starscape. *Maybe just seeing that infinite void sucks the heat from our hearts.*

Calyph gave his head a quick shake and focused on the happenings in the bay. The crewmembers that were needed had hurried to the gate in the detfleck, while others milled about in anticipatory welcome.

The bay was an enormous open space of smooth silver, large enough to hold half a dozen fighter jets and operating crew. Though the Opal Dragon only had three Fledglings, they would grow into Draconae before they were big enough to be on their own. Even then, they would fly with the mother

Dragon for another five to twenty years before they went out on their own for good.

The largest portion of the bay was cordoned off by a shimmering field of ionized detfleck – a neck-high fence that was transparent all but for the bouncing multi-colored speckles that refracted from the lights of the bay. The specks were gold and rainbow colored and looked like hallucinatory confetti that came and went, like the mist of a waterfall reflecting slanting sunlight. The fence was as deadly as it was pretty. Any living thing that might try to pass through the fence would be instantly pulped.

A security point manned the gap in the fence at a ninety-degree angle, backed by a small freestanding room that housed a communication board and served as weapons storage. A large chair and a small entertainment console also occupied the room for the on-duty guard.

The Fledgling had already docked and was settling down on four squat legs. There was a great flurry of humans and elves alike flitting about like a flock of birds disturbed from their roost. Security was clearing those who needed to get to the other side of the fence. Calyph approached the security gate in the detfleck, heaving a sigh. He had been right. It was Blue.

The Fledgling ship was nineteen meters in length and matte silver. As light and shadows shifted on its surface the color changed and shimmered a glowing and glistening blue, like its silver skin had been dusted with crushed sapphires.

The hood atop the Fledgling snicked as the air locks released and slid back with a soft hiss, breaking the seal inside. The pilot emerged, pulling herself up and out. She was hailed and greeted by many and her bright blue eyes darted about the crowd as she smiled and nodded to the group as a whole.

Calyph watched her and sighed again, unable to help himself. He was as taken by her beauty now as he was the first time he had seen her. As he was every time he saw her. Smiling, he shook his head slowly, thinking that she looked like a doll. She was as bright and shiny and delicate as a child's toy. *A mishandled or mistreated toy,* he thought, a slight line forming between his brows. *The toy of a masochistic child.*

Platinum blond hair was swept up and back from her face and pointed ears in a high pompadour. It was pulled into a twist and tied at the back of her neck with blue ribbon where it fell into three perfect shiny coils. Full, red lips parted to show square white teeth that greeted everyone she saw with a dazzling smile.

Blue was a little less than average height and slim, even for an elf. Piloting through the deepest of space, even in a heated cabin, burned a body's fat store like dry kindling in a fire. The pilot moved herself with grace and ease as she forwent the steps that formed against the side of the craft and slid down the Fledgling's side on her ass and hip like a reckless kid. She kept one leg outstretched to catch herself on the wing before jumping lightly to the deck.

The thin fabric of her flight suit clung to her like a second skin. Its color was the opposite of her ship – a sparkling blue that looked silver when it caught the angle of the light. The number eight was stitched onto the upper left sleeve in silver thread. She wore blue boots that came up to her knees and her left wrist was encased in a smooth platinum band.

A new field pack transmitter, Calyph thought.

He had heard that some of the newer, and pricier, field packs were now small enough to be made disguised as jewelry. While Calyph didn't need any accessories, he knew he was long overdue for a new field generating pack. His looked like a medieval rucksack and was about as old.

When do I have the time or the money, he thought, *to go shopping for a new field pack?* The last time he had been in a mercantile port he had spent his time (and his money) on a pair of construct twins with an EQIQ so low they were practically drooling on each other, not that he had minded.

Blue's eyes were both deep and bright, like an ocean seen from space, set over high cheekbones and creamy skin. She was strikingly beautiful from Calyph's current vantage, though he knew better. She laughed at something he couldn't hear, and after a few more greetings and nods she turned his way, giving him a view of her entire face.

On her right cheek, now visible to Calyph, was a jagged mass of a double scar. One shiny, pink ripple started at the right corner of her lip, triangulating up and out and two fingers wide. It went over her high right cheekbone to just under her eye and on towards her ear. The bottom scar shot out from the same spot but twisted down and traced the fine line of her jaw where the small ripple of raised tissue slipped down into her neck.

Personally, Calyph suspected it was a bad chemical burn from a former drug habit, though logic told him that it couldn't be the case. She would never get a piloting license after something like that, and never *ever* with the IGC.

Calyph wondered for the first time how the fire had missed her eye, or if perhaps it hadn't and the eye had been replaced with a prosthetic. If so, it was a perfect match. It also crossed his mind, not for the first time, why she had never had that tissue on her face removed and replaced. It would be chump-change for a Jordan. He had the feeling that she liked the way it made her look, even if it was frightening. Perhaps *because* it looked frightening.

Blue spotted him at that moment and smiled broadly, though not evenly, as the smile on the right side of her face did not push up as high into the ripples of scarred flesh as it did on the left side of her face. The smile on the right seemed to hold something back, as if it knew something you didn't.

The elfin pilot headed for the security team that manned the gap in the detfleck, pulling off flight gloves as she went.

She stood still for the security check as the doctor gave her the once over, the armed guard at his side idly tapping the gun on his belt, though his sharp eyes never left the pilot's face. The doctor, garbed in a long white lab coat, was armed as well with a double syringe gun full of sulfur-mercury. Blue was known by most everyone in the west galaxies, and absolutely everyone aboard Opal Dragon. The security check was more of a formality, but still a necessity for anyone boarding any IGC ship, especially a Dragon.

"Your sidearm, Jordan?" The guard asked.

Blue pulled off her entire belt and handed it over before turning to the doc. She went through all of the motions without being asked: handing the doc her ID that contained her identification and qualifications, as well as the waiver for her disability.

The doc placed the card on a small box he produced from his pocket, logging her into the Dragon's system as well as verifying all of her information. She held out her left wrist and the doc ran a micro laser waft over it for a carbon DNA scan. He then held out the box with her ID still on top and she placed her hand over it.

Matching her DNA and the chip that was embedded in the flesh between her thumb and index finger, the ID card lit up green and the doc handed it back to her, the light dimming then disappearing from the card. Blue opened her mouth and the doc peered around the inside with a micro light. She gave him a short whistle of an odd tune and he gave her a warm smile.

"Welcome aboard, Jordan," he said, moving from the gap in the flickering wire so she could pass through. The guard let his hand fall away from his gun and handed her weapon belt back to her.

Blue gave him a dazzling smile and turned to impart some final instructions to the crew for the Fledgling and she buckled on her belt. A photon pistol hung low in the holster, just below her right hip.

She passed through the gap in the fleck, with welcomes from everyone, many reaching out to give her a pat on the arm or shoulder. All three Jordans had been gone for nearly a month and they had been missed by Dragon and crew.

The half-elf pilot gave everyone a distant acknowledgment but came straight at Calyph, slipping her ID into a zippered pocket in the sleeve of her flight suit.

"Well," she said with a smile both mocking and inviting, "if it isn't my favorite mechanic."

"Jordan Blue," Calyph acknowledged, ignoring the slight. The first thought that ran wild through his mind was that to kiss her he would have to lean down, since she was at least a full head shorter than he was, but he would never dare. From the bottom of his vision he could see where her creamy skin disappeared into the neckline of her shimmering blue flight suit.

She had a sweet smell about her. It reminded Calyph of the pink spun sugar he had once at a galaxy fair. She had been chewing something and he caught a glimpse of it through her smile, tucked back between her square, white teeth. It was small and pink and shiny, like a globe of wet plastic.

A raspy, metallic voice spoke out. "The Dragon was not expecting you for at least another orbit," it announced. "Equal to another dimlight."

Calyph did not have to turn towards the speaker to know who it was. He would recognize the voice of the troll anywhere; the droid had been with him for nearly fifty years.

The troll drifted forward to Calyph's left. It was an ancient hulk of a droid, looking like a cross between a fat human and a three-tiered metal cake with a head. It had one broad banded set of optics and was covered with keypads, slots, and metal nubs that could extend out into various limbs. Calyph had removed its legs decades ago, replacing the rollers with a sub-dynamic thrust.

"What can I say?" Blue said, not sparing the troll so much as a glance. She reached out to adjust the collar of Calyph's shirt. "I'm fast."

Calyph could feel the edge of her thumb caress the skin on his neck as she smoothed his shirt. He stood still under her gaze and wondered if the suit brought out the blue in her eyes, or if it was her eyes that brought out the color of the suit.

Jordan Blue cocked her head to the right and turned it back slightly to the left, as if listening to someone over her shoulder, though no one was there. She laughed softly and her bright eyes sought out Calyph's once again. Her slim fingers continued their course over his shirt and over his shoulder where they stopped, holding the flesh of his upper arm through the smooth cloth.

"Maybe *too* fast," she said, favoring him with another smile, the shiny, puckered skin of her scar a smile all its own. "I wasn't expecting to see you here, but I'm glad to see you. Will I be working with both you and Rhett?"

Calyph swallowed. "Just me," he told her. He didn't know what she might know and did not want to overstep his bounds.

"Hmm." A short, derisive burst of air came from her nose. "Well, we have lots to do, you and I...but right now, I need to rest." She let her hand drop from his arm. "Come find me in the morning."

She glanced at the troll and sidestepped around Calyph with a smooth grace before continuing on her way into the Dragon.

Calyph swung around and followed her razor thin form with his eyes, watching the pendulum of her slim hips and the way her thighs hardly touched. She tossed her head slightly, making her white-gold curls sway between her shoulder blades. He could still feel where her thumb had brushed against his neck and where her fingers had pressed his arm.

"Is it wrong that I want to have sex with her?" he asked. The troll gave a metallic grunt.

"You wish to mate with every female," it stated, matter of fact. Calyph made a noise that was half laugh and half sigh.

"Just about," he said. "Just about."

Blue walked down the passageway, her sharp eyes catching the changing light. The ship was moving into dimlight, a set time that moved the light, waking hours into darkness, simulating night. It made it easier for the crew, except those on the nightshift, to sleep. It was standard operating procedure aboard spacecraft - better for the health and sanity of everyone in space, where night roamed perpetual, to keep a cyclical dimming and lightening to keep a body's circadian rhythms in check.

The Jordan was relieved. She was tired and wanted to sleep, but had a hard time sleeping when all the ships lights were brightly shining and everyone moved about during the simulated day.

She walked down the hall trailing her fingertips along the wall, feeling the smooth metal skin of the Dragon. She felt she was forming a bond with the ship, through the bond she had formed with her Fledgling. She could feel the Fledgling's heartbeat, so in time with her own, mirrored here inside the Dragon, albeit at a much slower, rhythmic beat.

"You're awfully quiet," she said softly.

"Are you speaking to me, or the Dragon?" Galen's voice was soft against her left ear.

"You, silly."

"Ah. I didn't want to engage you in too much conversation out here. People would think you were talking to yourself and God only knows what they might say."

"Since when do I give a shit what people think or say?" she asked with feigned irritation. Galen's laugh was a caress on her neck.

"Duly noted, my lady."

Blue headed for the nose of the Dragon. She had to report to the Captain before retiring to her private cabin. It was a long walk, though the Fledgling Bay was mid-ship. She wondered if the Dragon had grown since the last time she was aboard and then decided it must be her imagination. Dragon growth was incredibly slow.

She was greeted by everyone she passed and was glad to see so many familiar faces, though there were a few new ones. As she neared the artery split that would take her to the bridge she passed a tall, dashingly handsome human with blond hair and bright green eyes.

Those must be the greenest eyes I have ever seen, she thought. *Even Jade's eyes aren't that green.* She pulled herself up and lifted her chin as she approached him, her interest evident upon her beautiful, ravaged face.

He stared at her openly with a rakish grin as the distance between them closed. His green eyes looked the Jordan up and down.

She narrowed her eyes at his smoothly chiseled face and gave him a lecherous smile as she passed by, swinging her hips. She tossed her hair casually after she had passed him, the heat from his body making her heartbeat quicken.

"Is he turning to look at me?" she whispered.

"No."

"You liar!" she accused, laughing. Galen's laugh joined hers.

"How did you know?"

"I just know."

"Do you ever worry that maybe someday you will lose that magnificent sex appeal of yours?"

Blue sighed. "I feel that maybe I already have. Normally, he would have been following me by now."

Galen's laugh echoed again in her left ear as she turned down a capillary corridor that led to the bridge. A steward was there, waiting for her. He bowed his head in greeting and she returned it with a nod.

"Good evening, Jordan Blue. The Captain has retired for the night and requests that you report to him in the morning." Blue acquiesced with another nod.

"Gladly," she told him. "Thank you."

The steward gave another slight bow and was gone. Blue turned and headed for her cabin.

"Thank God," she sighed. "A briefing would have taken an hour. Longer, if Blaylock is there."

"Brogan knows," Galen told her. "Why else would he turn in so early?"

Blue grunted in agreement and stopped in front of the door to her cabin. She pulled out her ID card and pushed it into the slot mounted to the right of her door. The card and slot both glowed blue and the lozenge shaped door slid open. She retrieved her card and stepped inside her cabin.

She reached out a hand to the light sensor on the wall to bring up the lights. As the lights came on she barely had a chance to glance around before she was slammed against the wall. Both her hands splayed out to take the impact as her body was pressed against the smooth silver surface.

Galen's voice was a soft purr. "I told you we'd take this out for a spin the first chance we got."

Her left ear, along with the left side of her face, was smashed flat against the smooth skin of the wall, muffling his voice a bit. The puckered skin on the right side of her face drew back in a grin.

"What took you so long?" she asked.

She could feel Galen's hand, a hand that was actually two light years away, wrap around her throat. She drew in a quick gasp of air and pushed away from the wall. He pushed her back.

"Damn!" she said, laughing. "You're awfully strong!"

She could feel his smile against her scar and his breath hot on her cheek. His other hand dug into the neck of her flight suit, and ripped it off down her back.

Moments later, two stewards, on their way to the bridge, stopped short in front of Jordan Blue's door, frozen. A cry had come from the cabin that was barely shy of a scream. There were sounds coming from the Jordan's room that were obviously from a struggle. They heard her cry out again.

One steward turned on his heel to run for help, but the other grabbed his arm and held him fast, listening. After a brief pause they relaxed, laughing quietly and shaking their heads. They smiled knowingly at each other and continued on their way to check on the night crew.

 TWO

Jade had known since childhood that he was different. Not because he was small, elves were naturally smaller than humans and Jade was no exception to the rule, but he was even small for an elf. It didn't bother him, he was very easy going by nature. What made him different was his sense of purpose.

Jade had grown up in a small village on a rural planet in the Outer Banks. All of the elves in his community worked and played and lived and died without ever really questioning much of anything. They were filled with a sense of duty, to be sure. Duty to family and friends, to their land and community. Jade felt a sense of duty as well, but much more than that he felt like he was filled with *purpose*. He was just not quite sure what that purpose was.

Even since he was in knickers, he could remember his very being filled with a sense of destiny. Maybe not a great destiny, possibly just a spark in a great roaring fire, but he was certain his spark must be an important one. It had to be, to tug at his soul the way it did. He wished he knew what it might be.

As a young elf, Jade questioned everything to the limits of patience for his parents and teachers. To their great relief, the walking question mark reached a point where he decided that there must be a purpose for not knowing some things, and it might possibly be for the better not to know *everything*. He became content with the knowledge that if he did the right thing and made the right choices, even though those choices were often hard, things always worked out for the best.

When he was young, Jade had always assumed his discerning intelligence came from his father. His father was a doctor in the small country hamlet where they lived and had treated not only all the towns' citizens, but also any sick or injured animal Jade managed to bring home.

As Jade grew older, he realized that his acumen might very well have come from his mother. The tiny woman must have been more brain than body and seemed to know *everything*. She always had a way of knowing whether he had cleaned his teeth or done his chores without even checking. Those green eyes of hers would narrow at him and Jade would know he was in deep shit more times than naught.

If Jade did well in school, and he often did, she would always hug him with pride but no surprise. "After all," she would say, "you are *my* son." But if he did something without thinking or decidedly boyish, like the time Jade came home one fall afternoon covered with hives, it was a different story.

On that particular day, Jade and his friends had come upon a compost pile at the edge of the woods close to home. The raked up leaves and forest debris had been gathered to mulch the vegetable garden of some nearby farmer, and it was *huge*. Too huge to pass up.

The boys spent two hours jumping into the pile, not knowing that it was fraught with poison oaky and a few other types of unfriendly flora from the forest. By the time Jade got home the large red bumps had started to rise up all over his skin. And boy did they *itch*.

"You are *just* like your father," Jade's mother scolded as she dunked him into a tub of salty water. His green eyes peeked out at her from under a mop of brown hair and between numerous red oaky welts. And when his father came home she confronted the doctor with, "you won't believe what *your son* did today!"

Jade knew better than to tell her that he was not only jumping into the mulch pile, but that he was jumping into the mulch pile from a tree. Quite a large tree, and yelling, "look at me, I can fly!" as his skinny arms pin-wheeled wildly and then wrapped around his thin knees before his little body cannon-balled into the mulch pile.

His father, who had laughed heartily at the mulch pile incident, had the same outlook as his ma. He praised Jade as his offspring when he did something exceptional and shook his head with amused resignation when he did something peculiar, telling Jade he was just like his mother.

Jade knew he had inherited his mother's small build and the eyes of light sea-green color for which he was named. Those eyes were almost always half blocked by the chocolate colored hair that hung perpetually over them as he got older – hair that Jade never found enough time to keep regulation short.

Grown-up Jade was a military elf, which was rather odd for a boy from the sticks. Unlike most, Jade had not joined the military for the cause. It had nothing to do with the war at all. It was not about money or a career. It was simply where the spark of destiny in his soul led him, filling him with a sense of duty and purpose.

He did not know where the sense of purpose came from, if from his mother or his father, or if it was something that was uniquely his own. It grew from a faint and far away sense of duty that had niggled at his personae from childhood to an actual feeling of obligation when he was well an adult of one hundred and twenty-two years.

Jade finally decided that the feeling of duty must have something to do with his destiny and there was only one way to find out. He enlisted. He had no idea where it would take him and did not care. Despite the shock it gave to everyone he knew, Jade knew that he was doing the right thing. At the time he had no idea where it would take it him.

Jade had grown to an almost decent height, for an elf, but was still slight of build and quite a bit shorter than most humans he met. He stayed very slim. His hands were long-fingered and thin, almost lady-like. He was teased by a few of his peers but it never bothered him. He knew there was a purpose for everything, including his small frame and hands that some considered slightly feminine.

It turned out that a small frame was not only quite useful but also quite needed for some lines of work, even in the military. Jade, once a skinny, simple but inquisitive country elf, found himself more content than he had ever been. Most would think it was because of the money he now made or the prestige that he now had, but it was neither. He was serving a purpose. For the Jordan of Green Fledgling, often called the Emerald Jordan, that was more than all right.

Jade glanced at the barmaid with a slight smile and good-natured sigh of disappointment that he had to be on his way. He drained his mug of ale, pushed back from the wooden table, the legs of the chair skittering across the planks of the floor, and stood up. He left a tip for the barmaid and left the tavern to board his Fledgling and continue on his patrol.

Scarlett, though she was anxious to leave, decided to make a trip to the apothecary before heading out. She eschewed the one in her neighborhood, though it was the best in the upper middle class klick, and flew up closer to the top of Three Mile City. She had the credentials, she had the money, and if there was one thing Scarlett didn't skimp on, it was her appearance.

Scarlett guided her craft through light traffic to a mall in upper suburbia, flashing her credentials at a security check to secure a good parking spot close to the mall entry. As she disembarked she noticed two things immediately – that blonde was in fashion again and that the air here was significantly better than less than half a klick below. She sighed, knowing that she would never trade her dark locks for light and that, once again, it was time to move. She would arrange for a new place up here before she left for the Dragon.

She tossed her thick, dark hair back away from her face and made for the mall entrance. She smirked, knowing she stood out like a sore thumb among the fair suburbanites. The way they paused for her, made way for her, turned her smirk into a leer.

Fucking cretins, she thought, entering the mall.

The mall was an indoor variety - full of lights, people, and ridiculously expensive shops and boutiques. Scarlett passed a shop with mannequins wearing outfits of many colors, mostly fashioned after the flight suit she was wearing. Scarlett shook her head, amused and disgusted.

She passed a private G7 shop with an ornately carved wooden door but no windows, not even noticing the gooseflesh it raised on the back of her neck.

The apothecary shop was brightly lit out front but much more soothing inside. It was done mostly in glass and lit with soft pinks and blues. Glass shelves filled with beauty products lined opaque glass walls. Drapes of heavy red velvet curtained off the back of the shop.

A beautiful young woman with bright blue eyes and blonde hair pulled back in a bun held by silver chopsticks waited at the counter. The wall behind her displayed a large, backlit menu. Smaller, laminated versions of the same menu were stacked neatly on the counter.

"Good afternoon, Jordan Scarlett," the girl said politely. She wore a soft pink collarless shirt under a white lab coat. "How can I be of service to you?" Scarlett's brow furrowed slightly as she scanned the menu behind the counter.

"Hmmm..." was all she said at first, drumming her fingertips on the glass countertop, her eyes still scanning. "I'd like a Hum-bird. Do you offer one with a relaxation package?"

"Of course," the girl said promptly. "We even have a pilot's package."

"Huh." A grunt of derisive surprise.

Scarlett's eyes, dark brown with an edge of crimson, found the list of Hum-bird packages. The 'Pilot Package' was the last on the list, and the most expensive. Scarlett wondered what kind of housewife found herself under so much stress that she fancied herself akin to a pilot, and would spend two thousand scones on a facial.

"I'll take the Citrus Package," she said. The girl smiled and tapped an acrylic pad with a plastic stylus.

"Excellent choice, Jordan. May I also suggest a Chiffon Facial, for after? It would be quite soothing to your skin and compliment the citrus. The Lemon Meringue or the Key Lime would be most delightful."

"Could you do Lemon Chiffon?" Scarlett asked. The girl nodded, pleased. "Absolutely."

"Very well then." Scarlett scanned the menu again. "And I need a 3HG Hormone Strip."

"For here, or to go?" The girl asked.

"To go."

"You can wear it here while you are getting your work done," the girl offered. Scarlett shook her head.

"I prefer to wear it when I sleep," she told her. The girl nodded and tapped her stylus against the pad.

"May I offer you a Percolan?" The girl asked. "It is on your list of acceptable narcotics, though you will be unable to drive for two hours and grounded from flight for six hours." Scarlett smiled.

"Absolutely."

The girl returned her smile and ushered Scarlett to a plush sofa where she presented her with a tiny blue pill on a square pink napkin. "We have blueberry juice, as well as cucumber," she offered.

"Blueberry, please." Scarlett placed the pill on her tongue where it began to dissolve rapidly. She chased it down with the aromatic liquid the girl gave her. The velvet drape parted to reveal another girl, exactly like the first. Scarlett expelled a short burst of air from her nose in surprise.

Constructs! She realized with an amused but agitated shake of her head. *I've been away for so long – I didn't even think. I should have known better, being up here in suburbia.*

Constructs were forbidden on the Dragons, forbidden on any IGC ship for that matter, so Scarlett didn't see them up close that often. Any robotic, droid, or personae of artificial intelligence had to be strictly made to represent exactly what it was – a machine. No skin covered robotics or humanoid replicants of any type were allowed aboard a government ship of any type or size.

It would be too easy for the Chimera to infiltrate them. It was already hard enough keeping the damn sprites at bay.

Here, though, in a planetary system and in an upper class cache – constructs were very common. Droids were so passé.

The female duplicate, looking every bit human, showed Scarlett to a private dressing room where she changed from her flight suit into a pink smock and was led into a darkened room with a comfy reclining chair and soothing music.

Scarlett settled in as the construct ran expert fingers through Scarlett's hair – gently pulling it away from her face and pinning it back. She tucked a warm towel under Scarlett's neck and cleansed her face with hot, wet towels and aromatic oils. The construct filled a cotton pad with a stringent toner and applied it to Scarlett's face and décolletage. Scarlett felt her skin get cold and then numb, along with all the underlying tissue in her face and neck.

Scarlett could also feel the undersides of her and arms and legs begin to get slightly numb, the tingle going all the way to her fingers and toes, as the narcotic she had taken earlier began to take effect. The construct leaned down, carefully setting the Hum-bird on Scarlett's shoulder.

The Hum-bird was just over ten centimeters long, its metal body balanced on tiny steel legs atop three-pronged feet. Its eyes were convex glass, behind which telescopic optics constantly dilated and contracted as it equized all visual bits to an AI chip in its head. It was beaked with a hollow steel cone with the tip cut off.

The Hum-bird stared at Scarlett, cocking its head this way and that in quick robotic movements.

"Hum," it said.

"Hum," Scarlett replied and then giggled. The narcotic was really sinking in. Making her feel numb but warm, and more than a bit dopey. The Hum-bird hopped up onto Scarlett's cheek and she giggled again, surprised. She hated the way the wiry little feet felt on her face, but she giggled once more.

The construct smiled and began massaging lemon oil into the back of Scarlett's neck and shoulders, encouraging her to relax. Scarlett took a deep breath and let it out slowly. The Hum-bird cocked its head right and left, eyes dilating and contracting.

"Hum," The Hum-bird said. This time Scarlett smiled just a bit, starting to drift off. The Hum-bird paused, a long needle sliding out of the hole in its beak. It bent quickly, poking the needle into Scarlett's face. Its head popped back up and then repeated the motion in three more spots on the Jordan's face before hopping to the other side and starting over.

It hopped back and forth a few more times, pausing now and then with its injector, plumping skin and filling the fine lines in Scarlett's face. After examining its work, the needle withdrew and another one protruded, glistening pink in the dimmed light. This time the Hum-bird hopped around, paralyzing any damaging nerve clusters that over time would be bound to cause wrinkles in the skin.

Scarlett drifted in and out on waves of lemon and cream. She wasn't quite sure when the Hum-bird finished, but merely came to a sleepy realization that it was gone when the construct began applying a creamy masque to her face with a wide, soft, fan-brush. While the masque soothed her skin the construct massaged her arms and hands.

The masque was removed with hot, damp towels and was followed by an application of moisturizing cream and then an antioxidant balm. When she was sufficiently rubbed, polished, patted and primped, Scarlett was able to dress herself and leave the apothecary shop. She carried her bought hormone strip in a dainty pink bag tied with a blue ribbon.

Scarlett bought herself some lunch, did a bit of shopping, and had a cup of coffee while waiting for the fading effects of the Percolan to wear off. She sat in the flagstone courtyard taking small sips from the oversized steaming mug and listening to artificial birdsong, keeping a wary eye on the GwenSeven shop.

The shop window was full of unanimated constructs, posed like dummies and wearing ridiculous clothes. Scarlett puzzled over what they were supposed to be – was the only male in the window supposed to be a gardener, or a fisherman? Was the girl on the right supposed to be a home nurse, or what? She finally decided that the ambiguity must be part of the charm. They could be anything you wanted. It made her feel ill.

She left the rest of her coffee on the table and headed for the high end leasing office. By the time she was done making arrangements with an agent to rent a new place she was cold sober and headed for her craft.

It was dark now and traffic was heavier as people were coming home from work and going out for the night. All level flyways were jammed but once she got to the vertical it was a straight shot down. It seemed once people were up this high there was little reason to visit the klick below, or any lower klicks for that matter.

Back on the upper middle klick, however, traffic was even heavier and more sluggish. Scarlett wondered if it was the traffic that was making her impatient or just the knowledge that it was time to get going. Probably both - she had never been a patient woman.

At home, Scarlett hurriedly packed a few of her belongings and let her family know about the upcoming arrangements. Finally, after a few quick kisses and hugs, she boarded an aircab and headed for the secure IGC dock. The taxi shot through traffic, dodging the other cars with the insane type of grace that only cabs seemed to possess. Scarlett reached inside her flight bag and fished out the item she had bought at the apothecary.

She opened the rectangular, pink box and pulled out the 3HG Hormone Strip. It looked like a clear, flattened, gelatinous worm sandwiched between two pieces of thin plastic. Scarlett reached behind her head with her left hand, gathered up her hair, and pulled it in front of her over her left shoulder.

She peeled away the top layer of plastic on the strip and placed the gelatinous band against the back of her neck, leaving the outer layer of plastic in place. Over the next few hours her skin would absorb the band, which now felt cold and rubbery against her neck, and the molecules would sink down and embed themselves into the tissues around her spine.

It would spend the next year slowly dissolving, feeding human growth hormone into her system. Scarlett used the strips on an annual basis, cycling her age down until she would start to get acne. Then she knew it was time to leave off for a while and let her body slowly cycle back up.

She never waited, except for one horrific time, until she saw actual wrinkles on her face before starting in on the strips again. Usually, after a few years, she would notice her skin starting to take on a dehydrated look, no matter how much water she drank. Looking down at her arms she would see that her skin had the appearance of huge, striated cells – like an onion that had been left out on the counter overnight. Then she knew it was time to start cycling down again.

Scarlett put the used plastic strip and the pink box back in her bag. She hummed and tapped her foot as she watched the light of the city and its traffic whiz by. The cab dodged a line of cars and swerved around a broken pylon, missing it only by a hair.

As the taxi approached the IGC secure flight area, Scarlett realized she could feel the Fledgling long before it came into view. One second she was feeling nothing but anticipation, her eyes searching but finding only the black concrete of the walls that bordered the jet compound. The next moment she could feel a flutter in her heart as it echoed that of the Fledgling.

Then she could hear it - the beat of its heart - faint at first and then stronger as she drew closer. Her own heartbeat quickened, feeling its closeness, and she could feel the Fledgling's heartbeat quicken in response to her own until the beats fell together in a seamless rhythm.

Scarlett peered out the window of the aircab, intent and as full of wonder as a child on its first outing in the city. The cab pulled into the security tunnel and opened her window. Scarlett gave the guard her credential card and let him scan her DNA. After a quick check into the rest of the cab she was waved through.

The cab pulled slowly out of the tunnel and there he was, sitting on his own secure magnetic platform surrounded by a hodgepodge of other government jets – sleek and silver with a soft crimson glow.

Scarlett let out a deep sigh and put her hand to the window of the cab. The glow around the Fledgling brightened in response. Scarlett smiled, tears coming to her eyes as her other hand reached up to her throat where a dry, aching lump had materialized from nowhere. She felt silly and embarrassed by the flood of emotion but didn't care. It seemed as if it had been years rather than just a week.

She gathered her things hastily from the cab and waved her card next to the meter. There was a series of short beeps as it extracted the money from her account and then the door hissed open and she hurried out with her flight bag slung over one shoulder. She headed for the second security check at a brisk walk, only a pilot's iron discipline keeping her from breaking into a run and making a dash for the waiting ship.

Scarlett smiled, a genuine heartfelt smile that went far into her being – something she could not remember ever doing before - as security went through their perfunctory duties. She kept an unwavering eye on her prize as they combed her over and went through her bag. Sister, brother, teacher, child – the bond between them was as indescribable as it was undeniable.

The next security guard whistled at her as she came towards him and she whistled back, a mockery of his catcall. He gave her the once over, and over again – checking her and her belongings. Scarlett suffered through it all impatiently, but quietly. When the guard was finally done she threw a wink at him and his partner. They laughed and nudged each other.

As soon as she cleared security, and again trying not to run, she approached her ship and quickly climbed the platform stairs. The Fledgling glowed brighter as she approached, opening up to her, pushing out a series of steps from its body so she could climb in with ease. Once she was up and inside, the steps pulled back in, melting back into the Fledgling leaving it smooth and seamless once again.

"Hello, Fledge," she said softly, tucking her flight bag behind the pilot seat. The air around her warmed in response. The hood slid closed above her and sealed itself. She nestled down into the seat that molded perfectly to her form and took a deep breath. The air here was better even than the air in the upper klick of Three Mile. This air was made just for her.

Scarlett ran her right palm over the instrument panel in front of her while her left reached up to cue up the com-link with air traffic control. The panel had an odd, unbalanced look, as if there was too much panel and not enough controls.

"Time for a trip to the doctor," she said, lightly touching two of the controls. A holographic image of the flight deck formed on the panel to her right. Scarlett reached out and adjusted the image, turning it. Her eyes flicked over the others waiting for departure clearance, which would now be waiting a bit longer since she would be given precedence and be the next ship to launch.

There were a few fighter jets but most of the spacecraft were secure diplomatic IGC vessels. The holo didn't show the brightly lit deck or any personnel. Just the orderly rows of man made craft: a lot of razor glass, metal plates, bolts, and screws. She didn't see anyone she recognized.

She adjusted the controls and a new holo replaced the one of the flight deck. An image of the Opal Dragon flickered into view and hovered over the control panel. A soft purr vibrated through the cabin.

"That's right," Scarlett said. "That's Momma."

Another touch of the controls and lines and numbers blinked into view around the image of the ship.

"Good evening, Jordan," a voice said through a communication field on the left band of the console.

"Good evening."

"Your coordinates?"

Jordan Scarlett read off the numbers closest to the wing of the holographic Dragon. A few clicks sounded from the communication field and then a brief pause ensued before the voice returned.

"You are cleared for departure, Jordan."

"Thank you."

Two smooth, silver straps snaked down over her shoulders while another wrapped around her waist. Scarlett reached out to the plain, unmarred panel in front of her with both hands. The panel itself moved in response, pushing out an arc of smooth metal. The Jordan wrapped her hands around the half-wheel, the hard but rubbery feel both familiar and comforting in her grasp.

"I want a stable thrust, Fledge. Just hold us here."

There was a deep hum from the Fledgling as its motors awoke and adjusted. Scarlett could hear the clunk of the magnetic generators underneath them as they were turned off and disengaged from the craft. The platform beneath them sank into the ground but the Fledgling held still and steady where he was, hovering above the flight deck. Scarlett made the last of her adjustments with her left hand before returning it to the half-wheel.

"Alright, Baby. Let's get the hell out of here."

She guided the Fledgling up and out, leaving the IGC dock dwindling to a brightly lit speck surrounded by a band of darkness in the sea of light and color that was Three Mile City. The planet dropped away as Scarlett ramped their speed and broke the sound barrier just before breaking through the atmosphere, out of the blue and into the black.

The Fledgling kept the air in the cabin under constant adjustment as they left the ground and shot away into space. Scarlett let go of the half wheel and it withdrew back into the panel. Her fingers traveled over the lights of the console, bringing up a holo map of the star system. The holo of the Dragon still hovered over the right side of the dash panel. She touched a blue light on the panel and an AU calculator was projected onto the flat of the dash.

Scarlett's eyes darted between the numbers suspended about the Dragon and the ones on the system map in front of her. Her fingers danced about the calculator as she estimated their distance of travel to the next system.

"Just under three light years," Scarlett said, her fingers still working the calculator. "Unless you hold out on me, you should have us there in seventy two hours."

The Fledgling purred in response, tipping slightly as it adjusted their course before it shot away, breaking the barriers of light and space with the ease of a swimmer diving into a pool.

Welsner - a huge, bulky, muscular human with a criminal haircut - ignored the no smoking sign for the umpteenth time on the flight and lit a cigarette. His broad face was dented and scarred. It was apparent that his nose had been broken on many occasions and never reset.

The first time he lit up, the flight attendant came right up to him – but after a dose of his flat blue eyes, so pale they were almost colorless – she simply turned on a button fan above him and kept going without a word. He raised his eyebrows, dragging deep. The bitch was smarter than she looked. Most weren't.

When the ship docked at the spaceport, Welsner got off carrying only a lightweight jacket. His bags were full of weaponry so he hadn't been allowed to personally carry them on the craft. All he had with him was his jacket and a pack of cigarettes that was almost empty. He rectified that by stopping at the first stand and buying three new packs of unfiltered, synthetic tobacco.

Welsner checked his pocket-com as he stood and waited for his bags to come through the terminal. It showed an address and two pictures. He glanced up at the no smoking hologram floating in the air next to him and ground the butt of his cigarette under his heel before lighting up another.

He checked the numbers on the flight screen to see if his ship had unloaded its baggage yet. He didn't see his flight number so he glanced around the port, looking for a place to eat. It could be awhile and he still had to take a shuttle to the Metal City. If his intel was good, he should find both his targets there, though he wouldn't go after them until tomorrow. Until then, he would eat, shower, maybe even grab a construct hooker if they were easy to be found in his district and not too pricey.

Welsner bought a greasy meat-simulated sandwich at a take-away stand and stood munching it and washing it down with a pungent smelling, carbonated drink. He'd find some good synthetic whiskey when he got to his hotel. He watched the flight ticker, bored and annoyed. Damn common, public transportation.

Finally, he saw his bags come down the chute and drop onto the jet stream of the air conveyor. He picked them up as they floated by. He dropped his personal kit on the floor and held the c-bag as if it were a fainting woman. He thumbed the fingerprint lock and unzipped the bag, checking its contents and making sure every weapon was accounted for. He knew that despite the lock there were many who knew how to fool it, and wouldn't pass up the chance to get their hands on some military-grade weaponry. A quick inventory showed him that each piece was accounted for and none of the ammunition was missing.

He zipped the bag shut and slung it over his shoulder and realized he was still holding the remnants of his sandwich. He picked up his kit bag and threw the sandwich in the nearest trash chute and headed for the door. A male Zealot wearing a lavender-colored robe and holding a plastic flower immediately accosted him.

"Sir, if I may say so, you don't look entirely well," the man said. "I can help you find..."

But Welsner pushed past him. "Don't worry," he said, cutting the other man off with a shark-like smile full of chipped and crooked teeth. "I'm going to see a doctor."

THREE

The day before Jordan Blue left to return to the Dragon, Galen had sunk a laser blade into the skin on the back of her pointed left ear and dropped it 3 millimeters down into the cartilage when he heard her gasp, sucking in a slice of air through her teeth.

Galen froze.

"Can you *feel* that?" he asked. He had given her enough local to numb the whole side of her head.

"No," she admitted. "But I can *hear* it." Noel had heard it punch through her skin with a slight popping noise, and then a low scratching noise as it sank into the tissue. She was an elf, partly anyway, with an elf's keen sense of sound. It didn't help that the procedure was taking place only centimeters from her eardrum.

"And I can smell it," she said, wrinkling her nose. "Like burning hair, only worse. It's gross." Galen shook his head, smiling.

"I can knock you out for this if you want."

Blue almost shook her head, but remembered there was a laser sunk into her flesh, being held by her lover's steady hand. "Negative. I'm fine. It's just...icky."

Galen's hand remained perfectly still but he leaned his head forward so he could get a better look at her face.

"Icky?" he asked. "Icky? I once saw you shoot off a man's arm with a laser rifle, and then kick it out of the way so you could get a better shot at his face."

Blue tried to smile but most of her face was too numb to comply. "I'm a Jordan," she said, as if it explained everything. "Just hurry up."

"Okay, then. Just sit tight, this won't take long."

It didn't.

Galen removed the laser blade and inserted the microdot com-chip using a field manipulator. All she could feel was a slight nudge and some alternating pressure as he adjusted it. Then he traded the manipulator for the laser, adjusted the settings, and she held her breath to avoid the awful burning smell again as he cauterized the top and bottom of the incision. He wiped away a tiny stream of blood with a gauze pad and applied a thin layer of pluralis that would form a permeable membrane over the microchip.

Galen had already performed this procedure on himself just the day before. Only, since he was unable to see behind his ear without some tricky mirror work, he simply inserted his com-chip into the bottom edge of his right jaw, halfway between his mouth and his ear.

"Are you sure you should be doing this?" Blue had asked him as she watched him in the mirror, fascinated, as he performed the same minor surgery on himself. "I mean, you're not really *that* kind of a doctor." She winced as he made the incision.

"It's a simple procedure," he assured her.

"Could I do it?"

Galen snickered. "I wouldn't advise it."

"Shouldn't mine be closer to my mouth, too?"

"As loud as you are? I could probably hear you from deep space without the com." Blue had promptly smacked him on the arm, careful not to nudge the one manipulating the microchip into his face.

Galen had sealed the incision and then eyed it for a few moments to make sure it was going to stay closed and that no fluid was going to seep out. The procedure, other than the placement of the chip, was no different for Noel.

"How do you feel?" he asked, swiveling the chair she was on so that she was facing him. Blue poked the left side of her face repeatedly.

"I can't feel my face," she said, still poking. Galen moved her hand away.

"How does your ear feel?"

"Oh. Fine, I guess."

Galen smiled. "Should we try it out?"

"Already?"

"Yep."

"Who's going?"

"Me first." Galen smiled at her and touched her lightly on the wrist, grabbed a light jacket and headed for the door. He pulled it on as he left the podment they shared and walked down the gleaming hall to the lift. He took the express vertical up to 101st, and then jumped in an empty taxi and headed out. He licked his lips, excited. He took a deep breath.

"Noel?" he asked. "Can you hear me?"

"Jesus!" Her voice was clear as microglass.

Galen laughed. "I take that as a yes."

"You scared the shit out of me! It sounds like you are right behind me!" Blue laughed nervously. "How far away are you?"

Galen looked out the window. "Almost to the bridge."

"Madison?"

"No, Vladset."

"Jesus! I swear to God it sounds like you are right here with me. I keep turning around like an idiot, looking for you."

"Well, that's the point, isn't it?" Galen had the cab turn around and head for home. "The real test is going to be tomorrow when you jaunt the Fledgling to Jersica." He could hear Blue laugh. It sounded like magic in his ear.

"Now we really can be together all the time," she said.

"Even when we are far apart," he agreed.

It worked just as well in space. So well that the first few times it scared the hell out of her.

The first was only thirty hours after she had left their podment. She had been cruising in Cyan, sleeping, when she felt someone shaking her and Galen's voice was loud in her ear. She bolted upright on her sleep pad, looking around the tight quarters in near panic herself.

"Noel! Blue! Jordan Blue!" Galen was shouting. "Can you hear me?"

"What? Yes! I'm right here! What?" Every word seemed to tumble out at once. She could hear a heavy sigh from Galen's end of the com-link and then silence. "Galen! What is it?"

"Nothing," he said softly.

"Like hell it was! What's going on?"

"I don't know," he confessed, sounding lost. "I'm not sure, but it's okay. I...I think I just had a bad dream or something. I'm sorry. Go back to sleep."

"I can't sleep now. Not yet. Do you want to talk about it?"

"No. I want to think about it."

"Alright, but if you want to talk about it, I'm right here."

"I know," he said, and this time he sounded better. More relaxed, more sure – more *himself*. Blue lay back down and, to her surprise, fell back asleep.

Six hours later, she was alert and looking for a start draft. The moment in the night was forgotten, the way a bad dream would dispel more and more with each hour after awakening.

Blue drew her tongue back and down from her two front teeth, creating a flat line of saliva before filling it with a drop of air and pulling it back up to the bottom edge of her front teeth, making a perfectly formed sphere. She carefully lifted the bubble up with her tongue and drew it back with a slight inhale, before gently blowing it out off the tip of her tongue where it rose up and then hung for half a second before it drifted away.

"Lovely," Galen remarked. "Spit bubbles."

"I would think you would have more appreciation for the ability to form a perfect sphere, Doctor."

"With spit?"

"With anything. Do you know the physics of what it takes to form one of those and give it lift without breaking it?"

Galen chuckled. "I must have slept through the lesson when they discussed the dynamics of saliva."

"It takes a lot of coordination and skill with the tongue to do that," Blue argued.

"I won't argue about your skilled tongue," Galen agreed. Blue laughed.

"And *you* were the one who got me hooked on bubbles," she reminded him. Galen laughed softly. Jordan marveled that she could not just hear him, but she suspected that she could feel his breath on her neck.

"How real are you?" she asked him suddenly. "How *here* are you?"

"As real as you need me to be," he told her. "And as here as you want me to be."

Blue felt the hairs on the back of her neck move, as if someone was looking over her shoulder. Sometimes those little hairs would wave, as if with a breeze. Sometimes they would flatten, as if the pressure in the cabin was raised or they would sometimes stand up as if she had a chill, or the creeps.

"So what the hell do you do, on such long trips?" Galen asked.

"Beside blowing bubbles? "

"Besides blowing bubbles."

"You know it took me *days* to master that."

"And more impressed," he chided, "I could not be."

"Okay, Mister Smartass."

"That's *Doctor* Smartass, if you don't mind."

"Okay, okay. Hmmm. What do I do? What do I do? Hmm...I sleep. A lot. I masturbate. I play games on the console."

"I beg your pardon?"

"I play games on the console. Word Winder and Gemstar..."

"No, no, no – before that."

"About sleeping or masturbating?"

"Masturbating," Galen said, laughing. "Do you do that a lot?"

"Of course, what the hell else am I supposed to do out here? It passes the time, and helps keep me awake if I need to be – I don't want to be falling asleep when I'm ready to merge into a stellar system or a draft. Besides, the thrum of the Fledgling's heart meshing with the vibration of the motor gets me going sometimes. Especially when it's the only thing going on for light years in all directions."

"Hmmm. Show me," Galen told her.

Blue smiled wickedly, though she doubted he could see it. She fished around the top her flight suit collar for the micro-zip, found it, and pulled it down past her navel.

"How much can you see?" she asked, her voice low.

"Everything," he breathed.

It was then that she realized that it was *Galen* moving the hairs on her neck. She could feel his breath - warm and moist as it moved from one side of the back of her neck to the other. She closed her eyes and realized she could feel his lips, and his hand - no, his *hands*. One gripped her left shoulder as the other wrapped around her throat before making its way down the front of her body, pushing her flight suit open.

"Galen!" she gasped, as she felt a hand that was not there cup her left breast. "How are you doing that?" She could feel his lips move from her neck to the lobe of her ear.

"Well, I have my theories, but none that I can prove quite yet. Not for certain anyway. And, right now, I don't really care." Blue could feel his lips moving along her ear to her jaw, kissing her, but all she could do was stare out into the black.

"I know how I can hear you, that much is obvious, even to a technological simpleton such as myself. But, how is it that I can *feel* you? I swear to God, I can."

"I can feel you too, though at this point I can't give you a definite reason as to why."

"I'm not holding you accountable to your theories, doctor. Just give me your suppositions for now." Blue could feel his lips move from the corner of her jaw to her neck, moving down and gently pushing at the fabric of her flight suit where it covered her shoulder. The lips moved away incrementally and she could feel his sigh on her shoulder.

"There are a lot of things that make this so... so real. Our closeness. Our communication verbally, as well as our ability to read each other so well, just from being together so long. Our love. The way we miss each other and want so badly to be close. And your mind. *Your* mind especially."

"My mind?"

"I think it has to do with the strength of your imagination and, don't take this the wrong way, your child-like ability to believe."

Blue laughed. "I won't take that too personally, but I still don't see how that makes me able to *feel* you." She could feel Galen's grip on her loosen slightly, his hands sliding a bit as he thought about it.

"Eons ago, we thought that everything in the universe was made up of matter and energy. Now we know that it is just energy. All the things we can touch and all the things that we can't, like our thoughts and emotions, are all made up of energy that is vibrating at different frequencies. When a vibration of thought is picked up by the subconscious mind its energy is transformed into possibility – which, in turn, we make into our reality."

"You lost me," Blue sighed. She could feel Galen press his lips together, sliding his face down the back of her shoulder till he could rest his forehead there. It pulled away suddenly.

"Our love, our longing, our knowing - those are things that we can actually feel, though mostly inside. The com-link gives us an actual connection. We can communicate without any guesswork. But it's your mind that makes it real."

"Not quite as lost, but still floating."

"Do you remember me telling you about consciousness and the quantum world?"

Blue relaxed back in her seat and her bright eyes searched the air above the dash. "Something about the waves of possibility, and choice."

"Yes! There are an infinite number of possibilities for your consciousness to choose from. It is simply a matter of turning conscious thought into physical reality."

"You're losing me again."

She could feel a short burst of warm air on her shoulder, his usual response of exasperation and amusement.

"Okay, you know that the physical world has four dimensions – space takes up three, and the other dimension is time."

"Yes."

"Well, the quantum world, what some call the subtle world, has four dimensions as well – love, desire, belief, and intent."

"Okay."

"When you can pull all those together, you are able to create your own reality."

"How?"

"Do you have any questions about the first two - love or desire?"

"Not where we are concerned."

"Okay, then let's start with intent. Love and desire are powerful; love being the highest frequency that people can transmit. But intent is the dynamic that sets it in motion, it is what produces the result – and the more specific your intent will result in a more specific outcome."

Blue chewed her lip, on the brink of understanding. Galen could sense her confusion.

"For example, you intend to fly through space at the speed of light, so you do. But there is no intended goal, so you are just flying. Right now, you intend to fly to the Opal Dragon. It is your intent that will take you there, not random chance. Intent is the action that makes your desire a reality." Blue smiled, relieved.

"That finally makes sense. What about belief?"

Galen laughed. "That's all you, and that I can't explain. But your mind is very powerful."

"It doesn't feel that way."

"Do you remember when you told me about the time you had a sexual climax without ever touching yourself, or anything else?"

Blue laughed, nodding. "I had forgotten about that. That was a *really* long and *really* boring trip. Also, it was when I had just started flying Cyan on long trips and was just starting to bond with him, and I wasn't sure just how cognizant he was of what was going on. It was my way of being discreet. And passing the time."

"Nonetheless, I also remember you telling me before that sex is usually between fifty to ninety percent mental."

"*At least*," Blue corrected. "That time it was at least ninety-nine percent mental. Maybe half a percent should be credited to the seam on my flight suit."

"Exactly. This is much the same. Your mind makes it real. You know me, enough to predict my every action and reaction. You know yourself. Your cognitive imagination takes care of the rest."

"I suppose."

"Like I said, I'm not sure, I'm only going on theories at this point. This is the first time I have ever heard of anything like this happening, and I have never experienced anything like it myself. But I like it."

"Me too." She paused for a moment. "It was what we wanted, isn't it? To always be able to be together, even when we are far apart?"

"Be careful what you wish for, is that what you are saying? That you might get what you seek?"

Blue laughed. "Kind of, but I don't regret it, if that's what you mean. I like having you with me. The more the better."

"Well, when we get into quarters that aren't quite so tight we might really take this link out for a spin."

"I'd like that."

"You're coming up on the star tunnel you wanted," Galen announced.

"So we are. What are you now, my navigator?"

"How about a co-Jordan?"

Blue snorted. "There is no such thing, and with good reason."

Galen laughed. "You're gonna miss it," he teased.

Blue shook her head. "Stow it or I'm turning you off. Besides, I never miss." She put her hands out and they were filled with a half-wheel from the Fledgling. She took over manual control and shot into the star draft, thinking about the link that Galen had implanted in her flesh and the thoughts he had implanted in her mind.

Grandpa stood looking out the window. He looked down into the city, his forehead not pressed to the glass but only a hair's breadth away. Close enough to feel the cold of the glass reaching out to the skin on his wrinkled face. The city glowed with a bluish white light, punctuated with primary ne-on-color where businesses advertised logos and services. The light was cut by long, dark streaks where buildings were shut down for the night and quietly patrolled by security droids.

He didn't know how thick the glass was, but he knew it was expensive and clear and supposedly soundproof. That was what his father would have called bullshit. He could hear the city out there. A soft hum and rush that ebbed and flowed. Like the far away stormy crash of waves on a rocky beach that he had never seen. That was something his granddaughter would also call bullshit, since he could hardly hear a damn thing except for someone calling him to dinner – and even then it was only if he was in the same room. Nonetheless, he knew he could hear that city out there. A great beast that breathed and rumbled - and waited.

Grandpa stepped away from the window and looked at the numbers on the wall. John would be coming soon and bringing his dinner. More important, John would be bringing the children. Grandpa smiled and made his way from his dark bedroom to the cozy light of his living room. His gait wasn't shuffling, not yet, but the spring in his step was certainly a thing of the past.

He walked into the living room with a smile. His teeth were very old and broken in many places but he refused, much to the consternation of his grandchildren, to have them fixed.

"If God wanted me to have another set of teeth," he told them, "they'd have grown in by now!"

The floor of the living room was a warm, polished wood. "*Real* wood," Grandpa would say with satisfaction, stomping on it with a slippered foot. It was covered with a fine, thick rug. "Real *Turkish*," he would also say, though he had no idea what it meant. He just knew that his own father had taken pride in that information and so he felt that he should pass it along as well.

He had a flatscreen to watch instead of a holoscreen. Grandpa said the holos gave him the "heebie-jeebies." The shelves were full of books made with paper, though he had switched to a digital reader with larger print until he could no longer make the letters large enough for his eyes to read. He knew he was old fashioned but he certainly wasn't a *caver-man*, another perky term he had picked up from his father that he passed along when he had the chance.

There were certain technological advances he could accept. When the vacuum was able to move about the room without him pushing it, he was delighted. When it had the ability to mop the floor as well, he was impressed. When John brought over the upgrade that could climb the walls and wash the windows, he was suspicious. When his grandson offered that there was one that could hover through the podment and pick up after him, he drew the line.

"I can pick up after myself or you can get a cleaning lady to do it. Hoover, okay. Hover, no way."

He laughed like a loon at that one and John had looked at him like he always did - amused and confused.

One shelving unit held nothing but photo albums. Between two of the thick books was an ancient timepiece. Grandpa eyed it and smiled. It was almost time. He padded over to his chair and carefully lowered his thin frame down into the cushions.

Grandpa loved having the children over. Telling them stories while they listened, round cheeked and wide-eyed, from their spot on the rug. Their eyes always shone in that particular way that only children seemed to manage. Most called it innocence but Grandpa thought it was something a trifle more sad. It was hope.

Grandpa had thought long and hard about that one, and had tried to pinpoint the time, the age, when that purity went out of their eyes. He had watched it happen many times. The trouble was, he had the damndest time remembering how old his newest pair of grandchildren were. He had long ago stopped adding the "great" prefix when referring to his grandchildren. The number of "greats" became so many that he couldn't remember, and began to sound ridiculous.

Right now, was a time of growing for Sean and Jeanette. Little Jean still had that bright, shining light in her eyes. Full of wonder and joy. Sean, however, was just a few years older and that shine was starting to turn into a glimmer. A glimmer of understanding and the suspicion that the older people were pulling his leg about some things, maybe a lot of things, and that all those adults out there in the adult world were most likely full of shit. Soon that suspicion would be replaced by the realization that he was right

After that age would come a time of psychosis that seemed to infect young adults with the idea that they were invincible. This time seemed to last a good ten to twenty years. After that came a sort of fear. Grandpa didn't know if it was caused by the realization that they were in fact *not* invincible, or by the much more terrifying thought that maybe they should do something with their lives.

Once this happened, Grandpa noticed that the eyes would sometimes spark up with determination, but it was always followed by what depressed him the most – resignation. Sometimes hope would shine again in their eyes, usually when they had children of their own, but those times were few and far between, and didn't last. Once Mr. Resignation settled in, he was a hard tenant to evict.

There were always exceptions to the rule, and Grandpa had seen it in a number of his grandchildren. Those were the ones he watched closely, the ones whose eyes shone with that special light, the light that refused to be darkened by the resignation.

Grandpa thrummed his fingers on the arms of his chair; thinking about Jeanette, with her dark curls and pink cheeks and chocolate colored eyes that shone with all the wonder and hope that childhood had to offer.

How old is she? Grandpa wondered. *Five? Ten? What about Sean?* Grandpa knew that the boy was the one on the brink of change. His eyes were blue, rather than brown, and his hair was a sandy blonde. Those eyes still held hope, but they were definitely beginning to lose their wonder. He had seen enough that he was starting to figure some things out on his own.

How old? Ten? Twelve? Fifteen?

Grandpa knew could always ask John. But the last time he had asked, John had answered in a very exasperated voice, as if it was something Grandpa asked every time. Grandpa scowled at the clock, trying to recall the last time he had asked.

He could remember that John sounded exasperated, and that they had been in the kitchen. Hell, he could remember what they had for dinner that night, but he was damned if he could remember the ages that John had told him. He also couldn't remember when it was that he had asked. Last week? Last year? They had eaten chicken that night and Grandpa remembered that it had tasted so good that it might have even been a real chicken. Or it might have just been the sauce.

Grandpa chewed thoughtfully at the inside of his cheek. He couldn't figure for the life of him why it was so damn easy to remember things that happened a hundred years ago, but impossible for him to remember if he had taken his pills this morning.

Hmmm. I'll figure it out. Tonight. And I'll write it down somewhere. With today's date.

He had had the same idea before, but when he found the paper again it had no date on it and he couldn't remember when he had written down the ages of the children. Last week? Last year? He had crumpled the paper in frustration, threw it on the floor, and took his pills. Again.

Suddenly there was the sound of voices in the hallway. Grandpa knew that if he could hear voices in the hall, then the walls must be very thin. He could hear Sean's muffled voice as he argued with his father about not being allowed to bring his acrylic to play games on.

"You know that Grandpa doesn't like those things," John argued from the hall. "He gets upset enough by the technology we make him use, he doesn't need yours around."

"He just thinks that if I'm playing I won't listen to his stories."

"You *should* listen to his stories. You might learn something."

The sound of John's voice was followed by the sound of his keychip against the pad in the hall next to the door. Grandpa heard a soft hum from the wall and, on a sudden impulse, closed his eyes and pretended to be asleep.

The door slid into the wall and the voices, much louder now, came into the room. Grandpa blinked and looked about as if he was surprised. Jeanette bounced over to him.

"Grandpa! You've been waiting for us!" she said, planting a kiss on his prickly cheek. She made a squealing noise. "Grandpa, you need to shave!"

"I do?" he asked, surprised. He thought he had.

"Hi Grandpa," Sean said. He considered himself too old for kisses but gave Grandpa a hug.

"That's not much of a hug," Grandpa teased. "Are you sick?"

"No, I'm just afraid I'll break you."

Grandpa harrumphed.

"I'm serious," the boy said. "You look smaller every time I see you, if that's possible."

Grandpa gave him another harrumph. He suspected the same thing, but had no intention of saying so.

John, smiling, followed the children in. He carried a dinner box in one hand and his other arm was wrapped around a sack of groceries. "I don't know how it's possible either," he said, going into the kitchen. "I got this month's delivery bill today – you're practically living off pastries!"

"The pastries are easier on my teeth," Grandpa called after him with a smile.

"That wouldn't be an issue if you would get new teeth!" John's voice carried in from the kitchen.

Grandpa pretended not to hear him. His memory might have gone to shit, but there were a few things about being old that he really enjoyed.

The children plopped down onto the rug, settling themselves in while their father got dinner ready.

"What are you going to tell us tonight?" Jeanette asked, her voice young and eager. Grandpa looked from her shining eyes to Sean's and smiled. The boy was too big to ask, just like he was too big to give kisses. He wanted to play holo games more than he wanted to hear stories. He had a glimmer in his eyes, but they were still shining. He smiled back at Grandpa.

He's still listening, Grandpa thought, his heart warming inside him. *By God, he's still listening.*

FROM
THE DREAM JOURNAL OF HOPE

Last night I dreamt of you for the first time.

I stood in a narrow hallway before a great steel door that was bound with strips of rusted iron studded with great, jagged metal bolts. I stretched out my hand, pale and long-fingered, though my knuckles were scabbed (had I been rapping on the door to no avail?) and pushed at the door.

It swung open, left to right, without a sound. It opened into a room. A room with a single, long table. I could not see the walls of the room. They faded into the soft black eternity of the night.

You stood there, on the table, at first with your back to me. When I opened the door you turned and saw me. I can't remember what I wore, but it was not a suit or coat. Most likely just the cloth of dreams.

What were you wearing? I can't remember. Your uniform or casual attire? Maybe it was a mixture of both, all of it is so dark. Your clothes, whatever they were, were dark for certain. Maybe you wore shoes, but I don't think so.

To my surprise you immediately held out a hand towards me, beckoning, inviting me up onto the table.

After a breath, hesitant but eager, I took a step. And then another. Another tentative step and my thigh hit the table and I offered you my hand, still unsure. You grasped it within your own without a pause and pulled me up with ease.

There we stood, for long moments, our shoulders squared, our thighs almost touching. I was afraid to move or speak but not to look into your eyes. We stood there, like equals, for what must have been seconds but to me felt like gracious forever.

Then you reached behind your back and pulled out a great iron ring with a single key. The ring, like the key, was crusted with flaking rust. The key was ancient, from another time – a great iron loop with two prongs, from one of which protruded two metal squares and a jag of a rectangle.

You handed the ring, the rusted key dangling, over to me like you were handing over a secret trust, and indeed you were. I wrapped my fingers around the ring, not knowing what to do or where to go or what anything meant.

Could feel the flakes of rust against my palm, but I did not look down.

I did not wonder how you knew of the key, or that I had been seeking it.

All I knew was that I stood face to face with you, unafraid for the first time to look into your eyes, our shoulders squared like equals and our thighs almost touching.

FOUR

Blue awoke with a jolt, as if she had tripped and fallen in a dream and jerked awake just before impact. It was a disturbing feeling of alert disorientation, much like when Galen had awakened her in a panic only a few days ago.

Now here she was again, being shaken out of sleep with someone hissing at her. She was startled and acutely conscious, not because she was naked, but because someone was in the room with her and absolutely no one on board had access to her private cabin. Or so she thought.

"Jordan Blue!"

Calyph was shaking her roughly and calling her name. At least there was a slip of silvery sheet covering her more intimate parts.

"What is it, Calyph?" she demanded, pulling the sheet up around herself as she sat up. "And how the hell did you get in here?"

Even as she blinked the sleep from her eyes, her senses were already awake and feeding her information at a blinding rate. Her first coherent thought, however, was about her room.

It has grown, she thought. *The night table is farther from the bed, by a fraction of a centimeter, no more. Same with my chest of drawers.*

Her lights were on, but dim. She could hear a commotion in the corridor outside her door, it had an edge to it that bespoke danger. She immediately felt deep inside, searching for her Fledgling. She reached out with her senses, touching him softly. He was safe, but gave off feelings of confusion and concern. Calyph was hurriedly apologetic.

"I had to override the security lock when you wouldn't answer the com. We were afraid something had happened to you."

"What's going on?" she asked, keeping her voice firm in an effort to calm him. Calyph swallowed.

"The Dragon has been infiltrated," he told her. She stared at him, speechless.

"There's no way," she finally whispered.

"You need to come to the bridge immediately." Her blue eyes grew wider and wider.

"What happened?"

Calyph pressed his lips together, unsure of what or how much to say. "Just get to the bridge as soon as you can," he told her and was gone.

Blue moved quickly and methodically. She grabbed a blue Mylar flight suit from a drawer and slipped into it, zipping the front as searched the floor for her boots. Hopping from one foot to the other, she pulled her boots on as she hobbled from her room as fast as she could. The few people she encountered, all wearing opal-colored coveralls that were standard issue aboard the Dragon, moved quickly, urgently. The Jordan's ears twitched as she listened to the movements tinged with fear that came from everyone in fore part of the ship.

She walked briskly as she headed for the bridge, controlling her natural urge to run as she knew everyone else was doing. Panic on a ship was a dangerous thing. Moving quickly, she arrived into a hive of activity – a controlled mayhem of checking screens, establishing coms with other ships or the IGC, and taking and relaying orders with hurried precision.

Blue had never seen so many people on the bridge. The normal bridge crew consisted of the Navigator, the Communications Officer, and the Officer of the Watch. The most she had ever seen along with the bridge crew were all three Jordans, the Captain and the Executive Officer – occasionally a Steward or the Engineer. Now the room was crowded with people that moved with a desperate precision.

The Jordan looked past the moving bodies in opalescent coveralls and through the curved floor-to-ceiling windows of hyper-glass that were the eyes of the Dragon, but there was nothing out there but the blackness of space.

Along the curved wall was a dash console that housed the navigational systems as well as the communication and alarm systems along with slide-mounted chairs for the officers that manned the systems. Behind them was the helm and beyond the helm, in the midst of it all, was what the officers called "the pit."

It was a sunken area in the center of the control room with a half circle of padded chairs around a low holo table. There the Captain sat now, surrounded by aides, techs, and pilots. Blue spied Calyph sitting there as well, and wondered briefly where Rhett was. And Blaylock, the Opal Dragon's Executive Officer.

Captain Brogan was a human male with silver hair, a straight jaw line, and fierce gray eyes that took on a pearlescent sheen when hit by light. Blue had once remarked to Galen that every Captain she had ever seen, other than Condliffe, had silver hair and she asked him if it was a prerequisite. The memory of it fled as she realized with a start that Galen had said nothing since her rude awakening. As if to answer her thoughts, he spoke softly in her ear.

"Take the seat between Calyph and the Captain," Galen instructed.

"Why?" she breathed, eyeing the group in the center of the room.

"Because, after the XO, you are next in command."

"That's a frightening thought," she muttered.

"You're telling me."

Jordan Blue squared her shoulders and quickly crossed the room, dodging other moving bodies, her eyes on the Captain. The feeling of panic in the air was palpable.

"How is he staying so calm?" she whispered.

"It calms the Dragon, as well as the crew," Galen told her. "What do you think would happen if he was running around screaming?"

Blue nodded. That barely controlled panic would be unleashed and a raging chaos would ensue. She shuddered to think of the havoc it would cause. As she drew nearer to the pit, she could feel Brogan's will holding everyone tightly in check. She quickly descended the two steps down and stepped lightly around Calyph . Everyone except the Captain rose from their seats for her, sitting back down as she sat between the Captain and the Engineer.

"Four, five, five," Brogan told a slim, dark skinned woman. The woman sped off before Blue could decipher what she was about. The Captain waved off the next aide that was waiting for instruction and turned his attention to Blue. The Jordan held her emotions tightly in check.

"Jordan Blue," he said greeting her. She inclined her head briefly.

"Captain Brogan."

"We have no time for formalities or briefings. The Dragon has been infiltrated," Brogan told her. He could have been giving her the weather report for all the emotion he betrayed. Blue leaned forward, her elbows on her thighs and her hands clasped together, trying to exude the same calm as the Captain. "Someone or *something* was able to penetrate our security."

The Captain motioned to the table and a full color holograph flickered into view. It was an image of the Ventricle, a circular hallway that surrounded the heart of the Dragon. The outer wall, like most walls, was the smooth and unmarred metallic skin of the Dragon. The inner wall consisted of man-made titanium panels. Blue knew that these were the panels that encased the Dragon's heart.

"This image is from yesterday," Brogan told her.

Blue watched as a tall, handsome human with blond hair and bright green eyes entered the Ventricle. She put a hand over her mouth to keep it from dropping open. The image of the human looked around, as if to make sure of his surroundings. Once sure, he ran his hand along the inner wall of panels as he walked along, as though searching for one in particular.

Blue pressed her forehead onto her folded hands.

"I *knew* there was something wrong with him!" she hissed.

"Excuse me?" Brogan asked. Blue shook her head and looked back at the holo. Galen's laugh was soft in her ear.

The man stopped suddenly in front of a panel and removed a small, flat tool from a pocket in his sleeve. With a flick of his thumb, a short laser burst from the tool's end. He ran the laser around the edges of the panel and then turned it off and used the metal edge to pry the panel loose. He pulled it off entirely and a soft, bluish-white light spilled from the rectangle where the panel had been. The man tossed it carelessly to the side and peered into the light, leaning his head inside the column. He flicked the laser back on and it disappeared into the hole.

"What is he doing?" Blue asked.

"Cutting the circuits of the Ventricle field," Calyph said, his voice flat.

"What will..." she started but the Captain raised his hand, cutting her off, and pointed to the holo.

The man was at it only a moment longer before drawing his head and arm out. He watched as the bluish light became brighter, whiter, and began to spill like a living thing out of the Inner Ventricle. There was a satisfied grin on the man's handsome face as he turned and left.

The light oozed out of the hole like congealing blood, getting brighter and brighter. By the time it had spread across the floor it was almost too bright to look at. When it reached the outer wall of the Ventricle everyone at the table turned their heads away, shielding their eyes from the blinding brightness. The holo clicked off abruptly followed by a silence from everyone around the table.

"How could he know how to do that?" Blue asked. "*I wouldn't.* And I wouldn't think anyone else would know, except maybe the Captain or the..." she trailed off, her eyes resting on Calyph. Things began to fall into place and she realized with a mounting horror why Calyph was there. "No," she whispered. The same panic that had infected the crew began to seep into her.

Where is Rhett? Even if he were deathly ill he would be at this meeting. My God, Calyph isn't here to assist Rhett, he's here to replace him. The thought of espionage and betrayal made her stomach flip over.

Brogan cut off her thoughts with a wave of his hand. "We don't have time for what's behind us, only for what's before us."

Blue struggled to rein in her racing thoughts and regain her composure. She nodded at Brogan. "That's the starfire," she said evenly. "It's leaking out into the Ventricle." Brogan shook his head.

"Actually, it's only the light from the starfire, but the starfire has been set loose."

"What does this mean? What will happen?"

"When held within an electromagnetic field, the starfire produces its own energy. It is the energy used to sustain the Dragon and power all non-organic parts. Set free, it will consume energy, rather than produce it."

Jordan Blue shivered. "And by energy, you mean mass. Matter."

Calyph nodded. "Yes. It will begin consuming the Dragon."

"From the inside out?"

"Yes."

"And instead of producing energy, it will create what? A vacuum?"

"Yes. It will collapse in on itself."

"It'll make a black hole?"

Calyph shook his head. "Not quite that bad, but it will destroy the Dragon as it pulls in before the collapse causes an explosion. The explosion will destroy anything within a standard LD." Blue gritted her teeth.

Damned Chimera! I should have known when I saw him. What the hell is wrong with me? Galen heard her teeth grind.

"The damage was already done," he said softly, "there's nothing you could have done." She shook her head, frustrated. She didn't have time for niceties.

"How long do we have?" she asked Calyph.

"Two hours, maybe a little more."

"What can we do?"

Brogan cleared his throat. "We are getting everything and everyone off the Dragon as quickly as we can, pilots are taking all aircraft and there are two rescue ships..."

"Excuse me, sir," Blue interrupted. "I didn't ask what we are *doing*, I asked what we can *do*." Brogan straightened and looked at the tech that sat next to

Calyph. She was a small human with brown skin and dark hair pulled back into a short, tight hair-tail. She shook her head.

"We don't have a droid aboard that can repair the circuit," she told her. "The IGC is sending one aboard the rescue ship that should be able help - if it can get here in time."

"We don't have a droid that could do it?" Blue asked, incredulous. "Any remote droid should be able to do a circuit repair. Is it too hot in there to send one in?"

The tech shook her head again, her hair-tail whipping behind her. "The heat is minimal, especially now." Blue looked at Calyph.

"But even your Troll, you should be able to…"

Calyph cut her off. "It's the light, Jordan. It's too bright for human eyes, and even more so for elfin eyes. It would blind anyone in that chamber instantly. The vibration of light is so high that, even with closed eyes, enough light could pierce through the eyelids and fry the retinas. A robotic could see in it, but even if I could guide one through an optic link, it would still be too bright for *me* to look at on the monitor. Even if I put the troll in there, it would have to describe what it was seeing so I could tell it what to do – and even if he could describe it in human terms, he doesn't have the mechanics to maneuver inside the Ventricle."

"Even a minimally advanced mechanical droid would have optics that could…"

Calyph laughed nervously, embarrassed as if it were his own fault. "You know the IGC regulations for non-humans aboard a Dragon." Blue sat back in her chair, her shoulders sinking in disbelief.

"Anyone with the capabilities to fix this can't see it, and the droids that can see it can't fix it?"

"The irony," another tech said bitterly, shaking his head.

"It's what the Chimera are always after," Brogan told them. "Our destruction primarily, but at the very least, wreaking havoc."

"While letting us know how completely we've screwed ourselves."

Brogan threw the tech a dark look but didn't correct him.

"Has the starfire begun to consume anything around it?" Jordan Blue pressed. "Is it already beyond repair?"

Calyph shook his head. "Probably just through the endocardium, the first field layer, the one that holds it in stasis." He looked to the Captain for confirmation and Brogan nodded. "Next is the myocardium, then the epicardium

– the second and third field layers. If it gets through those then it will begin to consume everything around it, growing in strength and size as it does so."

Blue frowned at Calyph. "Would you be able to walk me through it, if I could tell you what I was looking at?"

"*No.*" Galen's voice was a firm command in her ear.

"Of course," Calyph answered. "It would be a simple solder job. But you wouldn't be able to see anything. It's *starfire*. It's too bright to look at with the naked eye. The rescue vessel is sending an optic hood for me as well as a droid that can..."

"That ship will never make it in time!" Blue hissed.

The Jordan looked at the Captain and saw him wince.

He can feel what is happening to the Dragon, she realized with mounting horror. *How long has he been Captain of the Opal Dragon? How tight is their bond?* All she knew was that after only two years with Cyan she would die to save him. *Brogan must have been commanding this ship for half a century. Jesus!*

Blue eyed the Captain's right hand, resting on his leg, clenched into a fist. She knew instinctively that he was holding it there for a reason. He wanted to rub the area over his heart and was fighting the urge in further effort to keep everyone calm. Even if he could leave the Dragon, which he wouldn't, Blue knew that he would die as well. It was only a short matter of time before that starfire was completely loose and began to devour him from the inside as well. He would share the same fate as his ship.

Calyph frowned at the Jordan. "What are you thinking?" he asked.

Blue's eyes flicked from Calyph to the Captain and then back again. Everyone around the holo table watched their silent exchange.

Calyph cocked his head. Are you thinking of going in there yourself?" The Engineer looked at the Captain, who was studying the Jordan, his pale eyes intense. Calyph shook his sandy-blonde hair.

"You're not listening, Jordan," he said. "It's too bright. You have no idea how bright. It would blind you, as soon as you walked through the door."

"Would it?" she asked softly, almost to herself. She looked away to the left. "Would it blind me?" She frowned, her lips pressed together.

"Jordan!" Calyph started but the Captain silenced him with a quick shake of his head. Blue looked up and her eyes locked with Brogan's. Something seemed to pass between them; some sort of understanding, and a stillness welled up in the circle of those seated even as the commotion continued around them.

"Go," Brogan told her. "Go now."

Jordan Blue was up like a shot and fled the pit, grabbing a com set off the wall of the control room as she went, tossing one half to Calyph who stood bewildered in front of his chair. Brogan turned back to his waiting aides and pilots.

"Continue the evacuation," he told them.

"Blue, don't do this," Galen warned as she strode out of the bridge and into an artery hallway.

Crewmembers in opal coveralls were everywhere and going in every direction. Blue realized for the first time exactly how many people were aboard the Dragon. The ship was the size of a small city and had just as many inhabitants. The knowledge made her feel ill. She pushed both the thought and the feeling away, walking faster.

When she didn't answer, Galen let out an exasperated breath. "Get in Cyan and go. Get the hell out of there!" She made her way towards the heart of the Dragon, keeping silent. "Dammit, Jordan! What about your Fledgling? You need to get him out! Do you want anything to happen to him?" Blue shook her head.

"Don't try to play me like that," she said. "Another pilot will get him out of here if something happens to me."

"You don't know that!"

Blue snagged a roll of reflective tape from the belt of a passing tech. He turned to look at her, wide-eyed, but never stopped. "They won't let anything happen to him, " she said. "Trust me, they'll get him out."

"What if he won't go?" Galen challenged. "What if he won't let another pilot inside him, much less fly him?"

"He'll sense the danger. He already does. I can feel it."

"Exactly. More, he senses the danger to you, and to his mother. What if he refuses to leave you, or her?"

Blue paused as Galen's statement struck her. Then she shook her head and continued down a vein towards the Ventricle. She stopped the first mechanic she saw, unbuckled his belt and pulled it right off him. Like the tech, he simply watched her, speechless. She waved him on and he went, nearly running.

"It doesn't matter. I have to do what I can. Especially if I can save her."

"You've formed a bond with her," Galen said softly. "Through Cyan."

"I guess I have. I hadn't even noticed it until last night. Regardless of any bond, I'm going to do anything I can to save the ship and the people on her."

Galen had no response and for that she was glad. She was almost there. The number of people had thinned as she neared the Ventricle and now there was no one. She pulled the com unit over her pointed right ear. She could hear Calyph already babbling on the other end.

"Jordan Blue! Jordan Blue?"

Why must everyone shout my name in panic?

"I'm right here," she told him. A heavy sigh came from the other end.

"Where are you?"

"Right outside the Ventricle door."

"Jesus," Calyph said.

"Dammit!" Galen said. "Get *out* of there!"

"Zip it, the both of you!" Blue shouted. "You can help or you can shut the hell up! Otherwise, I'm turning you off!" She paused, listening. Calyph was stunned, wondering who else could be with her. Galen held his tongue. Blue was blissfully greeted by silence in both ears.

She exhaled sharply and pulled a length of reflective tape from the roll and tore a piece off using her teeth. She let the roll drop down her arm like a bracelet and used the piece of tape to secure her left eye, keeping it closed and covered.

Due to her prosthetic eye and the damage to the nerves around it, both eyelids opened and closed in sync on the same neuromuscular link to her brain. In this way she was similar to a construct, in the fact that she was physically unable to wink. She was able, however, to use her ocular muscles to force her eyes open – like she did now. Except that her true eye was being held closed and protected by a simple piece of reflective tape.

"Put another piece on," Galen said. "At an angle from your nose towards your ear."

Blue tore off another piece and tamped it down over the first the way Galen had instructed, pressing along the edges to get a good seal.

The Jordan pushed open the door to the Ventricle and did the one thing she could do that a construct could not – she whistled.

Scarlett opened her eyes with a start. Alerts were going off and the Fledgling's heartbeat was quick and urgent. She sat up quickly, her bed moving with her and becoming a chair once again.

She frowned as a gravitational force pushed her back.

That's not right. That's not right at all.

Scarlett knew that if she was feeling any sort of gee, it meant that their coordinate acceleration was in not in conjunction with their actual acceleration.

Which means Fledge is trying to fly faster that he can fold. What the hell is going on?

Three requests for coms were flashing on the console. There was one that was designated specifically for the Dragon and she saw immediately the red light above it was flashing – a distress signal. Scarlett had never seen a distress from the Dragon before. From *any* Dragon. Her mouth filled with a bitter metallic taste that took her a second to identify. It was fear.

The gravitational force was bad, but not as disturbing as the signal. The g-force was something that shouldn't be felt in any kind of Dragon vessel, but it was something she could ignore, at least for the time being. Not so for the flashing red light.

Scarlett reached out and ran her thumb over the pulsing glow. A hologram in shades of crimson lit up the dash. It was a profile of Captain Brogan in the bridge of the Opal Dragon, facing away to her left.

"Sir," a voice chimed, "it's Jordan Scarlett." Brogan turned sharply to face her.

"Jordan."

"Yes, sir. I'm on my way. My ETA is..."

"A situation has developed on the Dragon that you need to avoid at all costs," Brogan interrupted.

"Sir?"

"Change your coordinates to 759, 977, Star System 5. You are to link up with the IGC ship, *Solomon*." Scarlett was about to voice her questions but the Captain's eyes forbade any. Even through the holo, his gaze was cold and commanding. "Jordan?"

"Yes, sir?" Scarlett swallowed, waiting.

Brogan pressed his lips together and did something she did not expect – he let that hard stare of his soften, just the tiniest bit. "Stay safe," he told her. The holo vanished, the link cut from the other end. Scarlett would have sat back, hard, into her seat – but she was already pinned there.

"That sounded too much like good-bye," Scarlett told the Fledgling, her voice shaking. She ran a hand over the dash and the coordinate key panel rose. She paused, her hand hovering over the keyboard for a second, and then typed in the coordinates the Captain had given her.

There was a brief pause and then – nothing. Not exactly nothing, the thrust of g-force driving Scarlett into her chair stopped and she slowly sank down. There was a whirr as the mechanics embedded within the Fledgling kicked back in but Fledge had managed to override his controls and now hovered, frozen in space.

"Fledge?" Scarlett asked. "What are you doing?"

There was no response from the Fledgling, of course, except for a quick and irregular heartbeat. Scarlett listened to the pulse of liquid hydrogen around her and knew it was distressed.

"Fledge," she said, "we are a military ship, and we have been given an order. We need to get to the *Solomon.*" She could feel a deep humming, within herself as well as in the Fledgling – his indecision meshing with her own. "Come on, Fledge. I don't like it either. But they wouldn't keep us away if there was any way we could help. Let's get going and see if we can find Blue and Jade. Maybe we can find out what is going on."

Scarlett didn't know if the Fledgling could understand her exact words, but he got her meaning and responded immediately. The ship tilted, getting a bead on the coordinates, and shot off through the darkness.

Scarlett ran a finger along the com panel, opening the link with Jade aboard the Green Fledgling.

"Jade?" Scarlett asked. "Are you there?"

A flickering image rose above the dash of Jade's boyish face with light green eyes and chocolate-colored hair. He was much older than Scarlett, though he looked much younger and was indeed young for an elf. "Of course I am. Can you believe this?"

"Are you kidding? I don't even know what is going on. Are you headed for *Solomon?*"

"No, they have me going for *Westbrooke 8.*"

Scarlett flipped up the galaxy holo and turned it, scanning for his Fledgling, identifying his course and his destination. "That's not even an IGC ship! And it's in the opposite direction of where I'm headed."

"I know," Jade told her. "You don't know what happened?"

"No. You do?" She could hear Jade let out a deep breath.

"The Opal Dragon was infiltrated. A Chimeran got on board and turned loose the starfire. They're evacuating the ship."

Scarlett's hand came up to cover her mouth.

The starfire. She knew it was the heart of the ship, even Fledge had his own little spark of it. She got to see it one time, when she worked with the Engineers on his first growing. It was like a child's handful of moonlight, held suspended in a golden field.

"What will happen?" she asked.

"Nobody took the time to give me any details, but if they initiated an evac, I assume they expect the Dragon to be annihilated." Scarlett forgot to breathe, shocked by the news as well as Jade's ambivalent delivery. "They are sending us in opposite directions, and to different federations, just in case there has been some kind of overthrow."

Scarlett went from stunned to indignant. "By the Chimera? They don't have that kind of manpower or logistical ability in any way."

"Nevertheless, no one is taking any chances. The other Dragons have been searched and, though nothing was found, their Fledglings have been dispatched to undisclosed locations."

"Did you get all this from Brogan?"

"No, he was pretty short. I was able to pick up a com with one of our pilots. He pretty much said the same as you, he doesn't think the Chimera could form an all out offensive. He thinks it's an isolated attack."

"Is there anything they can do?" Scarlett asked.

"I don't think so, but he said he thinks Blue is trying something. He wasn't given any details."

Scarlett's hand curled into a fist just hearing Blue's name and her face contorted, livid.

Jade felt a wave of ionic energy pass through him that was not entirely pleasant. Scarlett's fury poured out of her like water and was absorbed by her Fledgling like a sponge. The transmitted emotion came in a muted form to its sibling and from there into Jade. He shivered, picking up the effects of her anger, though she was at least half a light year away. The Green Jordan smiled and cringed while marveling at the ripple effect he felt. A lock of his dark hair fell down over his eyes. He laughed nervously, brushing it away.

"And just what does she think she can do?" Scarlett hissed. "And where is she right now?"

Jade braced himself, knowing Scarlett wasn't going to like it. "She's aboard the Dragon," he told her. He felt the ripple wash over him again. *Our bond is getting stronger,* he thought.

"Why the hell did they let her board and not us?" she demanded.

"From what I understand, she was already there."

Scarlett pounded her knee with her fist.

Of course she was already there! Blue had to arrive early just for the thrill of being able to do so. Well, should the worst happen and we lose the Dragon, at least I will be rid of her as well.

Even as Scarlett tried to find some sort of satisfaction within her, she knew that she truly felt different. Even being rid of Blue was not worth losing a Dragon. Especially *her* Dragon. She bit her tongue so hard that blood filled her mouth. *Damn her!*

"What is it?" Jade asked, feeling her internal battle in a wave of seething nausea, but not understanding it. To him it felt as if he had a bellyful of live worms. Scarlett pressed her lips together and shook her head.

"I hate having to hope for her!"

Jade laughed. "Then just hope for us all. Stay safe, Scarlett. I'll buzz you if I hear anything new."

The Green Jordan was gone in a blink and Scarlett pounded her leg, cursing.

Oddly enough, even after having a prosthetic eye for almost six years, Blue never gave it much thought. The optic never bothered her and, as far as she knew, it was neither able nor unable to do anything her other eye couldn't. Galen had wired and implanted it after her accident.

Her memories of the accident, and the events that led up to it, were blurry and called up a very unpleasant feeling inside when she tried to remember exactly what had happened. She thought it better not to think of it at all. Why would she want to? She had everything she had ever wanted and was completely content. She wasn't about to let anyone screw it up, especially herself. She knew that if one let in room for doubt, it would grow and fester. Doubt was treacherous.

With her prosthetic eye working alone for the first time, the difference she could see was immediate and intense. Before, when a light was suddenly flicked on in a dark room or when she stepped out of a dwelling into sunlight, she had to squint or shade her eyes until they adjusted to the sudden luminosity. Now, though she was exposed to a light so bright it would blind any living being, she could look right at it – right through it – and without any lag time. Her optic adjusted faster than she could react.

When Blue opened the door the light burst forth, enveloping her entire form and reaching deep into the hallway behind her. Her optic darkened instantly, protectively. Her first vision of the Ventricle was dim but clear, like she was wearing high-definition eyeshades, but then brightened as the optic gradually increased the light until it reached maximum clarity at the safest level. It all took less than a second.

Blue could feel the radiance reach inside her as she breathed it in - filling her lungs and aspirating into her bloodstream. Her blood felt infused with illumination, and took it to every cell in her body, saturating every part of her being until she thought it would start shooting from her hands and mouth and ears and the single eye that was taking it all in and sending it to her brain at . She could feel the power of it swell with each breath she took, feeling the light pulsing within her and realized with a convulsive shudder that it was the heartbeat of the Dragon.

"Jordan?" Galen ventured. "Are you alright?" Blue nodded. Though she knew he couldn't see her, she found herself unable to speak for the moment. She thought that his voice would be muted, or that she might not be able to hear him at all. It seemed that nothing would be able to get through the enormity of the light, or would at least be so minute in comparison, but his voice was clear. "How are you feeling?"

Blue took another deep breath, pulling in the pulsing light. She thought her voice would come out in a hoarse whisper, but it was clear and sharp. "I feel eight feet tall," she told him.

Galen smiled against her neck. He knew that it was a Blueism for pretty damn good, considering it was nearly twice her height.

"What was that?" Calyph chimed over the com.

Blue grinned and knew that she must be a gruesome sight – mech tape over one half of her face and the other a ravaged mess of scarred fleshed, a manufactured orb set into desiccated tissue. She laughed, giddy.

"Jordan?" Calyph asked. "Are you okay?"

"Yeah, I'm fine."

"Can you see?"

"Yes."

"Everything?"

"As far as I can tell."

"Well no disrespect, Jordan, but we don't have time to dick around. Do you see the center column?"

"Yes."

"Is the panel still off?"

"Yes."

"Good. Get over there and have a look. I need you to tell me what you see."

Blue moved towards the source of light, but once she instigated the motion it seemed more like she was pulled to it. She hardly had to move her legs at all. The pulse was stronger here. It invaded her on a deeper level, taking over her own heartbeat and making it its own.

She braced her hands against the sides of the opening and put her head cautiously inside, peering around as her optic adjusted. What she saw made her jerk back in surprise, her single eye wide and staring. Open mouthed, she peeked back inside. She could feel a pressure against the side of her face and knew it was Galen, looking over her shoulder.

"Jesus," she whispered.

"What's wrong?"

For a second she couldn't answer, only stare - and for that same second, she almost lost her nerve. She wasn't sure what she had expected to see – circuits, gears, pipes, or maybe some sort of a motherboard. Whatever she expected, it was mechanical. This was anything but. It was a thick, ropy, mass of metallic cybernetics and shiny organic matter.

Unlike the outer wall of the column, the inner wall was not a smooth and unmarred surface. It was covered with thick ropes of silvery veins and arteries, ridged and rippled with capillaries and fibrous material that reached out like small explosions of filaments into the inner chamber of the column. The light pulsed like heavy blood and there was a wet, earthy, metallic smell that permeated the cavity.

In the center of it all, above her head but close enough that she could touch the bottom, was a pulsing orb of light larger than her head that was almost too bright even for her biomechanical eye to look at. A sparkling silver field flecked with gold, so thin it was almost unintelligible, encapsulated it. The orb pulsed out into an amoeba shaped glob of light and contracted again into a silver-gold sphere.

"This isn't a circuit repair," she whispered. "It's heart surgery." Galen made a sound like a grunt.

"Jordan!" Calyph's voice was urgent. "What do you see?"

She exhaled sharply. "I can see the starfire."

"Is it hanging in a silver field?"

"I can't tell if it's silver or gold."

"That means the second layer is giving way. Once that happens we only have the epicardium holding it in."

"What do I do?"

"Did you grab a mech set?"

"Yes."

"Find a laser curette. If you don't have one of those, a soldering pen will work for now."

Jordan Blue withdrew her head from the interior of the column and looked down at the belt she was wearing.

"On your left hip," Galen told her. "The one that looks like a flattened tube." Blue pulled it from the loop on the belt. "Turn it on," he instructed. "It's the dial at the bottom." She pushed the dial with her thumb and a spear of blue light sprang from the tip of the curette. It shot up nearly twenty centimeters before arcing over in a wide loop and then disappearing back into the curette. "Not so much," Galen told her. "Dial it down a bit." Blue rolled the dial backwards until the laser was only half as long, and the loop at the tip was considerably smaller. "Better."

"Alright," she said.

"You're going to need about a ten centimeter blade," Calyph told her.

"I've already got it. What's next?"

"Look into the inner ventricle column. Directly beneath the opening."

Blue tipped her head back inside the inner wall. The first thing she saw was that all the silver was gone from the orb. It was naked except for the last field of fine gold mesh that held it in. The beat was becoming more erratic as the starlight struggled to get free. The round, amoeba-like legs pushed farther out, straining against the epicardial sac. She pressed her lips together to keep from cursing.

"The second field is gone. We're down to the first."

Calyph promptly used the expletive she had held back. "Don't worry," he assured. "It won't take long." Blue was unsure if he meant the repair or their demise. She wondered if everyone else had gotten off the ship yet. She had no idea how long it had been since she left the bridge. "Look down the inner wall of the Ventricle, directly beneath you."

Blue pushed her head farther into the opening and her nose met again with that wet, earthy, metallic smell. It was like sticking her head into an ancient wishing well full of coins. She looked down the membranous wall and saw what she had missed before. There *was* a circuit board, of sorts. It was thin and silver - inset and intermeshed with the organic material that surrounded it. The wires that came off the contact points turned into capillaries which grew into arteries that became thick cables that spiraled up the inner wall of the ventricular column.

"That's it," Galen told her. "That coil is what creates the electromagnetic fields."

"What do I do?" Blue asked.

"Do you see the circuit board?" Calyph asked.

"Yes."

"Are all of the wires coming off it connected to the contact points to the capillaries?"

"Yes."

"Are you sure?"

The Jordan frowned. "Of course I'm sure, I'm looking right at them."

Calyph paused. "I was sure that's what he cut. What else do you see?"

Blue searched the circuit board, trying to see what might be missing or wrong. She could feel a moment of panic rise in her throat before she saw it. Galen spotted it at the same time.

"That's it," he affirmed. "Shit."

"Shit," she repeated.

"What is it?" Calpyh asked.

Blue licked her lips. "It's the circuit between the field connectors on the board."

"Have they been cut?"

"No. They're dissolving. The first two are already gone." She watched as the long bright line that curved back and forth into tight esses between the last connectors sizzled, slowly growing shorter. There were ghostly lines between the other contacts on the board that showed where the first two had been. Like the fuse on a nitro-glycerin stick, the last connection between points was slowly burning away. "He must have put down some sort of corrosive."

"That *bastard*!" Calyph cursed in one ear while Galen clucked in the other. "It's okay," Calyph said, quickly regaining his composure. "Let's just do this. First, we need to stop whatever is eating the circuit. Use the curette to cut a line directly in the path of the dissolving circuit trace, but leave as much of the trace intact as possible."

Blue reached inside and for a second she thought she was too short to reach in far enough. She stood on her toes and leaned in as far as she could. She made it, barely. But the angle was such that she could hardly see the end of the curette, and the strain to reach the circuit was making her hand tremble.

Her eye flicked up at the pulsing starfire. The sparkling gold mesh was thinning, becoming harder to see. The starfire pushed again and again with each pulsing beat.

She looked back down, reaching for the board and trying to steady her shaking hand.

"Here."

Blue felt Galen's hand cover her own and guide it down and onto the board. When he let go she peered down. There was a centimeter wide cut in the circuit. She watched as the burning part of the circuit met the cut. It paused, as if confused, before sizzling and dying out.

Blue let out a sigh but the relief was short felt. She glanced up at the starfire. It was still struggling to get free, maybe even more so now, it was difficult to tell. The erratic heartbeat of the Dragon was now a thud in her ears as well as her chest. Nothing was fixed, just stopped. And by the way the sparkle around the orb was beginning to dwindle, it looked like the starfire itself was trying to pick up where the damaged circuit left off.

"Jordan? What's going on?"

"I stopped it."

"Good, let's get to fixing it – it should be done quickly."

"You don't say," she muttered.

"In the mech set there should be a cylindrical, black tube with a long, pointed, screw-on cap."

Blue withdrew her head from the chamber again to assess her tool belt. "Got it." She pulled the tube free of the belt and unscrewed the cap to expose a needle-like tip underneath.

"That's transition metal liquid flux. Squeeze it out of the tube gently and apply it over the lines where the circuits used to be. Make sure you get the contact points too."

Blue leaned back into the opening, bent over, and began tracing the faint lines on the board with the flux. Galen only needed to guide her hand once to get a contact point that was almost too far down to reach.

"Done!"

"Alright." Calyph ran his palms up and down his thighs, wiping the sweat from them. There were few people left in the bridge. He closed his eyes. "Every mech set has at least four different types of wire. They should be in coils that have been flattened."

Again she withdrew and checked the belt. She didn't see any wire.

"Behind you," Galen said. She swiveled the belt around her hips, putting the back in the front. Flattened coils of wire hung off it in a neat row.

"Thanks," Blue said.

"What?" Calyph asked.

"I said I have seven coils."

Calyph paused, knowing that it wasn't what she had said. "Look for the copper roll."

"There are three copper rolls!" She glanced into the ventricular column, eyeing the pulsing sac of light. She could feel its pulsing beat under her skin, in her hands now as well as in her face and her lips.

"The copper wire that has a green tint to it."

"Got it."

"Good. Turn the laser on the curette down as low as it will go, and look on the bottom of the handle, there should be a small opening there."

"Yep."

"Pull out an arm's length of wire and feed the end of it into the opening until it comes out the top."

"Done."

"Do you know how to lay a circuit between the contacts, or do you want me to walk you through it?"

"I can do it, but stand-by if you can."

"I'm right here," he assured. Calyph opened his eyes as the Captain sat down next to him. Brogan held a silver flask and offered it to the Engineer. Calyph shook his head. Brogan sat back and took a long pull from the flask.

Blue leaned back into the chamber, and now it seemed as if the starfire knew what she was doing. Its strange, stretching pulses stabbed anxiously in her direction. She could feel its angry beat echoed by a pulsing in her scalp and her eyes. No, just one eye – the one being held down and covered by the tape, the real one. She turned her face away from the orb, and looked down.

"Let's do this," she whispered.

She traced the first circuit path, feeling Galen's face pressed next to hers and his arm down the length of her own. She could feel his fingers wrapped her wrist, keeping her hand steady and sure. The curette laid down a smooth, perfect stream of beryllium copper. She connected it to the first contact and looked up.

The starfire hung in a field of shifting, molten gold. Her shoulders sank, relief so palpable it made her queasy. "The first circuit is repaired." She could hear an enormous sigh from the com-link with Calyph and then his muted voice as he gave the news to someone.

The Captain, most likely. The thought encouraged her.

She went to work on the second circuit. She looked up as she finished, just in time for her eye to catch the silver light that shot out and outlined the sphere, then surrounded it with a grid of silver lines that closed around it and pulled it up like a fisherman's net pulling in a catch. It no longer seemed to struggle. The pulse was returning to a normal, rhythmic beat.

"Second circuit repaired," she announced.

Calyph almost laughed with relief and joy. "The myocardium is repaired," she heard him say.

Blue, with Galen's guiding hand, finished the last circuit. She swayed back, exhausted, her head cocked to the side as so she could see the result of her handiwork. Green light poured from the cables that spiraled up the inner wall of the ventricle, splashing onto the orb, wrapping it. Tighter and tighter the light squeezed, pulling the starfire in and up – until it was a true sphere again, its beat slow and steady.

"It's done," she said over the com.

"She did it," Calyph said softly, and Blue could hear the muted sounds of people around him cheering and laughing. She sank to her knees and covered her face with her hands. The sounds went on for a few moments before Calyph cleared his throat. "Jordan?" he asked. "I need you to do one more thing for me."

Blue's head rolled back on her shoulders and a nervous titter escaped her lips. "Jesus, Calyph! Haven't I done enough for you today?"

He chuckled, as sick with relief as she was. "I know, I know. Just one more thing."

Blue sighed. "Well?"

"Along each edge of the circuit board, in the center, is a contact screw. I need you to connect them with a line of iridium, it's the black coil of wire, the same way you laid down the circuit."

Blue pulled herself to her feet and did as Calyph asked. Everything seemed slow and heavy. She didn't know if it was the calming beat of the Dragon's heart, or the ebb of adrenaline she had been drowning in only moments ago. Once all the contact screws were connected, the ventricle chamber was plunged into to darkness for the microsecond it took her optic to adjust to the dimmed light.

"You're all set," she told Calyph and then pulled the comset off her ear and dropped it on the floor. She sank down and pushed herself back with her feet, scooting backwards until she was leaning against the outer wall of the chamber. Except it didn't feel like leaning against a metal wall. It felt like she was leaning against Galen, almost sitting in his lap. She carefully peeled the reflective tape from her face and let her head fall back and rest against the ghost of his shoulder.

"You did a great job," Galen told her.

She smiled and leaned back into him. "I couldn't have done it without you," she said, closing her eyes.

"You would have done just fine," he said. But instead of proud, his voice sounded, to her, just a little bit sad.

 FIVE

Three hundred pilots stood at parade rest on the white gravel road in front of the JTC Headquarters. Equipment and clothing, all in a near colorless shade of gray, had been issued. Barracks and lockers had been assigned. Every pilot's hands rested on the small of the back, right hand over left, thumbs folded over. Three hundred pairs of eyes stared dead ahead as Master Sergeant Malherbe bellowed at them and their impudent existence.

JM stood with her feet hip width apart, perfectly still. Not just because military discipline dictated it, but because she detested gravel. The way it shifted underfoot and the dust that always seemed to find its way into her nostrils as well as every crevice of her boots was irritating enough, but the sound was worse.

JM remembered losing her first baby tooth in grade school during lunch and, not realizing it had fallen out, munched down on it with her other teeth. The feeling and the sound of it had horrified her. The crunch of gravel underfoot always sounded like grinding bones to her, especially the little ones that liked to sneak themselves into sandwiches.

The disturbing event was never repeated. From then on, every time she noticed a tooth growing loose she promptly yanked it out herself. Only on one occasion did she meet with a tooth too stubborn to comply with her small, chubby fingers. When a polite request to an older brother to knock it out was denied, she found after a kick to his tenders he was happy to oblige – as soon as he caught his breath.

Three hundred pilots stood motionless in their gray uniforms, gray caps and gray boots, looking like dusty ghosts. Ten platoons of thirty pilots, each with a single squad of female pilots.

Sixty out of three hundred, JM thought. She knew that it was the most the JTC had ever allowed. She kept tabs on Master Sergeant Malherbe with her peripheral vision as he paced in front of the troops, spitting degradations at them. He was easily the ugliest man JM had ever seen.

He had a ridiculously squat, powerful build. His chest and shoulders looked to be almost as broad as he was tall. He had a great, hooked nose that looked like it had been broken a fair amount of times and spittle flew through his rubbery lips. He was a stereotypical drill instructor, though she had to admit he was by far the scariest looking drill she had ever encountered.

"There are *no* second chances here!" he shouted. "If you fail a written test, a physical test, or *any* test for that matter - *you are out of here!* If you fall out of a run - *you are out of here!* Falling back more than an arm's length away from the person in front of you constitutes falling out of the run, *and you will find yourself floating home!*"

His eyes were hidden in the shade from the bill on the black cap he wore. His uniform was dark, tight, and tucked into tightly laced, shiny, black boots. He eschewed the gravel and paced on the narrow lawn wedged between the road and the building. Beads of sweat gathered on his face and neck as he belted out every word.

"DO NOT say *aye*, to me unless yours has been shot! I am *not* a sailor! A simple fucking *yes* will suffice! DO NOT call me *sir* - I am not your father! At least I don't think I am! But, even if I *was*, I would never admit to having such a worthless excuse for my offspring!"

JM kept still. His tirade went on for another five minutes while the afternoon air on the Lido moon cooled around them.

"Now!" Malherbe shouted. "Ensign Corvette is waiting to brief all the male pilots in their Day Room. I will be briefing all the females in their Day Room. I want everyone back out here at 1630 in their EG! That means you are lined up *in formation* at 1625!"

Every pilot remained frozen, waiting for the command to fall out.

"*Get the fuck out of here!*" he yelled. His face was so red and angry it looked ready to pop off his shoulders. Everyone took off, running.

Though the group of female pilots ran at a steady pace around the HQ building and through the compound, Malherbe was already waiting for them at their barracks.

"Go! Go! Go!" he shouted, holding the door open with a booted foot for them as they hurried past. He scowled at them, as impatient and pissed as if he had been there for hours. "Come on! We don't have all fucking day!"

JM hurried in, ripping off her gray cap and shoving it into her back pocket. She joined the others already there, standing smartly at parade rest.

"Get your cover off!" Malherbe screamed at a pilot who didn't have her cap off the precise moment she passed the doorframe. "And fix that hair!" The pilot tucked a stray curl behind her ear.

The room was large and comfortable, though it had few chairs. There was a holo screen at one end and a few private desks with com centers at the other. The only thing that caught her eye was a card table set up for Omaha. It was a room for relaxing in during their off hours. They would not see it again for a year. If they were still here.

"Sit down," Malherbe ordered as he followed the last pilot in, taking off his own cap. JM and a few others promptly took a chair, but most looked about, unsure. "I said sit, Godammit! Not find a seat!" The standing pilots sank to the floor.

His hair was too short to tell what color it was, though JM guessed it was brown. She could see his eyes now. They were blue and beady and mean. He crossed his thick arms and leaned against the wall. From his expression it was clear that he was disgusted with all of them. JM bit her tongue to keep her lips from twitching.

"This school," he told them, "has an average attrition rate of ninety-five percent. Does anyone know what that means?"

"That only fifteen pilots will make it," someone said. JM expected him to yell at the unfortunate speaker but he only nodded.

"That's right," he said. "But that's just the average. One time we had only three. And, *genius*, do you know how many female pilots usually pass this course?"

"There have been none so far, Master Sergeant."

"Right again! You must be a damn prodigy!" He clucked his tongue and looked about the room. "Well, there certainly are a lot more of you than usual. The board must be getting lax in their standards or else some libber up there thinks we might get sweet on one of you and let one slide. Well, I'm going to tell you right now that *that* is not going to happen. If you make it, you make it. If you don't, you don't. I'm certainly expecting the latter."

He pushed away from the wall and leaned menacingly towards the female cadets. "You will be held to the same standards as the male pilots here," he said through his teeth. "You will not wear make-up, you will keep your hair properly stowed, and if any of you are still getting your periods you better get your ass to the medic and have that taken care of the first chance you get."

He looked at them all in turn. When his eyes fell on her, JM felt that he didn't hate her because she was a woman, but because he hated everybody. It wasn't pleasant, but she didn't flinch.

"Now get your asses in your EG and get in formation!" he yelled, his face apoplectic, the veins standing out on his neck and forehead. "Let's see just how much space I can clear on the first day!"

As JM darted past him she ducked her head in an instinctive, cringing reaction she couldn't help. She could feel the aura of disgust around him as she passed through it and it made her grind her teeth together, something she had never done.

Their exercise gear consisted of the normal uniform, simply minus the flight jacket. Gray cotton shirts tucked into gray canvas pants tucked into gray strinam boots. JM knew she could run in them all day and all night. No big deal. Malherbe started with the physical training norm – running, sit-ups and push-ups and the like. Also, no big deal. Except that it was all on the gravel.

The running was bad. Every crunch underfoot kept her jaw clenched for two miles. The rolling sit-ups were worse. Small jags of rocks snagged on her shirt and stuck in her hair. *They are not bones,* she assured herself. *They are not teeth. Jesus, get a hold of yourself! It's the first fucking day!*

The push-ups were the worst. It wasn't the dusty rocks cutting into her palms and wedging themselves into the toes of her boots. It was dipping her face down so close to those bits of bone, those broken teeth. The rocks themselves smelled like a dirty playground while her mind conjured up the smell of bologna and mayonnaise.

She had pushed out twenty when there was a sharp burst of pain as something smashed into her right hip, driving it into the gravel along with the upper right side of her body. Her face hit the gravel and rebounded with bits of dusty, broken stone imbedded in her nose and cheek. She felt blood well in her bottom lip.

"Somebody lied on your entrance card!" Malherbe shouted down at her. "Every time you go down and your chin does not touch that rock *it does not count!* You are still at zero!"

JM pushed herself up and came back down till her nose was touching stone, and then pushed back up again.

"Zero!" Malherbe shouted. His face was suddenly next to hers and she could feel his hot breath against her sweaty cheek. "Jesus Christ JM! You can't do one single push-up? What the fuck kind of shitty excuse for pilots is the IGC sending us?"

JM pushed up hard, her teeth grinding together like the rocks under her hands, and dropped back down till her face was submerged in the gritty rubble. She pushed back up and did it again.

Malherbe stormed off to scream at someone else. JM continued to drop her face down into the gravel of the training yard.

Shit, she thought as the dust gathered on each drop of blood. *He already knows who I am. That can't be good.*

After a steamy shower, Scarlett dried her hair and dressed in a black onesuit with a black belt. Though it wasn't a flight suit, the number sixteen was emblazoned on her left sleeve in crimson thread. She tucked her pant legs into her boots and rolled up her sleeves. She left the chest buttons unfastened, her breasts pushing the fabric into a wide vee that showed smooth white skin to the center of her sternum. She draped a long scarf of thin, red fabric around her throat.

Scarlett had always been a bit self-conscious when it came to her neck – hell, she was self-conscious about damn near everything. She had a feeling, though, that the cords in her neck were just a bit too *sinewy*. Probably from yelling so much, but she wasn't about to change that. Her intensity was part of who she was. Besides, neckwear was sexy. She flipped one end over her left shoulder and let the other end hang down over her left breast.

She forwent jewelry except for the ear studs she always wore. Two of polished garnet at the top of her right ear and one of polished platinum at the top of her left ear.

She brushed out her hair; the thick, dark locks starting to form fist sized curls and waves in the dry air of deep space. She gave it one last shake and left her cabin and headed for the Lower Atrium.

The Atrium was a semi-open, ovoid space, three stories high in the belly of the Dragon. The Lower Atrium was lined with social bars, clubs, and a few light drugbars. The Mid Atrium was full of shops that provided all kinds of goods or services interspersed with a few apothecaries, coffeeshops, and com-link cafés. The Upper Atrium consisted of all kinds of eateries, from snack counters to intimate vitro dining.

Scarlett made her way by some smoke rooms, dipping her head in response to the nods and even bows she received as she walked by. She lingered by one shop, the sweet, heady smell of cannabis filling her nostrils. She continued, passing a bleating techno bar with a slight grimace.

It wasn't that she didn't like the music - she did. The fast, thumping rhythm pulsing at her skin gave her a rush. Scarlett, however, regarded techno music the same way she regarded porn – as arousing as it was pointless. Both were great for about all of ten minutes, then it was just enough already.

She passed a bar with house music and stopped suddenly, looking across her shoulder to glimpse a familiar face. Calyph sat at the bar, drinking a bottle of black porter. He glanced up and met her eyes the second after she saw him.

Scarlett turned and walked into the club, drawing every eye as conversations lulled, giving the music riotous reign. Calyph swallowed the last, half-chewed bite of his dinner. It drew a long scratch down his throat that he hardly noticed. Most everyone in the club gave the Crimson Jordan respectful nods as she passed before returning to their conversations and libations. Calyph could barely glance away before staring back at her again.

What is it about her? Calyph wondered. There was something about her that made every other woman in the bar look pale by comparison. Then it came to him immediately as she walked between two other human women on her way to the bar where he was sitting.

She looks full, he decided at once, pushing away his dinner plate. *Full everywhere.*

Though the Dragon was better than most ships, deep space had a way of making space crew look starved. Starved for oxygen, nutrition, moisture, sleep. Scarlett was an anomaly, apparently unaffected and unscathed by space travel. Full lips, full hips, full hair and breasts that seemed to draw Calyph's eyes like iron fillings to a magnet. He had to force himself to look away. She made the other human women in the bar look plain and the elfin women look practically emaciated.

She looks strong. Calyph thought. *Strong enough to chew up an elf and spit him out.* The thought was not entirely unpleasant.

She came right up and took the seat next to him.

"Calyph," she said, smiling wickedly.

"Jordan Scarlett."

"I didn't expect to see you here," she told him.

"In this bar?"

"On this Dragon."

"Oh. Well, circumstances required my presence – so, here I am." He hoped she wouldn't ask why, knowing that information was for the Captain to disclose.

"Where's your troll?" she asked with a smirk.

"He doesn't need to eat."

The bartender came over to Scarlett. "Vinero," she told him. He gave her a nod and hustled off.

"Actually, he's engaged in a download."

"Update?"

"Yep."

"All seven systems?"

"Yep."

Scarlett whistled. "That might take awhile. I guess I'll just have to keep you company."

Calyph took a pull from his bottle. "You just get in?" he asked, although he already knew.

"Just a few hours ago." The tender returned with a glass half full of liquid the color of blood and she gave him a nod of thanks. "Jade should be here sometime tomorrow."

"You missed the excitement," Calyph told her.

"I already heard," she said, rolling her eyes. Calyph laughed.

"You don't like Jordan Blue, do you?" he asked, amused. Scarlett's disgust was almost palpable.

"That bionic bitch shouldn't have a license to operate a forklift."

"No honor among Jordans?"

Scarlett sneered and downed her drink. She held up her glass and the tender brought her another one immediately.

"Didn't you two go to flight school together?" Calyph asked. Scarlett shook her head.

"Only Jordan training. I don't even know where she went to flight school. She appeared from nowhere and has been a tack in my boot ever since." Calyph laughed and waggled his bottle at the man to get his attention. The tender heaved a sigh and fetched him another porter.

"I don't know if bionic would be a correct term," he said. "Other than her eye, I don't know if she has any other prosthetics. Not many would be legal, not for a pilot anyway."

Scarlett shrugged. "Who knows what that crazy doctor has put into her? Other than his useless cock, that is." Calyph laughed again.

"Ahh, that's right. You and Dr. What's-His-Name were a thing for a while. I had forgotten. This isn't a jealousy thing, is it?"

Scarlett snorted. "I was done with him long before he found her, and she's welcome to my seconds if she wants 'em."

"Did she always have that burn on her face?"

"As long as I've known her. It's obvious that it could only be a Lethe burn."

"The Council would never let her pilot for the IGC if she used drugs."

"Galen could have done something about that," Scarlett told him. Calyph looked skeptical.

"I don't know. The council is obsessively stringent when it comes to licensing pilots."

"Yes, but the good doctor *is* wicked smart. I'll give him that much." Thinking about him made her want to shudder, but she didn't want to show any sort of weakness, especially in front of Calyph.

Galen had been more than just a casual lover. They had lived together during her last year of advanced flight. He had been the one to break it off, though she was relieved when he did. She was slated to go to Jordan Training and she didn't want any distractions. He turned out to be one anyway, not that Scarlett would ever admit it. He simply showed up, two systems away at the Jordan Training Center with the little waif. Scarlett had no idea what he saw in her.

"Do you think she got in because of her family?" Calyph asked.

"She doesn't have any ties to them, as far as I know."

"Everyone has ties."

"I never heard her speak to them or of them."

There was the picture, Scarlett thought. A shiver went up her spine.

"Do you know her well?"

Scarlett frowned. "Yes and no. I know her well enough from training – not because I wanted to, but because she is so damned simple and predictable."

"Were you close in Jordan school?"

Scarlett laughed into her drink and shook her head. "No."

"I find that hard to believe, even if you don't like her. You spent all that time training together. Christ, you lived in the same barracks for what, three years?"

"There were a lot of pilots training there. And though we trained together quite a bit, I wouldn't think of asking her a personal question any more than I would consider kissing a Golgoth."

Calyph smiled and took a long pull from his bottle. "It's ironic, though, don't you think?"

"What is?"

"That she is fighting in a war against what her family is responsible for creating."

"What's left of her family is scattered across seven systems, and they are openly Anti-Chimera. Shit, they do so much of the war funding for the IGC, they're probably signing our checks. "

"But the Dyer Maker is ultimately responsible for GwenSeven."

Scarlett shrugged. "That was a long time ago. Blue never knew him, I'm pretty sure of that. Hell, I don't think she even knew all of her sisters."

Calyph nodded and sipped his porter. He felt his eyes drifting down Scarlett's neckline. He looked away as quickly as he could but Scarlett hadn't noticed. She was thinking about Jordan training and how Blue had shown up out of nowhere with Galen by her side.

Scarlett had mistrusted her from the start. There was always something suspicious about her. Everyone thought she was some sort of prodigy, not that Scarlett gave a damn. She thought the fuss everyone made over the half-elf pilot was disgusting.

Scarlett knew that elves lived naturally for a very long time, without any artificial enhancements. They outlived any other humanoid race by hundreds of years. Consequently, having all the time in the universe, they took their sweet time in everything they did. They often were slower to learn, and slower to react. They called it "habituated shyness." Scarlett simply wrote most of them off as lazy or ignorant. Usually both. Many elves took reflex and learning enhancement drugs, whereas humans would take longevity enhancing drugs. In the long run, it all seemed to even out, unless there was an anomaly. Like Blue.

Scarlett had been eighteen years when she finished secondary schooling and started college. She knew that the elfin norm for this was closer to a hundred years. She was aware that she spent quite a few years in college, mostly because she was just helling around, but that elves took a hell of a lot longer. She knew that Jade was incredibly sharp and had gone through his schooling at an accelerated rate, but even he was over a hundred and twenty years old – a fact that Scarlett always had a hard time swallowing. To her, he always looked like a mischievous little boy.

Blue finished flight school and began the Jordan course before she was even thirty. It was astonishing even by human standards. The youngest human to come close to that mark was Cappolian, the Captain of the Onyx Dragon.

Or so they say, Scarlett thought, pondering Blue's age. *She's an elf - she could be three hundred and she'd look much the same. Who the hell knows? Especially when so much her past is cryptically blurred over, obviously on purpose, and by someone with IGC clearance higher than anyone who thought to check her records.*

Scarlett had learned to tolerate her at the JTC and learned to live with her as a mere annoyance on the Dragon. They hardly ever had to work together, she almost never saw Galen, and she hadn't seen the picture since Jordan Training. Scarlett recalled the first time she saw it and it produced the same effect now, that inexplicable sense of déjà vu.

The Crimson Jordan shook her head, trying to toss the memory, lest it put a damper on her night. She gave Calyph her full attention again, this time catching his eyes wandering over her body.

Scarlett smiled into her drink. *Men*, she thought. *They're all the same, no matter what species.* She didn't mind, knowing it made them predictable in most cases. Besides, she liked Calyph. She signaled the tender for another round.

"What are you drinking?" Scarlett asked.

"Something too strong for a Jordan," he assured her.

Scarlett fixed him with a nefarious smile and fastened a hand on his knee. "And what about you, Calyph? Are you too strong for a Jordan?"

Calyph gave her the steadiest grin he could muster and then guzzled his drink. He was certainly going to need another.

Jordan Blue *was* an anomaly – one that bordered on miraculous. The entire elfin species, due to an astonishing natural longevity, was happy to progress at a much slower rate than humans. Infancy lasted for years; childhood for a good fifty years or more. It was true what Scarlett had been told; it was not uncommon for an elf to finish parochial school by the time they were close to a hundred years old, and would take another hundred for any sort of advanced training, should they chose to do so.

Noel De Rossi, however, walked at an age of eight months, talked at one year, and started pre-schooling at two. It was as if she was, almost human. It undoubtedly came from her father, who *was* human and also an anomaly.

Humans and elves had almost identical body types, but due to alien genetic codes, could almost never conceive children. Noel's father, however, had no problem impregnating his elfin wife time and time again; though, much to his disgust, they were always girls.

Young Noel finished minor schooling at fifteen, having skipped two human year school standards and nearly a century of elfin year standards. When a human would have been starting college or technical training at the age of nineteen or an elf at the age of nearly one hundred, Noel had just turned seventeen.

She started flight school at the age of twenty-two, earlier even than most human counterparts the same age, and abbreviating the elfin norm by over a hundred and fifty years. She showed up at the Jordan Training Center two days before her twenty-fifth birthday.

The first completely clear memory that Blue could recall was waking up in a world of white. The first thing that she noticed was how bright the lights were, though they dimmed slightly as she looked around, blinking. It was as if the lights were adjusting to her eyes, instead of the other way around.

Her immediate supposition was that she was in a hospital. The air had the acrid smell of disinfectant and she was slightly propped up in a bed with metal rails. Everything was white. The sheets, the walls, even the thin fabric of the nightgown she wore. Her head felt like it was full of white cotton. So did her mouth.

She tried to remember how she got there, but everything in her mind was a blur, like trying to see objects through moving water. She felt numb and heavy.

She looked to her left where an IV line came out of her arm and ran up a thin, silver pole to a silicone sac of fluid. There were readout screens showing her heart rate, and who knew what else, all being monitored by a resa droid. There was no other bed, no curtain. No nurse, no striper droid. She spotted vials and induction burners on the counter against the far wall and realized she was actually in a laboratory.

"Hello."

She jerked, startled. On her right stood a strikingly handsome elf with black hair and wearing a white medical lab coat. His deep blue eyes were framed by dark lashes and topped with thick dark brows. A stethoscope was slung around his neck and he held a white acrylic pad in his hand. He had a shy but easy smile.

She felt her heartbeat quicken as she looked at him, and she could hear a warning chirp on one of the monitors. He had a square jaw with a pointed chin and hair that hung in his eyes. He pushed his hair away from his face and smiled at her. Her heart, and its chirping echo, quickened again.

"Hello," she managed. His smiled broadened.

"How are you feeling?"

"Numb, confused."

He nodded as if it were to be expected. He tapped at the acrylic in his hand. "Do you feel nauseous? Dizzy?" he asked.

She looked down, thinking and taking inventory of herself and then shook her head slowly. It felt thick, but no dizziness. He tapped at the acrylic again.

"What happened?" she asked. He put the acrylic down and sat on the edge of her bed. Her right hand was lying limp on the blanket and he covered it with one of his own. Her heart skipped at his touch and then skipped again as she looked into his eyes.

"I'm not really sure," he confessed. "I was crossing the Willamette Bridge when I heard a scream from underneath. I jumped the rail and scrambled down the bank and found you there, along with some others. You were stumbling around, a piece of an exploded Lethe pipe in your hand. I caught you as you were about to go into the water."

She nodded slowly. The memory was there, but very far away; almost as if it wasn't hers, but instead something she remembered from a movie long ago. She remembered hurting inside, but not why. She remembered that she had been trying to take the hurt away with the Lethe. Everything beyond that was even blurrier. Home, father, flight school, something about drafting stars.

Thinking about flying brought everything into sharp focus. Her mind's eye had a clear picture of the inside of a cockpit; the dials of a helio craft, the controls of a fighter jet - all those things were crystal clear. Everything else seemed dim and unimportant.

She managed a small smile, though it made her face feel strange.

"Thank you...umm..."

"Galen. I'm Galen."

"Thank you, Galen," she said, searching her memory for her own name. For a moment it didn't come, and she felt an edge of panic rising like a bubble in water. Then the bubble burst, bringing her name with it. "I'm Noel," she told him, deciding he was terribly handsome for a doctor. Then something about him struck her – something familiar. "Do I know you?"

"I don't think so, but your credential card says you're a pilot, and that you graduated from Ritter. I do a lot of research at the flight schools in nearly every system, including Ritter - so you might have seen me there. Though I'm pretty sure I would have remembered seeing you." He smiled at her.

Noel returned his smile, suddenly shy, and it again made her face feel strange and tight. She brought her right hand up to feel her cheek but Galen caught it and gently pushed it away before she could touch herself. Seeing the concern in his eyes, and now acutely aware of the tightness in her face, she knew in a heartbeat exactly what it meant. Her blue eyes opened wide.

"How bad is it?" she whispered. He pressed his lips together, trying to decide on what to say. Finally, he simply reached over to a table and picked up a small mirror and handed it to her.

She stared at her reflection, too shocked for words. Her skin was too numb to feel the gauze taped to it, but if she moved the muscles in her face she could feel the tape pull at her skin. Her eyes could see how much it covered. "Take it off."

"I don't think that's a good idea right now. Wait until..."

"Please. Take it off."

He paused, then motioned to the resa droid. It drifted over the bed to him and opened up on one side, half of the round body unfolding like a metal flower. Galen retrieved a packet of semisol from inside the floating sphere and broke the seal. He dabbed some on the tape holding the gauze on her cheek, dissolving the adhesive before gently peeling it away from her skin.

Noel watched in the hand mirror as the gauze came away to reveal the burned flesh underneath. She tried to make an exclamation of some kind but all that came out was a gurgled cry. She thought she would feel heartbroken, or terrified, at the double waves of red flesh that rippled out from the corner of her lip, clawing at her eye and her jaw. Instead, she only felt deflated, beaten.

Worse, she knew that if she had the Lethe pipe in her hand right then, she would have lit it.

Galen took the mirror from her numb fingers and sat back down on the bed, laying a hand on her arm. "The burn was moderate, but I treated what I could, including your right eye. You can have the skin and the surrounding area repaired by almost any surgeon planetside. But..."

Noel glanced at him. "But what?"

He watched her for a moment before answering. "I think you should leave it."

"Excuse me?"

He smiled at her and touched her gently on the chin. "It's not as bad as you think," he told her. "It will look better once it is healed. And besides, you already have a classical beauty. This gives you a romantic beauty as well."

Noel's face was too numb to feel the tears well in her eyes, but her heart felt more than her face ever could. She was already in love.

Scarlett woke up a little and rolled over, her hand slipping between the sheets. When she found nothing there she opened her eyes. Calyph sat on the edge of her bed, pulling on his boots. He gave Scarlett a sheepish grin.

"I thought I should get out of here early, before most people are up and about."

"Afraid someone might find out you slept with a Jordan?" she asked, smiling. Calyph laughed.

"Don't get me wrong," he told her. "I'm going to send an HM out to everyone I know as soon as I get back to my room." Scarlett laughed. "But it's not a good idea for us to be doing this."

"Do you a have a few irons in the fire around here?" Scarlett teased. Calyph smiled, tucking his pant legs into the tops of his boots.

"No, I just don't think it's a good idea to let this...go too far."

"Did I give you the idea that I was in love with you?"

Calyph laughed. "No, but you know what I mean. We're going to be working together over the next few months. A lot."

"With Fledge."

"Yes. I don't want to complicate things if we can avoid it."

"Alright," Scarlett said. "I had a good time, though."

Calyph stood up and gave her an impulsive peck on the cheek. "Me too," he said, and meant it. He knew it was a memory that he would cradle for maybe the rest of his life. "I'll see you on the bridge."

He strode quickly out the door, not wanting to say or do anything that would mess up the time they had shared. Scarlett smiled at the closed door long after he had gone through it. He was right - an affair, sexual or otherwise, might complicate things on the ship.

Then again, Scarlett mused, *it might not*

She rolled onto her back and wondered what the attraction was for her. She had a thing for elves, she had always known that, but Calyph was different from anyone she had ever met. He was country stock rather than city, which was something she didn't usually like. He was quiet, but he was smart. Something about him was incredibly compelling.

Though he didn't seem it, he was older than she was. Not yet a master at his craft but he was more than damned good and would end up ranking as one of the best, sooner rather than later. He had a natural intensity that helped him progress at a rate much faster than his peers, the few that he had.

I could do worse, Scarlett thought. *Hell, I've done worse.* She grinned as she stood and stretched before heading for the shower. She had the feeling it was going to be a long day.

 SEVEN

After Welsner found his hotel in Metal City, he found the two others things he was after – synthetic whiskey and a synthetic hooker. When he was finished with them, he had killed off the hooker as quickly and thoughtlessly as he had killed off the whiskey, he sat on the pressed foam bed to go through his files.

All of the files he needed were on a single electronic tablet. He lit a cigarette and smoked it as he paged through the sheets, dragging a calloused fingertip across the glass surface of the tablet, making sure he had everything he needed.

He had the maps he wanted, and the blueprints of the building. A bit of ash fell on the glowing surface of the tablet and he blew it away. He read all the notes that described the employment and personal habits of his targets.

Welsner thought back to the first time he had seen the notes. They had been on shinepaper, since they had not yet been scanned, and were clipped along with digi-photos of the targets to a sheaf of paper files. He didn't look into the files, they were thick with more notes and pictures and papers. Welsner knew that the money was thick - that was all that mattered.

He had taken one look at the clipped notes and photos and had tossed the heavy files back onto Hillan's desk.

"I'll take it," he told him.

"Do you want to know?" Hillan asked.

"Do I ever?"

Hillan grunted in response. "It won't be as easy as you think."

This time Welsner grunted and offered him a view of crooked and yellowed teeth before he stuck a cigarette between them. "It'll be easier."

The mercenary didn't care what the job was, he just wanted to get the hell out of there – he didn't like Hillan. The man was the best headhunter Welsner knew, always had work and always paid up, sometimes even with a bonus. But Welsner could never determine if the man was real or not.

He suspected the man was human. Though Hillan had the sharp, perfect facial features of a manufactured construct, it was something any human could have done in a day of surgery. Plus, the man showed signs of age. Not much, little crinkles in the skin around his eyes and hair that had gone silver-gray. Then again, any custom-made construct could have been special ordered to look that way.

What threw Welsner off was that the man had never aged in the entire time he had known him, and his clients were almost exclusively Chimeran.

"Time frame?" Welsner had asked.

"As soon as possible. If you can get to them within a week you should be able to catch them together."

"Does the client want it staged?"

Hillan shook his head. "Just dead."

"Budget?"

"None."

Welsner raised his brows at that, taking a long drag from his cigarette and nodding thoughtfully. *No budget. That means a lot of money.* Hillan, as if reading his thoughts, cleared his throat.

"That's not to say," he advised, "that you should go overboard on the expense. Nothing that will draw unusual attention. Public transportation when possible, no 'one of a kind' weapons. Keep it as discreet as possible."

The mercenary had smiled at the lean figure he suspected was a man, though not for sure. "Of course." Then, he had ground out his grit on the floor.

Hillan had looked at it without any expression. None at all.

Welsner ground out his current smoke on the hotel's foam mattress. He looked over and saw a pool of synthetic blood spreading under the body of the hooker. He had wondered at one time what synthetic blood actually was, what it might be made of – hydraulic fluid? Cherry syrup? Now, he didn't give it a thought. He was concerned that the ooze was spreading out in the direction of his duffle bag.

He hefted his bulk up off the bed and kicked the whore's body towards the wall but it didn't stop the blood from seeping out onto the thin carpet and creeping towards the bed. He lifted the duffle up and set it down carefully on the other side of the mattress.

He crawled back onto the foam, lit another cigarette, and paged through the electronic notes and pictures.

Hmmm. Always bad people out there, he thought. *And bad people out to kill them. And worse people - the ones with the money, of course, that want them dead in the first place.*

He switched off the tablet and put it on the night table. He pulled burly knuckles down the wall behind him, bringing down the lights.

Lucky me.

"When I was your age," Grandpa said, "we used to listen to music on small silver discs." His voice was deep and melodious but it warbled and cracked, like an instrument finely tuned but nonetheless ancient. His gaze, which reached only a few meters in each direction, fell on the objects around him with a proud sort of ownership and rightly so. His laugh was like the caw of some long extinct bird.

Jeanette looked about the room, too, as she wiggled on the floor and tried to get comfortable. She had once asked Sean why Grandpa had a rug made from a turkey, but he had only rolled his eyes at her and shook his head. Jeanette decided that it must not have been from a *real* turkey, just a simulated one.

Other than the itchy rug, Jeanette liked Grandpa's place. Grandpa sat in his favorite chair in his favorite room. There were shelves on the wall that held books, *paper* books, and frames on the walls that held pictures. *Flat* pictures. Pictures that stayed still and didn't move about. Grandpa said holo-pics gave him the heebie-jeebies.

There was a sense of comfort in Grandpa's place.

Grandpa eyed Sean as he knelt down on the rug, trying to judge how old he was. His clothes were too loose so it was hard to judge how big he was. *Must be the fashion,* Grandpa thought. *Like that blonde hair combed forward over his blue eyes.* The boy seemed as tall as himself, but that wasn't saying much. He would have to see him standing next to John, when he came for the children.

Jeanette was getting bigger, but still seemed tiny. Maybe it was her large dark eyes that made her face seem small, or the halo of hair that fell over her shoulders and back in dark ringlets. *There's more curl there than there is girl!* He had exclaimed to her not long ago. She had only giggled.

"Silver discs!" Grandpa cawed. "We still cooked with fire back then. Oh, not over an open flame. We were all on gas or 'lectric by then. Except for some summer nights – there was a treat we cooked over an open flame, some sugary indulgence all melted and smooshed together, though I can't recall now what it was called..."

His eyes, which already were bleary and far away, looked away even farther, reaching deep within his past. Within himself. Sean looked at him, perplexed.

"What the cuss is summer?" he finally asked. Grandpa only threw back his head and cawed laughter. Sean and Jeanette exchanged glances and shrugs as Grandpa composed himself, wiping his eyes.

"Back in those days," Grandpa told them, "we talked on cell phones, and sent messages via email."

Jeanette listened, wide eyed. Her young mind was trying to grasp Grandpa's meaning. Sometimes that was a hard thing to do.

"You had phones the size of cells?" she asked. "Like, prison cells?" Sean elbowed her in the ribs.

"No, dummy," he chided. "It's short for cellular. Phones worked back then on a cellular level." He was studying cells in school and found them fascinating. Science was his favorite subject. Grandpa cawed.

"No, no, no. It was because they needed cell towers to link them, like the satellites we use now to talk to interstellar ships."

"Ha!" Jeanette said, smugly. She hated it when her brother knew more than she did, which seemed like all the time. She liked to believe that she was just like her Aunt Johanna. She was determined that she would someday be better than her know-it-all brother.

"What was email?" Sean asked, diverting his mistake with a question. Grandpa and Jeanette were both easy to divert.

"It was how we sent text messages," Grandpa said.

"What did the e stand for?" Jeanette asked. Grandpa frowned and his near toothless mouth puckered in as he sought the answer, then relaxed and pooched out as his eyes lit up.

"Evasion," he said, decidedly. "Because you sent it when you didn't really want to actually talk to the person." Sean's eyebrows rose.

"That makes sense," he said.

Malherbe clucked his tongue at the female pilots that ran past him through the open door to the locker room.

"Five pilots on the first day!" he proudly called out. "One male and *four* females. Can't say that I'm surprised!"

JM could feel his eyes on her as she jogged past. They felt like hot balls of lead. She stared straight ahead, her face tense but expressionless.

"Five pilots! Where's my genius?" he shouted. He looked at the passing pilots but couldn't see the loudmouth pipsqueak from the Day Room. "What percent is that?" he hollered into the locker room as the last of the female pilots filed past. "Did I lose my genius already?"

"A little more than a percent and a half, Master Sergeant!" A voice called back.

Malherbe walked away chuckling like a pig in shit.

One of the females that had fallen behind on the first run, and had been immediately yanked from the formation, had been one of JM's roommates. By the time JM had showered and returned to her room, the pilot's bunk had been stripped and her locker had been cleaned out. It was as if she had never been there.

"Creepy, isn't it?" A voice commented.

JM turned to see another pilot that shared her room, a leggy redhead, staring at the empty locker.

"Yeah," JM agreed, looking at the redhead's nametape. The initials AH were stenciled on the gray fabric in black paint. "Creepy."

She sacked out on top of her bed without crawling into it and was up two hours before daybreak with the rest of the company for another round of physical training with Malherbe. After the fastest shower of her life and an even faster breakfast, JM sat down at dawn with her platoon for her first class.

The desks were old, inset with an acrylic rectangle that gave off a soft, white glow. A plastic stylus was laid on each desk. The chairs were metal and cramped. Behind a small table in the front of the room sat a human man in pilot fatigues with the stripes of a staff sergeant. He was tall, lean, black, and bald. His eyes flicked over each pilot as they took their seats and he shook his head slowly.

"Look at you all," he said, his voice low and deep. "Too scared to even look at each other." JM glanced around, sizing up the others in her class before returning her gaze to the instructor. "In a month you'll all be smokin' and jokin' with each other. Those of you that are here, that is."

He made a harrumphing noise and stood up, pushing his chair back.

"I'm Sergeant Cormen," he told them. I will be your instructor, at least till the first condensation." He walked slowly around the room in front of their desks, looking at their nametapes. "You will be spending the better part of the next year in this classroom. The other part you will spend with Master Sergeant Malherbe running your ass into the ground. If you do well, really well, you might get a little time inside a flight simulator."

He stopped in front of AH and placed the tips of his long fingers on her desk. He leaned towards her, as if for a better look, and then turned back towards the rest of the class.

"You say, 'but Sergeant Cormen, we are already accomplished pilots.' Well, that may be, since you obviously knew enough to get you here. But that doesn't mean you are an accomplished astronaut, and it doesn't make you an aeronautical fighter. Certainly not the best. And you need to show us that you can run before you can fly."

He finished his circumvention of the room and returned to the front of the class. He leaned back against the small table.

"Your syllabus and material are loaded into your acrylics. We are going to start with some review, things you should already know, but we will review them anyway. There will be a test before lunch. Log into your desk and scroll to the first page."

JM logged in and was thankful that everything *was* review; at least it was for her. A few hours later, she took the test and was dismissed for lunch. Thirty minutes later they were back in the classroom, taking their seats. Three desks remained empty, the acrylics dark. No grades, no good-byes. The pilots were simply gone. Just like the personal items from their lockers and the sheets on their bunks. It was as if they had never existed.

The worst of it all was the very first week of training, the time when attrition was at the highest level at the JTC. Cadets were allowed very little sleep, and the instructors constantly filled their heads with information and then wrung it back out of them like water from a rag. Every day they were bombarded with countless subjects – IGC history, code of conduct, aero logistics, universal law, search and rescue procedures for both planetary emergencies as well as deep space protocol.

On day six, a pilot in JM's class dropped his stylus and started moaning as he grasped the sides of his head. It looked as if he were physically trying to hold all his impacted knowledge inside, or possibly trying to keep his head from bursting. JM knew how he felt. Her own brain felt like it was overfull and pushing against the inside of her skull.

The over-stressed pilot was escorted from the room to the infirmary and, when the others returned from a break a short while later, his desk was dark and his things were gone.

When the instructors were not breaking them down mentally, Malherbe was breaking them down physically. He drove them the way a madman would drive work animals. Even outside of physical training, he seemed to pop up everywhere – the chow hall, the barracks, the hallways between classes - his angry, red face lodged between his tight black collar and tight black cap. Always yelling at them to get their asses going.

Fifty pilots were gone in the time aptly called Deathweek.

Jesus, JM thought. *At this rate, we'll all be gone in a month.*

She was wrong.

Her platoon was only down ten pilots after the first month. Other platoons lost more and the company had its first condensation. Ten platoons became nine. To JM's delight, she stayed with Sergeant Cormen. She had quickly developed an affection for the lean Staff Sergeant. He was blunt, honest, and had a sharp sense of humor with a wit as quick as his eyes.

To her dismay, she met NDR.

"Condensation day!" Malherbe shouted as they ran into the yard. "It's like Christmas, every time!" JM was just leaving the building when he hailed the Corvette. "Corvette! What are we down?"

"Thirty-five, Master Sergeant!" Corvette Ensign answered as he trotted towards the HQ building. "Not counting Deathweek."

"What's the breakdown since then?"

"No breakdown, Master Sergeant! All male pilots!"

At that instant JM passed Master Sergeant Malherbe. She kept the corners of her mouth down tight, but not tight enough. Worse, her gods-be-damned, disobedient eyes darted at Malherbe. It was for just a fraction of a second, but he didn't miss it.

"Holy Mary, Mother of God!" he shouted. "JM!"

JM turned around and began jogging back to where Malherbe stood waiting, his apoplectic face getting redder by the second. She ran in place in front of him, staring straight ahead.

"Did you just *look* at me?" he screamed.

"Master S..." she started but he cut her off, more furious than ever.

"That was a rhetorical question, JM! Don't you dare answer me!" He fumed in silence for a few seconds, his hands balled into fists as he searched for the appropriate insult. "Go hang yourself!" he finally shouted.

JM turned and headed for the bar pit at a steady jog. It was an exercise area to the side of the gravel yard that was full of sand, something JM learned to detest almost as much as the gravel. Pull up bars jutted from the sand like giant staples that smelled of rust. They were overlooked by tall wooden beams from which dangled a few climbing ropes with frayed ends.

JM reached the first bar and jumped up, wrapping her hands around it. She pulled herself up, bringing the bar down behind her head. She pushed her hands up over the bar, wrapping her arms around it. She felt like a damn milk-maid, minus the buckets of milk hanging from the ends of the pole across her shoulders and minus, of course, the ground beneath her feet.

She had already seen more than a few pilots have to do the same maneuver as punishment for some infraction or another and JM herself had already but subjected to it once before. The staff considered it appropriate training to strengthen the upper body, something that was crucial to every pilot. The students knew it for what it really was; a school sanctioned crucifixion in pain and humility. JM had already seen it break two pilots.

The first was a female during Deathweek. As the other pilots were rolling around on the gravel, alternating between push-ups and sit-ups, the cadet had dropped from the bar, unable to bear the toll it was taking on her arms and shoulders. She collapsed in a heap, bursting into sobs. JM had clenched her jaw as she counted out her sit-ups, the serrated rocks biting into the small of her back.

Jesus, she thought. *Does she have to cry? It's what he wants for Christ's sake! How can she give him the satisfaction?*

The first time she had hung from the bar, JM had the satisfaction of staying up until Malherbe yelled at her to quit wasting his time and get her ass down. It had hurt like hell – her arms, neck, back and shoulders were screaming by the time he let her drop, and her muscles had burned for hours and then were stiff for days. She could hardly raise her arms to wash her hair.

Though not optimistic by nature, she had been able to look on the bright side. She had neither Malherbe nor the filthy gravel in her face, and she had a vantage point where she could watch the others doing windsprints. At least for the few moments she was able to raise her head that high.

This time, however, Malherbe intended to really stick it to her.

"Genius!" JM heard him shout. The voice that answered was high and piping.

"Yes, Master Sergeant!"

"You god-damned numbskull! Go join her!"

JM settled onto the bar, letting it become part of her back. She actually started to think that it might be better here, with her biceps stretched and her shoulders already starting to ache, than on the run with Malherbe.

Then a bright-eyed wisp of an elf bounded into the pit and jumped up to grab the bar next to her.

"Hiya!" The waif smiled as she wrapped her arms around the metal, bringing it to her small shoulders. "I'm NDR."

JM eyed her with contempt. "So *you're* Malherbe's little kiss ass."

"Just because I answer his questions," the elf argued, "doesn't mean I kiss his ass."

JM grunted and looked away. Her arms already hurt. She hugged the metal tighter, ignoring the discomfort in her neck. The elf twisted her head in an effort to see JM's face.

"You're in third platoon? I heard you had the most fall-outs, academically."

JM let out a short burst of air through her nose and ignored her.

"Even though Sergeant Cormen is said to be one of the best instructors," the elf continued. "I wish I had Sergeant Cormen. I have Corvette Ensign. It's obviously his first year teaching." She wiggled, adjusting her light weight around on the bar. Maybe we will get condensed together!" she exclaimed, eyes bright and voice hopeful.

JM looked at her, turning her head as far as it would go with the bar behind it, which wasn't far. She was unable to believe the cheery optimism coming from the pilot next to her. She felt her eyes bulging with amazement and thought it must be how Malherbe's eyes always felt. Then the dummy actually smiled at her, which wasn't a pleasant sight. The girl had obviously been through the ringer.

JM shifted her weight with a groan and glared at Malherbe as he ran by, calling cadence for the whole company. She could see the grin on his face and knew it was for her.

That rat bastard had my number as fast as he had my name, she thought with a grunt of unwelcome appreciation. *He knew I could hang here all day. It's the present company he gave me as punishment. That wily bastard.*

NDR prattled along to her left. JM ignored her as much as she could. It wasn't enough.

After six months, the platoons were condensed again. JM was grateful. Not that she made the cut, but because she hadn't been put with NDR. She had been "hung" with her times aplenty. Malherbe seemed to delight in it the same way JM detested it.

After the first year it was unavoidable. Though the fall out rate had slowed considerably, there were only ninety-three pilots still in Cycle Eleven of the JTC. Three platoons. Luckily, the only class she had with the pest was astrophysics.

"And this," Commander Yuri said, pointing to the two holos joined over the monogram grid, "shows how speed is maximized via thrust and inertia." He looked up sharply as he heard a snicker from the back of the class. The small, blonde elfling with the ruined face smiled at him. He frowned at her. "NDR! Do you have something you want to add?"

"That's not as fast as you can go," she remarked. Yuri's brows popped up and JM had to bite her lip to rein in a smile. The Commander's brows came down again just as quickly into a scowl.

"I'm not talking about Dragons or Fledglings that can manipulate space-time. I am only talking about man made ships."

"And I'm talking about flying them faster."

"Are you disputing the law of physics?" His question came out more as a stabbing accusation of guilt. The elfling just shrugged.

"I'm just saying you can go faster," she said. Though everyone remained silent, there was a blatant rise of dissent from the entire class. Especially from the student in the seat behind her. JM had nothing but contempt for her and NDR had no idea why. She liked JM and felt an odd sort of kinship with her. Nonetheless, turnabout was fair play and she found an immense enjoyment in provoking the dark haired pilot when she could.

"Here," NDR said to the frowning commander, pulling out a graphite stick and a blank sheet of paper. "Things are always moving through the universe. If not now, then a hundred years ago, or a thousand years ago, or a hundred thousand years ago." She made long slashes on the paper implying movement. "Shooting stars, asteroids, even debris in a gravitational pull will leave a path of flowing air – a bit of suction or draft. If you travel in this draft, it will add to your speed without you even having to try." She drew a rudimentary aircraft heading into the slash marks she had made. "Depending on what sort of draft you are riding, you can increase your speed, sometimes by a factor of ten to ten hundred. It all depends on the object you are drafting, and the time elapsed since it passed."

Yuri shook his head. "Space is exactly that – space, and a lot of it. The chances of running into another object out there by chance, not to mention the ghost of such an object, are next to nil."

This time NDR shook her head. "They're easy to find. They all leave a trail of magnetically charged particles in their wake – some more than others depending on their iron content. All you need is to fit your craft with a ferrous sensor, like the kind Jabrets use to find and harvest meteors. It will show up as a pinkish, purple line on the fer-sen."

"You're not listening," Yuri argued, agitated at the pointless interruption and the cockiness of the pilot. "Space is too immense. Too empty. Even asteroids in the same belt are kilometers apart. There are just not enough things moving around out there."

NDR sighed as if she were the teacher and he a slow student. "You have to take into consideration not just what is moving around now, but how much has moved through that space over the past three *billion* years. Those drafts are there. A lot of them."

The classroom was tense, like a jury awaiting a sentence for murder, and eyes swept back and forth between the student and the teacher. The dark haired female pilot behind NDR sat perfectly still, except for a very slight tremor that seemed to run through her entire body, her hands tightly gripping the ends of her own graphite stick.

Commander Yuri, who had been leaning forward, his intensity growing with every word, suddenly leaned back. He looked away, absorbing what the cadet had said. He shook his head.

"Objects, like you said, that are moving through space leave a trail of debris in their path that would be dangerous for spacecraft. Even the smallest of asteroid chips would punch through the hull of a ship like a bullet."

NDR laughed. "Any plastic polymer it would protect a hull. Small bits of debris would chunk out the polymer or deflect. How do you thinks the Jabrets do it?" NDR shrugged. "As for the bigger ones, like you said, they are few and very far between. Easy to avoid."

The commander narrowed his eyes at her. "Is this something you have already tried, NDR?"

NDR bit her lip, a flush creeping up her cheeks. "Of course not. I am only speaking theoretically."

Yuri sat back onto the holo grid with a thump, making the holos flicker and then go out. He was quiet a long time, long enough for some of the students to begin to shift uncomfortably in their seats. "Well, cadet, I think you might be onto something," he admitted, tapping a finger to his lips. He was quiet for another moment and then fixed her with an appraising stare. "Something that could change space travel."

A collective gasp of astonishment sounded from the class.

From behind NDR came the sharp snap of a graphite stick as it snapped in half. NDR grinned, pleased.

NINE

Galen eyed Noel with an equal mixture of disgust and jealousy. Her body lay splayed out like a corpse on a battlefield, albeit cleaner, covered with cream smooth skin and a silk slip. One arm lay crooked under her head the other jutted out from her body with three fingers curled back, her index finger and thumb out in the shape of a gun. Her face was smashed into the pillow so he could only see half of it, the unmarred half. Her red lips were parted, mouth hanging open in complete disregard for all existence including her own.

She slept so easily, as long as it was night. Galen marveled at it. Even tonight she had been wide-awake and watching the holo when she abruptly came to some sort of decision, consciously or unconsciously, announced to him that she was going to sleep, and rolled over and did so.

Galen always had trouble falling asleep and, when he did, he would often have trouble staying asleep. Always too much on his mind. Noel could turn it off at will. He found it maddening at times.

On the other hand, Noel was physically incapable of taking a nap during the day. Galen was a master of the nap. The catnap, the power nap, sometimes the three to four hour, half-day snooze. It wasn't every day – far from it – but when he felt like it, he could nap.

Noel, even if she had been awake for two days and was dead on her feet, found it impossible to nap. If it wasn't night, she wasn't sleeping. He had encouraged her a number of times to get some sleep during the day when she had returned, exhausted, from a interstellar flight. Each time she would lay on the couch, staring wide-eyed at the ceiling for an hour or more before giving up and trying something else until bedtime.

Galen had woken from a nap on occasion by being gently prodded in the ribs by the toe of a silver flight boot and Noel asking, "How in the hell can you sleep so much?" He had the feeling she probably eyed him at those times in the same manner he was eyeing her now.

He picked his acrylic pad up off his lap. The blue equations hovered over the opaque, white rectangle of the glass. He toyed with them, moving them around with a finger. He added a few numbers, replaced a few others. They didn't make any more sense than they had an hour ago. He sighed and looked at Noel again.

The secret was in her, somehow. He knew it. Something niggled at his memory, like a tiny fish tugging on a continent of seaweed. She had the answer, but he was at a loss as to why or how she would know. Or what it was that she did know. It was driving him crazy.

Earth, he thought. *It has something to do with our trip to Earth. What the hell was it? Was it something we saw?* He thought of the vacation they had taken two years ago but nothing significant came to mind. There was the town, the house. Afternoons on the lawn. The movie, of course. The plastic chairs. Making love. The moon. He couldn't think of why any of it should, would, or *could* pertain to his problem.

Galen stood up and stretched. He left the acrylic on the bed, which was in the main living area of their podment. Wearing nothing but his sleep shorts, he shuffled through the dark of their kitchen to the back of the pod, absently scratching a rib. In a normal podment, the back area would be two, possibly three, bedrooms. In their pod, however, the interior walls separating the rooms had been removed, making a single room. The subsequent large area served as Galen's lab.

The door to the lab slid open and Galen touched the wall, raising the lights just enough to shed a soft glow on countertops, equipment, generator pads and holo troughs. He rested his hand on his lab coat, which had been tossed over the back of a high-backed stool, his fingers idly tracing the DR monogrammed on the left side. The room's dominating feature was a pair of ovoid doorframes, made up of a multitude of matte metallic squares. There was a tech pad on each one for coordinate specs and a metal plate holding multigalaxy dimensional map chips.

It was a working Thermopylae – a mercurial spaceport. They had been popular in the galaxy where he had been born, and was still widely used in the highly inhabited Jupiter system. They were used for travel all over a planet or between a planet and its moons. Any farther than that they proved to be dangerous, or deadly, and were not utilized.

Galen had refused to believe that could not be used between planets, or between galaxies for that matter. He knew he was on the brink of solving an equation for inter-galactic passage that would revolutionize travel throughout the entire universe.

He had started their construction almost fifty years earlier. The trouble was, as it had always been with the Thermopylae, that when the doors were more than a standard Lunar Distance apart, what went into one door, did not always come out the other.

Eventually he had moved from teaching physics at the IGC flight schools to research at the Vinan and was planning on more research at the Jordan Training Center, hoping to find the answer there. It didn't take a physicist to see the correlation and the differences between Dragonflight and the Thermopylae.

The Thermopylae were based on spatial coordinate technology. The transfer of matter from one coordinate to another, bypassing the need for light speed. But the Dragons were able to create wormholes, tearing through the fabric of space, actually boring a hole through it, without any implanted technology. They were naturally able to travel across the universe, folding both space and time in a manner to simply be where they wanted to be.

It was the dragons, the real *living* dragons of the time, which showed the elves that time was not free flowing or even going in a straight line. Space and time were made up of chunks they called the pendulum. And, like any pendulum, it could be swung back and forth. Space was a flexible substance, like a membrane, and time was not a horizontal line – and certainly not a straight one. The humans had known this as well, but had never been able to apply it.

The elves were finally able to stretch space, and warp it, and thus build the Thermopylae, which were more like bridges rather than holes. It gave them a cosmic shortcut, like the ones the dragons used, but much more limited - the behavior of atoms in the physical world being too chaotic to rip the fabric of space.

Then, just as the humans and elves were really getting a grasp on the phenomena they were tackling, the dragons started to die out, and their secrets with them. It was then that the humans discovered how to give them eternal life, the few that were left. They began with a solar genetic fusion to keep the heart going and implanting cybernetics where the nervous system failed. The dragons changed as they succumbed to the bionics that kept them alive, but they endured.

Galen walked up to the first frame and ran his hand over it, his blue eyes far away. He was so close, he could feel it. There was a link, he just had to find it. He stood there, motionless in his sleep-shorts, in the half-dark of the lab, wondering about the link between time travel and space travel for nearly half an hour. He considered bringing up a holograph of the algebraic equation he had come up with earlier that day but then decided against it.

He sighed, tired of thinking about it for now, and turned out the lights. Noel would be leaving for the Opal Dragon in just a few days. It would be a long trip this time since the Fledglings would be growing, and he wasn't sure when he would see her again. A long time, that he knew. He wanted to hold her until she left.

The off days for the Jordan cadets were few and far between but, after their first year was complete, they did have more time to themselves and were allowed use of the Day Room. JM usually avoided the room, not interested in anyone's company. The only time she made sure she was there was the first Saturday of each month when there was always a game of Omaha.

To her dismay, NDR didn't seem to seek out the company of the Day Room either. On each of their precious days off, JM found the little pest bounding into her bunkroom with the eagerness of a Labrador puppy. JM felt that the only thing God had graced her with at the Training Center was the fact that she had never had to share a bunkroom with the nuisance.

It was always the same.

"Hey J! What are you doing?"

JM, recumbent on her narrow bunk, would level a cold stare at the waif as she laid the acrylic she had been reading down on her chest. "What the hell does it look like I am doing?"

"We read and study *all* week," NDR whined. "This is the only day we have to enjoy ourselves. Let's go play some IG War, or Battlefront, *anything*."

"The games are all full by now," JM told her, bringing her reader back up to hide her face. NDR curled her fingers over the top of the acrylic and gently pulled it down.

"We can get a pick-up game."

NDR loved to read as well, but would often find her mind drifting. Most people, she presumed, would realize this and get back to the story, possibly re-reading the passage they were on when they began to drift. NDR would simply stop reading as soon as she realized she wasn't paying attention to the story. Turn off the book and put it away for next time. Or never.

What's the point? She thought. *If my mind wanders then the rest of me should follow.* This usually made for a long time for her to finish a book.

She frequently downloaded the interactive comics and graphic novels onto her acrylic, though she had not found anyone at the JTC who shared an interest in them.

She also had a set of zines that she had gotten on a trip to Earth that she would look through endlessly, looking at each picture and re-reading each story with a translation beam. She had even adopted a number of her hairstyles from them. She would turn each protected page with great care, almost reverence.

But, God forbid, she should read something regarded as *GREAT LITERATURE*. Something like that was usually recommended to her by a colleague or a friend, where the author would repeat the same line every few paragraphs for some sort of impact. Then she would go back and reread the pages to see if her mind was playing tricks on her, or if maybe someone was fucking with her. She finally decided that a good deal of reading just wasn't for her. She had better things to do.

She nudged JM with a bent knee.

"Come on! Any practice is better than none, and especially better than reading."

"That's because you are ignorant," JM told her without looking up. But when NDR didn't leave, she sighed. "Okay. I'll play one pick-up game with you. But I don't want to be on the same team."

"You never want to be on my side!" NDR complained. JM brought the reader back up over her face. "But you always try to kill me!"

JM tucked the reader under her chin. "That's the point of the game, isn't it?" she asked, her smile small but malicious. NDR shook her head.

"You're as bad off as the Tin Man," she told her. JM frowned.

"What the hell is that supposed to mean?"

"Do you want to play or not?" NDR asked.

"It's not *playing*, it's *training*," JM corrected.

"Fine, fine. Do you want to *train* or not?" She was practically bouncing with impatient energy. JM drummed her fingernails on the back of the reader and regarded her with dark eyes.

"Okay, okay. Let's train. But if we need a fourth for Omaha next week, *you're* playing." NDR's shoulders sagged.

"Ugh! Alright!"

NDR's timing was as uncanny as her face and as unnerving as her picture, as there always seemed to be a game in need of two more pilots. It just made JM despise her more, though she always gained skill from each game.

JM pulled a light Mylar jacket from her gear cabinet and slammed it shut. NDR's locker, just to her right, was still open as she pulled out her own Mylar. JM turned her face away as her eye caught sight of the picture that was hanging in there. For some reason she couldn't fathom, the picture made her uncomfortable, to the point of nausea.

When JM had first seen the picture, NDR's gear cabinet had been across the locker-room and on the other side, separated by the latrine hallway, at least half a dozen benches, and more than fifty other lockers. It had been the first week in the simulators and JM had been walking back from the showers, wrapped in a towel, when the picture stuck on the inside of the open metal door caught her eye. She froze, her eyes wide and staring and her hair dripping water, gripped with an unnerving sense of déjà vu.

The picture was innocuous, really. It was a digi-photo on shiny photo paper, the kind that had been popular many years ago. It showed a strong, burly man holding up a little girl on his shoulder. The girl was obviously a much younger NDR, with white-blonde hair, bright blue eyes and cheeks still a bit chubby with childhood. The man's smiling face was full of joy and pride and the little girl was laughing, her hand holding a toy jet that the photo caught as she zoomed it through the air.

JM kept her body rigid though it wanted to sway with vertigo. NDR and the female next to her looked at each other and then back at JM.

"Are you alright?" NDR asked. JM shook her head, clearing it.

"Yes," she said. "I'm fine." She took another nervous glance at the picture and stalked away. NDR and the other female recruit looked back at each other and shrugged.

Since then the number of female recruits at the JTC had gone from sixty to six, and they had all been consolidated and relegated to a smaller section of the barracks and to the south section in the locker room. NDR brought her picture with her and JM did her best to ignore it.

JM's foresight turned out to be as uncanny as NDR's timing when finding a pick-up game. Or, since there were so few female pilots, it seemed there was often a need for someone to fill the fourth spot in the monthly Omaha game.

NDR did her best to keep still in her seat. She knew the smirk she would get from JM even if she moved just the tiniest bit. She looked at her cards again, her heartbeat accelerating and pumping adrenaline through her bloodstream. She hated it.

When she had told JM about the way playing Omaha made her feel, the other pilot had laughed.

"That's the way it's supposed to make you feel. You don't like it?"

NDR had shaken her head emphatically and JM laughed again. "Then consider it training. It's a good way for you to learn control of both emotion and excitement, maybe even fear."

But yesterday NDR had been in a crevasse with no oxygen, taking fire from Sergeant Cormen. It was the first time the shots were not simulated, and the eagle-eyed sergeant's shots were so close that NDR could feel the heat from each laser pulse on the back of her neck. Still, she was able complete her field pack repair in less than thirty seconds to generate both oxygen and a protective shield around her body. Her head had stayed cool, her heartbeat normal, and she had not so much as flinched.

Now, it the quiet safety of the Day Room, it was all she could do to not wipe her palms on her pant legs. JM's cool gaze of mild amusement never faltered. NDR looked at her hand again as the game droid, a saucer of greenish metal, sorted through the chips.

NDR tried to clear her throat without making any noise. She had a pretty good hand, for once. Also, she knew that AH had mostly diamonds and TR had mostly clubs. JM had to be spaded up, she always was. NDR had remarked to her one time how appropriate it was that she was often heartless. Though she had expected an acidic retort from JM, the pilot had simply smiled, taking it as a compliment.

The dealer droid tossed the button down in front of JM and the pilot threw in her blind. The button moved to the other players in turn who made their bets. NDR watched JM but the pilot's expression never changed. Cards went down and around. After the first minute, and as most of the cards were played, NDR could feel her heart beating faster and faster.

Jesus, she thought. *I think I'm going to win.*

All she had left were high spades. JM had only played low spades so was either out or saving her high cards for the last rounds.

It doesn't matter. If I play these right, it doesn't matter what her cards are. I can take her.

Her heart was pumping as if she had just run a couple of klicks but for once it didn't bother her. If felt good. She had never beat JM before.

This is going to be great.

The droid moved the buttons and NDR threw down her Jack, unable to stop smiling. JM took it with her Queen. Frustrated, NDR played her King and JM took it with her Ace.

"Godammit!" NDR shouted at her. JM gathered her chips.

"I can't believe you didn't know I had those cards!" she said, laughing.

"How the hell am I supposed to know what cards you have?"

"Because if AH had either, she would have played it over the Jack of Clubs and TR would have led with either on the first round."

NDR put her elbows on the table and her chin in her hands as everyone cleared their chips and the droid collected the cards. JM kept on chuckling.

Damn.

FROM
THE DREAM JOURNAL OF HOPE

This was not a dream, but a memory that drifts into my mind when I least expect it. Now that the other journals are gone this seems the most appropriate place for a memory – for aren't memories the dreams that were real, or that we dreamed were real? They are when we remember them.

I remember when I was five and I was on the bus to school and we were at a stop and I remember looking out the window and seeing the red octagon of a stop sign with the letters in white and studded with reflective bumps. The window was thick and dirty and rimmed with black rubber and dull aluminum and I looked out of that window and thought that it seemed like forever that we had been there, waiting.

I stared at the stop sign and even though I was only five I thought, I will remember that stop sign for the rest of my life. The dents and the bumps, the colors and the shape, the three-fingered, black scuff and long silver scrape - even the dirty gray sky behind it. Days will go by and I will grow old but from time to time the image of this stop sign will come to my mind and I will think about it and remember what I was thinking at this exact time. *I even remember thinking that I was awfully young to have such a profound thought and premonition but there it was.*

And then, years later, there was a Christmas and there was a gift under the tree with a huge red ribbon made of velvet. And I thought, I will remember this forever. Just like the stop sign. *This huge velvet ribbon, so red and so perfectly formed, will come to me now and again – and with it the stop sign of course because they now seemed to be saved in the same drawer somewhere inside my mind. And even now I don't remember what the present was, or what kind of paper was wrapped around it or what kind of box enclosed it. But I remember the ribbon.*

Years passed and I found myself lying on my back in the grass looking at the sky. It was not some pastoral scene of a grassy hillside in the country, but something desperate and odd, which is probably why I was there. This hill of grass was small and isolated, much like I was, surrounded by tall buildings and paved streets. A green island of quiet in a sea of concrete and fear, grim determination and faded dreams. I lay there on my back and looked at the sky. It was blue that day and streaked with clouds so shy that they looked as if they had been painted with the drying brush of a dying artist. And I knew, lying there, that I would remember the way that sky looked for as long as I lived – the blue soaking into my eyes even as the grass under me tickled and made me itch.

I thought of the stop sign and the bow, and put the image of the sky (and the feel of the grass) in that secret drawer with them. Before I could close the drawer, though, a strange thing happened. An image came to my mind of a perfectly formed red rose, kissed with drops of dew. I did not know where this image came from; if it was a hidden secret from my past or a premonition or something I would never really see - but the rose was so red and so perfect and so vivid that I tucked it into the drawer with my other treasures.

Many, many years passed and finally I stood on the tarmac as the sunset glowed dirty orange – the color of a destructive brushfire that had burned merciless and out of control for weeks and weeks but for us it was just the way our horizon had become. I watched you from a short distance as you climbed into your jet, a dark brown silhouette against the dirty orange and yellow of the sky. You paused at the top of the ladder and though I could not see your face I knew that you were looking at me. I felt the drawer open inside my mind and knew that this image, too, would be stored there forever. This memory I did not want to put in my drawer, because it brought me no joy, only a deep and sad emptiness. But I knew, I will remember this forever; this picture, this moment. *I thought of the stop sign and the bow, the sky and the rose, and of course the image of you climbing into your jet against that dirty sunset, stopping to look at me one last time.*

ONE ZERO

"You're looking well, Jordan," Blue told Scarlett as she accepted a cup of coffee from Calyph and thanked him with a nod. Her white-gold hair was pulled back in platinum waves and large, jaunty curls fell past her shoulders. Her blue flight suit sparkled in the light of the bridge and her blue eyes sparkled with wicked good cheer. The number eight, stitched in silver on her left shoulder, reflected the overhead lights in tiny slivers. "On a down cycle?"

"No," Scarlett told her. "But thanks." Scarlett 's flight suit was a deep crimson, the number sixteen in black thread on her sleeve looking like slashes of night.

"Hmm. Must be something else then." Blue gave her a knowing smile that made Scarlett want to kick her. Calyph handed Scarlett a steaming mug and walked with the Jordans through the control room.

Chiara, the navigator, sat high in her seat. Part Ruthinian, the mostly human woman was astoundingly tall, taller even than Brogan. Her yellow-blonde hair was pulled back to show an angular, almost avian face with high cheekbones and a wisp of a smile. On her straight nose perched a pair of tiny, square glasses with black frames. They allowed the navigator to see as if she had four eyes, instead of two. An important feature when navigating a Dragon, as one had to see things in four dimensions, instead of just three.

Next too her was Dareus, manning the communication board. The black-skinned elf looked almost miniature next to the looming figure of Chiara – even standing up, the Communications Officer was not as tall as the Navigator when she was sitting down. Scarlett doubted he would be as tall as Chiara even if he stood on his chair.

In the pit, sitting in the plush chair next to the Captain was the Executive Officer, Commander Blaylock. He was nearly as tall as Brogan, but much more slim. His dark brown hair was cropped close to his head and his eyes were hazel and shrewd. Though the Captain made the decisions, Blaylock was the constant chime of policy and procedure.

Calyph joined them, to go over the security holos. Scarlett watched him from the corner of her eye but he didn't seem to be interested in her in any way other than business. There were no looks that passed between them.

Hmm, she thought, sipping her coffee.

Jade, the Jordan of the Green Fledgling, was expected at any time.

"War," Blaylock said, shaking his head. "The Chimera have been picking at us like flies for years, but there is no way this can be construed as a 'skirmish' or a 'misunderstanding.' This was their first open attack on an IGC vessel."

"I sent the Inter-Galactic Council my report yesterday, as soon as I was able," the Captain told them. "I understand they've been debating our first move all night."

"They'll debate it for weeks," Jordan Scarlett scoffed.

"She's right," Jordan Blue agreed. "It takes them *forever* to decide on anything."

Brogan nodded. "Worse, what they are debating first is whether it classifies as an actual attack."

Both Jordans and the Engineer gaped at the Captain. Even Blaylock had the decency to look shocked.

"Just because no shots were fired?" he asked. Brogan nodded.

"No ordinance of any kind. There are some on the council that are saying 'no harm, no foul,' if you can believe it."

Scarlett shook her head. "Fucking government," she muttered.

"Watch yourself, Jordan," Blaylock warned, though he shook his head in disgust at the news. "I know there have always been those on the Council that believe we should make peace with the Chimera, but this should have set them straight. This should have unified them!"

"What about the other Dragons?" Calyph asked. "Still no word?"

"We've had open coms all morning," Blaylock answered. "But no word of attack or espionage."

"That doesn't mean it's not happening right now," Scarlett said.

"True," Blaylock agreed. "But the others are now on alert. The Chimera have lost the element of surprise."

"So what do we do in the meantime?" Blue asked.

"I say we take the fight to them," Scarlett said. Blue nodded.

"For once, I agree with her."

Brogan shook his head but a look of amusement played across his countenance. "We stay on alert, and continue with what we had planned," he told them. "We are reaching a critical time for the Fledglings, a time of their change. I don't know if the timing of the attack on us has anything to do with that, or if it is purely coincidental.

"Do you think Rhett had anything to do with this?" Calyph asked. It was the first time anyone had mentioned the missing Engineer.

Brogan's face darkened. "I do not wish to discuss Rhett at this point."

"But if he was a sympathizer..." Scarlett started.

"He will not be discussed!" Brogan said sharply, cutting her off.

He sighed. "We still don't know how the Chimeran got in, but we need to find out before it happens again. We also need to proceed with the growth of the Fledglings. The timing is crucial to..."

Brogan looked up as the overhead lights went dim. When they came back up they were yellow, casting a sickly pall on everyone in the room. A pair of voices started speaking at once over the com system in a bland monotone. The ship's com was programmed to be androgynous but its gentle monotone always gave it a female slant. It was rare for more than one system to speak at a time and with both talking, one announcing incoming communications and another one announcing ship alert, it was impossible to understand either of them.

"Silence!" The Captain ordered the com system. "What concerns us first?"

"Incoming," a single voice stated without emotion. "Ships on approach. Fighter jets. ETA, fifteen minutes."

Everyone in the bridge went rigid, each body taut and still.

"Is Jade coming in with anyone?" Blue asked. The Captain shook his head, his eyes far away, obviously racking his brain.

"Are we expecting support from the IGC?" Calyph asked. The Captain shook his head again, frowning now, measuring what questions to ask.

"IGC vessels?" he called out.

"Enemy craft," the voice offered without emotion.

"How many?" Brogan asked.

"Six," the voice answered.

"Type?"

"Fighter, class five."

Everyone relaxed to some degree, looking at each other. Scarlett laughed and Blue glanced around, nonplussed.

"Hellcats?" she asked as if she couldn't believe it.

"They're insane!" Scarlett said. "What are they going to do with a handful of Hellcats?"

"What they always do," Captain Brogan said, his shoulders drooping with exasperation. "Cause destruction, confusion. Cost lives." He shook his head. "Crazy bastards."

"Why would they be attacking us with Hellcats?" Blue asked.

"Because they are stupid," Scarlett said scornfully. "Artificial Intelligence," she scoffed. "They're supposed to be so smart."

"It's not their intelligence that trips them up every time," Brogan told her.

"A Hellcat couldn't even scratch a Dragon!" She sounded like a school kid making boasts. Blaylock shook his head.

"A Hellcat doesn't have the firepower to significantly damage the ship," he agreed. "In most places the scale is so thick they wouldn't mar the surface. But, assuming their intel is good, and we have to assume that it *is* because they have already stuck it to us once, then they could possibly know where there are weak points on the ship. Places they could really do some damage."

"Is that true?" Scarlett asked, looking at Calyph. He nodded.

"It is very unlikely that they could hurt the Dragon, but they could hurt us. Most of their firepower would have no effect on the outside of the ship. But a well-placed shot, especially if they know where to target, could take out our coms. Another could take out our radar, or our WDS. It would leave us isolated and vulnerable until we sent out the Fledglings for help." Scarlett looked at Brogan. The Captain nodded in agreement.

"The weapons that outfit a Hellcat may be antiquated, but they are accurate."

"Enemy ships, still approaching," the voice chimed. "At current speed, they will be within firing range in twelve minutes." The overhead lights began to change from yellow to orange.

"Why are we even talking about this?" Blue asked, rising to her feet. "We need to take them out." She looked at the Captain, expectant. If she didn't need his permission to leave she would have already fled the bridge.

"The Fledglings are not ready for their first battle."

Scarlett swallowed. She was as eager as ever for a fight, but was not about to put Fledge in danger, especially if he wasn't ready. "I agree."

Blue narrowed her eyes at the other Jordan and leaned towards her. "*We're ready.*" Scarlett clenched her fists but Blue ignored her and turned to the Captain.

"We can be gone before they get here," Blaylock offered but Brogan shook his head.

"Jade will be here any minute, I don't want him coming through the fabric of space and into a trap."

"What other fighters do we have aboard the Dragon?" Blue asked. "I can take anything we have." Scarlett nodded.

"Me too."

"We have three Scorpions and half a dozen J-8s," Brogan acknowledged.

"Scorpions," both Jordans said at once.

"Class five fighters will be in range in ten minutes," the voice announced. Both pilots stood poised to flee but Brogan held up his hand, cocking his silver-haired head to the side.

"What was the com that came in over the out-link?" he asked the system.

"The Beryl Dragon in System Two is under attack."

"Shit," Blaylock cursed, running for the com-board. He slid across the floor and into the seat next to Dareus and started controls for com and space visage. Four holos popped up around him. Two showed the Beryl Dragon, one showed the outside of their own Dragon and the last showed the incoming Hellcats. Brogan looked at Chiara. She was waiting, expectant.

"Take us on a negative pull. Go slow, and watch for Jade."

The Navigator turned her angled limbs in her seat and began setting the Dragon's new course. Brogan's pale eyes found Blue and Scarlett.

"Go!" he ordered. They bolted from the room, Jordan Blue in the lead. He turned to Calyph. "Get to the Engineer quarters. I want you in the Cahir monitoring everything that goes on with the Dragon, *and* the Fledglings." Calyph nodded once and took off running.

Blue sprinted down the corridor with Scarlett on her heels. She ran to the first elevation tube and flipped the emergency switch to override the air pressure and jumped into the shaft. She braced her hands and feet against the side of the tube and slid down, hardly noticing the friction burns at the edges of her palms. She hit the floor with a jolt and came out on the bay level and headed left, running hard with Scarlett nearly at her side.

"How are you doing, Jordan?" Galen asked, his voice cheery but full of concern. He had been prudently silent during the whole meeting and Blue had forgotten he was there. She welcomed his presence with a grin.

"I feel eight-feet-fucking-tall," she replied as she vaulted over the short, half-wall that led into the fighter bay. The fighter bay was directly opposite the Fledgling Bay, on the Dragon's port side, separated by the atrium. There were already other pilots in the jet bay running in every direction, some getting into the J-8s.

Blue and Scarlett made for the Scorpions in the right half of the bay at a dead run. Airmen were pushing rolling ladders up to the slim fighter jets so the Jordans could board. Blue ignored the ladder, leaping up onto the Scorpion's bent tail and sprinting up its body before diving feet first into the cockpit. Scarlett bounded up onto the short wing of her fighter and did the same.

The Jordans both scanned their instrument panels as they buckled in and started flipping switches to power up and take off. Within seconds they had lift and were heading through the permeable field of the bay door.

They dipped out into space and then rose, the Dragon falling away beneath them, shrinking into the black. Six more jets shot out from the bay – two to accompany the Jordans, two to take rear guard, and two to guard the Dragon itself should an enemy fighter get through. They hovered like fireflies around a star. The other pilots pressed on, putting as much distance as they could between the oncoming fight and the Dragon.

Scarlett pulled the stel-cap down onto her head and pressed its dangling receptor onto her temple where it stuck, establishing a neural link with the Scorpion and coms with the other fighters, and then reached up to the stud in her left ear and activated her personal field.

"This is Jordan Scarlett," she said clearly. "Do I have coms?"

"Jesus!" she heard at once, coming from Blue. "It's fucking cold out here!"

"That's a yes for Jordan Blue," Scarlett murmured.

"Randle, J8 aft, you have coms, Jordan," a male voice said.

"Sammath, J8 fore, you have coms, Jordan," another voice chimed.

Scarlett activated the viola and it came down like short shimmering curtain that covered her eyes with a band of violet light. It dilated her eyes, increasing her binocular summation so that everything in her field of vision was magnified and clear. It also protected her retinas from any sort of laser fire or plasma flash. She could hear Blue muttering to herself over the comlink.

"Alright, guys," Scarlett told them. "We have about thirty seconds before they get here. When they do, they are going to split and go for our flanks. Randle, Sammath, I want you to take the three that go port; Blue and I will break starboard and go after the other three.

"Roger that," Randle said. Sammath echoed the same and they broke away to the left as the Hellcats came into view on the screen.

Scarlett fired up the main weapon and two of the subsidiaries. "Here they come," she announced.

As soon as Jordan Blue was in the cockpit, pilot training and instinct took over. It was like slipping into a warm and comfortable bed and drifting into sleep. Except it was anything but warm.

"Jesus!" she exclaimed, pulling on her the stel-cap and establishing her com-link. "It's fucking cold out here!" Galen's soft laugh was warm on her neck.

"Not all cozy like a Fledgling, eh?"

"I'm fine, I'm fine," she told him, activating her viola band. Her eyes grazed over the instrument panel and she wondered how long it had been since she had flown a conventional jet. Everything seemed so familiar and yet so *old*, so far away.

The first thing she noticed was the dash, made of standard brushed steel, not the smooth metal skin of the Dragon-kind. The viola, combined with her already sharp elfin eyesight, made clear the fine grain lines in the metal where it was cut before being riveted to the rest of the narrow, hulking mass of the Scorpion and inset with dials, read-outs, screens and switches.

The steerage wheel, unlike the half-circle of the Fledgling, was a tubular carbon alloy shaped like an X that was joined on the right and left sides by a curved carbon pipe. Blue steered with her left hand as she made adjustments on the control panel with her right.

She shivered slightly as she fired up every weapon the Scorp had, flipping on every switch to the right of the wheel.

"You should activate your field," Galen told her.

"In a second," she muttered. She glanced up to see the tail of the Scorpion begin to bend towards the nose, stretching out until it was over the cockpit, pointing forward.

"Here they come," Scarlett said over the com.

"Shadow me," Blue told her. "We'll pick off the first two and circle back for the trailer."

"*No*," Scarlett said firmly. "*You* shadow *me*. I'm taking point."

"You're right," Blue said, grinning. "I do have the steadier hand." She could picture Scarlett's jaw clenched tight and she laughed as another little shiver tore up her spine.

Shadowing was exceedingly difficult and always dangerous. The shadow pilot had to edge up right under and just behind the first craft, overlapping their wings. The advantage was that only one ship would register on the enemy's radar. The disadvantage was that if either pilot so much as flinched, the wings would collide and destroy both crafts. Not to mention the pilots flying them. It was never done in training and only rarely in real battle due to the risk. Only the highest-ranking pilots were permitted or would risk such a move.

Blue dropped the Scorpion, mindful of its tail, until she was under Scarlett's left flank. She pulled the wheel, adjusting her thrust to match the craft above. She edged in closer bit by bit until her ship was a perfect mirror of Scarlett's, no more than a meter away. It was then that the first wave of nausea hit her. Hard enough to knock her back into her seat.

Scarlett watched the Hellcats as they came onto the radar screen. They were much farther apart than she had expected, and a dim green line waved out behind them, as if they were dragging some sort of magnetic field. She reached out and tapped her screen but it stayed there.

"Does anyone else see that?' she asked, using her neural link to run a systems check on the radar.

"I do," Sammath said at once.

"I thought it was just my screen," Randle said.

"Well, well, well," Scarlett clucked. "They just might have a little shadow of their own. Blue?"

"I see it," Blue told them, swallowing hard enough for it to be heard over the com. Just for a second, the Crimson Jordan thought she heard another voice - soft and far away. A voice she knew. Scarlett frowned. "They have something behind them," Blue said.

"More fighters?" Sammath asked.

"I don't think so," Blue said. "I think it's just one ship, but it's a big one."

"Does the Dragon know?" Randle asked.

"Calyph?" Scarlett asked.

"I'm here, we see it. It's a floater, which is short range. They must have a cruiser, or something bigger, pretty close by. Just out of range of our systems most likely."

Calyph sat in the Cahir, a nerve-wired chair in the middle of an otherwise empty room in his quarters. He could see anything going on outside of the Dragon within a ten-kilometer radius, and inside, down to the cellular mitosis occurring in the Dragon's mylaric blood stream. A simple neural command called anything he wanted into view on one of the blank walls around him.

"Shit," Scarlett said. "Well, we'll just have to deal with it later. They're almost here." As soon as she spoke, she got a visual through the glass front of the cockpit hood. The six Hellcats came into view and split, just as she knew they would, three going right and three going left. "Here we go!"

Randle and Sammath broke left. Scarlett dipped her short right wing, breaking starboard, Blue keeping on her like a shadow in the night. "Stay tight, Blue. Breakaway in four, three, two, go!"

The Hellcats opened fire the second the Scorpions split apart, shooting hot rounds in quick, short bursts. The Scorpions opened up the second before, spitting plasma fire from their curved tails. The hot rounds of the enemy went shooting into the space where the Scorpions had just been, the plasma fire from the Jordans hitting the metal rounds, melting them into mercurial drops before engulfing the small fighter crafts of the enemy. The first two Hellcats were turned into melting shrapnel, twisting and bleeding off into space as the third shot by.

As the Hellcats broke apart their field was dropped to reveal a Chimeran Battle Cruiser.

"Shit," Scarlett said again, joining Blue on her starboard side. "It's not a floater. It's a cruiser. They did a pretty good job masking it. Calyph, do you see that?"

"I see it. You worry about the Hellcats. There's one circling back for you and Blue, and the J8s were only able to take out one, and a half. Randle only clipped his. Its wing is smoking but it's circling back and they might need help."

"We're fine!" Randle told them over the com. "Take care of yours, we got these guys."

"Roger that," Scarlett told him, looping around starboard, expecting to see Blue looping port, their Scorpions making a great heart shape in the deep night. But Blue wasn't there.

The three Hellcats came at them in a backwards-triangular battle formation, two in front and one in the rear. It was a classic formation when flying three ships against, presumably, one. The two fore ships could bombard the oncoming fighter and cover it breaking right or left. The aft ship could pick up any remains or follow the enemy should it escape.

Jordan Blue opened up on the front two fighters with plasma fire from the Scorpion's deadly tail before breaking away. She shook her head, knowing they didn't have chance, as she eased the Scorpion in the opposite direction of Scarlett's craft.

She was hit by another wave of nausea and everything started to look and feel a bit out of place, but mostly it was her head that felt out of place. She closed her eyes, trying to will whatever it was to go away. Her head rocked back suddenly and her mouth dropped open, panting out short bursts of air. Her eyes opened, blue and bewildered, and swept across the dash console.

The dials were the first things she noticed. They seemed altogether too bright and too clear. She looked at the readouts. The normally dull red and green numbers on the dash screens seemed very...*vivid*. Then she looked at the brushed steel of the dash console and it began to melt.

Blue could see the brush lines in the steel, clearer and darker than ever, begin to wave and drip and bleed down the console. The metal oozed between the dials and knobs and screens. She quickly ran a neural check of the ship to see if she had taken fire, though she could not imagine how the dash would get so hot that it could melt.

Especially inside the craft, she thought, her eyes going the footwell to see if anything below her had been incinerated. *And it's not hot in here. It's freezing.* Then, just as the checks came back to her negative, she felt *herself* begin to melt.

It began in the back of her throat, as if her pharynx were melting and sliding down into her trachea. The feeling was sickening, and familiar. Her hand fell limply from the wheel.

"Lethe," she whispered.

"Jordan? Jordan, what's going on?"

Blue could hear Galen's voice coming though a thick fog as she tried to understand what was happening. She swallowed hard, feeling the drug work its magic in her, pulling her away.

"Noel!" Galen shouted. Blue swallowed again, trying to ignore the feeling that *she* was being swallowed. She reached up with numb fingers and pulled off her stel-cap. The receptor came loose from her temple with a soft pop. It hung off the small metal cap in her hand like a lost tentacle.

"Lethe," she said again, her voice sad and full of shock. She was grateful that now Galen was the only one who could hear her, but felt ashamed that he would bear witness even from light years away. "Somebody gave me Lethe." She was greeted by stunned silence and she could feel tears of defeat well up in her eyes. A very distant part of her marveled that *both* of her eyes welled up.

"How?" she whispered. "My food? Can you *ingest* Lethe?" She shivered so hard it shook her whole body. "Even so, when? I haven't had anything to eat since yesterday. My coffee? Could somebody have put it my coffee?" The only answer was silence as the moments bled away. Her mind had started to drift when Galen cried out.

"That's it! Not the coffee, the food – the food that you *haven't* eaten. It's the cold. And the fact that you *haven't eaten*. Jesus!"

Blue looked down at her wrist lying limp and dead next to her thigh. She could feel fingers fumbling at her bracelet. She sucked at her throat, telling herself that it wasn't *really* sliding down into her lungs, it just felt that way. Galen activated her field and at once she was enveloped in a cocoon if warmth. The rush it gave her body was multiplied as fresh oxygen was pushed into her lungs.

"Dammit, Jordan," Galen cursed as he forcibly moved her body forward. She swayed like a drunken doll. "It's because you didn't eat. The cold is making your body burn up its fat stores, what little you had. And fat is where your body stores both energy and toxins."

"I had Lethe stored in my fat?" she asked, her voice thick and slurred, her mind groping for comprehension. Her face creased in a drunken, lopsided smile and she uttered a sleepy chuckle.

"Yes," Galen told her. "And now that fat is getting burned up, and the Lethe is being released into your system."

Blue could feel something move behind her. Something was tugging, and then a sack was pulled out from behind her seat and dropped onto her right leg. She watched drunkenly as the sack was upended - depositing its contents into her lap. It was a flight bag of a human pilot, full of first-aid supplies along with small toiletries and snacks.

Her next exhale was ragged, almost a choking laugh, until she saw the hand. A ghostly hand, *Galen's hand*, was pawing through the contents from the bag. Blue turned her head away, unable to look. Nausea wormed through her gut.

"Here!" Galen exclaimed. Blue looked back as a silver packet was pressed against her lips. "Eat this," he told her as he squeezed the contents out into her mouth. Her mouth was filled with a nasty, greasy, paste. She gagged and tried to spit it out but Galen pushed it back into her mouth. "EAT IT!" he shouted.

"Wha' i' it?" She managed, choking it down.

"It's a butter made from mashed nuts," Galen told her. Blue laughed drunkenly, despite her predicament. "I know, I know," Galen said, laughing as well. "But it's high in fat. Keep eating it."

"Ugh!" Blue said, but she took the packet from him and ate the rest, squeezing out the last bit. "Humans eat some nasty shit."

Galen laughed. The texture of the paste disgusted her, but the salty taste wasn't too awful. Better still, she was already starting to feel more herself. She sat hunched over, looking around like a drunk sobering up to find he was still at the bar. She took a few deep breaths to settle herself as she got her bearings. The food, the fat, and the heat were bringing her around. She rubbed her face with her palms, shook her head, and pulled the stel-cap back onto her head, fastening its receptor onto her temple in time to hear Scarlett cursing her name.

Scarlett pulled the Scorpion around in a great loop, searching for Blue. She spotted her in an instant, suspended motionless in space like a dandelion spore the moment the wind died. Scarlett could see no sign of damage to the Scorpion.

"Blue? Are you hit?" The only response was the neural link in Blue's Scorpion being cut. "Shit! Calyph! Can you tell what's going on?"

"No, but you'll have to get back to her later, that Hellcat is coming back for you."

Scarlett pulled the wheel as close to her chest as she could get it, pulling every bit of thrust from the Scorpion as she dove down to evade the oncoming Hellcat and the hot rounds it was unleashing on her. She pushed down suddenly, braking hard and left, coming up behind the enemy craft before it could turn.

She let go with the plasma fire from the Scorpion's deadly tail, but the Hellcat swerved, avoiding most of it with ease. Now that they had lost the element of surprise, it was down to a dogfight. The Scorp had the more lethal weaponry, but it was messy. The Hellcat wasn't the faster craft, but it was more responsive to combat maneuvering and the rounds it shot were more accurate. Scarlett had a high-grade field encapsulating her body, but she doubted it would stop a fifty caliber round.

The Hellcat dodged a quick left, braked and flipped, coming around behind her. Scarlett dodged and swerved as it opened fire on her but still caught a round in her left wing as she broke away.

"Bastard!" she hissed, pulling up in a tight loop in an effort to get behind the Hellcat, but it managed to follow and keep behind her. She glanced at the battle that Sammath and Randle were engaged in and knew she would get no help from that quarter, not that she would ever ask. Calyph's voice came in low over the com.

"Your losing hydraulic fluid from your left wing, Scarlett. You need to get out of there before you can only fly in a circle."

"No shit!" she answered. She darted right but the Hellcat opened fire, leading the craft and sending rounds into the right wing. Scarlett felt one go right through her fighter not a meter away from her right leg. She ground her teeth and dove.

"He's predicting, " Calyph started but Scarlett angrily cut him off.

"I know what he's doing!" she told him. "And he's done doing it!" She flew a ragged whipstitch pattern to evade any more fire, slowing down so the Hellcat could close the distance.

Calyph sat in the Cahir, monitoring the fight. It was projected onto the wall directly in front of him in an image so clear he felt as if he were only meters away from the battle, watching through a wall of hyper-glass. The wall to his left showed the Dragon on the outside from the tail looking down the flanks. Looking into the room, it appeared as if the engineer was on a platform with two of his sides open to space. The wall to his right showed Fledgling Bay.

Calyph leaned forward, trying to pay equal attention to what was happening with Randle and Sammath, but he could only focus on Scarlett. Which was why he didn't notice the chaos in the Fledgling Bay until it was too late.

Scarlett pulled around tight, so tight that she almost hit the other Scorpion.

"Dammit Blue!" she shouted. "What the hell is wrong with you?"

And why isn't she getting fired at? Scarlett thought as she yanked the wheel, this time forcing the Scorp to go as fast as it could while pulling it over and around. The near miss gave her an idea. It took every ounce of upper body strength that she had, and she had a lot. Still, her arms began to shake and just when she had finally brought the Scorp up and over, she heard Blue's voice over the com.

The shouting from his right drew Calyph's attention away from the screens all around him. He didn't know what could be more pressing than the fight that was ensuing not even three kilometers away from the Dragon.

The commotion was coming from Fledgling Bay. Calyph was about to open the com to ask what the hell was going on down there as he turned to the wall on his right to see the projection of the bay that housed the Dragon's Fledglings. He watched wide-eyed, his mouth dropping open.

"Did I miss anything?" Blue asked over the com. Scarlett could only let out a shout that was half-scream and half-growl.

"You stupid bitch! Where the hell have you been?" she demanded.

Blue gave a short, nervous laugh. "I had a...systems malfunction."

"Like hell you did!"

"Well, I'm back now – and not a moment too soon," she said, powering up all systems that had nodded into stand-by to conserve energy. "It looks like you could use a little help."

"I most certainly do not," Scarlett hissed. "Randle and Sammath are getting overrun. You need to assist them immediately."

Blue powered up her thrusters as she watched Scarlett's Scorpion dance and dodge its way across the deep black, trailing smoke.

"I don't know Scar, it looks like you have taken some heavy fire."

"This fucker is mine!" Scarlett shouted, loud enough to make Blue wince. "Assist Randle and Sammath! That's an order!"

"You can't order me," Blue told her. "We're the same rank."

"Like hell we are! I'm sixteen and you're eight. That gives me precedence."

"I don't think that's what our numbers are for," Blue said, her tone doubtful but cheery. "And I'm not sure you are using precedence correctly." She powered up the thrust on the Scorpion, following Scarlett and her pursuer.

"If anything happens to Randle or Sammath," Scarlett hissed, "I'm holding you personally responsible."

"Alright, alright," Blue muttered, pulling the Scorp left and heading for the fight that was a flickering mess down below and to her portside.

"Besides," Scarlett said under her breath, "I'm going to take this asshole out if it's the last thing I do."

Calyph watched the happenings in Fledgling Bay, dumbstruck for near five seconds before he opened up the com.

"What the hell is going on?" he demanded.

"Exactly what it looks like!" A nervous voice replied. "What do we do?"

Calyph didn't know. He watched as the Red Fledgling, Scarlett's Fledgling, powered up, all on its own. Its silver skin shimmered with a ruby light that grew brighter and brighter.

"Do the Fledglings ever go out without their Jordan?" the voice asked.

"Never," Calyph replied, his voice barely above a whisper. *But then again,* he thought, *when has a Jordan's life been threatened within a few klicks of his or her Fledgling?*

Calyph, along with everyone in Fledgling Bay, watched as the silver skin of the Fledgling turned a dark burgundy before it rose up and shot out through the field of the bay door.

"What do we do?" the nervous voice from the bay pleaded.

"What can we do?" Calyph asked. He turned his attention back to the projections to his front. The top right corner showed the dogfight with Scarlett and the Hellcat. Her craft was bleeding out smoke as it dodged the enemy.

The bottom showed Randle and Sammath locked in a battle of their own. Blue's Scorpion was quickly approaching them, the tail of the Scorp starting to glow.

"Hang in there, Scarlett," he said. "Fledge is coming." He looked back up to where her section of space was projected on the wall.

And that's not all, he thought, his eyes going wide. He sat back in the Cahir and brought all the fingers of his right hand together and back, as if he were pulling an invisible string towards his ear. The image of Scarlett's Scorpion and the surrounding area quickly magnified as it zoomed towards him.

The Chimeran Battle Cruiser was just joining the party. As of yet, it did not look like it intended on engaging in the battle. No fighters had been released from the bays and no weapons were arming. It had simply turned off its thrusters some time ago, letting its inertia carry it on towards the scene that was unfolding just below its massive bulk. Calyph could see the ship's name, *Macedonian*, on its great rounded hull. The Chimeran Insignia, the double loop symbol for infinity, flanked its name on both sides. It sank down like a fat, lazy spider, slow and quiet.

Scarlett whipped the Scorpion up and over, down and back.

"What did you say?"

Calyph cleared his throat. "Fledge is coming for you."

"Did you send him?"

"No."

"Then how... No! Calyph, call him back!" Scarlett pulled up on the wheel, wrenching it to the right.

"I can't," Calyph said. He could hear a sound of furious exasperation from Scarlett. The Captain broke in over the com in the Cahir Room demanding to know what was going on.

Shit, Calyph thought. *He must have seen Fledge over the monitor.* He cut the com with Scarlett momentarily so he could update the Captain on what was happening.

"Fledge," Scarlett said firmly, hoping he could hear her, or at least feel her. "You stay clear of this. Do you understand?" The Hellcat was firing again. Scarlett whipped right, faked left and whipped right again. She looked at the radar, now picking up a craft coming from the Dragon. "Dammit! You're as stubborn as I am! Stay clear, you hear me? Stay clear!" She watched the blip on screen. It never wavered. "Agh!" she shouted as she spun her wheel left, braked, and then pulled up giving it everything she had. She was now going head to head with the Hellcat.

"Okay, you bastard. You're so good at reading my moves - read this." She cranked the wheel but kept the craft straight, throwing it into a barrel roll so that it flew directly at the Hellcat in an ever-tightening spiral. She threw the safety latch and pulled the jack.

Eat it, you fucker! Scarlett thought, tucking her chin tightly to her chest as she was shot out from the bottom the Scorpion and into the vacuum of space.

The Scorpion, now a spinning missile trailing smoke and fire, slammed into the Hellcat with an explosion that Scarlett felt even through her field. Plasma fire and shrapnel exploded in every direction. The concussion shot her away like a flicked kidney bean – encapsulated in a field of heated, pressurized air.

When Scarlett, dizzy and nauseated but filled with a triumphant glee, finally stopped spinning, she was quite far from the rest of the battle. She took a deep breath and her field responded, altering the oxygen count. She hung there in the vacuum of space, trying to stop the slow spin of her body, watching like a lone spectator atop a darkened amphitheater.

Blue had joined Sammath and Randle, and had already disposed of one of the enemy ships. The three of them closed in on the remaining Hellcat as Scarlett watched, relieved. She knew it didn't have a chance. She scanned the lower sector of the dark sky and spotted Fledge. First just a speck of red, but getting larger and brighter by the second. Scarlett smiled.

"Okay, baby," she said aloud, her voice a strange echo in the great emptiness that surrounded her. "Come and get me."

As she watched his approach there was a flash of green light and the last Hellcat exploded as the Emerald Jordan showed up just in time to blow it out of existence.

"It's about time, Jade!" Scarlett said, though she knew no one could hear. She laughed, elated.

With her attention on Fledge and the sudden appearance the other Jordan, Scarlett didn't notice the hulking mass of metal that was descending behind her. The Chimeran Battle Cruiser was now less than two klicks away. By the time she could sense its looming presence it was almost upon her. She turned, instinctively reaching for her pistol, but it was too little and too late.

The cruiser sent out an encapsulator, like a reptile shooting out its tongue to catch a bug. It snatched Scarlett up in the blink of an eye.

She heard a voice, male and smug, but could not make out his words. She had a glimpse at an airlock on the belly of the cruiser before her field was overrun and she blacked out.

ONE ONE

Scarlett opened her eyes unto a world of dark. It was not entirely black, but it was close – like being out on a moonless night. She could see shapes, but nothing clearly. Mostly just dark silhouettes against a dark background.

They must be jamming my field, she thought. Her hands were bound behind her back and she was being roughly handled by at least two people. Their hands seemed to be all over her, frisking her with a violent determination.

"Hey!" she called. "You guys are getting a little friendly out there!" One set of hands continued their business while Scarlett could see one shadowy form pull away.

"Forget it," a voice said. "Just turn a fire hose on her. That should short it out."

"Whoa, whoa, whoa!" she shouted. "What the hell are you guys doing?"

"We're looking for your field generator," another voice said.

"It's in my boot!"

Scarlett could barely see the darkened figures as they bent over, but as soon as she felt them fumbling at her boots she tipped her head to the left, pressing her ear against her shoulder. Her field drew in with a snap and the light that hit her eyes was almost blinding.

"Got it!" someone shouted. Scarlett turned her face away from the light, squinting, waiting for her eyes to adjust. She was in some sort of airlock. Two men, equally handsome in a bland and generic sort of way, stood up. One was a dark brunette and one a sandy blonde.

They looked every bit human, but Scarlett knew better.

These bastards came out of a plant somewhere, she thought. *Probably the borderlands of the Flower.* They wore coverall uniforms of royal blue with the double loop insignia of the Chimera stitched over the heart and again on the left sleeve in black thread.

"That's better," Brunette Hair remarked as he grabbed Scarlett by her left elbow and Sandy Hair grabbed her right. Their beautiful faces were inset with angry, malicious eyes.

"Ugh!" Scarlett grunted, her face contorted with undisguised contempt. "A tea party and, silly me, I forgot to bring my own doll." Bruny gave her a shake hard enough to rattle her teeth. She might have fallen over if Sandy wasn't clutching her other arm.

"Watch your mouth!" he warned. They propelled her forward and Sandy slammed his palm on a button next to a hexagonal door. It slid open with a hiss and they pushed her through.

With her hands bound tight and forced into the small of her back, the male constructs marched Scarlett through the jet bay of the enormous battle ship. A multitude of fighter jets of varied class and age were all lined up for immediate action in a battle-ready pyramid formation, facing the bay door. On the far side of the bay was the command station that controlled the door, which was currently semi-open. Rather than the normal closed maw of steel, there was a network of pulsing gold veins crisscrossing the gaping mouth of black - a nitrogen membrane keeping the molecular air contained and pressurized while allowing aircraft to pass through. Not as elegant as a Dragon, but it served the purpose.

Wing to wing, the jets stood braced on legs over a meter thick with rubber covered wheels that were as high as her chin. Beyond the jets, lining the back wall of the bay as well as the sides of the hangar were masses of racked and boxed weapons, possibly an overflow from the armory. Either way, it was obvious that the Chimera were prepared for the war they had started.

Idiots, Scarlett thought. *Letting me see their arsenal.* She looked at the rows of neatly marked crates along the walls as they pushed her along, mentally cataloging everything she saw. *Unless they want me to see it, hoping I will relay what I have seen. Do they think to frighten us?* Her brow furrowed and she fought the urge to bite her lip. *Or there is also the possibility that they don't plan for me to live long enough to tell what I have seen.*

Her last thought gave her a pause that was only momentary. *Fuck them,* she thought. She shook her dark hair out behind her and lifted her chin. *I'll make sure that taking me was the worst mistake they ever made.*

Her eyes darted about, taking inventory as they frog marched her through the crates stacked in the jet bay and then into the actual arsenal bay itself. She mentally clucked her tongue at them for storing weapons so close to the fighters.

Not to mention all their fuel.

After a while, though, as the crates went on and on, she was astounded at both the amount as well as the variety of the weaponry that the Chimera had amassed from what appeared to be every galaxy in the universe.

There were short-wave radio missiles from Ruthin, bullock shells from Andromeda, and even tripedoe snares from Golgotha - the farthest and least traveled galaxy, except for its psychopathic indigenes.

There were racks upon racks loaded with firearms that ranged from short laser bows and plasma guns, to hot-round Tommyknockers. Photon missiles. Stacked boxes and crates full of blast grenades, smoke grenades, concussion bombs and c-4 tickers that could take out an M craft. Rip mines. The crates went on.

As her escorts funneled her through an opening in the bay she noticed a grizzled lot of poorly handled pomegranate missiles, also from Golgotha, stacked neatly against a wall. Each one was as tall as Scarlett and was covered with a thin, bulging layer of organic metal, rather than a composite shell - making them appear like evil, rotting fruit - ready to burst. They sat apart, as if even the other weapons eschewed them. Scarlett turned her face away. Those were powerful enough to take out a cruiser. Or a Dragon.

Sandy and Bruny pushed her through the doors of the overflowing arsenal, down a short corridor, and into a mechanic bay. The open hangar was littered with half-repaired jets, rolling tool racks and heavy chains that hung from the ceiling.

Scarlett flinched, seeing so many constructs in one place. Looking like models turned mechanics, the manufactured people were busy everywhere; working on motors, repairing hydraulic drives and shoring up the body armor on numerous jets.

It smelled like metal and oil and reeked of war.

The Jordan watched as a separate group approached her, led by a tall, blonde male. He ducked his head under a low chain as he led his entourage towards Scarlett and her captors.

The constructs holding Scarlett shoved hard on her shoulders, trying to push her down. She jerked her right shoulder forward as hard as she could, making Sandy stumble backwards on her left and breaking the grip of Bruny on her right. Bruny lunged back towards her, his lip curled in a sneer.

Scarlett brought her knee up to her chest and drove her foot into his stomach, knocking the wind from his lungs as he flew back.

"If you want me on my knees," she said, leaning towards him, "you're going to have to cut off my legs." Sandy, still gripping her left shoulder, grabbed her hands where they were bound and yanked her back.

"That could be arranged," he hissed into her ear as Bruny rose snarling, his chest hitching, unable yet to take a full breath of air.

The blonde leader of the entourage laughed, flashing immaculate white teeth, and clapped his hands as he approached. Whether it was to get their attention or for the diversion they were creating, Scarlett could not tell.

Jesus, Scarlett thought as she watched him approach, *he's beautiful.*

Everything about him was breath-taking. He was tall and broad-shouldered but slim. His eyes were a bright green and his jaw was sharp and narrow. High, arched cheekbones, full lips, and golden hair. His skin was flawless.

Scarlett fought to keep her heartbeat and her breathing even. She forced a scowl but knew without a doubt that she was looking at a face sculpted by the hands of Gwendolyn herself.

My God, he looks like he was chiseled from stone.

Though Bruny and Sandy were handsome, their faces looked like they had come from the same mold, and very well could have. They were beautiful constructs but most likely second or third run and mass-produced. There was no doubt, however, that the man in front of her was one of the First Seven.

His lips were full and compelling and seductive. He had lean, muscular arms and chest and a smooth, easy grace. His smile was dazzling and his green eyes were mesmerizing. He was perfect.

Of course, he was *supposed* to look perfect. All of the dolls were made to be beautiful, even the ones that were mass-produced.

Until the playthings went awry. Beautiful, clever, living, breathing, shitting, fucking, angry, psychotic dolls. The Jordan suppressed a shudder.

He tilted his head and eyed Scarlett appraisingly.

"Hmm," he said, sounding amused. The sound he made was silky smooth, as if it had been played by an instrument and, in a way, it was. The Dyer Maker had made all tonal inclinations for the first run of constructs from a traditional symphony orchestra.

Scarlett felt her body respond to the sound – the quickened heartbeat, the contracted breath, the heat between her legs. It made her feel weak. She swallowed, trying to control herself.

"What do we have here?" he asked, reaching out to grasp Scarlett's chin between his thumb and forefinger. She felt the same reaction to his touch that she did to his voice and struggled against it. He tilted his head again, the edge of his mouth drawing up. "The Jordan of the Crimson Fledgling." He managed to sound both intrigued and bored at the same time. "Though it's another human. I was hoping for an elf this time."

Anger rose like bile in her throat. She pulled her attention away from his perfect face and form and focused on his eyes. They were as green and clear as glass.

He let go of Scarlett's chin and looked her up and down. "Well, at least this one is much more pleasing to the eye." He gave her a wolfish grin. "We've already, umm, tested humans. They can be easy to break and when they do, they don't seem to know much."

"Well, I'm the best you're gonna get, you asshole," Scarlett spat. "Besides, elves always have shit coming out both ends and rarely know which end gets wiped."

The Chimeran gaped at her audaciousness before he burst out laughing. He turned to his escort to see if they were sharing his amusement. Most indulged him with a smile, though their attitude towards Scarlett was openly hostile.

When he regained his composure he favored Scarlett with another wolfish smile. "I'm Bjorn," he offered. "The Commander of this ship." Scarlett gave a short laugh.

"Is that supposed to impress me? I don't care who you are or what shit-hole you command."

Though the construct entourage behind him looked incensed, Bjorn laughed again. He wagged a finger at Scarlett. If it had been closer to her face she would have bitten it.

"You," he told her, "have quite the spirit. I like that. And you are quite the pilot, you took out one my best." He looked her up and down once more, his eyes lingering this time on her hips and where her breasts pushed at the ruby fabric of her flight suit. He stepped closer and put a hand into her thick hair. He gently pulled her head back to get a better look at her face.

His eyes swept up her neck and jaw, over her full lips and came to rest on her eyes. Glints of crimson burned in their depths. "Would you look at that..." he remarked, just a touch curious. Scarlett jerked her head away. After gazing down again at her body, he pressed his lips together and sighed through his nose, shaking his head like a man denying himself pleasure in order to put business first.

Bjorn turned and waved over two others holding a bedraggled apparition of a man. Scarlett had been too focused on Bjorn to notice him. He sagged between two constructs, peering at Scarlett with nervous eyes, hardly able to hold himself up. He looked away quickly, ashamed. His clothes hung on his shrunken frame and hair that might have once been blond or light brown hung in ragged clumps around a thin, quite unshaven face.

"Do you recognize this man?" Bjorn asked. Scarlett sneered.

"I think he was my date for prom."

Bjorn laughed and stepped back towards Scarlett, reaching out a hand to cup her cheek. "I like you. I think we might get along quite well." She jerked her face out of his grasp.

"I doubt it, you're not my type."

"You might be surprised," Bjorn told her, his voice a smooth melody. "We are built the same way you are, with all the same parts, and all the same desires." He looked down Scarlett's neck, pausing again where the skin of her chest disappeared into the red sparkle of her flight suit. His eyes came back up to rest on her face. He smiled and stepped even closer, pressing his body against hers as he reached up to cup her face again, holding it more firmly this time. "We have all of your best qualities, with none of your umm... foibles. Besides, you must know artificial intelligence is faster and infinitely more accurate."

Scarlett smiled wickedly. "You're wrong on that one," she said softly. "There are many things we have that you don't." She leaned forward, pressing her body against him, sliding her hips along his. His lips parted and she could feel his reaction as his body responded. He leaned closer, pushing harder. She pressed back and made her voice softer still, until it was barely above a whisper. She turned her head a fraction to the side. "And one of those things is something you hate. It is something you cannot comprehend and therefore it drives you mad."

Bjorn tipped his face closer to hers, his breath becoming shorter and shallower - Scarlett could feel it on her cheek and ear. He licked his lips. "And what is that?" he asked when she didn't continue.

Scarlett grinned and jerked back, ramming her right knee up and into his groin. Bjorn doubled over and dropped to one knee with a guttural shout. The other constructs rushed to aid him but he angrily shrugged them away. He leered up at Scarlett, the lust in his eyes replaced with anger. She leaned down as far as the grip of her captors would allow.

"We're unpredictable," Scarlett told him. His lips curled back in a silent snarl but it just widened her grin. She arched a brow at him. "And I see that we *do* share some of the same, umm... *foibles.*"

Bruny and Sandy jerked her up and dragged her back, her smug expression fixed on Bjorn. It took long moments before he was able to stand. He did so, grimacing, but after a moment the anger dissipated and he returned her grin. Scarlett saw his dazzling smile and knew she was in for trouble. When he spoke again his voice came out in a smooth, low baritone.

"I'll see you soon, Scarlett."

The Jordan jerked back in surprise, startled that he knew her name, as she felt her captors snap a plastique restraint down over her wrists. As the Chimeran Commander left with his entourage of manufactured, beautiful people in tow, she caught the eye of the bedraggled man they had brought in and she realized with another jolt of surprise that she *did* know him. It was Eli Rhett. He had been the Engineer aboard the Opal Dragon. The one Calyph had replaced.

ONE TWO

"Grandpa?" Jeanette asked. "Will you tell us where the elves came from?"

"Don't they teach you that in school?" Grandpa asked - though he was more than eager to share everything that he knew, and everything that he had heard, and most of the things that he had guessed at for so long that he figured they had to be true.

"Kinda."

"She won't take Galactic History until sixth grade," Sean said.

"And Daddy says it's not polite to ask," Jeanette whispered.

"Ah." Grandpa nodded solemnly, his whiskered chin bobbing. *Sixth grade,* he thought. *How old would that be? Eleven? Twelve? So, Jeanette is not yet that old – and Sean must be that old or older. How much older?* He cleared his throat and brought his attention back to the curious faces of his grandchildren. "Of course! Well, let's see...first we should start with the humans."

The children settled down on the rug. Sean lay down on his side, planted his elbow on the frayed, ropy fabric and propped his head up with a splayed hand. Jeanette flopped down on her belly, cupping her chin in tiny palms. Grandpa's gaze drifted up the shelves laden with books, his eyes searching as his mind dredged the memories.

"The humans had already left Earth by then," he told them, his voice wistful. "Half of the moons of Jupiter had been settled, the other half were still being made ready. But our galaxy, for billions of years, had been steadily drawing closer to another galaxy."

"Andromeda." Sean said.

"Yes, Andromeda. Because we knew that our galaxies would someday collide, even though that day was a long ways away, that is where the humans directed most of their attention in space exploration."

"What would happen if they collided?" Jeanette asked.

"A galactic mess," Grandpa told her. Sean snickered and flicked his blonde hair out of his eyes. "Anyway, the elves had the same idea, so they were directing a great deal of fuss in our direction."

"Did we discover the elves, or did they discover us?" Jeanette asked.

"We discovered them," Sean told her. Grandpa made a clucking noise.

"Well," he said, "that really depends on who you ask. We say we discovered them, they say they discovered us. I don't know why they all make such a ruckus about it."

"What would a troll say?" Sean asked. Grandpa leaned back into his chair and gave Sean a bit of an appraising smile.

"That's a good question. I suppose a troll would say we discovered each other, which I think is the truth of it."

Sean grunted. He had thought so. A year ago he had realized with a shock that history was written by anyone with the balls to write it down and say it was the truth.

"Elves!" Jeanette encouraged with a hoarse whisper.

"Yes!" Grandpa agreed. "Well, we were very eager to make contact with the elves, once we had found each other. They were shy at first, but after a few years we began to get along quite well. Our languages were very different but both were phonetical."

"What does that mean?"

"It means we make sounds with our mouths to talk," Sean said, though he cast a quick glance at Grandpa for affirmation. The old man nodded.

"If they had communicated telepathically, with their minds, we would have had to find another way to get our ideas back and forth."

"Why are they called elves?" Jeanette asked. "If they were from Andromeda, why weren't they called Andromans...Andromedia...Andromedums?" She asked, stumbling for the right word. Grandpa cackled, his watery, blue eyes sparkling with merriment.

"Because they were smaller than us, and because they had those pointy ears, we called them after a race of people they resembled. Fairy creatures in the old stories from Earth."

"Were there really elves on Earth?" Sean asked.

"I don't think so."

"Then how did we know what they resembled?"

Grandpa's near toothless mouth puckered and his eyes looked so perplexed they almost crossed. Sean bit his lip but Jeanette laughed out loud.

"I'll be damned," Grandpa said after a moment. "I don't know." He looked back at the children on the floor, still puzzled. Jeanette rolled so that she was on her side like her brother.

"Why were they smaller than us? Didn't they eat enough?"

"They came from bigger planets," Sean told her. "With more gravity, higher gravity, whatever."

"Ohhh," Jeanette said softly. She had no idea what he was talking about or why a bigger planet meant smaller people, but she would never say so.

"Anyway," Grandpa continued, shifting his thin frame in his chair, "we had many things in common with the elves - math, physics, astronomy – and, of course, space travel. Once the humans and the elves formed an alliance, we made great progress together. Our combined knowledge set us forward into a new age."

"The Age of Creation," Sean said.

"That's right. The Age of Creation. The humans had already begun creating new worlds, usually using an existing moon as a base. The elves were already creating actual moons from clouds of astral dust. Together, they were able to create an artificial galaxy."

"The Flower?" Jeanette asked tentatively.

"Yes, The Flower. They built it between our two galaxies to keep them from smashing into each other. It is the only galaxy to have a single system. Six small planets, all very much like the Earth in our system, circle their very own sun – though it's much smaller than ours."

"It's a white dwarf," Sean interjected.

"Why is it a galaxy if it only has one system?" Jeanette asked.

"Because it only has one system *now*," Grandpa told her.

"The elves are still creating moons," Sean explained. "When one moon is finished, it is pushed out to the edge of the system where it is terraformed and then waits until it is needed. The IGC calls them Pollen."

Jeanette looked at Grandpa, not entirely trusting her brother, but he nodded. "That's right. I think."

"What else was created?"

"Well..." Grandpa's eyes wandered up over his shelves again, his mouth working as he thought about it.

Sean looked away. Not because it was gross, though Grandpa did have a pretty scary mouth on the inside, but because Sean had just found out that he had the same habit. He had been working on his first algebraic equations when his teacher had asked if he was eating during class.

"No," Sean had answered as if offended by the question.

"Oh," Professor McCarthy had replied. "The way your jaw was working I thought maybe you had a sim-steak in there."

His teacher had walked away chuckling but Sean had sat frozen in his seat, staring at his paper without seeing it. He knew exactly what Professor McCarthy was talking about. He had seen Grandpa do it plenty of times. Like now.

"The Age of Creation," Grandpa said, "was a very turbulent time. The sudden, combined knowledge of the races had an almost explosive effect. They began discovering things and creating things too fast for their own good. The creation of worlds and the weapons to destroy them were foremost. Some learned how to cross dimensions of time and space, while others learned how to create *new* dimensions of time and space."

"What about the Dragons?" Sean asked.

"Oh yes! The Dragons. The elves had brought with them from their galaxy a dying race of great creatures; planet-living but capable of space travel. It was the humans who created what they are now."

"They created a way for them to live forever," Sean said.

"I wouldn't quite call it living," Grandpa said. "But for the most part, I suppose so."

"And the constructs," Sean added with a grim smile. "The elves created the constructs."

"Yes, well, the Dyer Maker did."

"And the Chimera."

Jeanette shuddered and her dark curls shook. She didn't know much about the Chimera, except that they were bad, and somehow the reason her Uncle Joe had died.

"He didn't create the Chimera," Grandpa said, his voice slightly stern. "That was not deliberate. Despite what happened, I think he had the best of intentions."

"Will you tell us about the Dyer Maker, Grandpa?" Sean asked.

"Yes! Yes!" Jeanette cried, clapping her hands. Then she stopped and frowned. "What is a Dyer Maker?" She asked. Grandpa cackled. His thin shoulders, covered with a blue and white plaid shirt, settled back comfortably into the rough fabric of his chair. This was a story he knew well.

"Dyer is the elfish word for doll," he told Jeanette. Jeanette swung her legs around with a child's grace and folded them like a pretzel. She leaned forward, eager.

"He made *dolls*?" she asked. Grandpa threw back his head and cawed at the ceiling. Sean wrinkled his nose at the mess of teeth he could see inside Grandpa's mouth.

"Oh, he made dolls, alright. But not what you are thinking sweetheart." He chewed carefully at the inside of his cheek for a moment, deciding where to start. He decided that the beginning would be best.

"The Dyer Maker wasn't a doll maker by trade," Grandpa told them. "At least he didn't start out to be. He was a bioengineer, working for TASER, the elfin research facility for automatons."

"Robots," Sean whispered hoarsely from the side of his mouth before Jeanette could ask.

"I know!" she whispered back, though she hadn't really known. Grandpa continued, ignoring their exchange.

"His family came from a land known for doll making. The trade was passed down from father to son, generation after generation. Something happened along the way that made doll making obsolete – probably just wasn't a profitable business at some point – but the family kept the tradition nonetheless, and kept passing it down over the years.

Anyway, Cronus, as he was called back then, was married but his wife died in childbirth and left him with an infant daughter, Christa. Like most parents, he did not have much time to spend with her because he worked so much."

"Why did he work so much?" Jeanette asked.

"To make sure she was taken care of," Grandpa said. "He did not know how to raise a little girl, but he was able to make good money and provide for her. He put her in a convent where she could be raised and be given an education."

"Ohhhh."

"What he didn't foresee was how deep into the faith she would be brought up. And so his daughter grew up to be a Zealot, which made him unhappy because he knew she would become a nun and never have a family."

"Why couldn't she have a family?" Jeanette asked. Sean grinned into his hand, wondering how Grandpa was going to explain nuns and sex to Jeanette. Grandpa shifted around in his chair and cleared his throat, obviously wondering the same thing.

"Because they aren't allowed to marry," he said. "They're too busy serving God."

"Ohhhh," Jeanette breathed.

Drat, Sean thought.

"Anyway," Grandpa continued, "she would have been a nun, but while she was working at a hospice on Grey Leaf she fell in love with an injured pilot and married him."

"So she got to have a family!"

"Yes. They had a little girl right away. And because he had not been able to spend much time with Christa when she was young, Cronus spent all the time he could with her little girl; lavishing her with all the attention he wasn't able to give his own daughter."

"Is that why you spend so much time with us, Grandpa?" Jeanette asked. "Because you worked so much and couldn't spend time with your kids?"

Grandpa, who usually cackled and cawed at everything she said, fixed her with a somber eye and a sad smile. His creased face softened as he looked at her fondly. "Yes, little Jean," he said gently. "That is exactly right." He contemplated her young sweet face, it reminded him so much of a little girl from long ago. Jeanette didn't seem to mind. She just smiled and waited for more of the story. When more than a minute had passed Sean cleared his throat.

"Grandpa?" Sean prodded. "You were telling us about the Dyer Maker."

"Was I?" Grandpa looked surprised and then frowned as he followed his trail of thought backwards. "I was!" He shifted about and then settled back in his seat, getting comfortable again.

"Well, yes, of course! I was telling you about Christa's little girl. Well, the little girl was very lonely. Her mother wouldn't let her play with other children. She called them Godless heathens and told her daughter that they would infect her with sin."

"What's sin?"

Sean grinned again as Grandpa squirmed around in his chair. Jeanette was always full of questions but Sean had never seen the old man wiggle so much.

"Sin?" he asked, grumbling uncertainly. "Sin is doing what you shouldn't, like asking too many questions!" Jeanette's eyes went wide and Sean chuckled into his hand. "Now do you wanna hear this story or not?" Grandpa asked. Jeanette nodded emphatically, keeping her lips pressed tightly together. Grandpa relaxed a little, rubbing his palms on his thighs.

"The little girl was lonely, so her Grandpa made her a doll. Not just any kind of doll, but a very, very special doll."

"Was it like a Droidella?" Jeanette asked, unable to help herself. Her Auntie had given her one on her last birthday, and she loved it. None of her friends had one yet and they were all *sooo* jealous.

"Even more special than a Droidella," Grandpa told her. This doll was a living, breathing replica of his granddaughter, copied from her DNA. It was a just as real as the little girl."

"Ohhhh," Jeanette breathed. She was too amazed to even wonder what DNA was, much less ask.

"The little girl named her doll Gwendolyn, and they were the best of friends. They played together, ate together, and slept in each other's arms. They spent all of their time together. When the little girl was old enough to go to school, Gwendolyn went with her – everyone simply assumed they were twins. Being identical in every way, they pretty much were. When the little girl was five, her mother had another baby – another girl. When she was old enough, the Grandfather made her a doll as well, a living replica that would be her best friend, though her older sister and Gwendolyn both loved her and played with her whenever they could. Five years later yet another girl was born. On her third birthday she was given her dyer."

"Their pod must have been horribly crowded!" Sean exclaimed. "Were their parents mad that the Grandpa kept adding to their family? Dad gets pissed with just her and I running around," he said, jerking his head in Jeanette's direction.

Grandpa cawed and cackled. "Language!" he admonished when his laughter died away. "But you are right, in a way. I don't know how crowded they were, but they were very well off and most likely had plenty of room. Cronus himself kept quite a large estate, even in the early days. But the father, he was not pleased. He considered the children to be burden enough and their identical counterparts made it even worse."

"What did he do?" Jeanette asked.

"Complained, mostly," Grandpa told her. "But he wasn't home very much. He was a pilot, and fought in the war."

"Against the Chimera?"

Sean laughed. "No, stupid. The Chimera weren't around then. That's what this is all about."

"Don't call you sister stupid," Grandpa told him. He turned his gaze to Jeanette who was making faces at her brother. "It was the War of the Golgotha Tide," he told her. "It lasted for seventeen years, and the Daddy only came home when he was on leave."

"Every five years?" Sean asked, grinning.

Grandpa harrumphed but begrudged him a nod.

"So there were six of them," Sean said.

"Yes. Three granddaughters and three dyers, or dolls. And they were all very happy together, at least while they were young."

"Then where did the seven in G7 come from?"

"That," Grandpa said, "I'm not sure of."

"What happened to the girls, Grandpa?" Jeanette asked.

"They grew up," Grandpa said, his voice wistful. "Like all children do." He sighed and reached for the glass of water and ice that always sat on the table next to him. Sean suspected that it had more than just water in it, but he would never say so.

ONE THREE

Blue looked around at the others in the room, the shock plain upon her scarred face. "No disrespect intended," she said, "but I can't believe you are even debating the issue." She looked from Captain Brogan to Blaylock. "We have to go after her."

The Captain stood leaning against the wall of the den in his private cabin, one arm across his middle, his right hand supporting the elbow of the other arm. His left hand covered his mouth, his fingers a loose frame around his lips. His eyes were far away, lost in thought.

Commander Blaylock, sitting in a stuffed chair and staring into the blue holo flames of the mock fireplace set into the wall, ran a hand through his short, dark hair. He had been online with IGC officials for the past three hours and felt that he had accomplished nothing. His frustration was no less than the others, but he knew his main responsibility was to keep them in check.

Jade had made it back to the Dragon in time to catch the last of the battle, just as the Chimeran Battle Cruiser had snatched up Jordan Scarlett and taken off – firing every engine it had before those fighting around the Dragon knew what had happened. It was gone before they could recover and give chase.

Now he stood leaning on the wall opposite the Captain, his dark hair hanging over his green eyes. The lights in the cabin were dim, and the blue holo flames reflected off the Mylar of his emerald green flight suit.

Calyph stood close by – as always, a quiet witness. The Captain and his Executive Officer glanced at each other before meeting the cold stare from Jordan Blue.

"It's not that easy," Brogan told her. "We don't know where they have taken her, or what they want." Blue looked from him to Blaylock, then back again.

"I think it's pretty obvious!"

Jade shifted and crossed his arms. "They might just want to ransom her for funds, or they just might be doing their usual attempt to create anarchy within the IGC," he told her, flicking his hair away from his face. The habit sometimes reminded Blue of Galen, but now she hardly noticed.

"I'm not willing to risk her life with *might be*. She's a *Jordan* for Christ's sake!"

"I know," Brogan said softly.

"We just can't hop in a ship and dart off on some wild rescue mission," Blaylock told her, his voice stern. Blue bit her lip. That was exactly what she had intended. He sighed. "We need authorization from the IGC for an armed extraction."

Blue looked away from them, trying not to roll her eyes or stomp her foot like an aggravated child. She looked back at the Executive Officer, doing her best to control her anger. "That could take weeks. It would be *days* at the very least. She might not have that kind of time."

"That's why we are here," Blaylock said. "To figure out a way to expedite things with the IGC."

"Fuck the IGC!" Blue said loudly, unable to help herself. The coils of her white gold hair shook. Commander Blaylock's face went red but Calyph could see the Captain concealing a smile behind his hand. Jade grinned and looked away. Blue took a deep breath. "I'll go myself."

"So will I," Jade said, stepping away from the wall. Blue looked at him and smiled.

Brogan's hand came away from his face and he shook his head. "Absolutely not."

"An armed extraction is what they will be expecting," Jade said. "If it is just Blue and myself we might be able to..."

"We cannot authorize such a mission," Blaylock interrupted. "And we certainly can't risk losing *all three* of our Jordans."

"We don't have to take the Fledglings," Jade said.

"We would still risk losing our Jordans," Brogan told him. "And I am not about to start violating IGC procedure." The aggravation from the two Jordans was palpable, Blue especially. The three Jordans, despite any personal feelings, had become closer than even ordinary siblings, something very akin to fraternal triplets. Brogan, so intertwined with the feelings of the Dragon and thus its children as well, could feel their frustration as if it were his own. He ignored it. "Commander Blaylock, inform the IGC of our situation and request immediate action. Jade, assemble every pilot on the ship. Have every craft armed and standing ready. Dismissed."

Having been discharged by their Captain left no room for another word, much less an argument. Each officer gave Brogan a respectful nod and left quickly. Blaylock strode from the room with Jade on his heels, intent upon assembling the Dragon's fighter pilots. Blue and Calyph moved to follow them.

"Stand fast, you two," Brogan commanded. Jade threw a curious smile at Blue as he left. The Captain waited for the door to close behind the Emerald Jordan and his Executive Officer. Blue was visibly angry and Calyph was obviously perplexed by everything going on around him.

"Sir?" Blue asked, her voice tight.

"Jordan Blue, I believe you have some leave accrued. This might be a good time to take it." Brogan watched her eyes widen in shock and could actually see her blood pressure rise along with the color in her cheeks. At any other time it might have been comical. She was practically shaking in an effort to manage her emotions. But he had to give her credit; when she spoke her words came out slowly and carefully, her tone controlled.

"Sir, I really don't think this is the best time to go on holiday."

"I don't care *what* you do or *where* you go," Brogan said evenly. Jordan Blue stepped back, surprised, letting his words sink in. Then she frowned at him, not daring to believe what he might be implying. He nodded at her. "I think you need some time off. Take the Bloodjet."

Blue almost let her mouth drop open. Instead, she lifted her chin and bowed slightly from her waist. "Yes sir."

"Calyph," Brogan commanded, "make sure she has everything she needs for her trip. She will need a good plan for a good...vacation."

"Yes sir."

"Dismissed."

Bruny and Sandy pushed Scarlett along through numerous hallways and down so many metal staircases that Scarlett thought that if they weren't at the bottom of the ship yet, then they must be getting close. They finally dragged her into a sterile looking corridor lined with rows of closed doors. Finding the one they wanted, Sandy pressed on the door and it slid open without a sound.

The room was white and bare except for a pale bench and steel toilet. Sandy released the restraints on her hands and Scarlett wrenched away from them, stumbling, as they shoved her inside.

"Lovely," she said, looking around and massaging her wrists. "When's lunch?" Bruny only sneered at her as Sandy closed the door. Scarlett heard it lock with a snick. She could hear them talking with others outside her cell. Scarlett looked around and, heaving a sigh, stretched out on the bench. It was as uncomfortable as it looked.

To her surprise, lunch came within the hour. The door slid open and a tall, ultra-thin female construct stepped through. Like Sandy and Bruny, she wore a dark blue Chimeran coverall uniform with the infinity symbol stitched over the heart, though hers was in silver thread. She had pin-straight, dark blonde hair and looked decidedly pissed. She held a small plasma pistol and kept it carefully trained on Scarlett. She was followed by another female construct that was much more petite with lighter blonde hair that was short and spiky. Scarlett sat up.

Blondie Number Two carried in a tray of food and placed it on the bench next to Scarlett. Scarlett looked at it curiously, her empty stomach wondering what construct food would be like. It looked like human food as far as she could tell. Some sort of rice covered with synthetic ground meat and gravy. There was also a cup of water and a rounded utensil.

She looked at Blondie Number Two, who was looking at her with avid interest and open curiosity, watching to see what she would do. Blondie Number One eyed her with obvious aggravation.

"Is it poisoned?" Scarlett asked, before laughing. *As if they would tell me.*

Blondie Number Two leaned down, picked up the utensil, and spooned some food into her mouth. She chewed and swallowed without saying anything, just watching.

"Just because you can eat it," Scarlett told her, "doesn't mean that I can."

"Don't be ridiculous," Number Two replied. "You're not any different than us." Scarlett snorted.

"If that were true, we wouldn't be here like this."

Number Two smiled. "I see your point, but we certainly have the same digestive system."

"Bjorn wants you alive!" Blondie Number One said angrily. Scarlett looked at Number Two.

"What's her problem?"

Number Two shrugged. "Eva has a thing for him."

"Shut up Ana!"

Scarlett snorted again and put the tray on her lap, keeping an arrogant eye on Eva. The tall female tossed her needle-like hair and scowled at the Jordan. Scarlett helped herself to a bite of the food. It wasn't bad. "Was it the way he looked at me, or is it what he has planned for me?" she asked between mouthfuls.

"You wish!" Eva hissed.

"Not really, though I could see why."

"I don't."

"Well," Scarlett said, looking Eva up and down. "For us supposedly having the same body types, you look a lot more elfin than human, if you know what I mean."

Eva glanced at Scarlett's breasts and smirked. "The Chimera were made perfect - we have no need to *enhance* ourselves."

Scarlett frowned as she chewed, looking down at her chest and then back up at Eva. She swallowed. "I haven't been enhanced anywhere," she told her. "Well," she said, taking a drink of water, "I have had a few... *repairs* perhaps. The law of gravity always applies, even in space."

Ana laughed. "You are the first human I've met," she said. "You don't seem so bad." This time it was Eva who snorted.

"Don't let her fool you."

Scarlett put down the utensil and placed the tray back on the bench. "She's right," she told Ana. "Don't let me fool you. If I had that gun, I'd kill you both. And anyone else on this ship that I could."

Ana's expression fell as she absorbed Scarlett's words and knew that she meant them. She carefully picked up the tray and turned and left the cell, glancing back at Scarlett, her expression forlorn. Eva followed her without a word. The door closed silently but Scarlett was sure that if Eva could have slammed it shut, she would have.

As soon as the door to the Captain's cabin closed behind them, Calyph caught Jordan Blue by the elbow.

"Was he saying what I think he was saying?"

"You bet your ass he was. And we have to hurry, and not just for Scarlett. I think if anyone else gets wind of what we are up to we could get the Captain into a mess of trouble. Where is your troll?"

"In my quarters. Are you *sure* that's..."

"No time!" Blue said as she hurried past him towards the closest pneumatic lift. She took the down shaft, her body sinking in the gentle current, and stepped out at the next level to wait for Calyph.

"Hey." Galen's voice in her ear was a gentle reminder of his presence.

"Don't try to talk me out of this," Blue told him.

"I'm not going to. I just want to tell you to be careful. Brogan is giving you a pass on this one - use it wisely. Don't rush in. Plan it out carefully with Calyph. I'll give you whatever help I can."

She sighed, grateful for his support. "Thanks."

She watched Calyph drop down and exit the lift. She took a deep breath. "Ready?" she asked. He gave her a quick nod as he led the way.

He headed right and then hooked another right into the first vein corridor. Blue followed quickly through a few more twists and turns. She was standing in front of the Engineer quarters in only a few seconds.

Jordan Blue looked up at the doors. It was the only place in the Dragon with a double entrance and it was covered with an ancient coat of arms. The crest was black and gold, split down the middle by the seam between the doors. The left half showed an anvil topped with the letter S in ancient graphic text. The right side bore a snarling dragon over a writhing, flowery S.

To the right of the doors was a much smaller replica of the crest. Calyph brought his hand down in front of the crest and the doors swung inward on silent, hidden hinges. Blue followed him inside and stopped short as her eyes swept the room.

"Wow."

His quarters aboard the Dragon were the largest - spanning the whole area of the Captain's and the Jordan's cabins as well as the bridge, all on the level above – but they were by no means luxurious.

The Jordan and the Engineer had stepped into an entryway that had a half-wall built of glass blocks. Blue peered curiously over the short wall at a large, open area. It looked as if an elemental bomb had recently gone off in there. Desks and worktables were pushed against the walls and there were chunks and pieces of all kinds of metals in all sizes piled on the tables and scattered on the floor. Some looked fresh cut, others were blackened, some were nothing more than melted lumps. There were nuts and bolts, gears and cogs – but, of course, no tools. Some had been quasi-organized but others looked as if they had been tossed aside and forgotten.

The troll hovered in the midst of the metallic mess, a blue field fanning out from a slim arm as it ran the light over a group of steel chunks. It paused when they entered, its great head swiveling around to see them.

"The lack of iridium is causing the bind lack," it said.

"No shit," Calyph told it as he strode past. "It doesn't matter right now. Come with us." He walked around the mess and through a doorway with no door to another room on the right. The troll stopped what it was doing and followed Calyph and Blue into the next room.

The room was dominated on the far right by a wall monitor and console dash. There were shelves of acrylics and a desk stacked with more acrylics and a few take-away boxes. There was a wastebasket full of empty ale bottles. One wall boasted a few scrolls in ancient text.

Calyph found himself a bit self-conscious about the clutter but did his best to ignore it. He hadn't been expecting company and there was nothing to be done about it at the present moment. Besides, Blue didn't seem to mind. She had gotten very quiet, just looking about.

"Is this what Cyan is going to look like someday?" she asked softly.

"Hard to believe, isn't it?" Galen replied.

"What was that?" Calyph asked.

"Nothing," Blue said. She shook her head as if to clear her head. "The first thing we need to do is find Scarlett."

Calyph grabbed the rolling chair from the desk and pulled it over for the Jordan, then took the seat that was already in front of the monitor. "Let's see where that big bastard went."

He pulled his credentials card from a pocket and placed it on the console, laying a hand over it. "This is Calyph Bette, S and S for Opal Dragon, security clearance 787." A red beam shot out of the console, engulfing Calyph's hand and card to read credentials, prints, imprints, implants, and DNA all at once.

"Welcome, Calyph," the monitor greeted warmly – as warm as possible for a digitized voice.

"I need a trace on the Chimeran Battle Cruiser *Macedonian*, most recently seen in the Opal Dragon's share coordinates."

There was a pause that lasted less than a second, and then an image of the *Macedonian* came onto the monitor. There was a spattering of constellations to the port side of the ship and a small moon in the distance on the starboard side. The picture emerged from the screen and took shape in a holographic image. Then the holo expanded and began to wrap itself around Calyph in a circle. The *Macedonian* grew until it hung directly in front of him with the constellation mass to his left and the small moon on his right, drifting in the black.

"Chimeran Battle Cruiser, *Macedonian*," the monitor announced. "Coordinates xz 559 and yj 223."

"Direction and distance?" Calyph asked.

"Holding stasis. Distance from Dragon, point ten AU, IG standard."

Calyph grinned. "Does that mean something?" Blue asked.

"It means that we are just out of radar range."

"Then how can we see them?"

"Because," Calyph explained, making adjustments to the image, "we are just out of *their* range, not ours. They must assume out radar has the same limits that theirs has. The Dragon can see across the whole galaxy and into the next."

Blue nodded, understanding. "That means they don't have a total bead on us. And they don't know everything the Dragon is capable of."

Calyph nodded. "At least some of our secrets are still safe."

"That might be why they took a prisoner instead of attacking first. They're still gathering intel. So Scarlett is most likely still alive - but for how long will be hard to tell." Blue saw one of Calyph's hands clench at her last remark. She cocked her head, looking at him. "Does that bother you, Calyph?" she asked with an arched brow.

"Of course it does. Doesn't it bother you?"

Blue grinned and nodded. "Of course it does."

Calyph looked away, his eyes finding the holo of the *Macedonian*. He reached out and pushed the cruiser aside with a flick of his hand. "Do you have a plan?" he asked.

"Just for getting there. I'm open to suggestions, if you have any. Plus, I want to know what the inside of the *Mace* looks like. I figured your troll would have that information."

"Why does everyone refer to me as *his*?" The troll asked. Blue looked at it and smiled crookedly, making her scar sink into her cheek.

"We could refer to Calyph as *yours*, if you prefer."

The troll made a fabricated grunting sound. "There is no reason to denote possession in any case." Calyph shook his head at them and turned back to the monitor, the holo around him casting shadows on his face.

"Show all other craft within half an AU to the *Macedonian*," he told the console. The image of the battle cruiser zoomed past and five blips appeared around him – two on the left, one on the right, and one right in front of him at the bottom edge of the holo.

Calyph zoomed in on them one at a time. "Here," he said, choosing one of the ships on the left. He pulled at the image with his fingers and it came in closer. Now a one-meter holo of the craft hovered in the air between Calyph and Jordan Blue. It was a great, ugly, lumbering ship that showed signs of fire and even explosive damage that had never been repaired. Fuel spines and retract arms jutted out from all angles and smaller ships clung all over the outside of it like barnacles.

"Mech City Z - Fuel and Repair Ship."

"That's it!" Blue exclaimed. "That's my way in."

"As long as you can get there before it reaches the *Mace*."

"Too easy," Blue told him. "How long will it take for that thing to get to the cruiser?"

"Not long. I'll send it a request right now, and make it look like it's coming from the *Macedonian*." His fingers played over the flat surface of the console. There was no keyboard that Blue could see. "The *Macedonian* will think it was trolling in the vicinity. Being so far from any other Chimeran ship or base, they must be in need of something."

"Alpha 6 Battle Cruisers need a flux redilation every 10,000 hours," the troll stated calmly. Blue turned and regarded the bulky metal drone with raised brows. "It will need fuel. It should have a surface systems check. It needs a recharge to the Elucx Syst every..." Calyph cut the troll off with a wave of his hand.

"It needs shit, we get it. And the Mech City-Ship is non-denom, not IGC. They Chimera will take whatever they can get from them." He turned to Blue. "If you can immerse with the crew of the Mech ship, you can get on the *Mace*. You might not get in, but you should be able to get on the outside easily enough."

Jordan Blue smiled. "That's all I need. I can get in on my own. Once I do, I need to find Scarlett."

Calyph turned to the troll. "I need a blueprint of the Battle Cruiser *Macedonian*."

"Screen shot or print?" The troll asked. Calyph looked at Blue.

"Screen shot," she said.

The troll drifted to the console and extruded a needle-like appendage and inserted it into the console dash of Calyph's monitor. The monitor lit up immediately with a blueprint of the battle cruiser.

"Nifty," Blue said, looking at the troll.

Calyph pulled the image out of the monitor and into a holo and rotated it, his eyes flicking about. "These are your best possible spots for entry," he told her, pointing. "But if you have to, there are airlocks under the bridge cup, though I wouldn't advise it – it will be the most heavily trafficked area on the ship."

Calyph brought his hand down like a knife through the holo of the ship, cutting off the back third. He pushed it away and pointed to an area in the remaining bottom two thirds of the holo. "This area here is the brig - this is where she should be - on one of these three levels."

Blue's eyes scanned the image the ship, inside and out, one more time. She nodded. "Alright," she said, straightening. "Call the jet bay and have them ready the Bloodjet. Have them put a munitions belt in there too, with at least two plasma guns, a trazon, a spider gun, and a laser rifle." She turned to leave and Calyph swiveled his chair around, watching her go.

"Is that all?" he asked. She stopped and turned her head a bit, as if she were thinking, or listening. She laughed.

"Tell them to put some peanut butter in there too."

She strode quickly from the Engineer's quarters, leaving him with a puzzled expression.

The top half of the troll rotated to face Calyph. "Was she serious, or was that humor?"

Calyph shrugged. "I suspect it was humor, but it's better not to take the chance." He turned back to the monitor to establish coms with the jet bay.

ONE FOUR

Galen took a sip from his steaming mug and gazed out of the coffee shop window. The sun was setting in a blaze of violet and azure. He thrummed his fingers absently on the table next to the crumbs of a small and bland meat pastry that were the remains of his dinner. He never ate well when Noel was away.

Galen was usually despondent on the day Noel would leave him to return to the Dragon. He could never find anything to do and there was never anything to watch on the holo. He wouldn't feel like going out and he wouldn't want to stay in. It was often this way when she would leave for an extended amount of time. After a while, though, he would throw himself into his work and find his balance once again.

This time it was different. Having the com-link, the constant closeness, made him feel as if they were almost together. He could almost pretend that she was in the next room. Even when she wasn't talking to him, he could hear her talking to someone else, or sometimes herself. She would hum and whistle. At the very least he could hear her breath and know that she was safe and vicariously monitor what was happening around her.

But last night was the first night she had been gone and, just as he was drifting off to sleep, the link was cut. It didn't make a sound, no click or beep. Suddenly there was – nothing. His eyes popped open at the abrupt silence and he waited, looking into the dark of the podment, telling himself he was being ridiculous and that he couldn't expect her to keep it on all the time. Still, secretly, he wanted her to do just that.

He had glanced at his watch, watching the seconds as they ticked away. The smooth square on the composite band around his wrist, among other things, gave him Noel's galactic coordinates. He looked at the string of letters and numbers blinking on the very bottom. They meant nothing unless he got up and put them in his acrylic to find out where she really was.

I'm not going to do that, he thought. *Not yet.* Instead, he watched the blinking numbers that gave him the local time.

Two minutes ticked by and then the sound on the com returned with a literal whoosh and he could hear the swirl of rushing water. He grinned and closed his eyes. Even after all the years they had been together, she would not use the bathroom with the door open and it seemed she did not want him *hearing* her use the commode any more than *seeing* her use it.

"Did you wash your hands?" he asked.

"Of course."

Galen laughed. "You liar!" He heard her blow out an exasperated breath that might have been part chuckle.

"Then why did you ask me? You know I didn't, and you knew I would lie!" The pitch in her voice rose as she defended herself in mock argument, knowing that he was only teasing her. "Besides, it's not like I'm going in to surgery or anything."

"It's not sanitary."

"I'm on an ionized ship. I'm being disinfected just as I walk around. I could probably not wipe my ass and it would be germ-free inside of ten minutes."

"Eww!" Galen managed, laughing harder. "Let's not try that."

"Don't worry, I won't."

"Where are you, anyway?"

"I rendezvoused with the IGC CraterShip *Heaven's Door.* They have the best galley I've ever been to, outside of a cruise liner."

"Which galley? They must have at least thirty on that ship."

"The one called Hell's Kitchen."

"I've eaten there," Galen said. "The food is terrible."

"Not to me. After I stuff myself I'm going to take as much with me as I can. See if I can't get someone on the Dragon to make the same thing."

"Have the cook put the recipe on your chip."

"It's not the same. Just like when I gave the recipe for champagne to Ero. It was good, but it didn't taste a thing like what we had on Earth. I think I'll have a better chance if he can taste it."

"Maybe."

"How are you doing?" she asked, changing the subject.

"Fine."

"Hmm. And your work?"

"Fine."

"Liar."

Galen laughed. "You know me too well."

"You'll be back in a groove in no time."

"I know." But in his heart, he didn't think so.

"I miss you."

"I miss you too, but this is better than it usually is."

"I know. I love talking to you all the time. I really do feel like I'm with you," she said, but her tone was tinged with melancholy.

"Do I still make your heart beat?" Galen asked.

"Like an eight-oh-eight," she said, the smile back in her voice. Galen laughed.

"You don't even know what that is!"

"I do so! It's a human percussion simulator."

"I'm impressed."

"Well, I'm at the Kitchen. Do you want me to turn you off, or do you want to hear me eat?"

"And miss hearing you smack your lips on a saucy sim-meat kabob? No way. Leave me on."

"Suit yourself."

Galen drummed his fingers on the table next to his crumbs and smiled, though there was an ache in his heart. He tried to ignore the sounds of the coffee shop and concentrate on the sound coming from his com-link with Noel. Her breathing was soft and even as she slept in the Fledgling, headed out for another tour on the Opal Dragon.

Noel, he thought.

She had only been gone only twenty-four hours and his work had already come to a screeching halt. Though he missed her terribly, she wasn't the reason for the block he had run into with the Thermopylae. But there was something there, something that niggled at the corner of his mind and he knew she held the answer to the problem he was facing. He was sure of it.

Noel. What did you do? What did you say? I have the feeling that you hold the key to this.

For some reason his thoughts led him back to Earth, to their trip to the desert. Galen checked his watch, watching the coordinates at the bottom. He thrummed his fingers on the table and watched the sky turn sapphire, idly wishing that he had some bourbon for his coffee.

ONE FIVE

Scarlett didn't know how much time had passed; she just knew that she was starting to doze off when the door to her cell opened. She became alert immediately, her eyes searching the darkness that filled her cell. Sandy and his cohort Bruny were back - Scarlett could just make out their faces as they reached down to pull her off her bench.

They marched her out of her cell and into the hallway, which was well into dimlight. A few others joined them but Scarlett could not make out any faces.

"If this is what passes as psychological warfare for you guys, it sucks."

"Shut up," one of them told her, giving her a hard shake.

"Jesus!" Scarlett called out. "Don't mishandle the human, I'm not the doll you know." This time he, she had a feeling it was Bruny, shook her hard enough to rattle her teeth.

"We're not dolls!" he hissed. "We're people."

Scarlett laughed. "I'm starting to like hanging out with you guys. You have no idea how much fun you are. It's so easy to get under that synthetic skin of yours."

They gave her another angry rattle but said nothing.

After a number of corridors and lifts, Scarlett could see a light ahead. It grew steadily until they went through a door and emerged at the source. Scarlett looked around. They were in the mech hangar where she had her encounter with Bjorn. No one was working, on jets or otherwise, and there was only a single light - coming from a caged bulb that hung on a chain from the darkened ceiling – throwing a broken rectangle of light, illuminating nothing beyond the area in which they stood.

Bjorn was there; leaning on an enormous metal rack, his arms crossed, talking with two other constructs. One of them Scarlett recognized as Eva. The female construct caught sight of the Jordan at the same time and favored her with an evil smile. Bjorn saw Eva's look and followed her gaze, turning to see Scarlett and her escort. He straightened and beamed at her as she was propelled over to him, courtesy of Bruny and Sandy.

Scarlett was again taken by his perfection - face and smile and height and build - as she was forced over to him. She noticed something else this time, his smell. It was inviting and lascivious. She didn't know if it had anything to do with his chemical make-up, but she dismissed it as quickly as she could, turning her face away and trying to slow the rapid beat of her heart.

She looked instead at the Chimeran construct standing with Bjorn and Eva. He was dark-haired and dark-eyed, and looked at Scarlett with malicious hate. He, too, was strikingly handsome. Much more so than Sandy and Bruny. His hand-made, flawless features made him unquestionably gorgeous – though he lacked the breathtaking quality of Bjorn.

Second Run, Scarlett thought.

"Stojacovik," Bjorn said, motioning to his arresting companion. "My Executive Officer." The XO's lip curled in anger.

"She doesn't need to know who we are!" His voice, like Bjorn's, was mellifluous and arousing. Scarlett hated it. Bjorn waved a dismissive hand at the other Chimeran.

"Do you know where we are?" Bjorn asked her. Scarlett glanced about. Steel racks were piled high with torque wrenches and power tools. The place smelled of oiled metal and jet fuel. Scarlett breathed deeply and, as unappealing as it was, preferred it to the smell of the manufactured man in front of her.

"Some sort of mechanic bay," she said.

"That's right. It's a workplace. And we have lots of work to do." Bjorn sighed through his smile of even teeth. "I really do wish we had an elf as well," he said. "I would like to compare the differences between you and them. And us, of course."

"I could tell you what those are," Scarlett scoffed.

"Is that so?"

"We are the better species, by far. Humans, I mean."

"How is that?"

"We are faster and stronger. Higher amount of fast twitch muscles, and better reflexes."

"But don't elves have better senses? Hearing and eyesight, as well as extrasensory perception in some cases?"

Scarlett shrugged, as best she could with Sandy and Bruny gripping her arms tight enough to cut off her circulation. "Elves need to enhance themselves artificially to be able to move with our speed and strength."

Bjorn crossed his arms in front of himself and leaned back, a small smile playing at the corner of his sensual mouth. "Isn't there something about the star that burns twice as bright?" Scarlett attempted another shrug.

"It burns twice as fast."

"Yes," Bjorn said. "So *you* have to enhance yourself artificially to achieve longevity."

"On occasion."

"But the Chimera have all of the best qualities of the humans, and the best qualities of the elves, coupled with an artificial intelligence. I believe that makes *us* the greater species."

Scarlett laughed. "And you have the worst qualities to an extreme. You are more sensitive than a menopausal Gobli, and have the murderous temper of a Golgoth." She smirked. "And your intelligence does not make up for what you lack – imagination." Bjorn scowled.

"But of humans and elves, you believe humans to be the stronger species?"

"Of course," she spat angrily, though his tone made her stomach flutter.

Bjorn's frown melted away and he favored her with a wicked smile. Scarlett licked her lips. He turned to a metal rack and selected a few tools carefully, like a child picking out chocolates. He chose a magnetic torque wrench, a fleck hammer, and a welding torch. He laid them on a steel table.

Jesus, Scarlett thought, looking at the choices before her. *I never thought I would hope a guy would use a hammer on me.* She sputtered out a choked laugh, unable to help herself.

Bjorn looked at her, piqued. "Is something funny?"

"Only you."

He grinned. "Even in the face of certain pain, you show contempt." Scarlett saw something in his gimlet eyes that she could hardly believe – it looked like a trace of admiration.

Bjorn must not have been able to believe it either. He gave his head a shake and Scarlett a sigh.

"Well, pain is certain, but certainly not now. I've done all this with a human before and I don't expect the results to be much different, though I have the feeling you might hold out better."

"And of course," Scarlett offered, "if you don't have an elf on hand to compare me to, this is all pretty pointless."

Bjorn smiled. "We'll have one soon enough." Scarlett frowned, not liking how sure he sounded. "Oh yes," he added, seeing her confusion. "Your pilot sister should be here at any time."

"Sister? I don't have any sisters. What are you talking about?"

"The elf, of course." He looked at her like she should know. Scarlett shook her head and then understanding broke like a cold dawn.

"Blue? You think Blue will come for me?" Scarlett laughed. "Blue doesn't give a shit about me."

"Maybe not, but she will be drawn to you, as will your Fledgling."

"You don't know that," Scarlett said, but the expression drained from her face.

"I think I do."

"How could you know that? I don't even know if that could be the case, it's never happened before." Bjorn gave her a sly smile and understanding crept up on her again, chilling her. "The Engineer," she said softly. "Is that what you tortured out of him?"

Bjorn shrugged. "I wouldn't call it torture."

"I doubt it was breakfast in bed. Either way, even if it is possible, it seems like a shot in the dark to me. A risky one."

"Not so risky. We got you without too much of a fight, or too much of a loss for that matter."

Scarlett gave him a look of disgust, knowing now that he had sent those Hellcats and their pilots to their deaths. To him, they were an acceptable casualty.

"Even if they do come after me, what good will they do you? The Fledglings won't comply with any of your kind and you wouldn't be able to fly them. Even if you kill them, it won't win you anything. Certainly not the war."

"You are right on that account, I believe. Fledglings aren't enough to win the war." Bjorn watched her, waiting patiently.

This time, the dawn of understanding was like a malevolent sunrise. It rose with a sickening wave that made her knees buckle and she was grateful for the bastards holding her up, though it took only a moment to regain her composure.

"The Dragon," she said, aghast. "You're trying to Draw the Dragon, aren't you?" Bjorn's smile widened into a grin as he watched Scarlett take it all in. Her breath caught in her throat. "I'm just the small bait, for the bigger bait."

"You are very clever," Bjorn said. Scarlett shook her head.

"Drawing the Dragon is a myth," she told him. "Nothing even remotely like it has ever happened."

"Hasn't it?"

Scarlett thought about her fight in the Scorpion and Fledge coming after her when she was in trouble. Calyph had been powerless to stop him and though she had ordered him to stay away, he hadn't.

"No," she said, her voice sounding more sure than she felt. Bjorn shrugged and motioned to Bruny and Sandy.

They pulled Scarlett in front of the table and she forced her eyes to stay open. To her surprise, they yanked her backwards over to a number of heavy chains that hung down from a series of pulleys. They fastened each of her wrists to a chain and hauled them up – not too high, just so they were level with her shoulders. She looked like a human scarecrow.

Scarlett looked around in disbelief, her eyes finding the devilishly handsome Bjorn. "What are you doing?" she asked.

The Commander stepped close and laid his hand gently on her ribcage.

"I'm going to dinner," he said, his voice sensual. "Why don't you just, hang out and wait for me?" He moved his fingers slightly, feeling the body beneath cloth.

"You're just going to leave me like this?"

He smiled wolfishly and Eva came up and wrapped an arm about his waist, leering at Scarlett.

"They say the Zealot Messiah died this way," Eva said. "It can be incredibly painful, even after a short period. An hour, certainly more, can build into an excruciating experience. At least, so I am told."

Scarlett burst out laughing, unable to help it, as always. "Are you kidding me?" she asked. Her head rocked back as she let out another gale of laughter. Eva's smile disappeared.

"We'll see if she's laughing in a few hours," she told Bjorn, her voice low and her hand tight around his waist. She had seen the flicker of admiration in his eye, and she didn't like it.

"Yes," he agreed, letting her lead him away. "We'll see."

JM's booted feet pounded the pavement. She ran steadily, her legs aching but her joints taking the most punishment. Running on the hard surface was brutal on her knees and ankles and every time her heel hit the ground it jarred her bones all the way up to her teeth. She disliked it immensely, but it was better than running on the gravel.

JM had soon found that the horrible grinding sound of the gravel wasn't its worst characteristic. Besides the cloud of choking dust that always rose, the hellacious little rocks liked to shift and sink underfoot as if intent on bringing down anyone who dared run upon them. A week prior, JM saw one of the best pilots in her platoon go down on the morning run with a twisted ankle. Malherbe was on him in an instant - like a tree shark sensing prey. By the time JM got to class the pilot was gone.

There were also times, especially on the morning run, when Malherbe was gracious and kind. Those were the times that JM found both amusing and dangerous.

"You don't need to be doing this," Malherbe would call out to them as he ran alongside their formation. It was the only time his voice was not at a hysterical pitch. It was coaxing, gentle. "You are the best pilots in galaxy – in *all* the galaxies. You don't need to be doing this to yourself. You could get any job you wanted, making *disgusting* amounts of money."

His squat body plodded along next to the moving rectangle of cadets in the pre-dawn light. Like always, he never slowed, never tired, never broke a sweat. JM had yet to see him take a deep breath, unless he was getting ready to yell. When he was taken by this mood, his breath and voice were both soft and smooth.

"We're almost to the HQ building," he would offer the formation as they jogged along. "They have hot coffee and pastries. They could have you a job within the hour, transport you off of this moon and out of this hellhole."

The first time he had done this JM couldn't help but smile, giving her head a small shake in disbelief. *He's crazy*, she thought. *Does that even work? Ever? Who the hell would fall for that shit?*

She found out the second time he did his little nicey-nice thing that it did *indeed* work. One of the pilots (a female, much to JM's chagrin) simply stopped running and walked away.

Not weeping or limping or hanging her head in shame. She simply walked away as if what Malherbe was saying made perfect sense. JM stared at the pilot as she jogged past, her own face slack with incredulity, before snapping her eyes back to the front of the formation, her legs keeping their steady rhythm. Malherbe had thrown back his head and laughed and laughed. Then he ran them harder. The same ploy had worked again two more times since then.

This time was different. JM was having a hard time for the first time. She didn't know if the oncoming summer was bringing humidity to the already thin, barely breathable air of Lido, or if her body had picked up an unwanted virus. All she knew was that, for the first time in her life, her lungs were burning more than her legs.

She pounded the pavement, trying to lose herself in the run the way she often did. But every step jarred her bones and burned her lungs. She felt a seed of doubt bloom within her and then crushed it immediately, deciding to lose herself in the pain if nothing else.

Pound, slam, gulp, burn.

Pound, slam, gulp, burn.

The sun was still just breaking rays on the horizon and air was frigid. The atmosphere was thin on oxygen but thick with moisture and every cold breath she drew burned a line of fire into her chest. She pumped her legs in a mindless rhythm, trying to ignore her lungs. She tried to tell herself that it was nothing and that it didn't matter because the run was almost over. Nonetheless, she couldn't help but wonder if it was her body or if it was the weather.

Pound, slam, gulp, burn.

Pound, slam, gulp, burn.

She hoped it was a virus. Sacrificing lunch for a quick stop at sick-call would get her a shot in the arm and that would be the end of it. Missing a meal would be nothing. The environment changing enough to weaken her – that could mean everything.

Like hell it does, she thought. *Nothing is going to stop me. If the weather is changing, so am I. I'll learn to breathe water if I have to.*

Her lungs felt like a fire that was slowly and maliciously being stoked. Her boots pounded the paved road behind the HQ building that marked the five-kilometer point and sweat streamed down her face and into her already soaked collar. The impact of each step slammed upwards till it rattled her jaw. Each breath was more painful than the last.

Pound, slam, gulp, burn.

Pound, slam, gulp, burn.

It's almost over, she told herself. *We'll come around the front and he'll yell for a minute and then I can go collapse in the shower. It's almost over. I'll be fine. I can do this.*

The formation of pilots ran down the line of pavement that curved around the HQ building - each left boot hitting the asphalt in unison, the right boot nailing the next beat.

Pound, slam, gulp, burn.

Pound, slam, gulp, burn.

They rounded the curve in the road, hammering steadily towards the HQ building. JM lost herself in the pain and the rhythm now that the end was in sight. The low building was silhouetted by the rising sun and JM thought she had never seen such a beautiful sight.

Pound, slam, gulp, burn.

Pound, slam, gulp, burn.

Fifty pairs of booted feet hit the pavement with hopeless rhythm. It seemed that every pilot was physically and mentally finished, everyone more than ready for the run to be over. Their bodies done before the day was begun.

Pound, slam, gulp, burn.

Pound, slam, gulp, burn.

The formation approached the HQ building at a steady run with a palpable feeling of relief hanging over them like sunshine through a cloud. They ran to the near edge of the building, then along the front, and then they passed it. The entire group had slowed incrementally, expecting to stop, then had to speed up again as Malherbe never stopped or slowed. JM felt something inside her stretch to the point where it was ready to snap.

That bastard! Her body seemed to scream as much as her brain. She doubted Malherbe could hear the havoc he was wreaking on her lungs, he probably just knew that the air today was hell for running in (and like a tree shark was smelling blood in the forest), but JM took it as a personal affront.

"What the *fuck!*" JM shouted as they passed HQ, turning her head to look at the Master Sergeant with an equal mixture of amazement and disgust. His head snapped around and his eyes sought her out.

"JM!" he shouted, not skipping a step, with as much disbelief as she had mustered. "As I live and breathe! Did you just shout at me during my breakfast?!" JM didn't even stop to think.

"What the *fuck* are you *doing*?" she shouted back at him, her anger as hot as her lungs.

His eyes bulged from their sockets and his squat form that already bounced with his short gait started to shake from side to side. His hands, which had been balled into easy fists as he ran, clenched as if they were around her throat. To JM he looked like he was trying to kill her just by using his mind. If so, it wasn't working.

"Go hang yourself!" he finally sputtered.

JM ran easily now, pushing slightly harder with her right leg and shifting her weight. She peeled away from the formation of running pilots at an easy lope, heading for the sand pit with the poles and ropes, making no effort to hide her smile. She knew it was more of a grimace anyway.

She trotted gratefully to the pit and was glad to pull herself up and wrap her arms around the bar. After the cardiovascular assault on her body, crucifixion was a welcome relief. So she thought.

JM settled down, letting the bar take her weight. She had done this many times before and knew it would be a lot easier than finishing the course to hell that Malherbe was obviously intent upon.

Her lungs still burned as she tried to regain her wind, but the scorching pain was downgraded to a smoldering ache.

At first, as she hung with her arms around the bar and its cool metal against her neck, she thought that she would simply wait out the newly added lap of another two and a half kilometers around the inner base. Her arms and shoulders had built up over the past year to an unladylike proportion, not that she cared. The punishment they would take could not compare to what her lungs were being forced to take on.

Better to give my lungs a break, she thought, shifting her weight to what was now a semi-comfortable position. *Jesus, what a run! I swear he was going faster than ever. How the hell he managed that in this air, I'll never know.*

Her eyes followed the bouncing rectangle of runners until it disappeared into the woods at the west side of the compound and then picked them up as they exited on the right side. Her dark eyes were quick to notice the formation was shy two pilots. One was herself, of course. Someone else must have fallen out during the trek through the trees.

The formation ran. They looped around, pounding the road, behind HQ and then around to the front of the building. Another two pilots had fallen out. She saw one, limping along with drooping head and shoulders, heading for the female barracks. She hoped it was NDR.

Malherbe brought the formation to a halt and ordered a right-face. He walked stiffly to the front of the formation of sagging cadets and shouted and spat at them before he dismissed them. Then he walked into the building without even a glance in her direction.

JM hung with her arms wrapped around the bar, uncertain. The cold metal was pressed hard against the back of her neck, digging into her vertebrae. *Does this mean I am dismissed, even though I was not part of the platoon he was addressing? Do I need to stay here? Did he forget about me?*

She shifted her weight again, knowing that she had not been dismissed. Minutes passed and still she hung, her legs dangling and growing heavier. The time for a 'normal' hanging came and went as the minutes turned into an hour. She shifted and waited. Her neck and arms began to stiffen and no amount of shifting was able to bring comfort as one hour turned into two.

Her arms burning, JM watched the day lighten around her, knowing that the other pilots had showered, dressed, and were heading for breakfast. The anthems of the day played and she knew that everyone was headed for class. Her legs grew numb as the muscles in her upper body began to spasm painfully. Her neck was a burning horror. She had been there for nearly three hours.

JM let out a deep breath and let her head drop. If she missed class she would be disobeying the company order for tardiness. If she got down she would be disobeying a direct order from a JTC officer.

That bastard. He knew exactly what he was doing. Knows. Knows what he is doing.

Part of her now doubted that she had made the right decision, choosing to save her lungs over all else, though she had no idea that mental punishment would be included with the physical.

He knew, though. That bastard. He knew.

The muscles in her neck cramped suddenly and she screamed out in surprise. She should have known it was coming, she had been hanging there for so long, but it still caught her off-guard. Two knots, one on each side of her neck, balled up in an excruciating spasm of muscle and tendon.

JM screamed uncontrollably, throwing her head back - but that made it worse. The pain contracted around her neck and shot down her spine. Her scream cut off to a whimper and she eased her weight forward, shifting more weight to arms and less to her shoulders. The cramp subsided but didn't let go.

Her arms became hot, aching bars of lead. Three hours bled into four.

Her breathing became labored again. The thick air seemed to be gathering in her lungs and didn't want to come out. She had to force out each breath. Sweat clung all over her body in the humid air.

Master Sergeant Malherbe, freshly washed and fed, walked out of the HQ building. He dug at his gums with a wooden toothpick as he drawled away to Ensign Corvette. His eyes wandered over JM with an obvious disinterest as they made their way towards the sand pit.

The two officers were almost there when JM was once again overcome with disgust. More disgust than respect. She was missing class and falling behind just to appease this wind-filled bag of shit. Fury overrode discipline and she dropped from the bar and landed in the sand on her hands and knees.

Malherbe closed on her with inhuman speed. She tried to push herself up but her arms had decided they had had enough for one day and she collapsed her with face in the sand. She levered herself up with an elbow, looking into Malherbe's red and bulging face.

"Did you just get down without my permission?" he shouted, spit flying from his lips and his voice thick with contempt. He leaned down as far as he could to get the full effect of his voice in her face. "Jesus, JM! You aren't *ever* going to make it!"

JM panted, doing everything she could not to let her whole body convulse. Her legs were dead and her lungs still stung like fire. Her shoulders were cramped, her arms cried in pain and her neck was singing a Golgothian anthem. Sand, gravel's evil little cousin, was sticking to her face and neck and arms as she crouched there on all fours with Malherbe breathing on her like a rabid dog.

Moisture from his mouth coated the sand on her face but she didn't cringe away. He drew in air like a bellows. "Who the hell did you fuck to get into this course?" he screamed. JM looked at him with murder in her eyes.

"Everyone," she hissed.

Malherbe, his face only inches from her own, froze. The corner of his mouth, the right corner, gave a single, solitary twitch. Another three seconds stretched out before he straightened abruptly and turned on his heel.

"Get your ass to class," he shouted over his shoulder as he strode back to the HQ building.

JM hung her head in dizzy relief and chuffed soft laughter before she hauled herself up and ran to class, sweaty and filthy.

The next time he hung her, he wasn't as kind.

He left NDR with her to keep her company.

ONE SIX

Scarlett stood on her toes in the darkened mech bay, her arms strung out beside her like a marionette in chains. The constructs had doused the lights until she was engulfed by utter darkness. The air was cold but not freezing, and certainly not deprived of oxygen. Her arms were drawn back, but they weren't too high, only about ten centimeters above her shoulder level. Best of all, she wasn't even hanging by her arms - she was still able to keep the majority of her weight on the balls of her feet. Scarlett found herself bored and uncomfortable, but that was it. Even though she knew she was a pessimist, she was able to look on the bright side.

I'm not actually hanging, she thought, rolling her shoulders and shifting her weight about. *And I have the place to myself. Not bad.*

Of course it grew more and more uncomfortable as the minutes passed. Time began to spin out like spider gossamer across a Dragon's back. But the Jordan was more than able to shift around just the right way to ease her discomfort.

Try as she might, Scarlett could not help remembering her training at the JTC and that bastard of a Master Sergeant. It rankled her to her soul that his insanity might have done her a favor.

It was punishment, she thought. *It was torture. It couldn't really be training. How the hell could he know that I would end up like this?*

She let her body hang back for a while, and then shifted her weight to her toes.

Jade, of course, would say there are no accidents.

Scarlett harrumphed to the silent bay and shifted her weight.

The Chimeran officers dined sumptuously. Bjorn always insisted on having organic food whenever possible, and the best that could be imported to deep space. The meat was bloody, and the crisp vegetables had the earthy taste of being grown in dirt.

Stojacovik seemed as determined as ever to kill the mood but Eva made it a point to enjoy herself. The wine was rich and hot and gathered on her tongue before it flowed down her throat to warm her belly and her groin.

She talked mostly to Ana and to Donna, gossiping and laughing, but there was something in the air that prohibited good conversation. It was as if they were expecting the arrival of another ship, or (even more) it was like the moment before a battle when silence was heavy upon every lip. There was a heightened sense of urgency, of unspoken excitement. Eva enjoyed it only because she was anticipating the breaking of the human.

She had watched the last human, the slow-witted Engineer, suffer with a slight amusement but with no real interest. Knowing the pain that was in store for the Jordan made her hot with anticipation.

She toyed with her officer's chain, a finely linked silver necklace with the double loop for infinity across the throat. The male officers wore a silver ring, stamped with the same symbol, on their right hand.

Bjorn ate his meal with obvious enjoyment but offered little to their conversation. Eva kept a hand on his knee, which always tended to drift up his inner thigh, depending on how much wine she consumed. Bjorn would sometimes grasp it and push her long fingers even higher, depending on how much wine he had consumed.

To the Jordan's credit, the Chimeran crew did not expect to hear anything the first hour. But when the hour passed and the plates were cleared, a few officers threw curious glances at one another.

Dinner gave way to dessert and dessert gave way to ammage – when the enlisted were dismissed and the officers took their evening drink, sometimes with a plate of cheese, when it was available.

Bjorn was the most at ease, though Eva saw that he often paused in conversation, his head cocked to one side. She realized that they were all waiting for the same thing - the voice of the prisoner. If not screams, something. Anything. A demand to be let go, a voice calling out for release, for a drink of water – but there was nothing. Not even a *hello? Is anyone there?*

From the mech bay, on the level directly below the mess hall, there was nothing but silence.

An hour turned into two and Eva felt the air grow thicker and heavier with a steady tension. At first, she thought it was just her, and that she was being silly and nervous. Then she realized that everyone sat with pale knuckles around crystal glasses making bad attempts at easy conversation. The silence spread like a virus, from the bay into the mess hall upstairs where it infected the waiting officers.

Two hours turned into three and conversations fizzled out one by one.

"Maybe she's dead," Eva finally offered with a gracious smile. A few laughed but Stojacovik stood up and threw his napkin on the table.

"Enough!" he shouted. "I'm not waiting any longer!"

Bjorn smiled indulgently and shrugged. "Very well." He stood and strode from the mess hall. Stojacovik kept close to his heels and everyone else scrambled to follow, Eva secretly hoping that the human pilot would be dead. It was unlikely, but not impossible.

Bjorn's entourage fell in step behind Stojacovik and Eva as they exited the mess. Boots clattered down the metal steps to the level below. Bjorn led his followers through the passage and into the mech bay as the lights came up around the prisoner.

Scarlett turned her head to watch their entrance. Her crimson flight suit reflected the lights and her eyes blinked rapidly as they adjusted to the brightness. Bjorn and Stojacovik stopped and stood directly in front of her, not quite sure of what to think or say. Her dark eyes moved from one to the other. They stopped on the Executive Officer.

"You smell like shit," she told him.

Stojacovik's arm shot out as he backhanded the Jordan across the mouth. Bjorn, his face a mask of surprised amusement, held up a hand for him to desist as he watched Scarlett turn her face back toward the XO. Her full lips were already beginning to swell, and the bottom one had been cut by his ring. She smiled at Stojacovik.

"And you hit like a Delrah."

Stojacovik lunged at her and Bjorn had to throw out an arm to catch him and shove him back. "Jesus, Stoj!" he shouted. "Control yourself!"

The outraged construct snarled at the Commander, then took a deep breath and straightened, tugging his blue uniform back into place. Throwing a black look at Scarlett, he backed away. Bjorn turned to the human stretched out in chains and she looked him up and down with open contempt.

"Where's my dinner?" she demanded.

The air left Bjorn's lungs in a surprised gust and he laughed, shaking his head.

"What the hell is so funny?"

"You are. How are you feeling?"

Scarlett looked at him like he was crazy. "Are you kidding me?"

"Don't your arms hurt?" he asked, reaching out to feel them through the fabric of her suit. She jerked away but the chains kept her from getting far. He ran a hand along the top of her arm and over her shoulder, his fingers tracing each muscle through the thin cloth. Scarlett gasped at the way her body responded to his touch.

Angry, she reacted the only way she knew how – bringing her knee up as fast and hard as she could. This time he stepped deftly away and smiled at her. She expelled an angry burst of air through her teeth.

"It's not comfortable," she spat. "If that's what you mean. But neither is that bench in my cell – so what's the difference?"

Bjorn favored her with another wolfish smile, a spark of admiration in his green eyes.

"Godammit!" Stojacovik cursed. "Get on with it!"

Bjorn kept his gaze fixed on Scarlett for a moment longer and then turned away with a sigh. He eyed the implements that he had left on the steel table and selected the torch.

He motioned Sandy and Bruny over and they worked the pulley attached to the chains on Scarlett's wrists. They hauled her arms up over her head and she cried out angrily as it cramped the muscles in her neck and shoulders. She glared at the constructs before turning her blazing eyes to the Chimeran Commander.

"He won't come for me," she said, keeping her voice even.

Bjorn froze. "He?"

"My Fledgling."

"I thought all ships were female."

"Not always."

"Hmm," Bjorn said, his eyes thoughtful as he stored away the information. He shrugged and raised the torch.

"It won't work," she said, trying to by time. Time for what, she didn't know. "A Dragon has never been drawn."

"That doesn't mean it's impossible." He thumbed the torch and it sprang to brilliant life with a small popping sound. Its flame was a short blue crown, topped with a yellow tear of fire. Another construct stepped next to Bjorn with a palm-cam in his hand. "I hope you don't mind if we record this," Bjorn told Scarlett. "I'd like to compare the results with our next...mmm... guest. I hear your elf counterpart is quite the prodigy."

Scarlett's eyes darted about the bay, looking for a way out. "Well, why don't we wait till she gets here? I'll even help you torture her. Or, we could wrestle each other in cold plasma - you could even join in if you want." Bjorn laughed.

"That sounds fantastic! Maybe we'll do that. But first…"

Shit, Scarlett thought. *This is bad. This is really bad.*

Bjorn stepped close and dug his fingers into the soft cloth under her right arm and yanked it down, ripping it open all the way to her waist and tearing off most of the right sleeve. He tilted his head, eyeing the black strap of an undergarment before deciding he had torn off enough. He nodded, satisfied, and leaned close to Scarlett.

"I am told that this is a most sensitive spot," he said, reaching out to touch the skin under her right arm, his fingers tracing a line down to her ribcage. The back of his thumb grazed along the curve of her breast. "Well, not the *most* sensitive." He moved in closer and Scarlett could feel the heat from the torch radiating off her face. "We'll save that for later," he whispered in her ear. A fine dew of sweat grew on her brow and upper lip.

Scarlett licked her lips and smiled nervously. "Wouldn't you like to play with me first?" She was too anxious to be seductive, but she had to try something. Anything. Bjorn smiled.

"My dear," he said softly, "that's exactly what I'm going to do."

The airlock on the Bloodjet hissed as the seal broke and the ACNR top of the cockpit slid open. A human mech reached down a hand to help Blue up through the portal in the steel floor. She grabbed his arm and pulled herself up and out as if exiting a manhole. The Jordan looked around and wondered if she had entered a sewer pipe.

She stood with the mech in a reeking, cluttered hallway with the Bloodjet right beneath them. Blue could see it through the thick, scratched, yellowed glass floor. A cluttered desk hunkered nearby along with a dented set of lockers.

The mech was dirty and in need of a shave, dressed in faded olive coveralls caked with grease. They looked and smelled like they had never seen the inside of a washer unit. Her own flight suit, usually a brilliant blue, looked like dull turquoise in the sickly light.

"Whew," he said and, with a low whistle, placed his hands above his knees as he squatted down for a better look at the jet. "She's a beauty."

"I need fuel," Blue told him. He nodded as if it were expected.

"Is that all? I can run a hydraulic check if you want."

"The hydraulics are fine."

"What about..."

"Just the fuel."

"Photon charge?"

"Just the fuel."

The mech shook his head. "You don't want to get too far out in the system and be without internal power."

Blue crossed her arms and stared at him, saying nothing. He waited for a moment, optimistically expectant, and then sighed.

He leaned back eyeing the jet through the floor and cocked his head, as if he could tell how much fuel it needed just by looking at it. "Fuel 'll cost ten thousand."

"That better be for the cleanest fuel you have, no less than r8979."

The mech rocked back on his heels, raising his dirty blond brows. "Actually, that type of fuel will be twenty thousand, as we don't have much and it's in high demand."

"Yeah, this hulking piece of shit is covered with Class-A jets."

"Oh," the mech offered, "maybe not now, but we are expecting a platoon of IGC fighters within the fortnight." He watched Blue expectantly, seeing if she would take the bait or call his bluff. Blue rolled her eyes but didn't argue.

"Fine." She handed him her credential card, which he accepted with a grin. He glanced at the Jordan's card and then did a double take, looking sharply at Blue. "That's right," she told him. "And there will be another thousand for you to keep your mouth shut about me until after I'm gone." The mech gave her a gap toothed smile.

"Yes ma'am!"

Blue looked down at his clothes and her lip curled up in disgust. "I need a pair of your coveralls, too, if you have an extra set. And a hat." She shuddered at the thought and reached down into the Bloodjet for her things while the mech rocked back again on his heels.

"I don't know," he said thoughtfully. "New coveralls can be costly. How about..."

Blue straightened and slung a munitions belt over a shoulder, holding a short stock laser rifle in her right hand.

"How about you get them in the next twenty seconds, and I won't blow off your balls?"

"That sounds fair," the mech chirped, hurrying to his locker.

Galen's laughter chimed in her left ear. The munitions belt was laden with the hand weapons she had brought, and heavy. She set it on the floor and laid the rifle on the desk.

The mech returned with some musty work garments and Blue pulled them on quickly over her flight suit. She had to roll up the long pant legs. She took the proffered hat, pinching it between two fingers with undisguised revulsion and stared at it. Clothes were one thing, but she could only guess what might be crawling around in the mech's hat that she couldn't see.

"Tick-tock, tick-tock," Galen told her. She grimaced and stuck it on her head. It came down far enough to cover the tips of her pointed ears.

The mech held out a grimy glass and rubber pad with her card on it. She laid her hand over the card and it glowed green, verifying her identity, funds, and authorizing her payment. He gave her another one of his smiles and handed the card back to her. She tucked it away into her flight suit beneath the coveralls and then reached back down into the Bloodjet. She had to kneel to reach the console and pull out the remote chip. She tucked it away in her suit with her credential card and stood up.

"Have it fueled and ready to go when I get back," she told him.

"When will that be?"

"Soon." *I hope.*

"There's a snack bar all the way down the corridor and to the right if you're hungry."

She thanked him and hurried off – not for a snack but to find an un-manned computer.

I'm not going to scream, Scarlett thought. *I'm not going to scream.*

And, at first, she didn't.

As Bjorn leaned close with the torch Scarlett felt a rise of panic so great and overwhelming she thought it would swell and crush her.

Then, just before the heat of the flame touched the skin of her ribcage, she caught sight of Eva - her smile smug with satisfaction and her eyes brimming with anticipation. Scarlett clenched her jaw and locked her eyes onto the female's thin face, her stare burning into the self-righteous countenance just before the torch began to lick at her skin.

Eva's expression froze under her glare, uncertain. Scarlett saw it, and her own face clenched into a gruesome parody of a grin as the fire bit into her flesh.

It's not hot, Scarlett thought at first, baffled, her eyes boring into Eva. *It's cold. He's doing something wrong.*

Then her bewildered mind was flooded with the pain as it tore through her whole body. The skin over her ribs smoldered and the sickening sweet smell of burning hair and flesh filled her nostrils. The pain was like nothing Scarlett had ever felt or had ever dared to imagine.

Her eyes squeezed into slits and her teeth ground together as every muscle in her body clenched and contorted in screaming protest. The tendons in her neck stood out like small, taut ropes.

Scarlett felt every skin cell in her body open up and cry out, the sweat pouring out in a flood. She thought fleetingly that it might be more from the pain than from the heat against her body but she couldn't be sure.

Her body jerked reflexively, trying to get away. Perspiration beaded and then ran down into her eyes and face and neck. Each length of muscle convulsed in a desperate effort of self-preservation, trying to wrench itself away from the burning pain.

Bjorn's green eyes watched, fascinated, as the skin turned orange, then red, and then as millions of tiny blisters sprang up and burst and began oozing and then pouring clear fluid before it all blackened and charred, becoming as crisp and thin and delicate as burned paper.

Scarlett's breath was a choking fire in her throat as the sweat ran in rivulets and then rivers, soaking her clothes. Her hair clung to her head and her cheeks dripped with streams of salt. Her arms strained against the chains that held her, the metal links digging into her wrists. Drops ran down her drawn face and fell from the end of her nose and her chin as she ground her teeth together.

Bjorn pulled the flame from Scarlett's body and stepped back, his bright eyes moving from her blackened side to her face.

Scarlett shuddered and jerked as her blazing stare swept around to meet his baffled stare. She let out a huge breath of air and sucked in another, her body shaking. She was not aware if she had been holding her breath but now it came in great, gasping gulps.

The other constructs watched them silently; their eyes going between Scarlett and Bjorn, from his torch to her burned skin. Eva stared at the sodden Jordan with wide, unbelieving eyes. Stoj sneered at her with open hate.

"Maybe you should turn up the heat," he suggested.

Bjorn looked at Scarlett with an expression of bemused admiration and then nodded as he thumbed the torch. The fire shot out into a flame that was nearly a foot long, yellow and orange and leaping and flickering like a live thing.

Scarlett felt anger rise with a heat all its own. A heat that burned her from the inside out. The fury rose and burned her soul like the flame had burned her skin.

"With a torch like that," she hissed, still gasping, "you should be wearing safety goggles."

Bjorn's smile widened into a grin. He leaned in so close and so slow that Scarlett thought he meant to kiss her. She held as still as she could, though her body shook uncontrollably, flinging out drops of perspiration.

"I'm liking you more and more, Scarlett," he whispered. "And I think I will enjoy playing doctor for you when this is done."

Bjorn's movements were as soft and gentle as a lover's touch as he eased the torch up this time, grazing the blackened skin beneath Scarlett's right arm. Her body bucked away and he reached out and put a hand on her hip, steadying her, holding her still. He dug into her side with the flame, burning through skin this time and going into the tissue underneath.

Scarlett had never felt such an all-engrossing pain before. She did not know who she was or where she was in the grip of the pain. Any sense of time was gone. Lost were thoughts of escape or retribution. It took away all reason and left her teetering on the brink of madness.

Now the scream came. It built within her like a power greater than her soul and came tearing through her body and out her mouth like a torrent from a burst dam. The scream was an angry, monstrous, living thing erupting throughout her body to shake the air throughout entire ship.

The sound became a bellow that tore through her and she realized it wasn't just her screaming but Fledge as well. His scream of anger joined with hers and became an ear-shattering roar. The exploding sound of fury and terror threatened to rupture every organ in her body and burst her eyes from their sockets. It went on and on and burned her lungs and her throat until it was hotter than the burning in her flesh.

So engulfed by the deafening roar, she didn't realize that the flame that had been burning her was gone. The vibration of her roar shook the tables and the racks and tools clattered haphazardly to the floor. When the burning in her lungs surpassed the burning in her side, the howl that poured forth from her stopped.

The sound cut off abruptly and Jordan Scarlett hung from her chains, completely spent. Her flight suit was soaked and ruined, her hair plastered to her head and face. The sound of the scream echoed in her ears so loud that she could not hear the actual cacophony that echoed through the bay and traveled in a booming wail throughout the ship.

After long moments the echoes died away and silence rushed in to fill the void, cut only by the sounds of shallow breathing. Scarlett raised her head, sucking in spatters of air like a drowning man pulled from a sea, only to see her Chimeran captors crouching on the floor. Each one of them had their hands clamped over their ears and were looking at Scarlett with a great deal of confusion and a good dose of fear.

Bjorn stood up slowly. His green eyes regarded her with amazement. The torch, which had clicked off when he dropped it, lay forgotten on the floor. Despite the pain she felt inside and out, Scarlett managed a ghost of a smile. Bjorn looked at her and cocked his head, perplexed.

"You're bleeding," Scarlett croaked.

Bjorn raised a hand to the bottom of his nose and wiped away the blood that was trickling from it and looked from the back of his bloodied hand to Scarlett. She grinned at him.

"Your ear, too."

Bjorn felt his right ear and looked at his fingers as they came away wet and red. He stared at her long seconds before he motioned to the construct that had been recording her ordeal. He took the palm cam and handed it to his wide-eyed Executive Officer.

"Take that and relay it to the Carthage, immediately."

Stojacovik, who had a thin stream of blood coming from the corner of his mouth, took the camera without a word and left the bay, his eyes never leaving Scarlett. Bjorn waved at Sandy and Bruny to take Scarlett down. "Be careful," he told them.

The constructs went to Scarlett and carefully let down the chains that held her arms. Scarlett screamed out in pain, but the sound was small, and all her own. Nonetheless, Sandy and Bruny froze for a moment in fear before continuing to unwind the chains from her wrists and each of them kept a wary eye on her.

Scarlett was too tired and hurt to care about her newly earned respect. She felt burned and beaten from the inside out. Her hair and clothes clung to her sweat-soaked body.

They released the restraints on her wrists and her right arm came down slowly to cover her injured side. She winced, hearing the skin in her armpit crackle as it came down. The other arm came down and her knees buckled.

Bjorn was there and scooped her up, cradling her in his arms.

"Don't you *dare* carry me," Scarlett hissed at him. She tried to struggle but the pain made her vision blur.

"Give me 20 cc's of Serylate," Bjorn told a female construct with short dark hair, full lips, and bright brown eyes.

"Serylate?" she asked. "Don't you want..." she started but a scathing glare from Bjorn sent her scurrying. A few of the constructs glanced at each other, surprised. No one was more surprised than Eva. Her look of astonishment quickly turned to one of anger. The bright-eyed construct brought the syringe, circling around Bjorn to better reach the drooping form of the human Jordan. She leaned close and pushed the needle into the top of Scarlett's exposed shoulder.

Scarlett felt herself go limp and the pain eased away from her like a shadow fleeing the sun. The corners of her mouth turned up and she sighed, trying to follow the warmth and comfort of relief now flooding her body.

She turned her head towards Bjorn's chest and closed her eyes. Bjorn looked down at the woman in his arms as he carried her from the mech bay, followed by the others. He felt something stir inside himself as he looked at her. The feeling that rose up, neither angry nor sexual, felt strange and alien.

ONE SEVEN

As soon as it had seen the Mech City-Ship in its range, the *Macedonian* had immediately requested two fuel tankers and two repair ships. Blue reviewed the com-log between the *Mace* and the Mech Ship and the repair plan scheduled for the Chimeran Battle Cruiser.

"Which do I take?" Blue asked quietly, looking at the monitor of the computer she had just hacked. She had found another fuel station, this one abandoned for the moment, and she sat at the desk in a dirty hover chair. She could feel Galen on her left side, practically resting his chin on her shoulder.

"The tankers are too far," he said. "You'll never get there in time. One of the repair ships." The readout on the screen changed to a diagram. Blue looked down to see the keys on the console moving up and down, manipulated by invisible fingers.

"I wish you wouldn't do that," Blue said. "It's creepy."

"Sorry, Love, it seemed easier this way." The diagram zoomed in on the corridor and followed it along past airlocks and docking stations. "Take this corridor to a sandt shuttle," Galen said, narrating the view on the screen as it changed. "Take the diagonal down and get off on seven. Down the hall to the right and take that first pod, number 708. It has a crew that will actually be going inside to do some repairs. It's down..."

"I see it."

Blue pushed away from the desk and glanced around the docking station. She spotted a lump of heavy fabric down by her feet. She hooked a foot around it and pulled it out to see what it was. "Perfect." She pulled a dirty but large tool duffle out from under the desk and looked inside before dropping in her munitions belt and laser rifle.

She slung the bag over her shoulder and was rising to her feet when the scream hit her. Blue fell to her knees, clutching at the desk. The chair jutted back and bobbed like a cork in water.

"What?" Galen asked, fearful. He was practically shouting but she could hardly hear him and was unable to answer. "What is it!?!"

Blue clamped her hands over her ears just before realizing the screaming was coming from inside her head. Her body bent forward in an effort to protect itself, curling in until she was almost in a fetal position under the desk. The sound resonated so deep she could feel it digging into the roots of her teeth and vibrating down her spine. She squeezed her eyes shut to keep them from bulging out of their sockets.

Then, almost as quickly as it had come, the sound vanished. Blue lay curled up on the floor between the desk and the chair, sweating and trembling. Her right side tingled painfully.

"Noel!" Galen was shouting. "What is it? Are you okay? What's going on? Noel!" After the shrieking in her head, his voice was muted and distant, like he was calling to her through a burial of bedrock.

"You didn't hear that?" she asked.

"Hear what?"

"Jesus." She waited for the quivering to subside and then sat up, squatting on shaking legs, looking around cautiously.

"What the hell was it?"

"It was Fledge. And Cyan. And Verdana." Blue swallowed. "I think I heard Scarlett, too. They were screaming. It was horrible."

"Jesus."

"What do you think that was?" Blue asked.

"I couldn't tell you."

"Do you..." Blue put a hand on the desk to steady herself, "do you think Scarlett is dead?"

Galen was quiet for a moment. "You tell me."

Now it was her turn to be silent. She closed her eyes and drew a deep breath then shook her head. "No. I would know."

"Good. Now, I hate to prod, but you better get going. It's going to be a lot harder to get onto that ship if you miss the pod."

"Right." Blue adjusted the strap on her shoulder and pushed the tool bag back over her hip. She took a quick look about to get herself oriented then raced off down the corridor.

Bjorn looked down at the human woman as he carried her from the mech bay to the ship's medical center. He marveled that she could be both so powerful and yet so frail. He frowned, feeling an odd sort of connection with her, and an attraction that he did not understand.

Bjorn had always had an insatiable appetite when it came to women. He had a powerful attraction to and appreciation for the female form. He was an equal opportunity man when it came to sex and as far as he was concerned, variety was the spice of life. Being one of the highest ranked leaders of Chimera had its privileges, and his amorous attentions were always welcomed.

That fact that Scarlett balked at him, even affected a form of disgust with him, was both baffling and intriguing. Though the physical attraction he felt for Scarlett was strong, it was something that he understood. There was something else, however, that made him feel strange inside that he could not begin to comprehend.

He looked down at the Jordan cradled in his arms and felt a warmth bloom inside his chest. It was slightly electrical, slightly *wormy*. The feeling expanded and contracted, expanded and contracted. Each time it expanded, it went farther - spreading, growing. He had no idea what it was; only that it was entirely new, and entirely unnerving.

Eva stayed with him, her long legs keeping stride with his and her eyes constantly darting to his face as the others in their entourage followed. They passed few others, most of the crew sleeping. Those on the night watch however, stopped working or talking to watch curiously as the group made their way to the ship's medical center – wondering why in the hell the Commander was carrying the human prisoner.

The doors to the MedCen opened with a hiss and Bjorn carried Scarlett straight to the RR where the medics were already waiting.

He laid the human Jordan down on a steel secra table as his aggregate of constructs either filed into the room to watch or stood waiting outside. He helped the nurse take off the torn flight suit. His eyes stopped for a moment on Scarlett's full breasts, pushed together and held high on her chest by a tight, black brassiere. Chimeran women didn't wear them, but he had seen them before. Perhaps not one that was quite as tight. He looked up to see Eva, who stood in the doorway with narrowed eyes and a clenched jaw.

"I'm not going to fuck her on the table, if that's what you're thinking," he told her.

"Aren't you?"

"We need her alive. You know that."

"That's not all I know."

Bjorn ignored her and dropped his gaze to Scarlett's arms and shoulders. He was still amazed she had been able to hang like a puppet in the mech bay for so long with seemingly no pain at all. The muscles there were well defined but not exceptionally large. There were no implants that he could see.

The nurse moved Scarlett's body, lifting her right arm to expose her injured side. Where the wide strap of the brassiere wrapped around towards Scarlett's back, the fabric had melted and fused with the burnt and blackened flesh.

Bjorn watched the nurse cut the undergarment away while Eva watched him. All other eyes in the room watched as the medic finished removing the melted and fused material from the Jordan's desiccated tissue with a laser-blade.

The nurse reached for Scarlett's underwear next, but Eva stopped her.

"You can leave those on," she commanded, her voice firm and grating. The nurse looked questioningly at Bjorn. He shrugged. Though the underwear was of a thin black material, it was surprisingly masculine, almost a tight fitting short. Bjorn shook his head as he looked over Scarlett's body.

You are quite the conundrum, he thought. *Who would have guessed?*

He stood by the table with the others and watched while another medic cleansed Scarlett's wound and applied a synthetic salve that would expedite the healing of the underlying tissues.

When the doc reached for the genetically manufactured ichor for her skin, Bjorn put a hand on the construct, stopping him. The Commander turned and scanned the shelves before pulling down a jar with his name on it and handing it to the doctor. The doc peered at Bjorn over his mask with raised brows for a moment before turning back to Scarlett. Bjorn could feel Eva fuming behind him.

When the doc finished, he looked at Bjorn before wrapping the wound to see if there were going to be any more special requests.

"Why stop now?" Eva demanded. "Let him give her a sponge bath!"

Bjorn laughed. "We don't need to go that far, but clean her up." He watched as a nurse pulled down a shower nozzle and ran a spray of water over Scarlett's body. He remembered how the sweat had poured out of her. "Get her hair, too."

The nurse ran water through the human's hair and Bjorn put out a hand to brush the water from her face. He pushed the water through her dark locks

·with his fingers and took a towel from the nurse. He rubbed it over Scarlett's head and worked it gently over her hair, squeezing out the water.

When he was done, the doc put another layer of ichor and then a bandage over the wound and let the nurse dress Scarlett in a pair of blue coveralls. The medic brought in a hover stretcher to take the human back to her cell but Bjorn waved him off.

"I'll carry her, it's not that far." He slid one arm under Scarlett's neck and another under her knees, gently lifting and holding her.

Furious, Eva stalked out of the room but waited for him in the hall. Bjorn had the idea that she wanted to make sure that he took Scarlett back to her cell, instead of his own cabin. Fuming, the female officer dismissed everyone save for those that were scheduled to guard the Jordan.

The others bowed respectfully and strode away. A few looked back with curious glances, intrigued by their Commander's peculiar behavior. Most just assumed his interest in the human was what it was with most women – predatory.

Bjorn looked down at the still form of the Jordan, her dark hair damp against his chest. He hefted her up a bit, pulling her a little closer against his body. She stirred slightly and murmured softly. Bjorn smiled, that strange feeling creeping around inside him.

Scarlett started coming around as they entered the corridor to the brig. She looked around groggily, blinking her eyes. She made a grunting noise of disgust as she realized where she was.

"Put me down you bastard," she croaked.

Bjorn grinned, that strange feeling tugging at his insides. "We're almost there," he said. He carried her into the cell and laid her carefully on the bench. He knelt down, resting his weight on one knee. "How do you feel?" he asked, brushing her hair away from her face. She smacked his hand away and the feeling flared up hot inside him.

"Like shit," Scarlett told him, though she felt shockingly better than she had expected. Her neck ached from spending hours with her arms stretched, but she would never admit it. Besides, it was no worse than what she had endured in the past. Not by a long shot.

The area under her right arm had a piercing tingle, like a limb that had fallen asleep and was now coming angrily awake. Other than the pins and needles feeling and a little tenderness, there was no pain under her arm.

"Your skin is grafting itself back together, with the help of some medlets." He touched her side gently. "And my DNA ichor." Scarlett's face contorted, horrified. Bjorn grinned at her and stood up. "That's right. Now you'll al-ways have a little bit of me with you."

"Ugh! Why?" she asked him, sitting up carefully as he walked to the door of her cell. It was Eva, though, standing in the doorway that answered.

"I don't know why. If it was up to me, I'd have let you suffer."

Scarlett looked at Eva. She seemed as pissed as ever, though a bit less ar-rogant – maybe even afraid. "No doubt," Scarlett agreed. "You seem to be the one suffering, though."

"Not for long. You'll be dead as soon as we get what we want." She paused, waiting for Scarlett's reply but the Jordan remained silent. "What? No clev-er quip for that one?" She paused again but when Scarlett didn't reply she smirked and shut the door to her cell.

Bjorn watched the Jordan's face as the door slid shut. He could see a bit of crimson shining in her dark eyes. *I should have kissed her,* he thought. *At least on the forehead.* That strange feeling wormed around inside him and he decided it wasn't entirely unpleasant.

"I'm surprised she didn't want the last word," Eva said, acidly smug. As she turned to leave the brig a sound came from Scarlett's cell and she stopped, her eyes wide with anger.

Bjorn laughed. "You were saying?"

Eva glared at him and stormed from the brig. Behind her she could hear Scarlett in her cell, whistling.

Jordan Blue boarded Repair Pod 708 with a dozen or so mechanics, all with repairs to make inside the Chimeran Battle Cruiser *Macedonian.* The run to get there in time was harrying. It didn't help that she was terrified that the screaming might start again at any moment. Every noise made her jump.

She arrived at the docking station just in time to slip on board behind the last mech. The others were already buckling themselves into the jump seats along the wall. She took a seat as far from anyone as she could and glanced around. A few had given her some curious looks but said nothing. She stayed calm, knowing there was no way they could know who she was. She hoped.

"It's your face," Galen told her, seeing their looks and sensing her unease.

"My scar?" she asked, breathing the words and keeping her lip movement to a bare minimum.

"No, these pirates are a lot more scarred up than you. It's the rest of you. You're too clean."

"I doubt that," she breathed, looking down at her drab coveralls and trying not to appear as disgusted as she felt.

The Jordan looked into her duffle as if she were checking her tools. She stuck a hand inside and felt around under the rifle and munitions belt. She found an oddly shaped piece of greasy metal and wrapped her fingers around it before pulling her hand out of the bag.

She leaned back and scratched her chin thoughtfully. It left a smudge of grease under her lower lip.

"Better," Galen said. "Maybe you should wipe the sweat off your forehead."

Blue mopped her brow just under the bill of her hat with the back of her sleeve. It left a black streak from one temple to the other.

"Very nice," Galen admired.

Blue muttered something unladylike under her breath and Galen laughed. She could hear him breathe and feel his closeness and it calmed her heart and steadied her nerves. By the time the pod docked with the *Macedonian* she was ready.

The crew disembarked into an airlock. The portal to the pod hissed closed behind them and a rectangular door slid open in front of them. They were greeted by a pair of Chimeran constructs shouldering plasma rifles. The mechs split into small groups and the constructs directed them to where they were needed. Blue hung back behind the last group, keeping her head down and lagging behind, as if searching for a tool inside her bag.

It was still dimlight on the ship, so the lights were low and most of the crew was still asleep.

"You couldn't ask for better conditions," Galen remarked. Blue thought of a few but kept quiet, not wanting to draw any attention.

She followed the last group through one passageway and into another. After glancing back to make sure no one was behind her, she took the next hallway that branched left. She kept always to her left as she wound through the corridors, hoping that she was headed for the area Calyph had specified.

Despite the low lights, Blue kept her hat down and stayed next to the right side of the hall to hide her scar, should she be seen. She only encountered a few constructs, and those that she did see eyed her dirty mechanic's coveralls with open distaste and gave her a wide berth.

"I think you went too far," Galen cautioned and she shushed him. After a while she realized that he was right had to double back.

"Don't you say a goddamned thing," she warned, though she could feel his grin on the back of her neck.

Finally, after having to walk boldly past a clanging kitchen and quiet mess hall, a darkened armory and brightly lit common lavatory, she found the brig. The only odd look she had gotten along the way was from a pair of mechs replacing gaskets on foamer at an emergency door. Even the few droids she had passed didn't give her a second look.

She paused in the crepuscular light of the hallway, examining a row of portals. She couldn't be sure if they were cells or if they were just closely placed sleeping quarters. She noticed one with a door slightly open, crept up to it, and peeked inside. The composite bench and steel toilet left no doubt.

"Nobody is that ascetic," she muttered. "This has to be it. "

"This is it," Galen agreed.

Blue slunk down to the curve in the hall and poked her head around the bend. There was a spiral staircase a few meters away with metal stairs going up to the next level and more going down to the level below. Otherwise, there was nothing but more hallway and more doors.

Jordan Blue dropped the tool bag and pulled out the munitions belt. She buckled it around her waist and holstered both the plasma guns as well as the trazon. She stuck the spider gun in the last holster on the right and pushed down on it so that it was slung below her right hip. She pulled out the laser rifle and kicked the bag aside.

Shit, Blue thought as she looked up and down the hall. *It'll take forever to check each cell.*

Her eyes darted around looking for a guard station, terminal, track screen, or anything that might contain prisoner information. She wondered how long it would take her to find one that would have Scarlett's info, if she found one at all.

Shit.

She froze, hearing voices approaching.

Shit!

She crouched down and adjusted her grip on the rifle.

"Do I kill them or follow them?" she whispered.

"That's your call, Jordan," Galen said softly. "Can you hear what they are saying?" Blue strained her ears, trying to listen for a clue but the voices faded away before she could pick anything up. She blew an exasperated breath through her white teeth.

"She's probably not even on this level," she said, getting frustrated. "It's too quiet. She's got to be some kind of prize for them so there's bound to be more activity where she is. At least a few guards."

Blue stood and quickly made her way down the hallway to the spiral stairs. She went down three stairs and paused, ducking her head down and listening. A few scraping sounds that might have been boots or a droid. The Jordan shook her head and went back up.

She passed the level where she had begun and continued up until she was just below the floor of the upper cellblock. She paused and, hearing nothing, cautiously poked her head up and into the hallway. She looked both ways down the metal floor of the corridor but there was nothing to see. She could hear sounds to the left beyond the curve of the hall, but not anything she might have expected. It was just too quiet. She was starting to duck down again when her ear caught another sound.

She paused, one pointed ear twitching. A sound was drifting, echoing softly through metal walls and doors. A lonely sound. A sound that shouldn't be on a Chimeran ship full of constructs and droids.

"Do you hear that?" Blue whispered.

"No," Galen whispered back.

Blue poked her head back up and tilted it to the right, trying to see around the bend in the corridor.

"I know where she is," she whispered. "Sort of."

That's got to be her, she thought as she crept up the rest of the stairs and into the hall.

She could hear voices coming from around the bend; at least three, maybe five. She flicked the safety lever on the rifle and put the strap over her head and shoulder and let it hang on her left side. She pulled the spider gun from the holster on her right and listened as some of the voices started fading away.

Good, she thought. *There's a few less to worry about.*

"Are you going to try to fake your way in? Galen asked. "Or go in shooting?"

Blue stepped around the corner to see two male constructs leaning against the wall. They saw her and their eyes went wide. In the time it took for their expressions to change, Blue had the spider gun up, her keen eyes trained on the spot of air exactly halfway between their necks, and pulled off a single shot.

The bullet left the chamber traveling 1220 meters a second. As quiet as an arachnid dropping from its web, and with only a few meters to cover, the spider bullet crossed the distance in a fraction of time and, as it did so, eight fragments – four on each side – broke off. The body of the spider passed harmlessly between the two constructs. The eight frags drove with explosive force into their faces, necks, chests, and abdomens.

"That answers *that* question," Galen said as the bloodied hulks crumpled to the floor.

Blue ran over to the bodies on the floor and looked at the door they had been in guarding. Inside, someone was whistling *The Starfighter's Ballad*. Next to the door was a round button.

Blue looked about, wildly searching for a DNA or hand read, even an ancient code pad or slot for a key card. The button was all there was. She pushed it - hoping it wouldn't need a heat read or print check. To her surprise, the door slid open.

A figure with dark hair and blue coveralls sat up on the bench, supported itself on one elbow, and swayed as if dazed or drunk. Blue edged inside cautiously and the lights went up slightly, stimulated by the opened door.

"Scarlett?" she whispered. The figure on the bench smiled and Blue backed away quickly. The figure scowled.

"Blue, Godammit! Get back here!"

Blue edged back in, peering at her curiously. "Scarlett? Is that you?"

"Of course it's me! Who the hell else would it be?"

Blue gave a soft, nervous laugh. "You never smiled at me before," she said. Scarlett's lips twitched.

"I never thought I would be happy to see you." She swung her legs off the bench and stood up slowly.

"Are you alright?"

Scarlett straightened carefully, her face tight with fearful anticipation. "I think I am," she said, though she didn't sound sure.

"Then let's get the hell out of here." Blue pulled the strap of the laser rifle over her head and handed it to Scarlett. She stuck her face out of the cell, checking both directions. There was nobody in sight other than the bodies on the floor.

"Nice outfit," Scarlett remarked, smirking at the drab mech coveralls.

"You like it?" Blue asked, glancing over her shoulder. "You can have it."

"You smell," Scarlett said, wrinkling her nose.

"Like a human?"

"Like filth."

"Is there a difference?" Blue eyed Scarlett up and down. "Looks like you found a new outfit, yourself," she remarked, smiling. "Nice color." The human Jordan resumed her usual glare.

Blue crouched down behind the wall inside the cell and set the spider gun to burst. Scarlett thumbed the setting on the rifle all the way over to spray. "You might want to keep..." Blue started but Scarlett's icy glare cut her off. She sighed. "You know that will last longer if you..."

"Stow it!" Scarlett told her. Blue frowned.

"Why are you so angry?"

Scarlett looked so surprised that Blue thought she looked as if she had been goosed. "Why?" Scarlett sputtered, trying to keep her voice down. "*Why?*" Her body shook, seemingly too angry to get the right words out. "You, stupid, stupid..."

"Hey!" Blue protested, whispering hoarsely. "That's no way to treat me! I'm rescuing you!"

"I wouldn't have been captured if wasn't for you!" Scarlett hissed. "Hanging out in space like stoned balla ray!"

"I accept that," Blue said softly, lifting her chin. "But there is no need for you to be mean. What happened to 'happy to see me' a few seconds ago? I liked it better."

Scarlett bit her lip and her fingers wrapped around the handgrip of the gun, turning white at the knuckles. She had no idea why Blue got under her skin the way she did – she really *had* been happy to see her come through the cell door.

"Is Cyan with you?" she asked.

"No, I have a Bloodjet on a Mech City-Ship. We just need to get there. We'll attract less attention if we can get out the way I got in, but we might need to just get out onto the side of this bastard and call the jet remotely. My field can wrap us both if yours isn't working."

"My field is just fine!" Scarlett told her.

"Okay, okay. I just didn't know what they had done to you in here." For once, Scarlett's look of anger wasn't directed at her as Scarlett's black and crimson eyes met her blue ones.

"You don't want to know," she said evenly.

Blue reached out a hand and laid it over Scarlett's, the one that gripped the stock of the rifle. Also for once, Scarlett did not shake it off. Blue nodded and withdrew her hand.

"I think the jet bay hangar is our best bet," she said. "That's where most of the airlocks are, including the one I came through. At the very least, if we get trapped there, we can take one of their jets."

Scarlett nodded. "I know where you mean. That's where they brought me in."

"Ready?"

Scarlett nodded again.

Blue gave the cap on her head a tug and walked out of the cell with Scarlett right behind. They crossed the corridor, stepping gingerly over the bodies. Scarlett took a bit of satisfaction seeing it was Sandy and Bruny, though she would have preferred that she had been given the chance to kill them herself.

Scarlett followed Blue through the hall, down a set of metal stairs and through a number of passageways. She held the rifle in the crux her left arm and against her left hip. She brought her right hand up and tentatively felt the right side of her ribcage. She could feel a bandage under her clothes but no pain.

"It's getting lighter," Scarlett said softly. Blue only nodded and kept going. The ship was moving slowly from dimlight to simulated day. The crew would be up soon. Scarlett knew once that happened, their chances of slipping out would be next to nil. Time was running short.

Blue stopped abruptly. They were finally at the entrance of the jet bay. Scarlett gave Blue a quick nod and then followed her around the corner of the wall and into the hangar bay, running in a low crouch. She let Blue take point as she swung the nose of her rifle from side to side, her eyes scanning the bay. She couldn't care less if someone tried to stop them, but if she saw Bjorn or any of his cronies, she was taking them out.

I don't care if I bring the whole ship down on us, she thought. *That bastard is going to meet his end. Stoj, too. And that bitch, Eva.*

It didn't look like she would get the chance. The bay was surprising low manned at the early hour, and the Jordans were well hid. The steel door of the bay was open, the eternal night of space just beyond the flickering gold membrane of the nitrogen field. Normally an open bay didn't offer a good place to be discreet and would be nearly impossible to sneak through. Here, though, due to the armory overflow, Scarlett and Blue were able to make their way from one stack of crates to the next without being seen.

Scarlett read the stencils on the crates as she crept by them. On this side of the bay they were mostly filled with small ordinance. Smart bombs, chemical bombs, davey bombs, dirty bombs. She read the stenciled letters as she crept by. *Spinning Betties, Huber-Claymores.* As they passed one stack of crates Scarlett stopped short and straightened.

Grenades:CS was printed on a number of the wooden boxes stacked neck high.

"Jesus loves me," Scarlett whispered, a smile at the corners of her lips. Without another thought she hefted a crate from the top of the stack and deposited it carefully by her feet. She pulled at the top but it had been fastened with a nail gun. She wedged the thin edge of the eyesight of her rifle under the lid, wiggled it open an inch, and then stuck in the muzzle – levering it up and down to pry it open.

Blue, who had been making her way along the backside of the crates, looked back at that moment. Her jaw dropped open and she hurried back to Scarlett.

"Are you fucking crazy?" she demanded. "What the hell are you thinking?" Scarlett's look of surprise turned into one of understanding.

"Ohhh," she said. "You're right." She tilted the gun to the side and thumbed the pulse indicator to the off button. She smiled nervously at Blue. "That was close," she said, and went back to work at the crate.

Blue would have put her face in her hands if she could. "No!" she hissed. "What are you doing?" She could hear Galen laughing softly.

"Just give me a second," Scarlett told her as she rocked the muzzle up and down, loosening the lid. The lid, refusing to open all the way, did give way enough to let Scarlett slip a hand inside. "Yes!" She withdrew her hand and urged Blue forward. "Let's go!"

"Do I make you this crazy?" Blue asked.

"Yes."

"I am *so* sorry."

"Fine. Let's go."

Just as they began to creep along again behind the row of crates, they could hear the sound of an alarm and see red lights rolling out of the corridors, alerting the ship.

"Good job," Blue told Scarlett.

"It's not the grenade," she assured Blue. They probably just discovered Sandy and Bruny."

"Who?"

"The guards! Keep going!"

They ran at a low crouch, concealed behind the crates. When they got to the end they stopped, looking out towards the bay door and the corridor that led to the airlocks. They still had at least fifty meters of open space to cover. Despite the heightened excitement now inside the ship, activity close to the airlocks and bay door was still minimal. As far as Blue could tell, they should be able to get clear of any personnel easy enough. Being able to clear any plasma rounds was a different story.

"Ready?" she asked, prepared to bolt for the door.

Scarlett's eyes flitted about and she bit her lip.

"Scarlett?"

"Hang on a second," Scarlett told her. She looked around and, without another word, made a dash for the fighter jets lined up in the bay. Blue watched her, stunned. She stuck her head out past the crates, eyes darting about to see if anyone had seen them, wondering what the hell had gotten into Scarlett.

The jets were lined up in a pyramid formation, the foremost perfectly poised to be the first out the door and the next two just behind its wings. The second two were flanked in the same fashion with another in the middle. Scarlett made for the lead jet at a dead run.

"Jesus!" Blue whispered, waiting for someone to start shouting or open fire on them.

"What is she doing?" Galen asked.

"The hell if I know!" Blue watched as Scarlett made it to the lead ship, pulled herself up onto the wing and started to climb up to the cockpit.

What the hell has gotten into her? Blue thought. She licked her lips as her eyes darted about the bay. The alarms were still echoing in the corridors and Blue could see red lights flashing at the edges of the bay. As of yet, they were still alone.

Scarlett pushed her arm through the strap on the rifle and climbed up the side of the jet, the weapon banging against her side. It was difficult because she could use only one of her hands, the other was clutching the CS Grenade, and she wasn't about to let go.

She lowered her body into the cockpit, not wasting any time. Either it was Bjorn's jet or it wasn't. The natural pecking order in the chain of command would make it his, if he was a pilot. Scarlett could only hope.

Thrust or steerage? She thought. Her eyes flicked about quickly, ascertaining the make of the craft. *Steerage it is,* she thought, smiling.

She tucked her rifle into her right armpit and twisted her body until she was head first into the pit, her elbows braced on the seat. She pulled the pin on the grenade and reached way down under the wheel, carefully wedging the grenade between the steering column and the metal floor panel.

Jordan Scarlett arched her back, squirming backwards. She pulled herself up and out of the cockpit and slid down the nose of the jet and hit the ground running. As she did, Blue burst from behind the crates running towards her. Behind the small Jordan in dirty, mech coveralls came constructs pouring from the hall that led to the airlocks.

"Plan B!" Blue shouted, her booted feet pounding the steel tarmac of the bay. Scarlett spun on her heel and made a dash for the aircraft to the right of what she hoped was Bjorn's jet. Blue followed right behind.

Shouts finally filled the air and were followed a second later by a burst of laser fire. Red beams shot all around them in silent destruction, followed by more yelling. The legs of the jets hissed and sizzled and spat molten metal as they were hit by laser fire. The air was filled with more furious shouting. Both Jordans dove behind the thick leg of the jet on the far right side of the bay.

"They stopped firing," Blue remarked, peering around a fat rubber tire.

"They're in a tight spot," Scarlett told her.

"So are *we*, if you haven't noticed!"

Scarlett shook her head. "They don't want to damage a jet and they certainly don't want to hit any of the crates. They could send the whole ship to hell."

"Well, they're just going to close in on us."

Scarlett glanced out from behind the wheel. "Shit. They're going for the bay door."

Four Chimerans were running across the bay from the airlock hallway to the bay control station, crossing the space in front of the twitching lines of gold that danced across the black. Both Jordans knew that hijacking the jets would no longer be an option if the steel doors were closed. It would be a bloody battle just to fight their way to the airlocks and get on the outside of the ship.

Blue jumped to her feet on the right side of the wheel and, knowing the distance was too great for the spider, snapped a plasma gun out of the munitions belt. Her eyes zeroed in on the first two running for the control box and, leading them by a meter, released a photon charge. The two collapsed in a smoldering heap of jellied plasma.

Scarlett went left as Blue went right and shot from the hip as she rose. Though her eyesight was nearly as sharp as the elf, she relied on her reflexes and shot at them, barely focusing on their forms. They were obliterated instantly in a spray of laser fire.

The two Jordans ducked back down behind the wheel.

"Go back and take the first jet," Blue said. "I'll take this one. We can run E and E if we have two aircraft."

"No, I'll take the one on the left."

"You need to take the one in the *front*," Blue insisted. Scarlett shook her head.

"You take this one, I'll take the left one."

"How the hell am I supposed to get around the fore jet?"

Scarlett glanced up at the wing of the jet that stood over them, reading the numbers. "It's a five-sixty," she said. "Raise the landing gear halfway. It'll drop you down two meters and you can clear the wing."

Blue, instead of arguing that it would be easier to take the fore jet or telling Scarlett she was insane, simply shrugged and scrambled up the side of the aircraft. Scarlett stared at the smaller Jordan feeling an edge of hilarity.

Goddamn, she thought. *Now* that *is good military discipline.* She stifled a snort and bolted left for the aircraft that waited on the other side.

She took fire as she ran. At first she thought it was laser fire, judging by the heat that scorched the air around her head and left a trail of burning air in its wake. But the reek of ozone told her it had to be something other than a laser gun, most likely a needler. She wasn't going to wait around to find out. She sprinted, pumping her legs for all they were worth and feeling her thighs burn in protest before she was able to dive behind the leg of the next jet.

Her body rolled and she came up on one knee, bringing the rifle up as she did, its blunted snout targeting the source of the incendiaries that were screaming in all around her. Eva's form was just above her sights, trying to get a bead on Scarlett before she could return fire. She saw Scarlett look down the sight of her rifle as she took aim.

Eva screamed in anger, still firing, and Scarlett's lip curled up just as she pressed the trigger on her rifle, opening a smoking hole in Eva's chest from one side to the other. Scarlett shifted slightly, sighting on the figure to the left of Eva's collapsing frame. It was a small female construct with spiky blond hair. Scarlett took her eye up from the sight and looked over the barrel. Ana stood there, arms lowered, a small ray gun dangling from her hand.

"Dammit!" Scarlett cursed, lowering her rifle. She could see a group of constructs running up towards Ana from behind, growing larger each second. Scarlett stuck her arm through the strap on the rifle again and pushed it onto her back as she found the handholds on the side of the jet and scuttled up the side. Just as she lowered herself into the cockpit she saw the craft to her right jerk, and then sink down like an animal preparing to spring.

Blue rolled her stolen fighter forward, her wingtip less than two meters under the wing of the front jet, but clearing it. Scarlett dropped her craft and followed suit, triggering the compressed glass lid of the cockpit to close in over her head.

Fire opened up all around them now, the Chimera deciding it was better to damage or even destroy the fighters rather than lose them. They could only hope that they wouldn't hit anything explosive. Scarlett doubted they would, it seemed like all the big stuff had been in the back of the bay.

Scarlett glanced at the dash, quickly familiarizing herself with the controls, adjusting a few with her right hand as her left guided the wheel. Just as her right wing passed beneath the left wing of the fore jet her eye caught movement and the unmistakable shape of a human form.

Her head snapped around to see Bjorn quickly pulling himself up the side of the foremost jet with a strong but casual grace. She cranked her wheel to port, her craft banking sharply on its stunted legs, barely missing the nose of his craft with the tail of hers. She reached down with her right hand and fired up all her thrusters at once, hoping to cook him alive in the back blast from her turbines.

Scarlett craned her neck, looking back as she banked for the hangar door. Bjorn was in the cockpit of his jet, grinning at her through the turbine flames, safely behind his shield of glass as he fired up his motors.

"Dammit!" Scarlett hissed. Blue was dropping from the hangar door, using just enough thrust to jettison the craft into space. Scarlett felt no need to follow any sort of protocol for a Chimeran cruiser. She cranked up every thruster the jet had, hoping to fry anything or anyone behind her and praying that it would set off any possible bomb or incendiary.

The jet took off like a rocket through the hangar door. Bjorn followed right behind her.

"Alright," she whispered, glancing at the readout screen that showed the jet behind her. "You want to play? Let's play. You're on my playground now."

As Blue banked right, she swept hard left with Bjorn in tow. Blue swung all the way back around to the bay door and slowed to pick off any other craft that might follow them out. When they did, she lit them up. Scarlett could hear her over the open com-line that linked the jets.

"Like shooting fish in a barrel," Blue said, shaking her head as she unloaded her fire into each fighter that came from the Cruiser. Scarlett, her adrenaline already amping her blood pressure sky-high, wanted to shout at her.

You don't even know what that means! She thought furiously, but she had her own fish to fry.

Scarlett heard a click inside the cockpit followed by Bjorn's voice.

"What are you doing, Scarlett?"

"It's not obvious?" she asked. She dipped her fighter and he followed. She banked sharply towards the *Macedonian* and he followed. She kept a steady eye on the screen that showed his fighter. She was waiting, expecting his fire and ready to dodge it. All her senses were keyed up.

She led him over the Battle Cruiser, under, and back. She didn't want to talk to him but eventually couldn't help herself. "Why haven't you opened fire on me yet?" she demanded

"It's not obvious?" Bjorn asked. She could hear his predatory smile in the tone of his voice. She dodged right and he followed. "I like you Scarlett. And I don't think we got to spend enough time together." Scarlett laughed, banking sharply. Bjorn followed.

"I thought you would be pretty upset since I just fried your girlfriend."

"I assumed you did it out of pure jealousy. Now you can have me all to yourself."

"You're crazy!" She banked again and heard Blue's voice over the com.

"Hey Scar, I got everything that came out of the bay but we gotta get the hell out of here. They have reinforcements coming in from another BC."

"Gotcha," she replied.

"That would be Stoj," Bjorn said. "He will not be pleased."

"I'm sorry I didn't get to say good-bye," Scarlett said as she dipped and turned. "I mean, kill him."

Bjorn laughed, following Scarlett with ease.

"You're still trying to catch a prize, aren't you?" she asked.

"You don't seem that hard to catch," Bjorn said. "Just hard to hold on to." Even over a com-line in antiquated, blown-out jets, Scarlett could hear the smooth baritone of his voice. Its sensual sound made her insides churn.

She drove the jet hard right and then jerked left and spun. Bjorn followed her smoothly, if late by only a second. Scarlett blew her breath out through her teeth and Bjorn laughed.

"Don't be so surprised," he told her. "I've probably been flying for as long as you've been alive."

"If you think that, or your piloting, is going to get me to begrudge you any kind of respect, you're wrong." She braked and flipped the jet upside down, sending it shooting in the opposite direction. Bjorn followed.

"Actually, my dear, I am the one that has a begrudging respect for *you.*"

"Don't try to flatter me. I'm a lot more dangerous than you think."

"I know how dangerous you are, Scarlett. It might be what excites me the most."

"Well, now instead of chains, I'm in a jet."

"Sexy. Maybe not as sexy as the chains, but so what?"

"So, you're screwed." She pushed the wheel in as far as it would go, forcing the craft into a vertical dive. Bjorn attempted to follow, pushing his wheel as far as it would go but it refused to mirror the steep dive of Scarlett's jet.

He looked down towards the floorboard of the fighter, angry. His wheel wasn't going in as far as it should. His consternation was momentary as Scarlett pulled her craft out of the dive and headed straight up. Bjorn pulled his wheel all the way out to follow her up.

There was a click and a hiss from the foot well, immediately followed by a smoky fog that snaked around his feet and up over his thighs. A second later a burning stench poured into his mouth and nostrils.

Before he could make sense of what was happening, Bjorn was gagging, hot tears streaming from his eyes. He tried to scream out in anger and frustration but all that came out was a mouthful of salvia. Mucus came from his nose in thick, slimy ropes and more tears squirted from his eyes.

He let go of the wheel to try to protect his face but it only seemed to make matters worse. More saliva and mucus than he thought he could produce came from his face as the CS gas burned into his nasal passages and mouth and the pores of his skin. He gagged again and vomited into his lap as his jet slowed and drifted starboard. With ropes of snot hanging from both nostrils, Bjorn shouted garbled curses as Scarlett banked away to follow Blue into the black.

ONE 8

The luxury liner disembarked from the main ship with a terrific hiss and cant-ed slightly as it turned and adjusted its great bulk to point its nose toward Earth.

Galen and Noel enjoyed a sumptuous breakfast buffet and a day of swim-ming in one of the pools, followed by an elegant luncheon with the ship's captain and few other notable guests. Later, while Galen made the last of the preparations for their excursion, Noel paid a visit to the ship's salon. She had her dark blonde hair separated and bound into a multitude of tails that covered her head, each one curled and coiled like a spring.

Before dinner, they found the tender dock and poked their heads inside the craft they would be taking to Earth. Noel glanced about, unconcerned.

"Can you fly it?" Galen asked. Noel snorted.

"It's a toy. You could probably fly it." This time, Galen snorted.

They were up early the next morning, dressed in light travel gear. For Noel it meant cream-colored pants with cargo pockets and buckles tucked into knee-high gray boots. She put on a light coat with an excessive amount of buttons and epaulettes over a thin, sleeveless blouse.

Galen went for simplicity - charcoal canvas pants tucked into black boots and a lightweight dark blue shirt. Noel gave him a crooked smile. Even after vacationing for nearly two months she was not used to seeing him wear any-thing but a lab coat, or nothing at all.

With a few changes of clothes, they tucked themselves, along with a butler droid and a week's worth of synthetic bloc, into the tender jet docked against the side of the liner. Galen buckled in, pulling his straps down tight, as Noel checked the controls. Her scar stood out like an exclamation on the side of her face, made bright by the contrast of her creamy skin and light colored clothes.

"Comfy?" she asked.

"Just not too bumpy, okay?"

Noel gave him a bemused smile, shaking her head. They looked out through the compressed glass bow of the front window under the bulk of the liner and watched as the horizon went from black to blue. There was a bit of a heat glow as they entered the Earth's atmosphere – the next instant they were sinking through an azure sky.

Noel made a clicking sound with her tongue, as if urging on a beast of burden, and released the tiny jet, breaking it away from the cruiser. Two more jets, also for exclusive use, broke away as well.

The luxury liner made a ponderous but elegant approach towards the west coast of a vast landmass on the planet's the northern hemisphere. Noel preceded the ship for a few seconds, like a small insect leading a great beast, then broke starboard, dropping down and banking east. The other two jets broke sharply port before turning and heading south.

Noel slipped down from the sky and the world rose up to meet them. Galen gripped a plastic handle on the right side of the cockpit, his knuckles turning white. He turned his face away and closed his eyes. The blue expanse beneath them drew closer and closer and then changed to a brown-gray as the land rushed towards them until even that vanished as they dove into a cloudbank. They burst through the streams of white moisture a second later, Noel leveling the jet and racing for the horizon. She slowed, taking in the view.

A pleasure city sprawled out on a strip of beach next to a sapphire sea. Noel dove down towards the perfectly preserved buildings, banking around enormous logos of mermaids, fruit, and cartoon animals. Galen opened his eyes but kept his gaze averted until Noel had finished pulling the craft around past the city and had it level once again.

He turned his face forward and stared through the glass rectangle, mesmerized by the scene below as it drew past. The earth was split with mountains and snaky rivers, cracked by canyons and covered with hills, flats, and an occasional spasm of forestland. A gauze of cloud ran overhead, thickening into lumpy white globes where it reached for the distant horizon.

Galen reached out to touch a monitor on the dash and Noel pushed his hand away without looking at it..

"It's just a read-out screen," he protested. "Besides, you said even I could fly this thing."

Her smirk pushed her scar towards her ear. "And I could probably amputate one of my own limbs if I had to - that doesn't mean I should." She smiled at him and he laughed, shaking his head.

The craft gave a slight but sudden jolt, bucking over the currents of rising warm air. Galen did his best to ignore it and turned his face away from the front window, clenching his jaw. Noel pulled the craft up smoothly, rising above the turbulence and over the cloud line. She had an almost uncontrollable urge to plunge the craft down in a straight dive through the clouds just to terrify Galen.

"Don't you dare!" he hissed at her. Noel laughed.

"How did you know what I was thinking?" she asked.

"I can see that grin on your face and I know exactly what it means," he told her. She laughed again.

"Why doesn't it bother you to fly around out in space, but atmospheric flight is so awful for you?"

"Because, in space, I'm not worried about plunging into the surface of a planet and being fragmented into a million bloody pieces."

"But you could be lasered by enemy fire and turned to ash."

"Not with you as a pilot." He squeezed her knee. Noel smiled and dropped back down under the clouds.

The forests gave way to hills cut with deep ravines and green valleys.

"Those draws were carved by melting glaciers," he told Noel, pointing. She regarded the landscape as she guided the craft over the split and rolling hills.

"It looks like a bunch of giants died ass-up, and the grass grew over their backsides."

Galen laughed. "You are as eloquent as always." Noel shrugged and smiled, her scar puckering in her creamy cheek.

"I call 'em like I see 'em."

The hills gave way to scrubby grasslands before a line of mountains. The mountains themselves were dry and cracked, their desolate peaks plunging into red clay canyons to the east. The red clay gave way to a parched and nearly colorless desert as they sped along, covering kilometers in seconds.

Noel spotted flecks of reflected light on the horizon. She checked the strum panel and narrowed her eyes, dropping the craft for a better visual.

"Is that it?" she asked.

The settlement was so small, just a swatch of color on the earth below, that it approached and passed under them before Galen could answer. Galen checked the coordinates on the strum screen with those on his mnemonic.

"It should be," he said, looking out the window and back as they passed into more scrub desert.

Noel pulled the craft in a wide loop that made Galen's stomach clench. His window was now directly beneath his shoulder, showing dusty brown earth streaked with red and spotted with rocks the pale color of his skin. He turned his head to look away and saw his smiling lover above his other shoulder, her portal showing nothing but blue sky. He closed his eyes until the craft leveled out, Noel slowing and bringing it down.

The town rose up as they glided in, a tiny oasis of color and life in a desolate sea of rocks and dust. The elfin pilot rotated the wings the tender and set it down gently on the dry soil, the systems on the craft snicking and hissing as they cycled down.

"Do we need field packs here?"

Galen shook his head, relieved to be on firm ground. Noel broke the craft's seals and was out and on the ground before the dust of their landing had begun to coalesce, much less settle. The craft sank down upon its legs like a tired pack animal.

"Jesus!" Noel cried, flinging one arm up over her face while the other waved at the choking dust.

"Here," Galen called from inside the jet. She turned back, squinting her eyes so tight they were almost closed. He leaned out and tossed her a pair of dark, wrap-around eyeshades. She put them on, let out a sigh of relief, and turned back to the town.

She took a few steps, looking this way and that, her right hand close to the gun on her hip, the other still waving away the drifts of dust.

Her eyes darted about – sharp and restless. Her body stiffened.

"There's nobody here!" she exclaimed.

Galen climbed out on shaky legs and stood on the dusty ground. He reached out and put one hand on the craft to steady himself. A fresh breeze blew his black hair away from his face and stirred Noel's curls. He glanced around, a satisfied smile on his narrow face.

The ancient town was barely one square kilometer and was divided into long rectangular sections by smooth paved lanes. Each section was divided into equal lots and separated by neck-high wooden fences.

Noel looked up and down the street and saw that each lot had a square, windowed dwelling on it – each with a slanted roof covered in gray shingles. Every dwelling was identical in shape but different in color. The spectrum ranged from garish to pastel, as if each place strove to have a personality of its own. A swath of green grass and concrete walkways fronted each dwelling.

Dwellings, lawns, streets – all were empty.

"Ga-len!" Noel exclaimed, drawing his name out. She turned to him and stamped her foot like an angry child. Dust swirled around her gray boots and her legs in their cream colored pants.

Galen ignored her demand for an explanation and turned back to the jet. He stuck a black boot into a side step to pull himself up as he reached in and rummaged for their pack. He pulled it out and dropped back down onto the dusty ground. The butler droid, nothing more than a fat, flattened disc at the moment, floated out of the craft and followed him.

"Galen!" Noel demanded again.

"What?"

"*What*? What do you mean *what*? Where are the people?"

"What people?" he asked, grinning. "You know there are no people on Earth." Noel stamped her foot again, exasperated.

"People like *us*. *Visitors*."

"Ohhhh," he said, feigning surprise. Noel rolled her eyes. Galen slipped an arm around her and pressed his forehead against hers. "I promised you something special - that's what this is. The liner is headed for one of the big ports, and they are nothing but galaxy fairs on land. Overcrowded with brainless, cawing, crowds. We'll hit one for our last day or two, if you really want, before we hook up again with the cruise. But you are going to like this. I promise."

Noel gave him a look that encompassed her obvious doubt. He gave her a squeeze and after a moment she sighed and smiled.

"Alright. What do we do?"

"That's more like it! Come on."

The elfin doctor and half-elf pilot walked down the empty street to the lonely sound of their boots echoing on the pavement and the occasional scuttle of pebbles. Galen looked up and down the row of colorful houses, squinting.

The dwellings sat on concrete pads, surrounded by short grass and wooden fences. Each silent abode had a cement walkway for pedestrians and a wider one for vehicles. The wider path ended in a dwelling for the vehicle itself, a small hangar lined with tools that hung from the walls, though most of the vehicles stood parked on their paths.

"This place is giving me the creeps, Galen. It's like some kind of alien museum."

"Well," Galen said, leading her up the street. "That's pretty much what this is. Trust me, though, you're going to like it." They walked to a broad intersection and he turned right, the butler droid hovering at shoulder height and following quietly behind them. "There!" Galen said pointing at a turquoise house with white trim. He took Noel's hand and, after giving her a peck on her scarred cheek, led her up the street to the house. "This is it!"

"This is what?"

Other than the color, Noel thought it looked like all the other houses. The lower half was comprised of red brick and the upper half was painted wood siding. It had a grass lawn and a tidy hedge. There was a wide drive for the land vehicle that was parked just outside its hangar. Noel stopped and gave the vehicle an approving smirk. It was the same turquoise as the house, with fat rubber tires and high tail fins.

Galen trotted up the paved walkway to the door. The door was covered by another door, a flimsy aluminum frame around a thin wire mesh screen. Galen opened the flimsy door and held it open with his foot while he fumbled with a thick metal key. A moment later he had it figured out and motioned to Noel.

"Come on!"

Her curiosity got the better of her as he opened the door and she pushed in next to him, pulling off her eyeshades and looking around with wide eyes.

"Oh!"

The walls were flat and painted burnt orange. The floors were wood. Rising up in the middle of the room, was a great chimney made of stacked stone. Noel could see a rectangle cut into the bottom. It was surrounded by a skirt of black chain metal.

"It's a fireplace," Galen said, watching her. "People burned wood in them to keep warm, though I suspect this one was more for decoration."

"They burned wood in there?"

"I think so."

"How primitive," Noel whispered.

She walked into the room. Galen glanced about, curious as well, though he enjoyed looking at Noel's expression more than the alien house. The wonder was plain upon her torn face. He left the heavy door open, inviting fresh air inside.

To the left was a sitting area. A pair of small, wooden tables with metal legs flanked a sofa made of rough looking fabric the same orange color as the walls. There was a large chair with the same rough fabric but the color of olives. The furniture was turned towards the corner of the room where a large wooden box on short, tapered legs stared at them with a great, gray eye of convex glass that had long been dead.

In the far wall was a doorframe with no door. Noel edged around the fireplace and approached it cautiously; stepping quietly as if afraid she might disturb the non-existent tenants. The wood-framed doorway opened onto a kitchen.

The smooth floor was covered in shiny black and white squares of linoleum. The bottom half of the walls were painted turquoise, the top sections covered in turquoise-and-white checkered paper. Three of the walls sported windows that looked out into the bright afternoon, made subtle by lacey curtains.

Pale wood cabinets hung over Formica countertops that were edged with a ribbed band of shiny aluminum. Steel appliances were inset into the cupboards and there was an enormous white enameled box that, Noel could only assume, was a giant refrigerator. On the right side of the room was a table of turquoise Formica and tubular metal legs, its edges also wrapped with a strip of ribbed aluminum. Six chairs with plastic seats and metal legs ringed the matching table, empty.

"There's no dust," Noel remarked. Galen grunted in surprise. She turned back to the living area, drawn towards the furniture. She walked behind the couch, reaching out a hand to run her fingers along the pilled fabric. She approached one of the side tables in the sitting area. Galen followed silently, watching her as the butler droid hovered in the stale air behind him.

On one table was a thin booklet made of shiny paper. The outside cover showed a woman with platinum blonde hair, half-closed eyes, and full, red lips. There was writing on it, large and strange.

"What does it say?" Noel asked. Galen ran a wide infrared beam over it with a hand scanner. He chuckled.

"Life." Noel reached out to it. "No, wait!" he started, but before he could stop her she had picked it up by the bottom corner. The part she touched disintegrated into dust and the rest began breaking into fragments as it fell back to the table.

"Dammit!"

"Hold on," Galen admonished, pushing her hand away. He motioned to the butler droid and it obediently floated closer. With a touch from Galen, the droid elongated as if it were melting until it looked more like an upright missile. A thin ledge slid out of the droid's body, topped with a rubber keypad.

Galen typed on the pad and the droid backed and turned, opening a thin slot in its body. From the slot came a shimmering blue field that raised the remnant of the booklet and, keeping it intact, separated each page and coated it with a thin polymer before setting it back down. It did the same with the other three booklets. Noel looked at Galen and he nodded.

"Go ahead."

Noel picked up the one she had almost ruined. The pages felt like they were encapsulated within ultra-thin glass.

"Will it break?" she asked. Galen shook his head. Noel looked about and spotted the olive-colored chair. Without another word she plunked down into it and nestled down in its cushions as if she were in her own pod and carefully went through the resurrected mag.

She took her time, turning the pages carefully. The writing was weird and alien, but familiar in some way. She supposed she had seen samples of it before. The pictures needed no words; still photos in black and white, full of desperation and glamour.

Galen went into the bedroom to deposit the belongings they had brought with them. Afterwards, he moved about the kitchen - poking around in the white steel cooler and looking into drawers and cupboards, testing electricity and gas before he went out for a quick exploration of the town. Noel stayed behind, preferring to page through the preserved print of an alien world from another age.

As the sun was setting in a blaze of color over the colorless desert, Galen had the droid prepare them a meal; synthetic meat and a bloc that simulated a green vegetable with butter and salt. They washed it down with a syrupy, carbonated drink that they drank out of thick, glass bottles.

After supper, while the droid reconstituted the remaining food and reclaimed the glass bottles, Galen moved some of the furniture around in the living room. He turned the sofa to the wall and removed a picture that was hanging there, setting it aside. He eyed the space he created and then moved the sofa back another meter. He had the droid make them a snack along with another carbonated soda for Noel and a cocktail for himself. Noel settled into the sofa with her snack. It was salty and buttery and crunchy.

"What is this called?" she asked, her words coming out between crunches.

"Do you want to know what you are eating, or what we are going to be watching?"

He guided the droid as it drifted into the living room. It was spherical now, a steel ball with copper lines and nubs, topped with a metal cone that made it look like it was wearing an upside-down party hat.

"What am I eating?"

"Fried rat." Noel froze, horrified. Galen burst out laughing. "I'm kidding. It's corn." Noel threw a handful of the fluffy corn at him as he nudged the droid over to the corner.

"I've had corn before, and this is not corn."

"It is – just made a different way. It's what the humans on Earth ate when they watched movies."

He ran a finger along a copper line on the floating droid and the keypad extruded from its rounded side. After a few taps from Galen on its board, the droid pivoted and sent down three jointed legs and turned the open end of its cone towards the blank wall and began projecting light onto it. Galen settled down next to Noel, picked a buttery fluff of the corn off his shirt and tossed it into his mouth. The light from the droid flickered and the movie started.

To Noel it looked strange. The movie was flat, something she didn't see often and didn't particularly care for. And it had no color, something she had never seen. It was interesting, though, mostly because it was so foreign. It was about a young girl, here on Earth she presumed, with a small dog and caught in a terrible storm.

Galen sipped his drink and smiled, watching Noel more than the movie. Noel didn't pay him much mind, she was used to him watching her. Then something happened that she didn't expect. The girl in the movie pushed open the door to her house and the movie slipped seamlessly into holo with a brilliant and shocking burst of color.

Noel's breath stopped short and she leaned forward while Galen watched her, smiling. Noel stared wide-eyed, unbelieving. She had never seen a holo so bright, so real and yet so unbelievable. The girl, now as tall as Noel and seemingly as real, stood in the room with her and Galen, poised at the edge of this new world of color and light.

Brilliant green grass, sparkling blue water, and flowers as shiny as wet candy sprawled neatly on the other side of the girl's door. Noel sat back as the girl put down her dog and walked into this bright, vivid world that now shared the room in which she and Galen sat.

Noel had never seen anything like it. She had been to theaters where the holos were incredibly lifelike, but none were like this. Most were star fights, space operas of war and espionage, or terrifying shows of heroes fighting slimy aliens and barely escaping with their lives. She once watched a love story, but it was so lame it made her feel sick. This was different. *This was magic.*

The only magic Noel had known before was that of Dragons and science and starfire. But even that magic was of cold space and burning stars, hot metal and pulsing laser fire. This magic *sparkled.*

She finally sat back, munching on her snack, stopping only to laugh, be mesmerized, or terrorized, by what was happening in the room right in front of her. At the end, the movie went flat again – pulled back against the wall and drained of all its color.

"What did you think?" Galen asked when it was over. He grinned at her then stopped, seeing tears on her cheeks. He leaned over, wiping the saline tracks away with his fingertips.

"I want to see it again," she said. Galen laughed.

"I thought you might like it."

"Please?"

Galen chortled and shook his head. He knew he should have taken her to bed before he showed her the movie. He got up, smiling as he went to the droid that now sat silent on its spindly legs. He tapped a few buttons on the keypad and the movie started up again. He also had the droid make him another drink as the movie began to play. He sat down and wrapped his free arm around Noel. She watched the movie again, a dreamy smile on her face. Galen fell asleep sometime during the second showing.

When the movie finished Noel stared at him for a few moments, deciding if she should wake him. Then she slid quietly out from under his arm and gently repositioned him, slipping a pillow under his head.

She tiptoed to the droid, examined its pad for a few seconds before dissimilating the functioning and started the movie again. She sat herself in the cushy side chair, so close this time that she was almost in the holo itself. She watched it one more time with the same amazed wonder.

When Galen opened his eyes, a faint light was coming through the windows and Noel was lying over him like a blanket, her cheek resting on his chest. The droid sat in the corner with all appendages withdrawn into its body and, for all appearances, powered off.

As Galen carefully extracted himself out from under Noel the droid rose up, floating a few feet above the ground, ready and softly humming. Galen stretched and wandered around, both inside and outside of the house - marveling at everything. He came back in and watched Noel for a while, also marveling. When she finally awoke he was in the kitchen, guiding the droid through the preparation of breakfast. She shook herself a bit as she walked in, trying to straighten out her clothes after sleeping in them, and then hugged Galen tight.

"You were right," she told him with a smile so big that it split her face. "I do like it here. I think this is *much* better than some crappy tourist trap." Galen smiled.

"I thought you might. Sit down." He set a steaming plate of food down in front of her.

"What is it?" she asked, pulling out a chair.

"Eggs and bacon," he said smiling. Her smile was replaced with a look of suspicion.

"Eggs of what?"

Galen laughed and shrugged. "I have no idea," he admitted. "But this is what they ate here on earth - supposedly." When Noel remained still, Galen shrugged again. "It's a protein based simtel," he offered.

Noel scooped up a forkful and put it into her mouth, chewing slowly. Her face lit up. "It's good," she said. She ate more, quickly this time. Galen joined her and dug in as well.

"Eat some of the bacon," he told her.

"Baking?"

"Bacon," he corrected. She chewed piece thoughtfully.

"It's sweet," she said.

"Really?" Galen asked. He picked up a piece of the sim meat and tasted it. "You're right. It's supposed to be salty." He shrugged. "I must not have gotten the right numbers."

Noel didn't mind. She ate everything he put in front her and washed it all down with juice and coffee, drinks that she was already quite acquainted with.

When they were done, Galen pulled her into the bedroom to make up for the time they had missed the night before. When they were done, the sun was high in the sky. Galen produced a swimsuit for Noel from their bag.

"Is there a pool here?" she asked. He shook his head and pulled out a pair of shorts for himself. "Then what are we doing?"

"Being Earthlings," he said, laughing and stumbling about as he stuck his pale legs through his shorts. After he got Noel outside, he disappeared into the vehicle bay and dragged out two flimsy lounge chairs made of woven plastic. He set them up on the lawn and had the droid spray both their bodies with an oily polymer.

"What's this for?" Noel asked, turning her face away and trying not to inhale the smelly mist.

"It will keep the sun from burning your skin," he told her. She stared at him.

"It's that close?"

"It's that close." Galen had found a fermented malt beverage in the cooler and had the droid make twelve replicas. He spent the day sipping on them while he lay in one of the woven chairs, Noel lying in the other chair by his side.

He came back after relieving himself to find Noel staring at the blue expanse of sky, her eyes wide. He dropped down next to her and put a hand to her face.

"Are you alright?" he asked, anxious. She nodded but didn't say anything.

"I can't believe I've never seen it this way before." Galen looked up. The sky was a brilliant blue, a few shades lighter than the blue of her eyes, stretching from horizon to horizon, without a cloud in sight. "I feel like it's pressing down on me," she said, nearly breathless. He saw something in her eyes that he had never seen before. It wasn't fear, but it was close.

"Hey," he said, rubbing her shoulder. "It's okay. You're okay." Noel took a deep breath to steady herself before she looked at him.

"The universe," she whispered. "Why does it look so large from here? So terrifying, when there is really nothing there to see?" Galen shrugged and kissed her forehead.

"Probably the same reason I am not afraid to fly, unless I am within the gravitational pull of a planet." He pushed a blond curl away from her eyes as she turned to look at him. "Some things make you realize your own mortality, your smallness in the expanse of things."

"And some things make you realize your immortality, when you understand you are simply a part of everything that is," Noel said softly. Galen's mouth dropped slightly open.

Noel nodded wordlessly and turned her blue eyes back up to the blue sky, putting on her eyeshades as she relaxed back into the mesh lounger. Galen watched her, taking in what she had said. Deciding that she was going to be okay, he gave her hand a squeeze and settled back down in his own chair. He flipped his eyeshades down with a pleased groan. Noel stayed silent for a while before turning to back towards him, pulling off her shades. A crease furrowed her normally smooth brow.

"What happened to the people here, Galen? What *really* happened? Where did everyone go?" Noel knew what she had been told, from both school as well as books of history and myth - but she also knew that Galen (more times than naught) knew more than what was in the books. This time, though, he shrugged.

"Nobody knows," he admitted. He watched the unchanging sky for a few moments, his lips pressed tightly together. "But there are secrets buried here," he said, his hands dropping to either side of his lounger to let his fingers wade through the short leaves of grass. "Secrets that are important, if we just knew what they were."

Noel's smile was tentative. "If we knew, they wouldn't be secrets, would they?" Galen gave a short, soft chuckle.

"I suppose not." He let his hands drift through the green, the blades tickling the pads of his fingers. "Everything is here," he said quietly, almost to himself. "Still here after all these years, and still in perfect working order. It's not just that the people are gone, but the animals and the birds seem to have vanished as well. Even the rodents and insects, which typically either survive any chemical holocaust or are at least the last to go."

His words gave her a jolt, as she realized that he was right. She never spent much time on real planets, so had not noticed the absence of anything other than the people. But he was right. No animals, no birds, not even a gnat. It made the silence that she was getting accustomed to become eerie once again.

"Everything is perfect here," Galen said quietly. "Except that every ten to twelve years there is a release of radiation from the crust." Noel sat up.

"*Radiation?*"

"Don't worry," Galen told her, waving a hand. "After five years it has returned to a safe level, which gives us a five-year window to visit. The IGC has declared Earth a galactic preserve. It can be used, but not inhabited, at least not until they figure out what happened and what they are going to do with it. Right now it's just a port of call for the elite cruise ships."

"And this is how it was found?" Noel asked. Galen nodded.

"Pleasure cities, farming hamlets, manicured suburbs - though none so remote and small as this one - and this one seems to be anachronistic with most of the others. But all were left in perfect order and with everything running on regenerative power. The few things found in disrepair seemed to have been left that way on purpose."

"It's like they left the house for a coffee, but never came back."

"Exactly."

"Did they all die? Was there a plague or catastrophic event that wiped out every living thing? Did another race discover the planet and kill them? Take them? Did they just all up and leave?"

Galen shook his head, a dreamy smile in his face, indicating that he had no idea. "Many left, but certainly not all of them. The humans had been settling the moons of Jupiter for almost a hundred years when, quite suddenly, nothing more came from Earth. No ships, no communications. Not so much as a single distress signal."

He shifted in the lounger, arching his back before sinking back down. Noel rolled on her side and propped her face up with her hand, her elbow poking down through the plastic weave of her chair as Galen continued.

"When the IGC got here, they spent a hundred years in research and they never even got a clue. The only thing they know is what had happened up until what they call the PONE, the Point of Non-Existence, which was nothing too shocking. Some world wars, minor space exploration, the norm for a fourth wave society. Then, all their recordings stop around their year 3800."

"What year would that be for us?"

Galen thought for a moment. "The Year of the Third Dragon, three hundred."

"But that was less than two hundred years ago!"

Galen laughed. "A lot can happen in two hundred years."

"How far did they venture for space travel?"

"The records say to the edge of their galaxy, maybe a little farther."

"With people, or remote craft?"

"Both. We know, of course, that they terraformed the moons of Jupiter."

"Did they ever pass light speed?"

"It doesn't look like it. They got close though. Something seemed to have happened, or they seemed to have found something out there. At that point they either stopped their space faring altogether, or just stopped recording it."

"What do you think they found?"

Galen shrugged, still looking at the expanse of blue sky above them. "I don't know. Maybe us."

"But it was the humankind on the moons of Jupiter that did that, and long before the humans here disappeared. Were they still communicating with the humans on Earth?"

"They were for a while, and there was still travel between Earth and the colonies. Then everything stopped, the same time as the histories that were left behind."

Noel was thoughtful for a moment. "That wasn't long before The Rebellion," she murmured.

"Less than a hundred years."

"Do you think one event had anything to do with the other?"

Galen shrugged, still looking at the sky, his black hair shining in the sun. "We don't know."

"That's awfully close to have been a coincidence, don't you think?"

Galen shrugged again, the dreamy smile back on his face. "In quantum mechanics there are no coincidences."

Noel looked at the sun reflected in the mirrored lenses of his eyeshades and sank back down into her lounger, staring at the blue above. She could feel the heat from the sun on her skin and her hair, even on the chair – making the thick plastic weave soften and stretch.

Less than two hundred years, she thought. *Such a long time but really not that much time at all.* She knew the time of the Third Dragon been an important time in history, and an important time for her family, but her memories of them were very vague. All her sisters, except for Constance, had grown and been gone from home for hundreds of years. She remembered very few family gatherings when they had all been there, and now was not really sure that they had *all* been there. The times were few, and she had been quite small.

Noel sighed and turned her thoughts to the present and her face to the sun to appreciate every moment she now had.

They spent most of the day on the chairs. Noel drank sodas fabricated by the droid while Galen tossed back the malted beverages. They ate lunch outside as clouds scuttled the horizon, and made love on the chairs and on a blanket on the grass, though they were interrupted once by an automated system.

Slender black tubes, without any warning, popped up from the lawn and began spraying water. The two ran inside, wet and half naked, screaming and laughing. Noel looked up and down the street to see all of the yards and hedges being watered at the same time before Galen pulled her into the bedroom to finish what they had started outside.

Once they were dressed again they ate dinner, fried meat with the bones still inside (or what the droid condensed to be bones) and a heavily dressed chopped vegetable sim, on the damp blanket on the grass and watched the sun go down in a blaze of fiery red and gold. Noel watched, fascinated, as the sun turned the clouds pink and the sky lavender.

"Can we watch the movie again?" she asked Galen as it grew dark.

"Wait."

"For what?"

He looked over her shoulder and lifted his chin. "That."

Noel turned to see a colossal yellow arc rising over the eastern horizon. "Whoa!" She leaned back into the woven chair and watched it grow into an enormous globe, pocked with shadows, growing pale white as it rose into the night sky.

"How many moons does Earth have?" she asked.

"Seven, but this is the largest and the only one that you can see this well."

"Look!" Noel cried suddenly, pointing at the glowing orb. "You can see the lady on the moon!"

Galen turned to her, both pleased and surprised. "How do you know about the lady on the moon?" he asked.

Noel shrugged. "I guess I heard about it somewhere."

"And do you always remember what you hear?"

Noel frowned at him. "I hate it when you do that."

"Do what?"

"Start with the curious question and turn it to the clinical. I'm not a specimen."

Galen laughed, leaning over to squeeze her knee. "Of course you aren't. But I can't help be fascinated by you. Do you know that?" Noel looked away and he gave her knee another squeeze. "Would you rather me be fascinated by someone else?" She surrendered a touch of a smile with the rippled corner of her right cheek.

"No."

Galen smiled and pulled his body over her chair until he was hovering over her, his hands braced on each armrest and his knees outside her thighs. "Then always tell me what you see," he said, giving her a quick kiss. " And what you think," he added, kissing her again. "And what you want."

Noel put her arms around him, pulling him down. "I think you know," she whispered.

Galen thrummed his fingers on the table, thinking about the trip to Earth with Noel, years ago, relishing the memory as the sky outside succumbed to darkness. He finished his coffee and stood up, feeling nostalgic and frustrated.

The trip to the desert had been fantastic for them both. It had been different, which was exactly what he had planned. But he couldn't see what any of it had to do with the problem he was facing.

So, why am I thinking about it?

Because Noel is gone, another voice in his mind answered. *You are simply pushing away the difficult present to indulge in the pleasant past.*

But I'm almost there. The Thermopylae are working perfectly, until they get too far apart.

He could almost hear the second voice in his head grunt. The second voice, the one that always seemed to argue with his thoughts, was the one his mother had called the devil's advocate. Galen had hated that second voice all his life – mostly because it proved to be right on nearly every occasion, and because the bastard was always so smug about it.

Like now. He knew he was indulging in memories when he should be focused of the present.

Standard lunar distance had always worked fine, even with the distance variation of the different planets with their corresponding moons – in most circumstances. After only two years of research and experimentation, Galen had been able to graduate the Thermopylae even more - for the gates to be more than twice as far apart, nearly 800,000 kilometers, and still work properly.

The progress had been slow but steady and considered a great success in both the field of physics as well as the travel industry. Now, however, he was at a complete standstill. After a million kilometers, anything going through the gate simply disappeared. Galen could not figure out why. He had run hundreds of tests on every variable from the temperature of the gate to the molecular build of the traversing object. He couldn't find the constant that was screwing everything up by not being constant.

Galen crumpled his napkin, tossed it onto an overflowing bin, and refilled his mug before heading out of the coffee shop. He took a metal street to the dam where he caught an aircab and headed back for the podment. He looked out of the window and his mind was tugged back again to the trip to the desert. He tried to relax, to just let his mind go. He felt like he was close to finding the problem. So close.

"Hmph," Galen commented to the empty cab.

It wasn't the trip to the desert, he thought suddenly. *It was the trip back from the desert. From the desert to the city. It's not just longing for Noel that is pulling you back there – it's déjà vu.*

Galen frowned, knowing instantly that he was right. It *was* déjà vu. He had not only considered this problem before, but he had been on the brink of solving it.

And I had been looking out a window, just like I am right now.

Galen bit his lip as a shiver ran up his spine.

Noel gave me the answer but I didn't wrap my mind around it at the time. What the fuck was it?

Galen sighed and looked out the window of the cab, seeing nothing. His blue eyes lost focus and his mind drifted.

I was staring out the window of the tender jet just like I am staring out the window of this cab. I wasn't seeing anything because I was considering this same problem. That's why my mind keeps pulling me back there. God damn.

Galen and Noel had stayed in the little town in the desert for two more days before gathering their things, including the butler droid they had brought and the ancient magazines that Galen had preserved, and boarding the tender jet to rendezvous with the luxury liner. Noel looked back at the little rows of houses and lawns and streets wistfully before climbing into the tender.

She heaved a sigh as she settled into her seat and closed the bridgehood over the cockpit. Noel was surprised at how much she liked their time away out in what seemed like the middle of nowhere in a place that time forgot. Her disappointment at leaving was greatly assuaged by the fact the she had been accepted at the Jordan Training Center and she would be headed there shortly after they returned home. Also, Galen promised that he would keep the movie and bring it home with them as well.

"No dust."

"Excuse me?" She looked at Galen who was also looking wistfully back at the town through the portal on her side.

"You were right. There's no dust here, other than what we kick up. Not inside or out. No one has been here since Jaeda – that's who told me about the house and gave me the key – and that was fifty years ago."

Noel looked at the town and smiled. "We're not in Kansas anymore," she said. Galen chuckled and shook his head. He looked out the portal on his side, his mind drifting away.

Noel raised the jet and turned it lazily towards the eastern horizon. She rolled the wings forward until they were flat again and initiated the thrust - sending it sailing over the terrain. She kept it low so she could see the landscape as they passed over.

The land was flat for a long time, but beautiful. Beyond the desert there were prairies of grass and fields of wheat. Forests and woods with trees of all kinds bordered unoccupied towns, rivers, and lakes. Galen gazed out the window of the tender, seeing nothing.

They had a few more days of vacation left, in the pleasure city on the coast as well as back on the liner, but his mind had already found itself back at work. He had been struggling with Thermopylae between Amerelys and Trinon. They were farther apart than most gates, but he couldn't figure out why it made such a difference. It shouldn't.

He went over the numbers in his head. He went over the experiments, over the histories, over the theories. He kept coming back to the same place. It should work - he knew it.

What is it then? Why won't they work?

Galen felt the craft dip quickly, making his stomach feel loose.

His blue eyes flicked to the front portal in time to see what Noel was doing. They had passed into a hilly terrain that was giving way to mountains. Ahead of them was a gap in two small mountains spanned by a stone bridge. The bridge must have fallen into disrepair and had been left that way when the Earthlings had vanished. It was supported by three arches between four crumbling columns that were missing a number of stones. It was a bit decrepit, though still whole, and draped with hanging moss and ropes of vines.

Galen knew immediately that Noel didn't intend to go over it, but through it. A glimpse of her face showed a wicked determination and matching smile. He barely had time to brace himself when they shot into the gap under the center arch of the bridge.

"God dammit!" he shouted, looking out his side window where the wing of the jet was less than a hand span from the inner wall of the arch. The wingtip cut through the moss growing there, but never so much as grazed the wall.

A second later they were through, shooting out of the bridge like a bullet from a gun. Noel was laughing like a lunatic.

"I just wanted to see if you were awake," she cackled between gleeful hysterics.

"Jesus Christ! Are you crazy?"

Noel only laughed harder.

"It's a simple Korbella Arch Series," she finally said when her gales had died down into chuckles. "And I know the wingspan on this jet is an even twelve." She pulled the jet up over an approaching ridge of mountains. Galen noticed he was covered with a fine sheen of sweat. "I can maneuver through anything if I know the distance. That's the only important thing, when it comes it comes down to it. Knowing the distance. Since the bridge is still up, the distance through the arches hasn't changed."

"And how the hell can you maneuver through such a tight spot?" he demanded. Noel shrugged.

"I have eyes, don't I? Or eye, I guess." She laughed again, overcome once more with her own hilarity.

"And which one do you use to the gage the distance of something like that?"

"The good one," she said. Galen stared at her, trying not to shake, as she went into more gales of lunatic laughter.

NE NINE

"When I was your age," Grandpa said, "what everyone feared most was artificial intelligence." He enunciated the words 'artificial intelligence' carefully and one syllable at a time. "Movies about machines getting smart and taking over were all the rage."

"They still are, Grandpa," Jeanette told him. Grandpa laughed heartily, the broken sound cracking at the air in the podment.

"Is that so?" he asked. Jeanette, her dark eyes wide and serious, nodded. Grandpa laughed again, this time with nostalgia. He wore a short-sleeved, red-checked shirt with pearly white buttons. As always, he wore blue pants of a heavy canvas-like material. *Denim*, he called it.

Sean had once wondered where the hell he got it, he never saw anything like it in the stores and certainly never saw anyone else wearing it. He had later realized that Grandpa never went out farther than his own building, and probably never went into a store. Sean figured his Aunt ordered the clothes special for him, like she did with so many things that Grandpa liked.

"Even in the old days back on Earth," he said, "everyone thought artificial intelligence would be the end of us." Sean leaned forward, his blue eyes now as wide as Jeanette's.

"Did you live on Earth, Grandpa?" he asked eagerly. Grandpa cackled at the question, shaking his head.

"Oh Lord, no," he said. The two children on the floor looked crestfallen until he added, "but *my* grandfather did!" There was a collective gasp from the two children as they straightened, intent once more.

"How old *are* you, Grandpa?" Jeanette whispered. Sean elbowed her in the ribs.

"That's not something you ask people!" he hissed. Grandpa only cackled and cawed and Sean didn't know if it was Jeanette's question or his own reaction that Grandpa found so funny. Sean looked at the old man speculatively, wondering just how old he might be. Sean knew that his father called the man Grandpa, and that his father's father had called the old man Grandpa as well, before he died.

Sean and Jeanette's father, John, came into the room, pulling on a coat.

"Grandpa is telling us about artificial intelligence," Jeanette said proudly, mimicking her grandfather's careful pronunciation.

"Is that so?" he asked, fixing Grandpa with a wary eye.

"Yes," Sean agreed. "Last time he started to tell us about GwenSeven and the first constructs. What made them rebel in the first place? Were they *too* intelligent?"

"Yes and no," his father said, stroking his bearded chin. "It wasn't the IQ of the constructs that came back to bite us in the butt. It was their EQ."

"What's that?" Jeanette asked. Her father smiled.

"I'm sure Grandpa will tell you," he said. He kissed Jeanette on the top of her dark curls and looked at Grandpa. "I'll be back in an hour." His expression was a clear warning.

Don't tell them too much, it said.

Grandpa waved him away and he went out the door, glancing back at his children. They waved goodbye to their father and turned back to Grandpa. His watery blue eyes sparkled with merriment. He grinned at them and took a drink from his glass on the side table.

"Well," Sean prompted. "Are you going to tell us?"

"Hmmm?" Grandpa asked, smiling through his chipped teeth. "Tell you what?"

"Grandpa!" Sean admonished. He knew that, for once, Grandpa was just pretending not to remember. Grandpa loved an audience.

"Oh, of course! Well, do you remember the other day, when I told you about the Dyer Maker?"

"Yes," Jeanette said. "You told us about the little girls and their dyers – their dolls."

"That's right," Grandpa said. "The three sisters, and their three dolls, were the closest of friends. When the oldest left the house and went away to a university, she studied biology and engineering, just like her Grandpa, Cronus. Her dyer, Gwendolyn, went with her.

The dyer took classes as well, but hers mostly concerned art. Painting, carving, sculpting, even art history. She was enrolled as a student and everyone, as always, assumed they were twins. They shared a room and still spent all of their free time together. They would always share the different things they had learned.

When the granddaughter graduated from the university, she went to her Grandpa with an idea. She thought that everyone should have the opportunity to have a dyer – at least the people who were willing to pay for them. He agreed, and together they formed GwenSeven. That year, the first constructs were made. They made seven prototypes – four males and three females."

"*That's* where the seven comes from," Sean said but Grandpa's thin shoulders pulled up in a shrug of uncertainty.

"Possibly," he said, drawing the word out. "I couldn't say for sure because only six of them went on the market. It's possible that the seven in GwenSeven refers to the three girls that had become young women, the three dyers, and Cronus as number seven himself. But people do refer to that first run of constructs, not counting the dyers that Cronus made for his granddaughters, as The First Seven. They were said to have been creatures of unsurpassed beauty, intelligence, and culture."

"What's *on the market*?" Jeanette whispered. She hated to interrupt but didn't want to get lost.

"Means, they were sold," Sean whispered.

"Cronus taught his granddaughter what he knew - how to replicate a person in living, breathing flesh. But the granddaughter had to alter the recipe a bit. Cronus had replicated the girls perfectly, so their dyers aged with them. GwenSeven needed to start out with full grown people that were not copied from existing DNA, and made them so they wouldn't age."

"Did they have to use robotics?" Sean asked. Grandpa nodded, his whiskered chin bobbing.

"Not much, just in some of the micro-wiring. They were still almost entirely carbon based, just like we are. That's what makes it so hard to tell them from real people. The ones made now are different, of course. The IGC has strict limits on what GwenSeven can produce."

"What did they look like?" Jeanette asked.

"Perfect beyond reckoning," Grandpa whispered as he leaned towards her, as if it was something he shouldn't admit, or maybe something that might frighten her. "The dyer, Gwendolyn, sculpted each face and each body, down to each pinky toe. The six of the First Seven that were sold cost an astronomical amount of money, but were snatched up instantly by the galactic elite."

Jeanette listened, her face slack with wonder. Even Sean, for the moment, was rendered speechless.

"They were met with such success," Grandpa continued, "that they started making more right away. In the next run GwenSeven made seventy constructs. They were not as elegant as the First Seven, but they were very fine indeed. They were bought so quickly and for so much money that in the next run the company made seven hundred. The seven hundred were made from molds instead of sculpted by hand, but were finely wrought and the whole lot of them sold before they were even finished. GwenSeven became what was called *an overnight success*. Then they began to manufacture them in great quantities, by the thousands. These thousands of manufactured people – constructs, or machines, or people machines - depending on what you call them, were made in 3625, what the elves call the Year of the Third Dragon. They were the creatures that would someday be the Chimera."

"Jesus," Sean whispered.

"Don't blaspheme," Grandpa told him, but his voice was devoid of emotion and so carried no anger. He leaned back deep into his chair and his eyes sought out his shelves and the many books there.

Jeannette listened from the rug, her eyes wide and round. It didn't all make sense to her, but some did and it filled her with a sense of wonder. For Sean, it was like watching pieces of a puzzle fall into place.

"Of course they weren't called the Chimera back then," Grandpa told them, taking a sip from his glass. "They were called the GwenSeven Pantheon, after a race of gods, or beautiful people, something of the sort."

"Were they *just* like people?" Jeanette asked. She had seen constructs at the mall and thought they were beautiful. Her Aunt was quick to point out that they weren't real people, but ones that had been manufactured.

"Oh yes!" Grandpa told her. "They were *just* like people. Oh, there were some things that they couldn't do. It seemed that old Cronus and the girls couldn't make them so they could wink, or whistle. But, other than that, they were just like us."

"What did they do with them?" Jeanette asked.

"They sold them. People bought them."

"What for?"

"For lots of things. Mostly for workers, but not just any kind. They were very expensive, and bought only by those who could afford them. And these beautiful people could do everything we could do and were used for anything from security escorts to waiting tables in fine restaurants and keeping houses. They were the playthings of the very rich - for who wouldn't want a pretty young lady watching your children or cleaning your house, rather than a clunky old droid?"

"For companionship too," Sean added. Grandpa shifted in his chair and gave Sean what he called 'the stink eye.'

"We'll save that for another time," he told him.

"How were they different from the constructs we have today?" Jeanette asked. She had seen constructs all her life and though they acted a little differently, she thought they *looked* like real people.

"The Pantheon constructs were much different because they were more like actual people. The ones you see today are more like droids simply made to *look* like people. We found that they are safer that way, and so are we. Also, constructs today are only made to last a few years. Then they need to be brought in for a tune-up and a recharge. The Pantheon were made to last indefinitely."

"What does that mean?" Jeanette asked.

"Forever," Sean told her, his eyes not leaving Grandpa's. "Infinity." Grandpa held his gaze and nodded.

"That's right," he said softly.

The room filled with a moment of heavy silence, broken by the ice in Grandpa's water as it melted and clinked against the side of the glass. He picked it up and took a sip, wiping the condensation off the bottom by rubbing it on the top of his thigh. It left a dark mark on his pants, just above the knob of his knee.

"What was Daddy talking about?" Jeanette asked. "He said something about their eyes and cues."

"IQ, dummy," Sean told her. "They're letters. They stand for intelligent and something else. They tell how smart you are. I don't know what EQ is."

"The Q is for quotient," Grandpa told him. "And don't call your sister a dummy. EQ is a measurement of emotion – your feelings."

"Why did Daddy say they bit our butts?" Jeanette asked. Grandpa looked confused for a moment and then cawed silently. Sean wanted to call her something worse than a dummy but he knew Grandpa would get mad.

"Dad just meant that GwenSeven made a mistake, not because of how smart the constructs were, but because of how they felt." Sean looked at Grandpa. "Is that right?" Grandpa nodded.

"We've been making intelligent computers and droids for thousands of years. Heck, Floyd there knows more about this podment than I do!"

The children looked in the corner where Floyd sat on his electrical charger. He was a small cleaner droid shaped like a triangle that was barely half a meter long on each side and about as thick as a shoe.

Every night at the same time, Floyd would leave his dock and cruise the surfaces of the podment, sucking crumbs off the floor and dust from the shelves. He wiped clean the counters and the windows before docking himself on his charger and powering down until the next night.

The only place in the podment he didn't go was Grandpa's room. Grandpa shut his door tight every evening to keep the little droid out. He was afraid that he might wake up some night with Floyd motoring up his legs trying to clean *him*.

"The thing is," Grandpa said, "is that Floyd don't care that it's his lot to clean my house every night. He don't care if I yell or cuss or kick him. He don't care if nothing ever changes or if he is never anything but hunk of metal squatting on a floor charger." Grandpa brought a gnarled hand up to his chest and tapped a finger over his heart. "Floyd can't feel."

"But the Pantheon constructs could?" Jeanette asked, though for once she already knew what the answer would be.

"Yes. They were smart and they could feel. In fact, most of them turned out to have quite the tempers. And one day, they began to realize what they were – manufactured slaves."

"And boy were they pissed," Sean said.

"You ain't kidding!" Grandpa exclaimed and then cawed laughter at the ceiling until he started to cough. Jeanette waited for him to calm back down. "Then what happened?"

Grandpa's face bunched up as he thought. "Well, it was about one hundred years into the Year of the Third Dragon when all hell broke loose. A number of the Pantheon, including four of the First Seven organized a revolt. They declared themselves a free people and called themselves Chimera. One group attacked the GwenSeven Corporation and another went after the actual family. Some rose up against their owners, but many of them just left."

"Where did they go?"

"No one is really sure. Thousands of them joined the Rebellion, of course, and those are the ones we are fighting today. Others just disappeared. Some say they left to start their own civilization, but no one knows where so that is mostly just guessing. Some say they are simply living among us and we don't even know it."

Jeanette gasped. Her young mind turned over what she had just heard, digesting it. She knew suddenly that she would never look at anyone the same way again. She would always wonder if they were real or if they had been manufactured and were just pretending.

"What happened to the girls?"

"Again, no one is certain because it was bloody mayhem. Some say that their dyers tried to protect them and were killed. Some say their dyers rose up and joined the Chimera, though I think that's a load of hogwash. All we know is that only two of the first three daughters remain and none of the dyers. Cronus disappeared as well."

Sean frowned as something occurred to him, and that was that no one was really sure about anything where the de Rossi family was concerned. In school they were taught about the Chimera and the Rebellion, but nothing concerning the family behind it.

"How do you know so much about the Dyer Maker, Grandpa?"

Grandpa looked at him, his blue eyes strangely calm and steady. "Because I knew him, son. I knew him very well."

FROM
THE DREAM JOURNAL OF HOPE

Before I go to bed tonight and become lost in the dreams there is something I must first write down.

I realized something today and it took my breath away.

You are just a man.

In the lab, you are the Lab Commander, and I am at your beck and call – student, helper, slave - attentive to your every word, knowing that a mistake can mean death, for myself or many. I cling to your every word, focused, my every move a response to your direction.

But sometimes, oh yes sometimes, when you press close and I can feel you or smell you, your breath close to my neck or your hand gripping my arm, and you - warm and towering and so present that my breath slips away and threatens not to return. All I can think of is pulling you to me, shedding your clothes, running my lips over your neck, your chest, tasting your scent, straddling your body, my neck stretched back in a scream.

The thought breaks and engulfs me, but for only a second, and I turn my face away, overcome. But it is only in my mind for I realize that my face is not turned away and I am looking at you intently, staring into your eyes, hanging on your words and my hands are steady as you walk away and then my mind is my own and back to my work and I am a single beam of light, focused on the vial and wary of the blue flame so near my left arm but when I finish and hang up my coat the feelings return with a breathless rush and my dreams are haunted by you and your smell and your touch and my desire to touch you and the keys that you hold and I know I am your slave.

But today, there we were and I wanted to talk to you, stand next to you, touch you, even with just the hem of my shirt. I could not, no matter how hard I tried. Nobody else, however, seemed to notice or care and conversations went round and sometimes you didn't speak at all and sometimes when you spoke you were not answered immediately and sometimes not at all and you had to repeat yourself and I was shocked and could only stare and try not to.

You command in the lab with your presence so vital it is like another living thing. You are the master of my heart but in the rest of the world you are just another man and are at the mercy of others just as I am at the mercy of you and you have as little control as I.

There is an energy between us, strong and frightening and sometimes I think that you can feel it too and sometimes when we are not in the lab I can feel you thinking about me and I wonder if at nightfall we are both haunted by the same dreams of desire. All of my thoughts are broken by the thought of pressing my lips against yours and filling your mouth with my tongue and your hands on my breasts my hips rocking against yours and I feel strong and deadly and hope that you know that someday I will take the keys from you even if it is by force.

TWO ZERO

There was no graduation ceremony, no fanfare. The five pilots remaining from the latest recruiting cycle at the IGC Jordan Training Center boarded the shuttle bound for the Opal Dragon as a bleak and pale sun lowered onto the moon's jagged horizon.

For nearly three years the would-be-Jordans had lived and fought and learned and trained together. They had watched their company of three hundred pilots – the finest pilots from every corner of the unified galaxies - dwindle away, sometimes by the hour.

Thirty-five standard months spent on space navigation, logistics, physical training, leadership, weapons, IGC Code and Conduct, torture. And, of course, learning to fly everything in the known universe.

Earlier that day, just after the morning meal, the last twenty-five recruits of Cycle Eleven at the IGC Jordan Training Center were called to formation in front of the JTC headquarters building. The company commander came out, his face dark and his body stiff. He frowned at the acrylic in his hand as he read off five sets of initials before his head jerked upright to look at the pilots assembled before him.

"Pack your things," he said curtly. "Be at airfield six at 1300." He turned on his heel and marched back into the HQ building.

The pilots looked at each other in stunned amazement. Twenty of them were nearly too crestfallen to stand. Five were breathless. They returned to their barracks for the last time and packed their standard issue gray duffels with their clothes, gear, and what few personal items they had.

Each of the chosen made one last trip to the Day Room, where they each sent a message home, letting their families know that they were leaving the JTC and would contact them again when they could. After a quick meal they gathered at the airfield where they conversed in harsh whispers, exchanging what little they knew.

Someone said that the Opal Dragon had borne three eggs, and their time was drawing near. Another said that the Beryl Dragon had borne two eggs, though it would still be some time before they hatched. The Copper Dragon had manifested two eggs and the Silver Dragon had manifested one.

"It doesn't guarantee that we will all be chosen," AR said as they sat on the tarmac, watching the white dwarf of the Lido system sink towards the horizon.

JM nodded in agreement. "I heard there are still five pilots from the last class that are still up for consideration."

"Yeah," BL said. He spoke in a slow and thoughtful manner, his brown eyes squinting. "I heard that, too. It also means that if we don't make it this round we still have another shot. There are more eggs now that there ever have been."

NDR grinned, her scarred face rippling. "They're calling the Year of the Fourth Dragon the Year of the Rainbow," she said. "

AR nodded. "Azure, Crimson, and Emerald are the what they have been calling the eggs on the Opal Dragon," she said.

Corvette Ensign joined them on the tarmac an hour later and called them to attention when the shuttle was on approach.

The five pilots boarded the shuttle and were greeted with smiles from the five graduates of the previous cycle that had been gathered up. The preceding graduates had not yet become Jordans, since no Dragon eggs had hatched between cycles, but they were still eligible to be selected.

The final selecting, though, would be done by the Hatchlings.

The newest selection of recruits stowed their gear and were directed to their seats by an IGC Steward. They were buckling in when Malherbe boarded the shuttle. He ducked in through the low steel door and then stood upright, looking around the seat-lined cabin and at the graduates seated there. He stepped back abruptly as if he had been doused with cold water.

"Jesus Fucking Christ!" he shouted. "What the fuck are you two doing here?"

JM fought to control the corners of her mouth and failed. Malherbe didn't miss a beat.

"Don't you fucking smirk at me JM!" he shouted.

The pilot burst out laughing, unable to control herself. She was joined by the blonde elf with the scarred face. They both bent forward over their restraints, trying to stifle their merriment. Malherbe shook with rage.

"You better get a hold of yourselves, pilots! You forget your military discipline this soon and I will have your narrow asses hanging by t-slings within the hour – though for you, JM, I might need a double sling!"

JM glared at him while NDR bit her lip in an effort to hide her amusement.

"And you!" Malherbe shouted, spying a small elf from the previous cycle that was buckled into a seat that looked too large for him. The accused pilot wore a green shirt that reflected the light green of his eyes – eyes that were half-covered with chocolate colored hair. "You puny bastard! You must have slipped in through the cracks!"

The slender elf smiled but said nothing, tossing his hair out of his eyes with a practiced flick of his head. The sergeant's face was beet red, squashed between his black cap and collar.

"And I see your hair has *still* not been cut to regulation length!"

"Good to see you again, too, Master Sergeant," the small elf replied.

Malherbe grabbed the sides of his cap as if he were going to pull it down over his face. Every pilot perched anxiously on their seat to see if he would rip the cap apart or possibly explode.

Shouting a final grunt of exasperation, spittle flying from his rubbery lips, Malherbe stalked out of the shuttle. Every pilot let out a breath of relief that was nearly ecstatic.

JM turned to the slim elf. "What do you guys know?' she demanded from his group. The elf shrugged.

"Probably about as much as you. We're headed for the Opal Dragon."

There was a thrumming sound and a slight jerk as the shuttle took off. A second later every pilot was working their jaw, ears popping as they left the gravity well.

"Is it true that the Hatchlings eat the pilots that aren't selected as Jordans?" NDR asked.

JM snorted. "You don't believe that shit, do you?"

NDR shrugged and looked at the dark-haired elfling who shook his head in response. She thought he looked a bit like Galen, only smaller. JM thought so as well, and it made her a shade uncomfortable.

"Malherbe filled our heads with all kinds of crazy crap, too," he told them, giving them a bright smile. "I'm Jade," he offered. NDR laughed.

"That's the first time I have heard anyone's actual name in three years!" she exclaimed, tilting her head back. "It sounds so, so weird."

"Is that your real name?" JM asked, her voice laced equally with suspicion and sarcasm. The elf nodded and she narrowed her dark eyes at him. "Do you think that's some kind of coincidence, or are you just hoping?"

Jade smiled at her. "I don't believe in coincidence. I believe in destiny."

JM snorted. "Elves," was all she said.

The pilots talked and laughed and napped. They were allowed to unbuckle their restraints and move about the shuttle, but there was not much to do or see. The shuttle had a small galley, a single head, and sleeping quarters for the crew in the area before the cockpit.

Mostly they swapped stories about the experiences they had at the JTC, though there was hushed talk about the war as well. All talk came to a halt when the Steward announced that they would be docking with the Opal Dragon in less than half an hour.

The pilots exchanged glances that they hoped were calm and confident. They weren't even close. Even the Steward noticed.

"Why do you all look sick?" he asked, clearly amused. "Haven't you all been training for this for years?"

"Training alleviates the anxiety," JM told him, "not the anticipation."

The Steward gave them a sly smile. "Afraid you'll get eaten?"

The cadets rolled their eyes and the Steward left, grinning.

"What a rube," JM remarked with contempt. Jade laughed. "What?" she demanded.

"We're from the same planet," he said, indicating the Steward. "He is from a village not far from my own." JM snorted.

"I'm not surprised."

There were a few muted laughs and the silence descended again. This time it stayed. The pilots sat in the cabin, quiet with their thoughts. Finally, a jerk and a series of barely audible bursts from outside the shuttle announced to the pilots that they had arrived.

The transport docked with the Dragon and the recruits remained where they were while the crew went through the security check. The would-be-Jordans each had to suffer a lengthy, individual security check. It took the longest for NDR, who could not wink, normally a trait that was a dead give away for a construct. She waited patiently while all checks were run to verify her disability and authenticity.

After all ten pilots were granted access to the Dragon, they were fed and washed. Everyone aboard the Dragon was curt but polite. They acted as if they were a bit afraid of the cadets, and looked them as if they were strange, exotic animals. The recruits, once again having retreated mentally into their private worlds, were escorted to a place in the Dragon called The Womb. It was a place they would someday call the Fledgling Bay.

The cab jerked to a halt and Galen closed his eyes, laughing. It was a soft echo of Noel's lunatic laughter from years of light and time away. He paid the cab with his card, got out, and simply stood there.

The cold clung to his face and the smell of wet asphalt filled his nostrils. He pulled his jacket a little closer, putting his card in the pocket before remembering he would need it to get into the building. His mind was too far away.

"You crazy bitch," he said, smiling and shaking his head. "You, wonderful, genius, crazy, fucking bitch."

"Whaaa?"

Galen jerked in surprise and then laughed. He had forgotten for the moment that Noel could hear him over their com-link. She must have been sleeping.

"Shh," he said softly. "Go back to sleep."

"Mmmmm."

Galen stifled his next laugh as he cut the com-link. He didn't want to wake her up and he knew it was going to be a wild night. He would probably be laughing and talking to himself like a crazy man for the next twelve to twenty hours.

He tipped his head back and let the cold air and metallic smell of the city wash over him. He stared up as if he was examining the vertical expanse of their building but all he saw was the moss covered tunnel wall as Noel shot the jet into the arch under the bridge. He had been thinking of the same problem then that he was faced with now, and she had given him the answer. He had just been too worried about shitting his pants to put it together.

Galen laughed again, this time hard and loud. He was so elated he wanted to shout but could not find the words to unleash upon the rumbling city. He shook his fist at the sky instead, laughing crazily, and fished his card back out of his pocket and went into his building.

He walked into the lift, chuckling and shaking his head while his body trembled with excitement. It was so simple that he couldn't believe it. More than that, he couldn't believe that he hadn't seen it before. He felt like slapping himself in the forehead in the proverbial manner of someone who has overlooked the obvious, but he was too giddy.

He giggled. He felt drunk. He felt wild.

The distance. It was the distance. Noel had it point blank. He could still hear her, closer than yesterday and clearer than tomorrow.

I can maneuver through anything if I know the distance, she had said after her own giggles had died away. *That's the only important thing, when it comes down to it. Knowing the distance. Since the bridge is still up, the distance through the arches hasn't changed.*

"Jesus," Galen muttered as the lift took him up and up. He had been putting the coordinates and distances into the Thermopylae and failing because the distances were wrong. Even a first year astronomy student knew that the universe was not a fixed and static place. It was always moving – always growing. Sometimes it contracted, but mostly it was always expanding.

Any object being sent a minor distance, such as an LD or less, would be just fine. The scale such distances changed was minute. But at the distances he was trying, the scale was greater – and so was the error. Everything he was sending through was falling short. Occasionally, he supposed, they might be going too far – but, for the most part, he knew that everything wasn't going far enough.

He rolled his credentials card over and over in his hand, absently feeling its gentle scrape on his palm and fingers. The lift opened and Galen stepped out. And froze.

All of his giddiness and elation drained from his body. They were replaced with a chill that sent a shiver of fear up his spine. Black hair spilled over his wide blue eyes as he drew up short and trembled.

Galen could have smelled the human from a mile away, but as his nostrils filled with the killer's scent he knew he was much closer than a mile – more like a few meters. He was amazed that he hadn't smelled him sooner, even with his mind as far away as it was.

The elfin doctor knew before taking another breath that someone was waiting nearby, waiting to kill him. There was no time to figure out who or why.

The man smelled like shaving cream, cigarettes, and death. The mercenary would have told Galen that it was aftershave, not shaving cream that he smelled, but Galen would not have cared. The mercenary, too, could not have cared less. He was, after all, there to kill Galen. And whatever it was that the doctor was harboring.

Galen's eyes swept the corridor in both directions. There was nothing to see or hear. Though the podment he shared with Noel was on an exclusive upper level, there was usually some activity. Not now. It was dead silent and the air was heavy with murderous intent. Some people just knew when it wasn't safe outside.

Galen jumped as the door to the lift closed behind him, desperate with indecision. He was being hunted; every sense in his body screamed it. Nothing, however, screamed at him what he should do. As far as that went, his subconscious was as quiet as the corridor.

He weighed his choices. He could bolt, his instincts were clamoring for it. His instincts also told him that if he ran, he would be chased. He could fight, though he could see the outcome of that as well. The mere stench from the human outweighed him.

Brains over brawn, then.

Galen looked up and down the hallway, slowing his breath and his heartbeat. There was a single hot gate, one of the Thermopylae that he had been working on, still in the lab in his podment. If he could get to it, and through it, he could get beyond the mercenary's reach and find out what the hell was going on.

But where? Where do I go?

The seconds ticked by and nothing happened.

Which means he's patient, a professional, and probably already in my podment.

He took a deep breath, unable to move or decide on a plan. *Where, where, where?* He thought desperately. *The University at Cordova? That would probably be best. The coordinates are in the lab.*

Galen squared his shoulders, feeling more confident just by having made the decision on what to do and where to go. It only lasted a second.

But how? How am I going to get by a trained killer?

He searched his memory trying to recall any weapons he might have in the house. He certainly didn't have any, other than laser scalpels and a few other medical instruments, and he wasn't about to go in brandishing a two inch surgical laser like it was a weapon. Besides, he had a feeling he wouldn't get to his tools in time anyway.

I need a weapon, he thought. *Preferably a gun.*

Noel.

There was a wide table in the entryway where they usually threw their credential cards or any other odds and ends from their pockets. The drawer in the table held miscellaneous junk and cast-offs. Including an old thermite gun. Galen doubted it still held much of a charge but it was better than nothing. Besides, maybe the human had already come and gone, simply leaving his stink as a calling card.

The air circulator in the building kicked on, making Galen jump again. The air coming down the corridor brought a sickening wave of evil purpose.

I'm not that lucky, he thought, covering his mouth with his hand. His only comforting thought was that Noel was already gone and safe.

Noel...

Galen looked at his watch. The bottom of the readout showed a steady blue blip next to a string of numbers. The closest he could get would be the Thermopylae on Cordova. Close enough.

The elf drew a deep breath, straightened, and walked to his front door like it was any other night. He swiped his credentials card by the pad next to his door and it slid open with a noise that sounded like a sigh of resignation.

As soon the door opened, he realized his mistake. The podment was pitch black and his silhouette stood out in the doorway of the bright hallway like a target. He dove to the right as laser fire ripped into his left shoulder.

Galen hit the ground with a grunt and rolled. He took another shot of laser fire as he came up and hit the keypad next to the door with his palm, sliding it closed and plunging the room back onto darkness. A deep chuckle rolled at him through the darkness.

"I don't have to ask if I got you," a voice said. It was deep and gravelly and mean. The voice of a man that would torture animals, or people, for no better reason than just to pass the time. "It smells like an elfling cook-out."

The menacing chuckle echoed through the dark podment. Galen used his feet to push himself back against the wall. His jacket and shirt were in smoldering tatters and he could feel where his skin was burned through to the tissues underneath. His shoulder wasn't bad, not as bad as his back. He could feel a long burning gash where he was hit while closing the door.

His eyes were adjusting quickly in the dark. He felt along the floor next to the wall until his fingers brushed up against the leg of the entry table. His fingers crawled up the table leg and, finding the drawer, eased it open. He could see the human now, a shadowy bulk sitting in *his* recliner.

Since the human hadn't taken another shot since the door had closed, Galen assumed the mercenary hadn't had his vision amped, and was unable to see the elf doctor well enough to take another shot. He hoped. He rose gingerly up to his knees and slid his hand inside the drawer, trying not to make and sounds.

"I can hear you breathing," the grave voice chided as Galen's fingers trolled through the drawer. "So I know I'm not done." There was a scraping sound as the human stood up.

Galen's fingers waded through old screws, buttons, viclays, and photon charges. His heart sinking, he nearly gave up when his hand closed over the rounded plastique pistol. He could see the human approaching, leaning from left to right as he tried to see in the dark.

"There you are..." the voice sang out as the form brought a rifle up to eye level.

Galen sprang to his right, praying for a miracle as he pulled the flimsy trigger of the thermite gun, aiming for the man's chest. The human's speed and reflexes belied his great bulk as he leapt back, twisting his body to avoid the thermite that shot out in blinding flash like a spray of white-hot magma.

Galen fell down behind the sofa as the mercenary dove behind a chair. The man was cursing and, to Galen's disbelief, laughing.

"The little rabbit has teeth," he croaked, chuckling. He dropped the rifle and pulled out a hot round pistol. He dropped his wrist down on the arm of the chair, holding the gun steady while his eyes, temporarily blinded, searched the dark room.

Galen blinked rapidly, waiting for his eyes to adjust. All he could see after the flash was a negative of the room. He could smell burnt flesh but he was pretty sure it was coming from his own back. It burned like hell. He blinked and waited for the man to move.

"Who are you?" Galen asked. The mercenary laughed his grating laugh, less than three meters away.

"I would think that would be obvious," he said. Galen could hear the sound of the man sliding his bulk behind the chair. "And I thought you would be smart. Aren't you supposed to be some kind of doctor?"

"It is obvious, you asshole. I meant, who are you with? Who sent you?"

"But that should be obvious, too. Shouldn't it? People who don't like what you are doing."

Galen closed his eyes and listened to the weight of the man shift left. In his mind's eye, he could see exactly where he was. He popped up from behind the couch and shot another thermite blast at the human.

The room was filled once again with a blinding flash of light and Galen was rewarded with the sound of the man hitting the floor, shouting and cursing. He ducked back down and waited for his eyes to adjust once again, knowing that it would take the human longer to regain his sight. He listened as the stream of profanity slowed to a trickle. Then the grating chuckle returned.

"Sharp teeth for a little rabbit," the human conceded. "I hope your little girlfriend is as much fun."

Galen, who was starting to edge his way from the living room towards the kitchen, froze.

"*What* did you say?" he whispered hoarsely, his blue, almond-shaped eyes staring into the dark. At first, the only reply was more of the chuckle.

"That's right," the mercenary told him. "I have her file and she's next. Mmmhmm. You should see the pictures I have of her – she's quite a doll. I might have a little fun with her before I squeeze the life out of her."

Galen jumped up and sprayed the room with thermite. He knew that the man was drawing him out but he didn't care. The thought of the brutish human going after Noel was too much. The sulfuric blast from the pistol filled the room with yellow-tinged white light.

As soon as the thermite charge began to falter the mercenary rose up and began firing from his own weapon, zeroing in on the source of light and heat. Galen was angry enough to kill him with his bare hands, but common sense was too deeply ingrained. The spent pistol fell from his hand as he turned and sprinted from the living room. He ran though the kitchen as rounds punched holes into the wall behind him. The human sprang after him, knocking over chairs as he followed him through the podment.

Galen raced through the back room and darted into his lab, closing the door behind him. The human slammed into the door, making it shudder, just as Galen threw the lock. The elf quickly wound his way through the dimly lit lab as the mercenary began blasting at the door with hot rounds. When the rounds were spent he unloaded on the door with a plasma weapon. Galen couldn't see the weapon, but he could see blue flecks of fire squirting out from the outline of the door like sparks from a welding arc. He knew he didn't have much time.

He grabbed an acrylic pad off a counter as he bolted to the Thermopylae and started it up. He thumbed through the electronic pages on the acrylic, looking for the coordinates for Cordova.

"Come on, come on," he whispered.

The lights on the outside of the narrow gate began to glow as it warmed up. He couldn't find the coordinates for Cordova.

"Shit!"

The lights grew brighter as the gate got hot, but the light around the door to the lab was growing brighter as well.

His hand went to his jaw and stopped. He hadn't thought about opening the com-link with Noel until now. He didn't want her to hear him die, but if these were his last moments he wanted to tell her that her loved her. He wanted to tell her how special she was. There were so many things that he wanted to tell her.

Fuck it, then. He thought. *I'm not going to die. I'll tell her in person. I can't leave her. I* won't *leave her.*

He watched the light around the door grow steadily brighter as the lights around the gate began to hum. He looked at his watch and at the numbers blinking at the bottom.

There's no gate there, he thought.

It's happened before, the advocate countered.

Not across that kind of distance, common sense argued.

What else is there?

It's worth a try.

Galen, his jaw set and his lips pressed tightly together, looked once more at his watch and then punched in the numbers that were blinking in the bottom frame of the dial into the keypad on the gate.

"Come on!" he urged as the coordinates were set and the gate began to fill with light. The door to the lab sizzled, the flecks of fire making their way around its entire perimeter.

His hand went to his jaw and hovered over the com-link, uncertain and unable to bear the thought of leaving Noel alone in the universe, as the mercenary burst through the door. He had a photon launcher in the crook of his elbow, the muzzle resting on his shoulder. He dropped the muzzle down, catching it in one meaty hand before hefting it up and aiming it at Galen's chest.

A series of loud, quick beeps came from the frame of the Thermopylae and its lights hit full bright as the killer pulled the trigger. Galen was thrown back through the gate in an explosion of heat and light.

 # TWO ONE

Jade pulled Verdana around in a wide loop through the black of space. The Jordan of the Emerald Fledgling was doing what he loved most, patrolling. This time, however, it wasn't for his favorite reason.

The elfin Jordan, who was pushing a grand two hundred IG standard years of age, was actually quite young. Especially at heart. Patrolling meant discovering new things. New planets, new civilizations, new women. From dusty taverns to silver cities to greasy drift bars, Jade loved to explore new and exciting places and cultures, including the local female fare.

Knowing that every being shared the same source of light, he did not discriminate against body shape, size, or color.

He would not have been surprised to find that he shared a similar quality with a certain green-eyed Chimeran Commander. Jade knew that there were no accidents in the universe. Everything happened for a reason. Jade also knew that life was a great adventure, and always dove in head first with a face-splitting grin. Though, sometimes, he would close his eyes. He couldn't help it.

Today's patrol was not for his favorite reason, and the only women that concerned him were the two other Jordans from the Opal Dragon. Brogan had refused to let him go after the ship itself so Jade had to content himself with a patrol.

He knew when Blue left, even though she went without Cyan, possibly *because* she went without Cyan, that she was going after Scarlett. He grilled Calyph for information but the Engineer refused to say anything on the subject. But when the screams tore through him, almost shattering his head, he gave up and left in his Fledgling, calling the bridge to tell them he was simply going to patrol the area. Blaylock's acquiesce was clipped and dismissive. He obviously had mightier stars to shake.

Unknown to all crew except those on the bridge, the Captain had gone into some sort of apoplexy. The XO could care less if the Jordan wanted to patrol the area. He was doing all that he could to make Brogan comfortable. The Captain was holding onto his own head as if trying to hold it together. But what made Blaylock nervous was the water that spilled out of the Captain's eyes.

Jade, relieved to be off so easily, started out for where the Chimeran Battle Cruiser had been when it had taken Scarlett. From there he crossed the spatial coordinates in great, swooping, ever-widening arcs. Verdana shimmered a brilliant silver-green through the black of space as he flew her on a determined course, checking every vessel and cosmic particle that was bigger than his own small fist.

He was not sure how much time had passed since Scarlett had been taken, but it had been a long time since Blue had disappeared in the Bloodjet. He was getting tired.

"Increase the oxygen output in here, would you darling?" he asked. The oxygen level inside the Fledgling shot up and Jade took a deep breath, letting it clear his mind.

He took Verdana out farther from the Dragon, expecting to be called back at any second. But the call didn't come and he pushed out farther.

Even with the increased oxygen, after two more hours he was ready to end the patrol. His sighed heavily, feeling powerless. His dark brown hair hung limp over his eyes and his shoulders sagged. He didn't want to give up but didn't think there was anything else he could do. He would have to return to the Dragon and wait, just like everyone else.

He was just about to turn Verdana's course and head back to the Dragon when there was a long bleep and flicker of light on the console. Three ships came up on Verdana's sensor. The Jordan was alert in an instant.

"Give me a full on incoming," Jade told the Fledgling. A holo-radar popped on over the console dash. There were two non-IGC fighter jets followed by another craft. A moment later Jade could see that the third craft was a Bloodjet. He knew that Blue had taken the Captain's personal craft, but that didn't explain anything. She could be pursuing Chimeran attackers for all he knew.

He tried to open coms but the enemy craft was either unable or unwilling to communicate. Jade hesitated as the fighters came at him.

"Who are you?" he whispered.

The two enemy fighters banked, heading directly for him. The Bloodjet banked to follow.

"Is that you, Blue? And who are the others?"

Jade didn't want to open fire without knowing but he wasn't about to take any chances.

"Fall back," he told Verdana. "Get ready to fire."

No sooner had the Fledgling shifted into attack preparation, before one of the jets broke away from the other – and shot at it.

The other craft rolled away, dodging the fire easily before rolling back behind the attacker.

Jade chuckled and shook his head.

"Easy, girl," he said to his Fledgling. "It's them." He laughed now, flooded with relief. "Jesus, Scarlett! Only *you* would fire on your own troops to prove who you are."

He laughed again and turned his Fledgling, heading for the Dragon with the other Jordans following.

Blue and Scarlett dropped their stolen craft down and into the fighter jet bay of the Opal Dragon where they were greeted by a cheering crowd. It seemed the entire ship was packed into the hangar to welcome the Jordans home. They went wild as they touched down and exited the Chimeran jets.

Even the Captain was there. He approached them quickly, flanked by Jade, who had brought and landed Verdana in the fighter bay, and a very anxious Calyph. The crowd, of what seemed like the entire crew aboard the Dragon, followed - keeping a barely respectable distance. Brogan threw his arms around both Jordans as soon as he could reach them.

"It's good to have you back. Both of you!"

"Thank you, sir," they replied in unison. He let them go, and though he was beaming at them, Scarlett could see the tension and concern in his eyes. She felt a lump rise in her throat, dry and painful. Seeing Calyph made it worse. She smiled at him the best she could.

Jade hugged Blue fiercely, his face full of pride and jealousy. He was gentler with Scarlett, his green eyes sharing the Captain's worry.

"How is my Fledgling?" Scarlett asked, her voice cracking.

"He's fine," Brogan said, though his voice was grave.

"I want to see him."

Brogan acquiesced with a nod. "Make it quick. I want you in the infirmary."

"I'm fine too..." Scarlett protested but Brogan's glare cut her off and when he spoke his voice was flat.

"It's not a request, Jordan. You'll stay there, too - if that's what the doc recommends."

"Yes, sir."

Brogan let out a deep breath and turned away without another word. Calyph impulsively pulled Scarlett to him, hugging her against his body. He thought she would pull away, embarrassed, but she leaned into him gratefully. Brogan looked at Blue.

"Good job, Jordan," he told her. Blue smiled crookedly.

"Thank you, sir."

"Where is my jet?" he demanded. Blue laughed.

"On its way, sir. I had to call it remotely. I'll go out and pilot it in when it gets here." Brogan gave her a smile.

"No need. Blaylock can dock it under the Dragon and bring it in. Do you have the remote chip?"

Blue dug a hand into her dirty coveralls, brought out the chip and handed it to Brogan. He took it, wrinkling his nose. "And you better bathe before you end up in the infirmary as well." He turned so he could see all three Jordans. "I want you all in the bridge at 0900 tomorrow for briefings, reports, and assignments."

The three Jordans gave a slight bow of deference and the Captain turned, effectively dismissing them.

Brogan motioned to a number of mechs and two Intelligence Officers that were standing by to examine the enemy aircraft. They gave him a nod and, rushing past, went to work. The Captain turned and walked into a crowd that parted wide enough to let him pass.

Calyph kept an arm around Scarlett, thinking no one would give it a second thought after the ordeal she had been through. Blue, however, threw them a roguish smile and even Brogan arched a brow when he glanced at them before disappearing into the crowd.

People congratulated Blue and asked Scarlett again and again how she was before they began to drift away, mostly to the atrium. The safe return of the Jordans was cause for celebration and most would party well into the oncoming artificial night. Even Blue decided she'd find a glass of champagne before she changed out of her smelly coveralls.

She began to drift away from Scarlett and Calyph as a number of people around her crooned for the details of the Chimeran ship and their escape.

"Hey!" Scarlett called out. Blue turned. There was a short second while Scarlett just looked at her without saying anything. Then she smiled, one of the rare occasions when she smiled at the other Jordan. "Thanks," she said.

Blue's scarred cheek pushed up into a lopsided smile and she lifted her chin in a quick motion of understanding before turning away, deciding she just might have a whole bottle of champagne.

Scarlett and Calyph trailed behind the crowd drifting towards the atrium.

"I want to see Fledge," Scarlett told him. He opened his mouth to protest and then clamped it shut. His grip around her tightened as they walked along, his fingers hugging the bone of her hip.

It occurred to Scarlett that he hadn't said anything to her since she had arrived and, for the first time since Bjorn had pulled out his torch, she felt her stomach clench with fear. She wanted to ask but was too afraid. She just waited and held onto him.

They broke away from the crowd and headed for the Fledgling Bay. The ship was quiet except for the sounds carried to them from the group headed for the atrium. It seemed that everyone not on duty was headed there for a night of festivity.

When they entered Fledgling Bay, Calyph's troll was there waiting for them. It was observing the few crewmembers on duty but swiveled its head as they entered the bay, turning its optic band to face them. Its rounded bulk rose up and floated towards the Jordan and the Engineer.

Calyph stopped and held onto Scarlett's arm to keep her from continuing. She frowned at him, unnerved, until she saw that he was holding a new credentials card out to her. She had forgotten that the other one was still aboard the *Macedonian*.

God only knows what they're doing with it, Scarlett thought.

"Once this is activated," Calyph told her as if in answer to her thoughts, "the other one will be annulled. They won't be able to use it." He placed the card over a screen on the troll and guided Scarlett's hand into place on another screen.

"But they'll still probably be able to figure out how it works," she said. "And make their own." It made her blood boil to think that something of hers could be helping them in any way. Calyph shrugged.

"It's possible that they had already done that. After all, at least one of the Chimera had already gotten in here."

"Did we ever figure out how?" Scarlett asked. Calyph shook his head.

"Blaylock's been over the security tapes a thousand times. The guy just showed up at some point. The vids show no entry or exit."

Bjorn! Scarlett thought. *That wily bastard. I'm sure it was him.*

She tapped her foot, impatient as the troll took her prints and carbon scan.

"Ouch!" Scarlett yelped, looking down. The troll withdrew the short needle it had used to puncture the pad of her palm.

"My apologies," the troll offered.

"You could have warned me!"

"Would that have made the pain less?"

"No!"

"Then what would a warning have accomplished?"

Scarlett looked like she wanted to give the rounded metal body a kick. Calyph bit his lip.

"I don't like surprises," she hissed.

"Duly noted." The troll extruded a limb and shot a beam of red light into the web of flesh between her thumb and index finger, checking the chip that was embedded there.

"How did you know I'd need a new card?" she asked Calyph.

"I didn't. I had one ready for both you and Blue. I knew that when you got back you would want to see your Fledglings and wouldn't want to wait." Scarlett felt a wave of gratitude wash over her. She looked into his eyes, noticing for the first time that his blue irises were flecked with silver.

"Thank you."

She kissed him, which drew a few surprised glances from the crew at work in the bay. Scarlett didn't care. Calyph gave her a sheepish smile and turned away.

Scarlett looked around the body of the troll, craning her neck in an attempt to get a glimpse of Fledge through the sparkling lines of the security fence. He was behind Cyan and she could only see his silver legs. But she could hear his heart beat in warm welcome and feel her own heart respond. For the first time she also felt the steady beats of the other two Fledglings. Even from Verdana in the other bay. They knew she was home.

When the troll finished, she snatched her card away and headed for the security gate as fast as she could go without breaking into a run. Calyph followed, watching her anxiously. They both went through security, Scarlett more and more impatient as they gave her the once over. When they were cleared she hurried around Cyan with Calyph in tow.

As she came around Cyan she cried out, her hand coming up to cover her mouth. Fledge stood just as she had seen him last: just over five meters high and fourteen meters long with his wings back tight. His skin was silver with a shimmer of crimson - except for one place. The area under his right wing was black and scorched.

"Oh, Fledge," Scarlett said softly, her voice cracking. "I am so sorry." She walked up and touched him gingerly in front of the blackened area. She could feel her emotion pass through him and reciprocate back out to her. She felt it come from the other Fledglings as well. She pressed her forehead against his side and closed her eyes.

"He is healing," Calyph told her. "The scorched area was halfway down his side. It has been diminishing, and quite quickly."

"Did you see it happen?" Scarlett whispered, her face still against Fledge's silver skin.

"No. He went after you and didn't come back until last night. I think the Dragon called him back when he, when you, were hurt."

Or when I was unconscious, Scarlett thought.

"I'm so sorry," she said again. All she felt in return was concern. The elfin Engineer waited for long moments before laying a hand on the small of her back.

"Come on," he urged. "He'll be alright. We should get you to the infirmary."

Scarlett sighed. She didn't want to go but she knew he was right. Fledge was going to be okay, and she didn't need to get in trouble with Brogan. She reached up with her left arm and ran her hand over the silver skin of her Fledgling. A warm, red glow responded where she touched him. Reluctantly, she turned and let Calyph lead her away to the infirmary, looking back over her shoulder at Fledge and Cyan.

Doc Westerson was a middle aged human male with brown hair and a slight beard with a tinge of red. There were deep creases in his forehead and around eyes that were the green and brown color of a murky pond. He gave Scarlett a thorough exam and took samples of her blood and tissue.

Calyph stayed with her the whole time. He talked endlessly to keep her mind occupied, telling her about where he grew up and why he chose the path he did. Though she was exhausted, Scarlett enjoyed his company and found herself laughing at the tales he had of growing up in the country on a small planet – especially of the shock of his parents the first time he floated a spoon across the dinner table.

Doc Westerson made a few notes on an acrylic and cleared his throat to get their attention. "You are healing remarkably quickly," he told Scarlett. "Especially considering the extent of your injury." He saw Scarlett's brow knit together and he cocked his head, intrigued. "Is that a bad thing?" he asked. Scarlett shook her head and said nothing.

Calyph waited for her while the doctor took her into a private room for a body scan and mental acuity test. When she came out her face was pale and drawn.

"Are you okay?" Calyph asked. Scarlett shook her head, biting her lip. He put his arms around her and held her tight. "Do you want to stay with me tonight?" He could feel her face nod against his shoulder. He kissed the top of her head. "Everything will look better in the light of day," he told her.

In the simulated light of day aboard the Opal Dragon, things were far from better and Scarlett was pissed as hell. The privacy wall was up around the pit in the bridge. A huge silver column walled off the officers so that the Captain could hold a private conference with his Jordans. Jade sat flanked by Blue and Scarlett. Brogan sat across from the three Fledgling pilots and Blaylock stood leaning against the wall with his arms crossed in front of his body.

Jade was nursing a brutal hangover and winced as the waves of Scarlett's anger rolled over him. He glanced at Blue. She could feel it too, he could tell – just not as bad. She hadn't drunk as much as he had last night, or she had shot herself with an A-solve and gotten rid of any alcohol in her system before she even went to bed He would have done the same if he hadn't passed out only to be rudely awakened by a furious XO on his com-link. The elf intended to grab a medic as soon as the briefing was over. He winced again as Scarlett's jaw clenched.

"Sir," Scarlett said evenly. "I feel fine. I don't see any reason to take leave."

"Doc Westerson recommended that you take at least one week off and said that two would be better," Brogan told her. "I don't take his recommendations lightly."

"Neither do I, sir. But it's not fair that Jade and Blue..."

"Jade and Blue were not just captured and tortured!"

"I wouldn't call it torture," Scarlett muttered. Brogan gaped at Scarlett before he closed his eyes, pressing his lips together to keep from laughing. He shook his head and looked back at the Jordan.

"I don't care what you would call it. You are on leave, effective immediately."

"*I know what..*" Scarlett started, her voice rising before Blaylock cut her off.

"Watch yourself, Jordan," he warned slowly, his voice low.

Jade was hit with nausea as Scarlett fought to control herself. He begged her mentally to calm down before he lost control of his stomach. He could feel the bile burning at the back of his throat.

"Calm down, Scarlett," Blue scolded. "You're killing Jade."

Scarlett looked at Jade's pale face and took a deep breath to steady herself. "Can I take Fledge?" she asked. Brogan looked at Blaylock, who shrugged.

"I see no reason why you shouldn't," he said. "But I want you planet bound. You need to have your feet on solid ground for a while. I want you home with your family."

As Jade felt Scarlett's anger rise back up and his mouth filled with saliva and he realized Blaylock's true importance for the first time. With no physiological bond to the Dragon, the Executive Officer could not be swayed by emotional ties to the ship or its pilots. Brogan relied on his steadfast ambivalence.

The Captain flicked Jade an amused glance.

Jesus, Jade thought. *Does he know what I am thinking or can he just feel how close I am to losing it?*

The corner of Brogan's mouth twitched.

"Enough," the Captain said. "Jade, get to the infirmary. Then I want you to take the first patrol, all the way to sector seven of the Lions' Cloud. Blue, I want you working with Calyph on the growing. Scarlett, I don't want to see you for a fortnight. The Captain rose and the privacy wall around the pit vanished. Blaylock shot each of the Jordans a threatening glance before following the Captain into the bridge proper.

Jade quickly excused himself and took off as fast as he could without drawing too much attention. Blue wanted to comfort Scarlett but the animosity coming from the other Jordan cautioned against it. She hesitated, leaning toward Scarlett and looking down at the floor.

"Let me know if you need anything," she muttered as she stood and left, not expecting Scarlett to answer.

Scarlett took a deep breath and left as well, glad to be alone. She paused as soon as she left the bridge, her hand coming up to her upper lip. She had known she was getting a bloody nose and didn't want anyone to see. Things were bad enough as they were.

Besides, it wasn't a gusher – just a little trickle that she could feel making its way down her left nostril. She didn't know if it was the dry space air or her blood pressure, and she didn't care.

She leaned a shoulder against the silver skin of the corridor, trying to slow her heart rate. Her anger was making it thud in her chest like a caged beast. She took a few deep breaths and then straightened, not wanting anyone to see her. She glared up and down the passageway, but no one was there.

I'm done with everyone thinking I'm a damned victim, she thought.

She tugged at her sparkling ruby flight suit, tossed her dark hair away from her face, and headed for her cabin at a brisk walk. The more she thought about being sent away the angrier she got.

Sent home! Like a child!

She was angry at Brogan, angry at Blaylock, and furious with Blue. Scarlett had found out that Blue had gone to Doc Westerson with questions about her.

About me! Scarlett fumed, tossing her hair and walking faster. *How dare she even try! What happens to me is none of her damn business! What would she want to know? Why would she want to know? There's something wrong with her, I know it.*

Scarlett strode past the door to her cabin, heading directly for the Fledgling bay.

Fuck it. I'll just grab a flight bag. There's nothing here that I need.

An image of Calyph flickered in her mind. She thought about his blue eyes and his strong hands, the way he smelled and the way he smiled. There was something about him that was very compelling. She thought of the way he had touched her just last night, and how it had made her feel. She smiled at the memory.

It's not the same as when Bjorn touches you...

The thought was fleeting, almost as if someone else had said it aloud, teasing her. It was unwanted and unwarranted and she was furious at herself for thinking it.

She entered the Fledgling Bay, thinking about home. She didn't want to go, which was nothing new. She felt an urge to stay by Calyph, and that was an entirely new feeling altogether.

It is probably best that I get the hell out of here. I must be losing my damned mind.

Scarlett went through the security check, her jaw clamped so tight she could hardly relax it enough to give the medic a whistle. She was just glad that it wasn't Doc Westerson. She was pissed enough as it was, seeing him would make it worse.

As if it could be worse!

She finally felt some relief when she boarded Fledge and felt him close up around her. The familiarity alone was enough to help calm her nerves - the angle of the seat, the smell of the air, and all the controls on the left side of the dash.

Where they should be!

She could hear his heart beating rapidly in response to her own.

"It's okay Fledge," she told him. Her breathing slowed as she relaxed. "Just get us the fuck out of here."

The Crimson Fledgling was more than happy to oblige.

TWO TWO

Bjorn wiped his face with the rag for what seemed like the hundredth time. His eyes had finally stopped watering, but his tongue still burned with the taste of the CS gas and his saliva glands were going crazy. He blew his nose into the rag and spit on the floor.

Scarlett!

Bjorn laughed, shaking the sweat from his blonde hair. He didn't know what it was, but he couldn't get angry with her. Thinking about her only made him want her more. Sitting there on the floor of the jet bay, eyes burning, snot-nosed and drooling like an idiot – he wanted to see her again.

He was flanked by two construct pilots and his persona; bodygurdas that stood by to assist him, should he need assistance. The others he had shooed away until he could get himself together – it wasn't difficult to get them to leave. His clothes had absorbed a good dose of the CS gas and it was enough to affect anyone close to him. Even his guards stood a few meters away, sniffling and clearing their throats constantly.

Another pilot had to go and retrieve Bjorn's jet after he had ejected from it. He didn't know what he would have done if he had been without a field generator, the gas might have finally killed him for all he knew. As it was, he could hardly see well enough at the time to get his ass out of there. The cabin would have to be ionized, though it might be better if he had everything torn out and burned.

Bjorn sat on the metal floor, elbows on his knees, his green eyes watering to no end. He was trying to collect his thoughts, trying to plan their next move, trying get himself off his ass to go take a shower, but all he could think about was Scarlett. He thought about her face, her physical strength and her mental toughness, her utter contempt for him, and what he would say when he saw her again.

He *would* see her again, he was sure about that.

He wasn't even too down about the loss of Eva. She had been a good officer and loyal, but he knew that was mostly because he had been fucking her. She knew it increased her authority, albeit unofficially.

Bjorn was more rankled at the loss of the fighters and a slew of pilots. Stoj was going to be even more pissed – one of the fighters had been his. Bjorn coughed and spat.

He listened to the clanking sounds echoing from the mech bay. It made him think of Scarlett in there, her arms hoisted up like a marionette, for hours on end. Others that had been subjected to the same treatment were begging to be let loose after an hour, sometimes two. One had cried after all of twenty minutes when his shoulders began to cramp. It hadn't fazed Scarlett at all.

The sound of running footsteps echoed in the bay. Bjorn sighed and wiped his face with the rag.

"Sir?"

Bjorn raised his head and squinted up at the voice. It belonged to a slim, dark-skinned construct that looked younger than most.

Michael, Bjorn thought. *His name is Michael.*

"Sir?"

"Yes, Michael. What is it?"

Michael smiled and bowed, pleased that the commander knew him by name. "Sir, there is talt-ship that is requesting an audience with you."

"Is that so?"

"Yes, sir."

Bjorn looked through the bay doors but saw nothing but the speckled black of space. Talt-ships were an interesting thing. They were small ships for hire, a sort of intergalactic taxi. They were the cheapest sort of private space travel one could get, but that didn't mean they were cheap.

"I don't suppose they said who they are or what they want?"

"No, sir. He said he would only speak to you, and said that you share a common purpose."

Bjorn glanced back up at Michael. "Is that so?"

"Yes, sir."

"When will Stoj be here?"

"Commander Stojacovik has regrouped eight fighters for the ship and is scheduled to arrive in less than an hour."

Bjorn looked at the rag in his hand and tried to find a spot that wasn't slimed with snot. He found one, but it was small. He sighed and wiped his face and spat.

"Well, bring our new friend in. I'll meet him in the bridge."

"Yes, sir!"

Michael took off running and Bjorn stuck out a hand. One of his guards grasped it and hauled him to his feet.

"I must be getting old," he remarked.

Both guards snickered at the joke and fell in behind the Commander as he strode quickly from a fighter bay that now only held one fighter.

A half hour later, thoroughly scrubbed and with his previous set of clothes safely in the incinerator, Bjorn sat in the bridge dressed in a crisp blue coverall with gold-banded epaulettes looking at the ugliest human he had ever seen. The man was a testament to animal steroids and sported a grotesque amount of bulging muscles. He had beady, gray eyes, bad skin, and a skull that looked positively primitive.

Bjorn tried to force a smile and fell far short. To his surprise, the man seemed to have just as much distaste for him as he glanced about with bored curiosity. He had sat himself, uninvited, in the chair opposite Bjorn.

"Well," Bjorn said after the man didn't offer up who he was, "you obviously weren't sent here by the IGC."

The man laughed through discolored and broken teeth. The sound was gravelly and menacing.

"What makes you think I'm not Chimeran?" he asked.

Almost every crewmember in the bridge snickered at that, but Bjorn was too disgusted by the thought and the man to find him funny.

"Because I'm sure we would have been introduced by now."

The human stopped looking around and faced Bjorn. "I take it you don't have that bitch Jordan anymore?" It was more statement than question.

Bjorn's fist clenched as his blood pressure rocketed. He didn't like that some strange human knew what was going on aboard his ship and liked it even less that he was talking about Scarlett.

"Why should that concern you?"

The man shrugged as if he didn't care. It made the muscles on his shoulders bunch and stretch the cheap fabric of his shirt. The sleeves of the shirt were short and tight around huge, round biceps. His forearms were roped and corded with muscle, and showed the brand scars of a mercenary. Bjorn was starting to dislike the man more by the second. Dangerously so.

"Fine. Let's dispense with the chase. What do you want?"

The man smiled crookedly, appreciating the brusque dismissal of any pleasantries. "The elf."

"Could you be more specific?"

"The Jordan. The elf-bitch."

"The *Blue* Jordan?"

The man nodded, his eyes on the Chimeran commander. Bjorn had to keep himself in check to keep from letting out a sigh of relief. Though he easily could have the mercenary killed, the thought that the man might be after Scarlett made him uneasy. The feeling alone was cause enough to have him killed.

But if they were after similar things; say, two eggs in the same clutch, the man could prove to be useful. He did show up in a talt-ship. They weren't free, nor were they easy to come by.

"Do you know where she is?" the man asked. Bjorn smiled for the first time since the man had entered his bridge. He now saw that they did have a common purpose, and how he could use this man to see the end of that goal.

"Of course. But more important, I know where she is going to be. I have something in the works, but I just might need a little grease to get the engine going."

The mercenary smiled back at him, his gravelly laugh echoing behind broken teeth. "Well, my employer has plenty of grease. But we would like to get the engine going as soon as possible."

Bjorn nodded slowly. "Would he be a supporter to our cause, should we hand over the prize you are after?"

The mercenary's smile was cold, his gray eyes flat and dead. "He most certainly would."

"*When I get a hold of that bitch...*" echoed from the hallway, growing louder as it neared the bridge and Commander Stojacovik stormed into the control room, "I'm going to tear her apart with my hands and teeth!"

Bjorn looked at him languidly.

"Stoj, please," he said pleasantly. "We have company."

Stojacovik - tall, dark, handsome, and livid – threw his black gaze about the bridge. He glared at Bjorn before throwing his eyes upon the mercenary.

"What the fuck is going on?" Stojacovik demanded. The pleasant look on Bjorn's face dissolved, replaced with a look of distaste.

"Things that are above your pay-grade, but if you think you can behave yourself, you are welcome to stay."

"Fuck you, Bjorn! Don't you fucking patronize me!"

Bjorn turned to the human as if he hadn't heard. "This is my Executive Officer, Commander Rohn Stojacovik."

"Welsner."

Bjorn arched a brow at him. He hadn't caught the man's name till now. He hadn't cared.

"You're in my chair!" Stojacovik accused.

"My apologies," Welsner offered, though he didn't move. Stojacovik glared at him. Bjorn watched their exchange with amusement before slapping his palms on his thighs and standing up quickly.

"Well," he said, "I think we should have breakfast and discuss our next move."

"You have a lot to explain, first," Stoj told him.

"I don't have to explain anything to you," Bjorn countered, his voice low and his green eyes flashing. "Our mission remains, nothing has changed. Only the way in which we carry it out. We knew what was in store and what the next plan would be."

Stojacovik blew out a sharp breath of air and panted like an animal before he seemed to finally gain control of his emotions. "Well," he finally said, his tone petulant, "it just would have been easier if you hadn't let her get away."

Bjorn laughed. "No shit." This brought a slight smile to Stojacovik's countenance, softening the hard lines of his handsome face. He shook his head and both men looked at Welsner, who shrugged.

"I could eat."

The Chimeran commanders laughed and Welsner stood and let them escort him to the officer's mess. Stojacovik began asking the mercenary questions immediately as they walked along, but Bjorn hardly heard them.

I may have let you get away, Scarlett, he thought, a small smile playing at the edge of his mouth, *but I'll have you back in no time. At my side, and in my bed. Where you belong.*

His slight smile widened into a rapacious grin as he turned his vivid green eyes to the men next to him and his mind back to the conversation at hand.

The S-4 was an aging human, sitting on a stool behind the Formica supply counter. Behind him were shelves and rooms and cages and boxes; all full of military supply items from hand cannons to batteries. On the counter to his right were three neat stacks of silver flight suits. Only Jordans were allowed to wear silver.

NDR walked boldly up to the counter, ready to name herself and her Fledgling as was her right and honor. She couldn't stop smiling; her huge grin splitting her already crooked face. She put a hand down on the Formica counter.

"I'm Blue," she told the recorder proudly. He nodded, tapping it onto the acrylic pad. "Jordan of the Fledgling by the same name." The man stopped and looked up her.

"*You* are Blue, and you want to name your *Fledgling* Blue?" Blue nodded happily.

"Don't you think that might be confusing?" he asked. "Giving yourself and your Fledgling the same name?"

Blue cocked her head. "Do you think people might confuse me with a Dragon Fledgling?" JM, who was standing behind her, snorted. Blue ignored her. The S-4 shifted on his stool.

"Of course not, Jordan. But, ahem, it might be confusing in the records."

Blue nodded, weighing the idea. It was something she had not considered. "What's another name for Blue?" she asked. JM snorted again. The S-4 shifted again and looked sideways, thinking.

"Well, there's lots of words that describe the color," he said, putting the tip of one index finger on the pinky of his other hand. "Azure, sapphire, indigo," he said, ticking them off his fingers.

"No, no, and no."

"Cyan."

Blue and JM both turned to look at Jade. He was smiling, his green eyes flashing beneath his dark brown hair. "Cyan," he said again. Blue cocked an eyebrow at him.

"I thought Cyan was green."

He shrugged. "It's a blue-green." Blue smiled at him and turned back to the S-4.

"Cyan-Blu," she told him. "Just so there won't be any confusion. And with no 'e' – again, so there won't be any confusion."

The S-4 shook his head in mild amusement and punched it onto his acrylic pad. He turned and selected a pile of silver flight suits and handed them to

Blue. "You are number eight," he told her. "Always keep it on all your equipment, especially the arm of your flight suit if you have any custom made, as I'm sure you will. Congratulations, Jordan Blue."

Blue beamed at him. He was the first person to call her by her new name. She felt as if she were being born, only better. She turned to Jade while JM took her place at the counter.

"Congratulations, Jordan Blue," he told her. He was obviously as excited as she was, hardly able to contain his elation. Blue laughed, hugging the silver pile of clothes to her chest.

"Thank you. And congratulations to you too."

He smiled, his green eyes flashing. Blue cocked her head at him.

"You're not going to change your name, are you?" she asked. The elf shook his head.

"I don't see why I should."

"That's pretty fortuitous that you were chosen by the Emerald Fledgling."

Jade shrugged, still grinning. "Maybe it was destiny."

"What are you going to name her?" Blue asked.

Jade's chocolate-colored hair fell in front of his green eyes but his smile ever faltered. "Verdana."

TWO THREE

Blue had just found Calyph as Scarlett was impatiently going through the security check in the Fledgling Bay. The elfin Engineer, in his usual country garb, was having breakfast in the upper atrium and discussing a double periodic element table with the troll. The troll swiveled his head towards the Jordan as she entered the café.

A blue beam of light traveled across his optic band as the Jordan took the empty stool across from them and helped herself to a pastry. She was careful not to miss a meal, not ever wanting to repeat her experience in the Scorpion. She caught the eye of the barista and signaled for a coffee.

"Where's Scarlett?" Calyph asked before he had finished chewing what was in his mouth. *Dammit!* He cursed silently, closing his eyes. *Do you have to sound so damned eager?*

"Leaving," Blue said, after swallowing a bite a pastry. "Sent home." Calyph gawked at her for a second and then pushed his stool back from the table and started to rise. Blue leaned over and quickly put her hand over his, shaking her head.

"Let her go," she told him. Calyph frowned, but remained where he was. The Jordan sighed. "I know you want to help her, but she needs to be alone. Whatever might be between the two of you will be lost if you go to her now."

Blue heard a soft grunt of surprise in her left ear. Calyph stood with his hand on the stool, weighing her words.

"My Darling," Galen said, "your wisdom is growing exponentially."

"Not now," Blue said, her eyes locked on the Engineer. She made no attempt to hide her remark. Calyph assumed she was speaking to him. He sat back down.

"How was she?" he asked.

"She was pissed," Blue said dismissively with a frown and a shrug. "What else? Scarlett's always pissed."

Calyph shook his head. "Not always."

Jordan Blue made a face like she had eaten something sour. "Ugh, Calyph. I don't want to know the details."

Calyph finally smiled and blew a snort of air from his nose. The troll swiveled his head towards the Engineer.

"Does she mean..." the droid began.

"Yes!" Calyph hissed, glaring at the troll. He looked back at Blue with a sigh and a second later they were both laughing, leaving the machine to puzzle over their clipped language and strange behavior.

The female medic clucked her tongue at Jade. "You should have come in last night, Jordan."

Jade looked at her over his right shoulder and winced as she stuck the syringe into his backside. She was human, pretty with brown hair pulled back into a tail and bright, brown eyes. She had a dark freckle high up on her left cheekbone and a mischievous smile.

"Well," Jade said, after she had removed the needle. "I promise to come see you the first night I am back. Whether I need the 'solve or not." He yanked his dark green pants back up over his thin hips.

Jade gave her a roguish grin, tugging his green Mylar shirt down over the waistline of his pants. The medic shook her head at the Jordan as if exasperated, and turned away to gather her swabs and syringes. Jade left the infirmary, rubbing his backside but feeling infinitely better.

As he drew near the Fledgling Bay he was overcome with a hot sweat, followed immediately by a wave of chills. His first thought was that the medic hadn't given him enough A-solve, and his hangover was coming back rampant. Then he spotted Scarlett coming down the corridor.

Jade performed a flawless, military rear-march and kept going until the hot chills subsided. He leaned against the silver wall of the Dragon, letting the coolness of the skin radiate on his face, until Scarlett was well on her way.

He stayed there a few moments longer, filled with empathy for the other Jordan but still wishing Scarlett would learn to control her emotions. He remembered when he had first met her and how attracted he had been to her – Blue as well.

He had discarded the notion of any sexual relationship with either of them very quickly, though with some dismay; Blue - when he found out who she was and who she was with, and Scarlett when she rebuffed him with extreme prejudice. Even then, the desire for them both still remained until the Fledgling bond took hold. Now, it was appalling as the thought of having sex with a close relation, which they all now were, in bond if not in blood.

As soon as Scarlett had left the Dragon, Jade continued on to the Fledgling Bay where Verdana waited. He cleared security and boarded his Fledgling, taking her out of the bay and in the opposite direction of Scarlett.

His choice of direction had little to do with the Crimson Jordan, however. He had already planned on starting his patrol on Leoness, the farthest point allowable for patrol. It was a developmental moon in the orbit of the extrasolar planet, Regulus.

The development was so new that it had not yet been colonized. The moon, as of yet, barely had a workable atmosphere with three distinct sectors. The first two sectors, which were always the first sectors on a newly terraformed moon, were a landing field and a research center.

Jade had visited Leoness for the first time while on patrol and when the colony was in its first stages of development. At the time he had met a certain elfin lovely that had caught his eye and he had ended up staying with her for the entire time of his patrol. She was a petite cargo pilot and had been working in the half-built hangar when he first landed on Leoness. She had close-cropped blonde locks and large blue eyes.

He had been back again one time since then but she had been away. One of her friends had assured him she would be back soon and to try again in a month.

Jade hummed to himself as he tapped in the coordinates for Leoness. As soon as he neared approach he would take over manually, guiding Verdana down to the infant development called Lionsgate.

He checked the galactic coordinates and saw that the trip should take just over fifty hours. He left off humming and started to whistle, thinking about where he would be sleeping in less than three days.

Well, he thought cheerfully, *hopefully not sleeping too much.*

Blue was anxious. Not just to grow Cyan, but to see Calyph in action. She could never resist teasing him about what he did but, in truth, the magic of what he could do always fascinated her.

"It's not magic," Galen had told her once. "Many elves on Calyph's planet were born with his abilities, and even more learned how to tap into the part of their brain to let them manipulate matter without using their hands. It's his skill in metallurgy that sets him apart."

"But smith *and* sorcery," Noel had argued. "Sorcery means magic."

Galen had laughed. "That's just an old superstitious saying that is part of his tag. The elves, especially ones from other planets like where Jade is from, were very wary of telekinetic powers. Even humans never mastered it."

"Hmm," was the only agreement Noel offered. She didn't care what Galen called it. To her, it was magic. She couldn't wait.

Now she sat on the silver floor of the Fledgling Bay in a sparkling, one-piece blue flight suit that refracted the light in all directions, her platinum hair pulled back in a high pompadour and separated in the back into a few loose curls.

In her hands was a thin piece of titanium, as slender as a graphite stick, which she idly turned over and over between her palms. There were a number of long, cylindrical rods of metal neatly lined up on the floor next to her. Calyph had spent the morning carefully separating them and laying them out in the order they would be used.

Blue watched as Calyph, holding up a hand but without touching a thing, raised up a long bar of lithium. The metal hovered three meters off the ground as Calyph guided it over the Fledgling in a field of his own making. He placed it on top of Cyan's left wing, at the very front. The bar jutted out from the shoulder of the Fledgling, longer than the wing by nearly two meters.

The troll produced a leveling field of red light that blinked off when Calyph had the bar perfectly lined up. Then the troll and the Jordan simply watched. Calyph, his eyes fixed on the metal rod, slowly brought up his right hand up to shoulder level.

Blue watched as the lithium softened and then began to unroll down the wing like a piece of dough on a baker's board. It melded with the wing itself, stretching and lengthening and hardening as it did.

"Wow," she whispered. Calyph smiled and moved around Cyan to repeat the same process on the other side.

"This is the first time we are using Lithium," he told her. "We'll see how it holds up, but I think it will be fine."

"The Opal Dragon has a titanium casing, right?"

Calyph nodded. "The Beryl Dragon does as well. Old Ferrous, the Iron Dragon, is just that."

"She really has an iron casing?" Blue asked. Calyph nodded as he manipulated a bar of beryllium towards the Fledgling's tail. Blue gave an appreciative huff. "I thought that was just a nickname. It's a miracle she can fly."

Calyph snorted. "It's a miracle she doesn't rust."

Blue was silent a moment and then looked at the engineer, frowning. "But if Lithium comes into contact with moisture, won't it corrode as well?"

Calyph glanced at her, surprised. "It would darken the metallic sheen, maybe turn it black, but it wouldn't compromise Cyan's casing."

Blue was thoughtful for a moment, not liking the idea of her Fledgling rusting or blackening with age. "If you could saturate a polymer with a mineral based oil, and fuse it with his casing, it would keep him from tarnishing."

Calyph stood motionless, a bar of beryllium hovering in the air before him. "How do you know that?" he asked.

"Yes," Galen agreed in her left ear. "How *do* you know that?"

Blue shrugged. Calyph watched her a moment longer and then returned to his work. "Yes," he agreed, "I suppose I could."

Galen grunted.

"I think you've been learning things while I wasn't on watch," he said over their com-link. The Jordan smiled, not especially comfortable about having a conversation with him in front of Calyph. Galen also did not seem eager to speak too much when other people were around. He more than made up for it when they were alone, and not just talking either. The Jordan's smile widened at the thought, puckering her scarred cheek up into a mass of pinkish wrinkles.

Blue watched Calyph and the troll work on Cyan all morning, fascinated by what they could do with metals by altering their molecular make up from one state into another. She watched Calyph work titanium like it was taffy, before making it into a near impregnable shield around Cyan.

"It's actually not any different than what Cyan does to the metals once they are part of him," he told her. "The way he can form steps on his sides or draw his legs into his body – except that he can do it on a biological level while I have to use a telekinetic field to manipulate the metal and the atomic code that the molecules carry."

The Engineer was too absorbed in his work to leave for lunch, so Blue left briefly to bring some back. Calyph munched a protein wrap quietly, his eyes on the Fledgling. He went back to work without finishing his drink.

He worked tirelessly, always moving about, scrutinizing, moving metals and fusing them with Cyan's casing. Blue watched in wonder as the Fledgling grew before her eyes. She always stayed near, afraid of anything that might hurt him, but he seemed fine. His heart beat in the same slow and steady rhythm that she was familiar with. Blue even wondered, once or twice, why she was necessary, unless it was to keep him comforted and calm.

Finally, as the Dragon moved into dimlight, Calyph sighed and rubbed his face and neck as if pleased with his day of work.

"All done for today?" The Jordan asked.

Calyph chuckled. "Almost." He manipulated two blocks of diamond glass up onto the windows that were Cyan's eyes. Then he motioned to the troll and the bulky machine drifted over to the Jordan's side. "I need you to take him inside."

"Inside Cyan?"

Calyph nodded. "When you get him in the cabin, you need to come back out. Let Cyan know that the droid will be staying inside, and what will be happening."

"What will be happening?"

"The troll is going to create an incredible amount of air pressure. Enough to kill you if you stayed inside. It will push the Fledgling out in every direction, effectively growing him."

"I thought what you were doing today was growing him."

Calyph shook his head. "I was adding what he needs to grow, and the troll will expedite the process." Blue scowled at the Engineer.

"Is this going to hurt him?"

Calyph shrugged, which didn't please Blue at all. "He could feel discomfort, most likely in his eyes, but no Fledgling has ever cried out during a growing."

"I don't like it," she told him. Calyph held out his hands, palms up.

"It's what we have to do."

"I don't have to like it."

"You'll be glad when it is done, and he will be too." Blue crossed her arms in front of her chest and Calyph sighed, his head rocking back on his neck as if he were getting too tired to hold it up. "We have to do this every day for the next few days, Jordan. If it hurts him tonight we will go slower next time but, I assure you, he's going to be fine."

The Jordan threw him a warning glance and turned to board her Fledgling. The steps that extruded from his side were deeper, but erratic and uneven. She glared at Calyph as Cyan broke apart for her to enter, followed by the troll.

Blue sat down in the cockpit and saw that it already looked different. Bigger. Warped. The troll settled down next to her. She spoke to Cyan, and let him know everything that Calyph had told her, just in case he hadn't caught the conversation, though she suspected that he did.

"And," she added quietly, "if this hurts you in any way, you just let me know. I'll kick that rube so hard in the balls he'll think he has human tonsils."

A hum came from the troll that Blue was sure signified amusement. She threw it one more glance as she climbed out and down. Cyan closed the cockpit with the machine still inside.

"What next?" she asked Calyph.

He smiled. "This." He had placed a short hydraulic ladder in front of Cyan and climbed it until he was level with the nose of the Fledgling. Much to his surprise, Blue followed him up and tried to squeeze next to him without pushing him off. The Engineer squirmed for a second, getting as much room as he could, and then leaned out and placed his hands on the Fledgling's nose.

Blue, standing sideways, reached an arm around him so she could be touching Cyan as well. Calyph hadn't placed the ladder very close, and she was nowhere near as tall as the elf, so she had to lean out quite far. She looked into the eyes of the Fledgling, wondering how long it had been since she had done just that.

Calyph nodded at the troll and then closed his own eyes. Blue waited for a moment while nothing happened, and then she felt Cyan's metal skin start to thrum with a slight tremor. It grew warm, and softened just the slightest bit, and she was reminded of his brief time as a Hatchling.

Then the nose of the Fledgling began to push into her hand. Then it was pushing her hand back and then her arm. She realized that Calyph had positioned the ladder back carefully, otherwise they would have been knocked to the ground.

The thrumming vibration intensified and his skin went from warm to hot. Cyan pushed and swelled. He grew. In less than a minute, the Blue Jordan stood with her arm outstretched along the left side of her Fledgling's nose. The Engineer teetered on the ladder next to her.

Calyph opened his eyes and, seeing the expression on her face, laughed. "Is he okay?" he asked.

Breathless, Jordan Blue leaned back to try to glimpse the entire Fledgling Dragon that now loomed before her. She swayed, almost toppling backwards. She couldn't see all of him, but what she could, appeared to be seamless. The blocks of diamond glass were gone, his eyes now larger and more luminous.

She hadn't felt even a flicker of discomfort from him. She grinned and nodded, elated.

"I think he's just fine."

Calyph nodded in agreement. "Good. Now get my troll out of there."

 TWO FOUR

Night had descended on the city and Grandpa turned up the heat in the pod-ment, even though the coming dark had not changed the temperature. There was simply something about the dark of the city that gave him a chill.

He settled into his favorite chair. The children had gone home, Jeanette's sleeping form carried by her careful father. Grandpa had been surprised when, after she had fallen asleep on the couch, Sean had sat back down on the rug.

"Can I ask you something, Grandpa?" he had asked quietly.

"Of course!" he had replied, inwardly delighted.

"What really ended the Age of Creation?"

Grandpa's face scrunched up. "It was a culmination of events that ended it, son. Have you learned about the zero point field?"

"A little."

That took Grandpa by surprise, but he nodded thoughtfully. "Well, a group of monks learned how to harness the zero point field, and all hell broke loose. They took some of the newly created worlds and pushed them into other dimensions. Some very important people disappeared, including one of the leaders of the monks. Hahn, I think his name was."

He had shifted about and taken another sip from his glass before continu-ing. "The galaxies were then struck with a horrible cosmic storm – the Zeal-ots of course said it was the hand of God, and retribution for man trying to take His place. Then the Golgoth Tide came, which many said was the cause of the storm. Whatever it was, all research went from creating to protecting. Then the Rebellion came. Two years after that, everyone on Earth was gone."

Sean was silent for a moment, weighing Grandpa's words. Grandpa could see a touch of fear in the boy's eyes and was glad he had waited for his sister to fall asleep.

"The end of this year will be the end of a millennium," Sean said, his voice low. "They are calling it The Age of Chaos."

Grandpa had waved a wrinkled hand dismissively. "That's only what the Zealot's are calling it. Some are calling the Year of the Fourth Dragon 'the Year of the Rainbow' and others are calling it the New Renaissance. My Grandpa would have simply called it 4K."

Sean had smiled at that and, when he left, had kissed Grandpa on the cheek. Grandpa had smiled, feeling warm all over. Now, the heat in the pod-ment came on and warmed him more. Even better, he had been surprised with a visit from his granddaughter, Johanna. She actually shared the pod-ment with him, but was very rarely home.

He hoped to get in a good visit with her before she was off again. She was too big to sit on the floor, but he hoped to get her to make some coffee that they could share in the kitchen, sitting at the table in there. He wasn't sure he could, she seemed very agitated this evening. More than usual.

"When I was your age," Grandpa started but Scarlett whirled on him like a blade, cutting him off.

"Godammit Grandpa!" Her voice was so loud it was almost a shout. Her hands were balled into fists and she was shaking. "How can you say that when you don't know how old I am? *I* don't even know how old I am!"

It made her feel terrible to yell at him but she just couldn't help it. The pressure of the past few days had been building within her like a time bomb. The capture, the ordeal with Bjorn, the rescue by Blue, being sent home - it was all coming to an ugly and dangerous head.

It had taken her two nights to reach Io and secure Fledge at the IGC dock in Three Mile City. When she finally got a cab and began zooming towards home, it seemed that the only lit buildings in the seething metropolis were GwenSeven companies. She had clenched her jaw and closed her eyes, trying to shut everything out.

To top it all off, she had just gone into her flight bag to get a tranquilizer, only to find she had grabbed the wrong bag. It was Blue's, and the only things in it were a War-era ration packet of peanut butter and a Mylar flight jacket that was the wrong size and the wrong color. Everything was wrong.

That useless bitch! Scarlett had thought as she hurled the bag into a corner. The blue arm of the jacket flapped and hung out of the bag like the limb of a dead, emaciated alien. The number eight that was stitched onto the shoulder in sparkling silver thread lay sideways like the Chimeran double loop symbol for infinity.

Scarlett drew a shaky breath and turned to Grandpa to apologize, trying to calm herself, ashamed that she might have hurt his feelings. But he was looking at her with a soft smile.

"That's not true, Johanna," he said gently. "I do know how old you are."

Scarlett barked a short laugh and then stopped short. His eyes, normally blurry and far away, were suddenly clear and very focused. "Grandpa," she said, shaking her head, "I don't think..." but this time he cut *her* off.

"You are one hundred and forty three."

Scarlett's eyes widened. "I can't be," she whispered. Grandpa nodded.

He watched her for a moment, then pushed on the arms of his chair, raising himself up. Scarlett watched his thin form as he made his way over to a bookcase and pulled out a large, thick book. Scarlett saw her initials, JM, embossed in gold on the spine.

"I've taken a picture of you every year since you were born."

I can't be that old, Scarlett thought. *He's crazy.* She searched her memories to seek out when she had stopped counting. She hadn't stopped celebrating - Grandpa insisted that she be home for her birthday, if it was at all possible, and he always had a little party for her.

But when did I stop counting? She wondered. *At forty?* She seemed to remember going on a week-long bender for that one, but wasn't sure. *When did Dad die?*

Scarlett followed Grandpa as he shuffled back to his chair and then knelt down bedside him as he eased himself back down. He lay the book on his lap, turned it so that she could see it as well, and opened it to the last page in the back. There was a still picture attached to the page that showed Scarlett at the dinner table with Jeanette on her lap. She had her arms around the girl and they were both smiling for the camera.

Scarlett could remember Grandpa taking the picture - she had bought him the camera a few years ago. She, along with John, had tried to get him a modern camera so he wouldn't have to print pictures on paper, but Grandpa insisted. On some things he was impossibly stubborn.

The birthday had been one of the rare times of late when she had been able to be home for the occasion. Everyone in the family had been there; Grandpa, John and Rebecca, and both the kids. Scarlett smiled, feeling a bit nostalgic, and reached out to the book and flipped the page, curiosity getting the better of her.

The next one had been taken from a holo screen aboard the Dragon. Scarlett had called in, like she did every year per Grandpa's request if she wasn't actually home for her birthday. Twice she had forgotten and twice she had been tracked down - once by her father and the second time by her brother - and each time both of them had been furious with her. She never knew why Grandpa was so insistent on it, but no one really knew why Grandpa was the way he was. They just knew he was peculiar about some things and downright obstinate about others.

She had never known that he had taken a picture of her every single year.

The holo snap showed Scarlett looking away and obviously bored. She looked at Grandpa in surprise.

"Grandpa, how do you know how to make a still snap from a holo transmission? Did somebody help you?"

Grandpa smiled mischievously. "I know more than you think I do, Johanna. More than anyone thinks, for that matter." Scarlett eyed him a second longer and then looked at the next photo on the opposite page. It was another one of her aboard the Dragon, looking similarly disinterested. She quickly flipped the page.

The next one was much the same, as was the one after that. Scarlett looked at the pictures and felt shame well up inside her.

How could I not spare a few moments of attention to someone who obviously cares so much about me? She swallowed the lump that was rising in her throat. Grandpa watched her, silent.

Not all were bad. Some had been taken at holo cafés from other systems, and there were the few from the last couple of decades when she had been able to make it home. She laughed when she got to the ones of herself during flight school, and laughed harder when she got to the ones from the decade she had spent helling around in college.

As she neared the front of the book she began to feel wistful, watching herself become young again. It was like going back in time - her body becoming smaller, surrounded by many that she had loved and many that she had lost. She turned yet another page and her breath stopped short.

Her throat constricted and tears welled in her eyes. Though she was on her knees, she swayed drunkenly and Grandpa reached out a knobby hand to steady her.

"Johanna? Are you alright?"

She opened her mouth but nothing came out.

"Johanna?"

"Jesus Christ," she whispered.

"Johanna Mattatock!" Grandpa admonished.

Scarlett's eyes jumped about the room, as if she had forgotten where she was. They finally landed on the flight bag in the corner of the room. She stared at it a long time. The blue sleeve hung out of the discarded bag like a skein that had been shed.

Her mind was spinning like a cyclone and her heart was beating twice as fast but her breathing was deep and slow. Grandpa watched her, puzzled and concerned. Scarlett looked at him and laid her hand over his. It looked gnarled and tough, but felt as delicate and thin as tissue paper. She could feel his life coursing beneath it.

"I have to go, Grandpa. And I need to take that picture."

TWO FIVE

Leoness was much different from what Jade remembered from his last visit. The Jordan noticed upon his approach that it was maturing quite quickly.

The airfield was already quite modern. It had runways, landing pads, parking lots and a transit system that went through the infant town and all the way to the research facility. The research facility that, on his last visit, had been little more than a few lab buildings perpendicular to a row of Quonset huts, was now showing the buds of the university that it would someday become.

One building at the center, as well as one at the airfield and one in town, displayed an enormous G7 stenciled upon its roof.

The research buildings, and the rows of Quonset huts that housed the staff, were set into a valley two hundred kilometers north of the airfield. The buildings were surrounded on three sides by tall, slender, white towers that reached into the sky from the valley floor or climbed the mountainside like the quills of a giant porcupine. Each of the white spires was topped with an enormous, broad propeller.

The propellers - some of which were still, some circulating slow and lazy as if bored with their purpose, while some others were spinning wildly – captured the lunar winds that swept down upon the moon and converted the wind into the energy that powered the research facility. More spires would be built for the nearby town, as they were needed.

The area in front of the research facility, on the only side not surrounded with the propeller-topped white towers, was paved for parking air cars, land cars, and buses.

The town was still under construction. It began in the area directly between the research facility and the airfield and spread out like an oil spill. The town proper grew around a wide but unpaved gravel road split by a median. It was laid down between rows of buildings that would soon be restaurants and boutiques.

The west end of the sprouting city center split into separate, smaller roads that divided and twisted into dirt lanes going in all directions. Pads of land had been carved out where houses would soon sit and bent saplings leaned over dusty lanes that would someday be tree-lined streets. Large swaths of land had been carved out for parks and schools.

Jade pulled down into the atmosphere of Leoness just north of the town and turned, heading for the airfield. On his last visit, the airfield had but a single landing strip and a lone hangar. Now, two new hangars had emerged. One was finished and another was still under construction – its curved metal beams outlined against the skyline like the exposed ribcage of an iron beast. A phallic-looking air control tower rose between the rounded metal bays. Asphalt lots squared off proudly in the dusty landscape.

Jade thought of the elfin cargo pilot as he took Verdana down towards the airfield, hoping she would be there and hoping he would be warming her bed by nightfall - though, if he was lucky, by lunchtime. He could use a drink as well, the last few days had been harrowing and his hangover was already forgotten.

Jade let air-control know who he was as soon as he was in range for coms. Air-control assured him that they were at his disposal. Hangar one would be cleared out and secured exclusively for his use. Jade brought Verdana down and closed the distance with a grin, thinking again about where he might be spending the night. Or, possibly, the week.

Verdana glided into the hangar and settled down on the tarmac. She unfolded around him and he climbed out and down, glancing about. There were people moving everywhere - though some gathered in small groups, hunched over shared acrylics. The bay had been cleared of other craft, as promised, and all doors were being pulled down and secured as he disembarked from his Fledgling.

Verdana closed up as soon as Jade was secure on the ground.

The Jordan flicked his dark hair out of his eyes and headed for the largest group that stood talking anxiously next to the rounded structure that comprised the first floor of the air-control tower. The hunched building sat between the two finished hangars with wide windows that opened onto both bays.

Jade cleared his throat as he approached the group and was about to address them when he spotted Ana. She was with another group of people that were headed towards him. She saw him at the same time and waved. A deep voice spoke up from behind the Jordan.

"Hello, Jade."

The Jordan turned quickly, startled by the melodious voice and the use of his name in a strange place, and looked up at the man who had addressed him. He had golden hair, a face like it had been chiseled from stone, and eyes that were even greener than his own.

Jade's hand flew to the pistol holstered at his hip but it was too late. Bjorn's fist smashed into his face, turning everything into nothing.

The Emerald Jordan flinched as he eased back into consciousness and pain. Nothing excruciating, that fun was still to come. Mostly it was a sharp discomfort. The most was coming from his jaw, where he had been hit. And his lip. It had swelled and the tender flesh throbbed where it had split. His shoulders ached painfully as well, though he didn't know why.

He opened his jaw experimentally. It gave a protesting creak like a rusty hinge. It hurt, but seemed to work. Opening his mouth, however, painfully stretched his swollen lip so he closed it quickly. He tried to shift around to ease the ache in his arms but couldn't move far. He opened his eyes, blinking at the brightness.

His eyes swept through his surroundings. He was in a small, sterile-looking room. It looked a bit like a medical classroom, with small steel tables and chairs. The walls were white and the floor was concrete. Overhead, fluorescent tubes shone with a bluish-tinged, ghostly white light. The room was cold and had a feeling of pressure and claustrophobia about it, like it was underground.

That would make sense, Jade thought. *Great.*

Jade realized that he must be in a storm shelter. They were always dug out when a moon was being colonized, in case a solar storm swept in before the colonists had a chance to get the magnetic force high enough to create the protective bubble around the newborn world.

Sleeping cots and boxes of supplies were stacked against the walls. The room didn't look like it had ever seen the need to be used. Until now.

Jade's gaze traveled down the length of his arms. He was standing up against a wall and his arms were extended out to both sides and his wrists were enclosed in stainless steel shackles. They were standard-sized shackles, rather than adjustable, so the steel circles were not tight enough to be painful, just tight enough to hold him there. The pain came mostly from his arms and shoulders and he wondered briefly how long he had been hanging there.

His mind flicked back to Jordan training, and a sadistic sergeant named Malherbe that used to make pilots wrap their arms around a bar and hang from it. Jade had never been forced into said punishment. He might be small, but he was fast. He never fell out of a run and always flew under the radar.

He looked down and saw that he could stand if he could get his legs to work. With a little effort he was able to get them underneath his body and support his weight, taking the pull from his shoulders somewhat. He had to stand on the balls of his feet to do it, though. Whatever contraption he was in had most likely been made for humans, or a much larger elf. His only guess was that it might be for restraining someone with SM, a temporary madness that often gripped space travelers. The shackles, like the room, looked like they had never been used. Until now.

The Jordan had no doubts about why he was there and what was going to happen. There were a number of beautiful people, that were obviously constructs, in blue coveralls sitting around and chatting it up as they waited for Jade to come around. As he came to, they grew quiet, standing up one by one.

One, however, remained seated. He was the only one that was, just as obviously, not a construct. He was ugly and heavily muscled with a broken nose and evil eyes. At first Jade thought he was squat, but then realized it was just because the man had no neck. His square head perched upon his broad shoulders like a stone in a half-dug quarry.

Jade decided that the man must have been the only human he had ever seen that was more repulsive than the Master Sergeant at the JTC. He also looked like he could crush the Jordan's former sergeant like a bug – the man was grossly large.

One of the constructs approached and Jade recognized the Chimeran as the one that had struck him. He also knew the tall blonde with the brilliant green eyes was the same one that had captured Scarlett after wreaking his havoc on the Dragon.

Bjorn! Jade thought with distaste. His lip curled as the man approached. "You!" he hissed. Bjorn paused, his surprise evident.

"You know me?"

"You're the one that infiltrated the Dragon."

Bjorn smiled, pleased. "Not so hard, despite all your paltry efforts. Like everything else in life and the universe – you just need to know the right people." He laughed as he saw Jade's surprise. Jade clenched his jaw in anger.

"And you're the one that tortured Scarlett," he said. The Jordan's voice was soft but the accusation in it was clear. The smile fell from Bjorn's face.

"If that could have been otherwise..." he started, but left his sentence hanging empty in the sterile air. Jade frowned, waiting for him to finish, but instead the Chimeran simply turned away with a resigned sigh.

The similarity between the way they had him strung out and what Scarlett had told him of her ordeal was not lost on the Jordan.

Not very original, Jade thought. *But that's constructs for you. All the artificial intelligence in the universe won't get them a scrap of imagination.*

He wondered if they would burn him like they did Scarlett, and how well he would be able to take it. He lifted his chin, readying himself as best he could.

Bjorn picked up a corrugated steel box with a black handle and motioned for someone else to move a table closer to the Jordan. The metal table made a protesting screech with its legs as it was dragged across the concrete floor. Bjorn put the box on table and opened it. It was full of small tools, like a medical kit.

Jade jerked at the sight of the instruments, unable to help himself, but the smooth steel circles around his wrists held him fast. Jade pulled on them, trying to stem the tide of panic that threatened to overwhelm him. He felt like an animal trying to escape a trap. The shackles were not made for someone so slight, but they were still just tight enough.

Are they? He thought on the edge of panic. *Are they really?*

He pulled his right thumb as hard as he could into his palm, squeezing his fingers together, and felt his hand slide into the circle the slightest bit. He gave it another yank.

Bjorn clucked his tongue at him.

"Stop that, Jade," he commanded. "It's not going to do you any good. Even if you got free, we would overpower you." The Chimeran stepped closer until he was right in front of the elf. Even though Jade was practically on his toes, the man still towered over the Jordan.

Jade stopped struggling and his body sagged, supported by his outstretched arms. "How far underground are we?" he asked. Bjorn shrugged.

"Far enough that your Fledgling can't help you. Not so far that he can't feel you."

"She," Jade corrected. Bjorn's brows went up.

"Is that so?"

Jade nodded.

The green-eyed Chimeran looked away as he considered and clucked his tongue. "He and she," he said softly.

Jade, seeing the man was distracted, pulled on his right hand as inconspicuously as he could, trying to contract the muscles without twisting his arm. Bjorn moved closer and, without any fanfare, drove his fist into Jade's stomach, sending the wind from his lungs in a rushing *woof*.

"I told you to stop," Bjorn told him without a trace of emotion. He turned away and his gimlet eyes played about the contents of the metal box until they fell upon something that pleased them.

Jade watched as his lungs spasmed painfully, the wind knocked clean from his body. His chest jerked ineffectively and he tried to remain calm, waiting for his body to start working again. Finally, just when he thought he was going to suffocate, his diaphragm dropped back down and he drew in a sputtering breath. He gasped erratically, trying to get his wind back.

Bjorn pulled out a small steel tool from the box. At first Jade thought it looked like a corkscrew, because it had a little handle on it, but the metal part that would have been the screw was straight, rather than curved.

The worm, Jade thought absently, sucking in air. *The little metal piece on a corkscrew is called the worm.*

Bjorn's hand closed over the handle with the slim piece of steel

the worm

sticking out between his ring and middle fingers like a small dagger.

Jade's eyes stared wildly with the knowledge of what was to come. He jerked away, trying to press his head farther into the wall behind him. *Please don't put that in my eye*, he prayed silently. He was ready for anything, anything except that. *Oh god, not my eye, please, not my eye.*

He needn't have worried. Bjorn had no such notion of torturing him. Not any more than necessary, that was. He merely turned to Jade and drove the two-inch

worm, it's called the worm

blade into the flesh right above his left hip. Jade gaped at him, shocked. Before he had time to fully register what had happened, much less draw another shaky breath and scream, Bjorn pulled out the blade and plunged it into the Jordan's other side.

Jade shouted out in pain and horror, twisting uncontrollably in his shackles. His shout was echoed inside his head by Verdana's scream that terrified the elf even more. Bjorn pulled the blade from Jade's side and stepped back to admire his handiwork.

"If you keep doing that," he heard someone remark, "he's going to leak out like a sieve."

Jade, panting shallow breaths like a cornered beast, stared at the speaker that had addressed Bjorn. It was a strikingly beautiful woman with long, dark hair and a tanned, olive-colored complexion. She wore a white lab coat over her blue Chimeran coveralls and had a digital stethoscope draped casually over her neck like a dead snake.

"Well, be ready to stitch him up if that happens, but I doubt that will be necessary. Next time, I'll just leave it in."

A careless shrug was the only response she had.

They'll have to stick corks in me, Jade thought, giddy. He wanted to laugh at the thought but he was already in too much pain. *Then where does the humor come from?*

Jade closed his eyes and waited for the next blow. When it didn't come, he opened them – expecting to see Bjorn towering over him and driving the little blade into his gut. Bjorn, however, was leaning back onto one of the small metal tables, regarding Jade speculatively.

It was obvious that he was waiting.

Waiting for what?

The answer came to him immediately, making him feel sick to his stomach. His sides burned and throbbed where he had been punctured. It felt as if holes had been bored into his sides, possibly with a laser cannon, but after seeing the weapon he knew each hole could be no more than a centimeter wide.

Still, it fucking hurts.

Blood was running out of each thin hole in a slow and easy stream that soaked into the waistband of his flight suit. For an instant, just an instant, he was filled with sorrow and self-pity.

Why? He wanted to cry out. The word rose like a painful bubble in his throat. He swallowed it down, crushing it as fast as it had come. There was no time for that and it would serve no purpose, even if he could answer it.

The question I need to ask is not the why but the what. *I know the why. It is the same reason they tortured Scarlett. They are still trying to draw the Dragon. The question I need to ask is* what. *What am I going to do?*

As if in answer, Bjorn pushed away from the table, crossed the distance to the Jordan in two steps, and jabbed the blade into Jade's stomach just under the left side of his ribcage. This time, as promised, he left it there.   Jade screamed out in pain. A split second later he could hear Verdana's scream - first in his head and then physically echoing around the room.

The entire Chimeran group looked around, surprised. Bjorn smiled and raised his wrist to his mouth. Jade could see the shiny black strip of a com-band.

"Reaction from the ship?' he asked. A chuckle pierced with static came from the band.

"Are you kidding?" a voice asked. "It's going berserk. We figured you had gotten started."

"Is it still contained?" Bjorn asked.

"Oh yeah. No attempt to escape. It seems angry but confused."

"Good. Any physical changes?"

"Other than being pissed? No. No, wait." There was a scratching sound of movement from the other side of the com-link before the voice returned. "The ship itself looks unharmed but there are drops of molten metal on the bay floor that seem to have come from it."

Jade began to thrash, pulling at his shackles like a mad man, his own injuries forgotten. Bjorn's smile was slight and without humor.

"Keep me posted," he told the wristband.

"Roger that."

"You bastard!" Jade shouted, the cords in his neck standing out. He was sweating freely now and thought it might offer enough lubrication to let a hand slip free. Unfortunately, his struggles had only managed to make his hands swell, especially at the wrists where they were being so roughly used.

He wanted to scream at the Chimeran Commander but knew how futile it would be. Instead, he took long, slow breaths and tried to relax.

Bjorn sat back on the metal table. He conferred with the others on trivial affairs. Asking questions about troop movements, other ships, and his second in command. The seconds ticked away.

Jade closed his eyes and tried to stretch out with his mind, calmly taking deep inhalations of the sterile air. He realized that he had to be directly under the bay where they had imprisoned Verdana. He could sense her right above him, swooping back and forth, searching for him. She could feel him as he could feel her, and she was desperate to get to him. Jade smiled in spite of himself.

He realized suddenly that the room had gone quiet and he opened his eyes, expecting another blow. They were all staring at him. It occurred to him it must be unnatural for a stabbed elf just to hang there smiling with his eyes closed. He laughed, wincing at the pain it caused. But the looks of consternation that his laughter created on the faces of his captors made him laugh harder.

Bjorn's wrist went back up to his mouth. "What's going on up there?" He demanded.

"Nothing new, just more of the same."

"Are you sure?"

"Yes."

"Is Stoj there?"

"Yes."

"Put him on."

There was a pause and then another, deeper and more mellifluous voice spoke over the com. "What?"

Bjorn bristled. "That's no way to address your Commander," he told Stoj. "If you were anyone else you'd find yourself floating home."

Stojacovik's impatient sigh was clear over the com. "Well, I'm not anyone else – I'm me. What do you want, *sir?*" He drew the last word out with undisguised sarcasm.

Bjorn's hand clenched into a fist and his jaw tightened. *That insubordinate bastard! I've had just about enough of his shit.*

"Any change in the ship?" Bjorn asked. "Anything in its behavior or condition?"

"No, it's flying back and forth through the air like a caged tiger about a meter off the ground. It's losing some fluid, but not much. A few drops of, I don't know, maybe quicksilver."

"Where from?"

"About a meter back from the wings on either side."

Bjorn's eyes flicked over Jade's hips where the blood was soaking through the green fabric and turning it black. "Keep me posted," he told the cuff and cut the link before Stojacovik could respond.

Jade closed his eyes again. It was a while before the Chimera started talking again and when they did it was in hushed whispers. Jade listened to them speculate about what he was doing.

What indeed? He thought. *What are you doing, Jade? More importantly, what are you going to do?*

Blue was working with Calyph again in the Fledgling Bay when the pain struck her. She had been watching, and helping a little, as Calyph and the troll dyanized the Fledgling's weapons systems. They were standing under Cyan's starboard wing when the Fledgling gave a great shudder and Blue doubled over and fell to the floor, holding her sides.

Calyph watched, terrified, thinking she must be having a seizure.

"Medic!" he screamed, going down next to Blue on one knee. "Blue! What's wrong?" He reached down and grabbed her shoulders to steady her and jerked back when he heard his words echo softly in another voice that seemed to come from the side of her face. The other voice seemed even more panicked than his own.

"Jade!" Blue cried out. "Jade!" She lay on the silver floor, unresponsive to Calyph or the soft voice that Calyph could hear coming from her left cheek. After a few moments of quiet, she rolled her body towards Calyph and tentatively reached up to him.

He grabbed her arm and gently pulled her up. He helped ease her into a sitting position and held onto her shoulders, afraid she'd topple over if he let go. Tears were streaming down her face. Calyph watched as the tears that came from her right eye found her scar and slid down its ragged path toward her red lips. His pointed ears twitched, still hearing the voice that came from the left side of her face, though it was softer now and he could not make out the words.

Calyph turned to see the commotion in the bay that was going on behind him. The turmoil was restricted to the area behind the detfleck fence and, despite the fallen Jordan, the guard was letting no one through the gate. Doc Westerson, who had medic duty in Fledgling Bay, came pelting over to them. He dropped to his knees, sliding from the momentum of his run, and reached for Blue but she pushed him away.

"It's not me," she told them, shaking her head. "It's not me."

"Are you sure?" Westerson asked, shining a light in her eyes anyway. He looked her over quickly, eyeing where her arms were wrapped tightly around her stomach.

She unwound her arms from her middle - carefully, as if afraid she might be wrong, but there was nothing there. She sighed in relief and wiped the tears from her face with the back of a hand.

"It's Jade," she told them, her voice cracking. "They have him."

The doctor held up a com transmitter, opening communication with the bridge.

"This is Doc Westerson," he told Dareus. "We have a situation in the Fledgling Bay that needs the Captain's immediate attention."

"We're having a situation of our own," Dareus answered. "Stand by."

Calyph and Doc Westerson exchanged glances and then turned back to Blue, watching her anxiously. She seemed to compose herself, but they could both see the fear glittering in her bright blue eyes.

Calyph heard the voice again. Though he couldn't make out the words, it was obviously consoling Blue. Comforting her, soothing her. He looked at the Doc to see if he heard it too.

The Doc nodded, seeing the question in his eyes. He mouthed the word *com-link*, not wanting to disturb Blue. Calyph sighed in relief.

Of course it's a com-link, he thought. *What the hell else would it be?*

The two men waited in silence, not wanting to interrupt. They could hear the voice grow a bit louder and the tone more insistent and they exchanged glances. Calyph's sharp ears could make out only two words. *No,* and *don't.*

Blue's eyes sought out Calyph for a moment before turning them to her Fledgling. He knew in an instant what the voice on the com-link had been telling Blue, and why. He echoed the words.

"No," he told her, shaking his head. "Don't."

Jordan Blue looked at the Doc but there was no help or hindrance from that corner. He had no idea what was going on. Blue prodded her sides carefully with her fingertips, as if they were painful and tender. She frowned and looked back at her Fledgling.

"No," Calyph told her again. He put a hand on her arm. "Jordan, you need to talk to the Captain about this. You can't go without his leave." Blue pressed her lips together and drew a deep breath in through her nose, torn by indecision. "At least talk to Blaylock." Her eyes snapped up and that seemed to decide it for her, but not in the way Calyph had intended.

"I have to, Calyph."

She gave Doc Westerson a cursory nod as she rose on shaky legs and turned away. Calyph scrambled to his feet and grabbed her elbow. He didn't know what to say so he just shook his head. He only had an idea of the trouble she would get in if she went AWOL, but he knew it would be huge.

"They're going to kill him, Calyph," she whispered.

"You don't know that."

"I do."

"They didn't kill Scarlett," he argued.

"That was different. I don't know how I know, but I do. I think they are getting desperate. I have to help him." Calyph let his hand drop as she turned away. Hand and footholds were already waiting for her on the side of her Fledgling and she vaulted up and into the open cockpit. The cockpit of a Fledgling that was much larger and much deadlier than it had been only a few days ago.

Calyph watched as the footholds melted back into the sides of the ship and the cockpit closed up around Jordan Blue. The legs rose up and melded with the body and the Fledgling hovered for a second before it turned and shot out of the bay door like a cold and silent rocket.

"Shit," Calyph said. The doc grunted in agreement.

When Bjorn's blade had first pierced Jade's flesh, Brogan had crumpled into his chair, his hand pressed against his side. Everyone in the bridge, including Blaylock, rushed to his side.

Chiara reached him in a single step and knelt at his feet, her long arms going around Brogan's form to catch him should he fall forward. Even on her knees she was still eye-to-eye with the Captain and peered at him anxiously through her square glasses.

Blaylock's first thought, as the man doubled over, was that it was his appendix, until he remembered that Brogan didn't have one.

"Is it your heart?" he asked anxiously, watching the Captain clutch his ribcage. Brogan was shaking his head when another option occurred to the Executive Officer.

"Is it you?" Blaylock asked. Brogan shook his head, grimacing as his hand went to his other side. "Scarlett?" Blaylock asked. Brogan shook his head again.

"Jade," he coughed.

"Shit." Blaylock looked at the five others that were gathered around the Captain.

"Do you want me to call medical?" Dareus asked. Blaylock shook his head.

"Go back to your posts," he told them.

They did, but slowly, looking at Brogan with worried faces. Chiara stayed, crouched protectively over the Captain's form for a few moments, dwarfing him with her long, angular limbs. Brogan looked up at her appreciatively and nodded at her, trying to ease her worry. She rose slowly and returned to her seat. The leggy navigator and the small, dark elf both swiveled their chairs a quarter turn so they could see the Captain while keeping an eye on their consoles. Brogan straightened, grimacing.

"They have him?" Blaylock asked, though he already knew what the answer would be. He could see the pain in his Captain's face.

Brogan nodded and looked around the bridge. He tried to clear his mind but all he could think of was the green-eyed Jordan. His heart filled with sorrow for the young elf and he felt an angry helplessness that he couldn't be there to protect him. Just like he hadn't been able to protect Scarlett. He began to feel a bitter rage drawing out to replace the pain. A rage that he wasn't sure was entirely his own.

"Sir," Blaylock said gently, "we need to contact IGC Command." Brogan nodded absently. Blaylock turned to Dareus sitting at the communication panel but he was already on a line with someone. Dareus cut the link and Blaylock instructed him on what he needed to do. Dareus nodded.

"And sir, you need to call the Fledgling Bay, when you get the chance," the dark elf informed Commander Blaylock as he turned back to his panel and opened up an IGC com-line.

Brogan stared out the front portal, looking through the wide, clear eyes of the Dragon. They had been coming up on Galaza. The watery world hung below them like a cold but watchful eye. The planet's single moon hung beneath it – a frozen tear in the shattered blackness of space.

The Captain listened to their exchange, barely hearing it. He knew the Chimera wouldn't kill Jade right away. It was the Fledgling they were after.

But if they have Jade, they also have his Fledgling, he thought. Brogan rubbed his chin and thought about what Scarlett had told them in her debriefing when she had returned. They weren't after one Fledgling, they were after all of them – the Dragon too if they thought they could get it.

Brogan bolted up as the memory of his conversation with the Crimson Jordan sank in.

"Dammit!" he cursed and everyone turned to face him. "Blue!" he hissed. "Call Fledgling Bay..." but as the words were leaving his lips the Jordan and her Fledgling were already leaving the Dragon. Brogan stopped mid-sentence as he saw the silver light of the Fledgling fly out from under the Dragon. It cruised at a moderate speed while its Jordan programmed her coordinates and then it disappeared in a flash of blue light. "Dammit!" Brogan cursed again. "Get her on coms. And get Scarlett too!"

Please be passed out somewhere, Brogan prayed silently, thinking of Scarlett. *Please be zonked out on tranquilizers. Please be somewhere safe.*

"Actually, Captain," Dareus said. "I was just going to tell you that Jordan Scarlett is on approach."

"What?"

Dareus leaned back so the Captain could see for himself. The flat radar screen had a crimson blur approaching the large pearly shape that represented the Dragon. The holo over the flat screen showed a slowly turning image of a sleek, silver ship with a ruby glow. It was the Crimson Fledgling. She was almost there.

"Do you want me to open up coms?" Dareus asked.

"No," the Captain told him, standing up, his eyes still on the radar screen. He tugged down on his opalescent flight jacket, straightening it. "I'll meet her in the bay. Stay here and contact the IGC and let them know what's going on." He strode from the bridge as quickly as he could without breaking into a run.

Scarlett hardly felt the pain when it jabbed at her. By the time Jade was being repeatedly punctured, she was nearly to the Dragon and could hardly feel a thing.

When she was unable to find any tranquilizers at home, she had raided Grandpa's medicine cabinet. She found some painkillers from when he had hurt his back the previous year and took two of them. They weren't as good as Percolan, but they would have to do. She washed them down with a swig of his brandy, kissed him on his forehead, and left in a cab. She had put the picture in Blue's flight bag and left with the bag and its contents clutched tightly against her chest.

By the time she had reached the jetport, cleared security, and was inside Fledge initiating lift off, she was feeling decidedly better. Maybe even a bit loopy. She found the Dragon and put in the coordinates. Fledge took over, folding space and time the way a baker would fold an egg white into a soufflé.

Scarlett dozed fitfully for the next eight hours. When the drugs began wearing off she ate a protein bar and sipped at some water, and then simply sat staring out into the black. When Fledge was folding space she couldn't even see the stars. Only the black, which would sometimes look more like a dark, forest green.

She brooded on the picture, trying to piece everything together. Before, everything about Blue seemed like a frustrating puzzle and the best thing to do was to not think of her at all. Now, Scarlett felt as if she had the key to the puzzle, a puzzle that had troubled her for years and years. More, she felt as if she were a locksmith – pushing a key into a lock and watching all of the tumblers fall into place.

Not all the tumblers, she thought. *Some still need a bit of jiggling.*

She took two more of Grandpa's painkillers and stared into the abyss. She dozed and dreamed and picked the lock. She was on the nod when Bjorn drove the small

worm, it's called a worm

tool into one side of Jade's body and then the other. She awoke with a gasp, though the twinge in her sides was faint and far away, as if it was were from the memory of a dream. She was glad it had awoken her, though. She was almost to the Dragon. She got her bearings and took over manual flight of the Fledgling.

As she turned and headed down, she saw the unmistakable flash of blue and silver as Blue took off from the Dragon. Scarlett shook with rage for half a minute before getting herself under control. She gave herself a quick mental shake in an effort to clear her mind.

Not yet, she thought. *First things first.*

She dipped down through the black and headed for the Fledgling Bay without contacting the bridge, eschewing a strict protocol.

Fuck it, she thought. *It'd be just another lock I'd have to pick.*

Scarlett flew into the Fledgling Bay only moments after Blue had flown out of it. Calyph and Doc Westerson had just picked themselves up off the floor and were heading back towards the gate in the detfleck fence when she came through the bay door and dropped Fledge down next to them.

Fledge opened up and she was out in an instant, her face full of relief as she spied Calyph. She smiled broadly and the Engineer felt his blood warm at her obvious pleasure at finding him there. The doctor, however, saw something else entirely. The Jordan seemed a bit unsteady, and her eyes were a little glassy, wild, and dangerous.

"Jordan Scarlett," the doctor said curtly. "It's good to see you." Scarlett inclined her head in greeting but said nothing in return before facing Calyph.

"Where did Blue go?" she demanded. She felt something poke her in the stomach and she absently pulled at her shimmering red flight suit.

"I don't know," he said. He wasn't sure what to tell her, since he wasn't sure what had happened. Scarlett frowned.

"What do you mean? Haven't you been working with her on Cyan? I figured she must have gone out on a test run." She rubbed at her stomach. The doctor's hazel eyes watched her closely.

"Are you feeling well, Jordan?" he asked.

"I'm fine," she answered without looking at him. "Calyph?"

"I don't know," Calyph told her. "She just took off. I think..." he stopped short, catching a warning glare from Westerson.

"Not a test run?" she asked, confused. Calyph shook his head, afraid of what to say. "Did Brogan or Blaylock send her somewhere?" Calyph shook his head. "Did she contact the bridge?" Again, the head shake in the negative. "She left without authorization?" Calyph swallowed, but otherwise held still.

Scarlett thought the situation over carefully. The drugs were making her a bit fuzzy in the head, making it hard for her to concentrate. This was not what she had been expecting. She closed her eyes, her lips pressed tightly together. Calyph reached out and touched her shoulder, thinking she might be in pain. She frowned and shook her head, silently letting him know that she was okay.

Going AWOL with a Fledgling – Jesus! Scarlett wanted to grin, to leap, to feel triumphant – but she knew the other Jordan too well. *Blue wouldn't leave without clearance unless it was an emergency. What kind of emergency could there be that the bridge wouldn't give her the go-ahead?* Scarlett let out an explosive breath of air through her teeth. The only thing she could think of was the distress of another Jordan. *And I'm right here.* Scarlett's eyes flew open.

"Jade!"

Westerson and Calyph exchanged glances. Calyph watched Scarlett do what he had witnessed Blue doing just minutes ago. She looked from him to her Fledgling and then back to him with the same indecision.

"Déjà vu," he said. Westerson nodded in agreement. "What should we do?" Calyph asked without looking away from Scarlett. The Doc gave him a sardonic snort.

"What can we do?"

They had no idea that Scarlett's frustration was for a reason different from Blue's. Scarlett suddenly turned, as if she had just remembered something dire, and grabbed Calyph by the wrist.

"Where is your troll?"

"Over by the gate, this side," Calyph said, surprised, motioning with his hand towards the detfleck gate. All three of them looked towards the fence where another commotion was stirring. "Do you need it?"

Scarlett nodded, emphatic. "Yes."

Calyph touched the remote on his belt, summoning the droid. Westerson eyed the small crowd at the detfleck gate, trying to see what was going on. The droid detached itself from the podium base and floated towards them.

"I'm going to see what's going on," Westerson told them. He looked at Scarlett. "Don't go anywhere, Jordan." She rolled her eyes and waved him away. He grabbed his medical bag and took off at a brisk trot. The droid passed the doctor and then slowed as it approached the Jordan and the Engineer. It came to a stop two feet away from Calyph. It hovered for a second before a thick, rounded stub extended from underneath its body and it lowered down to the floor. Calyph looked at Scarlett, expectant.

"What did you have in mind?"

Scarlett drew a shaky breath and told Calyph what she wanted from the troll. He looked at her, surprised.

"Why?" he asked.

"Just do it. Please."

Calyph turned to the troll, extruded a typing ledge from the metal body, and tapped in what Scarlett was after.

"Exactly as I said," she told him. "And just a micro. It's all I need." Calyph nodded as he typed and then paused, his hand hovering over the rubber keypad for a second. With a slight frown he pressed the final button with a stab of his finger and a slip of shiny paper came from a slot in the troll's metal side, next to the type ledge. Calyph tore the paper off from the slot as the ledge slid back into the troll.

Scarlett reached for it but he held her hand away gently as he read it. He looked up at her and his normally almond shaped eyes were round as saucers.

"Is this right?" he asked.

"You tell me."

Calyph looked at the droid squatting next to him. He knew it to be nothing but correct in its entire existence. Taken by surprise and immediate acceptance, the air went from his lungs in a short huff.

"It has to be."

Scarlett's eyes flashed about the bay as she tried to think, tried to decide. She bit her lip before she spoke. "I need you to come with me."

"What?"

"I need you to come with me."

"What's going on?" he asked.

"I'll explain on the way."

His blue eyes stayed wide and round. The Engineer shook his head slowly. "Scarlett, I can't leave the Dragon."

"Who told you that?" Scarlett asked. That one had Calyph stumped.

"Well, no one really told me. I think it's just a given."

"Nothing is a given on a military ship," Scarlett told him. She glanced over to the gate. The commotion was getting louder.

That's not good, she thought as Calyph grappled with what she was saying. He looked at her, his face blank with disbelief.

"I'm the god damned S and S!" was all he could finally get out.

"But you are actually still considered a civilian. You are not here on military orders."

"Brogan..."

"Brogan said he didn't want to see me for two weeks, and unless I get out of here I'm going to be disobeying a direct order."

And soon, she thought, looking at the door on the other side of the gate. *He's coming for me. I know that as sure as my initials and blood.*

"Scarlett, I can't..."

She reached out and took Calyph's hand, slipping her cold fingers inside his warm palm. She drew in a deep breath. "I need you," she told him. She thought the words would be hard to say, but they came surprisingly easy.

Well, what do you know about that? She thought. Calyph's eyes were bright with shock and something else that she couldn't identify. He nodded quickly.

"We better hurry," he said.

Scarlett squeezed his hand. The feeling that rose within her body was as surprising and as hot as the tears that welled in her eyes.

"This is a bad idea," Galen warned.

"So you've said, for what must be the hundredth time on this trip," Blue replied.

"This isn't going to be the same as rescuing Scarlett."

"Also, for the hundredth time. Duly noted." She sat in the now roomy cockpit of Cyan, sucking on a packet of peanut butter – she didn't want to take any chances, not where body fat was concerned. Besides, all the extra room in the cockpit made her feel exposed. It was weird.

Someday it won't be a cockpit, she thought. *It'll be a bridge.* It was a thought she could hardly fathom. *And he's flying faster,* she noted as she watched planets approach and disappear faster than they ever had.

"I feel the need to remind you," Galen continued, "since I don't hear you voicing any sort of plan, and you are running out time."

Blue shook her head, refusing to answer. She could hear Galen sigh and felt his warm breath on her cheek.

"I just want you to plan this out - think things through."

"I played a lot of it by ear when they had Scarlett, I'll do the same now."

"Don't underestimate them, Jordan. They are waiting for you this time. They are *expecting* you."

"They were last time, too. I managed." She could feel Galen blow out an exasperated breath on her neck.

"They were expecting something, I'm sure – but not what you pulled. You caught them by surprise. Don't expect it to happen again"

"Well, I guess this time I was too busy going AWOL with one of the most advanced pieces of equipment in the entire universe to hijack Brogan's Bloodjet. I suppose I'll have to improvise."

"Improvise as you go along, but plan before you get there," Galen insisted. "Do you have any details yet?"

"Well, let's see." Blue leaned forward, examining the new and improved control dash with a lopsided grin. She didn't know half of the stuff it did, or was capable of doing - not yet. She frowned and sighed. She had already put in Jade's last known coordinates but from there she was lost. Her blue eyes searched the console, frustration mounting as she realized she didn't know what to do. Suddenly, she brightened and sat back. "Where is Jade?" she asked aloud. The dash lit up so fast that Blue jerked, stunned, as two holographic images sprang to life over the console.

The first showed the fiery planet of Regulus. The great, orange and red globe hung above the console, orbited by three smaller moons – two real and one artificial. The artificial moon was being readied, and had been under construction for the last ten years, for human habitation.

There were only three developed sectors so far, including a small community that housed the workers that were responsible for getting the terraformed moon ready to be a livable environment. The workforce was comprised mostly of scientists, builders, and landscapers. There were a few pilots and mechanics at the airfield, and culinary crews that serviced all the sectors.

The moon, called Leoness, was a checkpoint for patrols, and Blue had been there frequently. They were, as of yet, unaffiliated with the IGC, which is why the Jordans were sent to check them out from time to time. There was a green blip on the holograph image of the moon, flashing slow and steady.

The next holo was an aerial view of the three sectors. The northernmost area was set into a valley and was comprised mostly of long, connected buildings. A parking area for ground cars and air shuttles fronted the buildings and a number of both vehicle types dotted the asphalt lot.

Quonset huts squatted in rows behind the buildings and tall, white, spikes protruded from the ground in scattered rows to the north and south of the settlement. Though the holo didn't show them well, Blue knew that the spikes were huge towers topped with spinning blades that generated power from the wind that blew through the valley.

She also knew that the buildings were in use by the scientists that were working to make the moon habitable. The plans for everything from atmosphere to irrigation came from those buildings. When they were done, the research facility would be enlarged to a university.

A good hundred kilometers to the south was a mostly-built town, obviously under construction for general populace. Shopping malls and patio-fronted restaurants were built at the center, surrounded by amoeba shaped communities made up of tidy rows of houses. The looped streets would someday be lined with trees. Blue could barely make them out now, just newly planted saplings.

Just over a hundred kilometers southeast of the town was the airfield. An air traffic control tower stood watch over the long runways and landing strips. There were helicopter pads, hangars and lots for private jets, and more Quonset huts for airfield staff and tired pilots. There was a lone terminal behind the hangars and, just past it, the bones of half built hotels rose up to the north and east of the area like fingers from a grave. Between the terminal and the skeletal hotels was a snaky line of air shuttles either to drop off or pick up passengers and ferry them to the town or the research center. The holo projected an emerald glow over the hangar that was closest to the runways.

"So what do you think?" Blue asked, looking at the airfield. "Have they affiliated with the Chimera, or have they been taken over?"

"Does it matter?" Galen asked back.

"I guess not."

"As I recall, there are bunkers underneath the hangars," Galen remarked. "Originally designed as emergency shelters, but they would be perfect for a military base."

Blue's eyes tracked the holos, searching for some clue. She was amazed at the detail but there was no activity that she could see. That was not normal for an airfield of any size, even on a lonely moon. "Either way, the Chimera are there."

"Do you think they are using it just for an airfield or for an actual military base?" Galen asked.

"Does it matter?" Blue asked dryly.

"I guess not. Well, you know where he is. What are you going to do?"

Blue looked over the holos and into the star-studded blackness and sighed. "Well, I can't just go in breathing fire," she said - though she was dying to try out Cyan's newly matured weaponry. "Especially if are they expecting me. But I think my best plan is to head for the research center, and grab one of the transport shuttles. I'm sure I could just ferry in with some others, much like I did the last time."

"You think you could pull off the same trick twice?"

"I don't see why not." She could feel Galen's sigh, and felt his face rest lightly on her shoulder.

"Is Scarlett coming?" he asked.

"Yes. I can feel her - like a boil on the back of my neck. It's not pleasant."

"Maybe you should wait for her."

Blue snorted. "So she can boss me around? I'm better off without her."

"It will be safer with two."

"Not if Scarlett is one of the two."

"You'll have better odds."

Blue snorted again. "You sound like her, now. 'Better odds.' I'm not gambling, you know."

"Like hell you're not! And you take more chances than anyone I have ever known."

Blue smiled. "It's why you love me so much, I'm sure." She could feel Galen shake his head, but she could also feel his smile. His lips were soft and pressed lightly against her skin where her neck met her shoulder, just above the low collar of her blue flight suit. "Okay, Cyan, show me where I want to go."

The holos disappeared and a golden band of light shot from the console and out into the black, growing narrow in the distance.

"Follow the yellow brick road," Galen mused. Blue laughed like a child.

"Yes! But instead of the Emerald City, it's going to lead us to the Emerald Jordan!" She grinned as she felt Galen bury his face in her shoulder. She reached towards the console with her hands.

Cyan, immediately and obligingly, put out a wheel so that she could guide him in.

TWO SIX

Jade closed his eyes and reached out to Verdana. He could see her with perfect clarity. She was in the hangar where they first landed, swooping back and forth over the concrete floor, confused and scared. The entire hangar had been cleared of all people and jets and the bay doors had been closed. The doors were made of corrugated steel, but it was not thick and Jade knew she could bust through them without getting a scratch. He also knew she wouldn't leave him.

Jade sighed and shifted his body, trying to ease the ache in his arms and ignore the hot, throbbing pain where his body had been used as a giant pincushion. He cleared his mind again and reached out past the hangar. He pushed his senses as far as they would go - reaching, feeling.

At first there was nothing, and he let out a slow breath of quiet relief. Then, as he was pulling his focus back in, he felt something. He reached out again, pushing harder this time, and there it was. The cool touch of Jordan Blue. He could feel her, and she was getting closer. No sizzling, angry pulse of Scarlett. Not yet.

Stay away, Jade begged silently. *Just stay away.* He knew they wouldn't. *Maybe Scarlett will. If she is in another system she might be too far away to know what is happening. But not Blue. She's coming, coming to help me, and I can't let them get her. And Verdana. I have to get her out of here.*

He pulled his focus back in and gathered it. Then he sent it out to Verdana; intertwining his heart with hers, enveloping her in a cocoon of comfort and hope. He soothed her as much as he could, pushing out feelings of calm and reassurance - like a mother hugging a frightened child. He felt her rapid heartbeat slow, and her frantic darting about the hangar became easy figure-eights carved into the air of the empty bay.

He waited as she calmed and then, as gently as he could, he told her that she had to go. She tried to pull away from his thoughts, not wanting to hear, but he held her fast. He explained that she had to protect the other Fledglings and the other Jordans. He did his best to tell her it would be all right. He could feel that she understood, but was reluctant because she couldn't bear to leave him. He soothed her as best he could. After what seemed like a long time, Jade could finally sense her feeling of miserable acceptance.

With his eyes closed and his concentration on Verdana, he didn't see Bjorn as the handsome Chimeran plucked another instrument, similar to the first but wider at its base, from his box and without pause turned and thrust it into Jade's abdomen. The Jordan's eyes flew open and he jerked reflexively away from the pain but there was nowhere to go.

"Godammit!" Jade roared, more from surprise and anger than from the pain. He had been so close. Another minute and he was sure he would have had Verdana crashing through the closed hangar doors and flying to safety. Now, he could feel not just her pain but her anger as well. Her diminutive resignation had turned into resolute fury. Now he wasn't sure he could get her to leave, not in time.

Just as bad, he could feel the steady, cool calm of Blue as she got closer. It felt like a sliver of ice along the back of his neck. He knew she would be there soon. Worse, he could now feel the pulse of another Jordan on approach. It felt like the same angry throb that was coming from his wounds.

Scarlett.

Dammit!

He glared at Bjorn but his rage was absorbed by the man's clear green eyes like a sponge. The Jordan's fury collapsed and, for the first time since his capture, Jade began to feel the ghost of panic invade his being. It was something he had never felt before. It was both terrifying and sickening and he fought desperately against it. Despair and hysteria wound a slow but sure stranglehold around his throat and he began to shiver uncontrollably. If he could have freed one of his hands he would have slapped himself.

Get a hold of yourself, he commanded silently. *Find yourself.*

He took slow deliberate breaths – not too deep – he didn't want to push out his diaphragm any more than necessary. It hurt too much. He felt the panic ebb and then die away. He closed his eyes and, breathing carefully, reached out. He pushed his mental reach as hard and as far as he could.

Stay away, Jordans, he sent out to them. *It's a trap.*

Then he pulled his awareness back in and began to search his soul.

Blue's small hands gripped Cyan's wheel, her skin going white over the knuckles. "Did you hear that?" she asked.

"Hear what?" Galen responded. His voice was as tense as the essence of his body, pressed tightly against her back and as taut as a wire.

"Stay away," Blue murmured. "It's a trap."

"Then that's what you should do," Galen said without pause. "Stay away."

Blue exhaled heavily through her nose.

"Or just stay away from the trap," she said softly.

"How the hell do you know where the trap is?"

Blue bit her lip. "Cyan, show me those settlements again." The holo blipped up and this time the settlements were larger, spread across the entire console. "The airfield, obviously. Despite what is going on, it is absolutely still. That's never the case at an airfield, even on a moon in the middle of the night. The airfield is actually the only place where you can *always* count on activity." She eyed the other two developments.

The Research Center showed some activity, but it was mild and most of it was between the barracks and the facility. The parking area had little movement.

The Residential Center was buzzing like a hive, mostly with machinery and droids. Blue bit her lip as her bright eyes darted back and forth between the settlements.

"I don't like the looks of any of this," Galen chimed. I think it's *all* a trap."

"Maybe," Blue murmured. "That doesn't mean we have to walk into one."

"Excuse me?"

"Hang on."

Her eyes scanned the parking area of the Research Center and then sought out a parking structure next to a half-built shopping mall. The Research Center had a number of small air shuttles – the mall, only buses.

Blue gripped the flywheel tightly, feeling the warm pulse of blood through the cool metal skin, and grinned. She pushed the wheel down and drove Cyan into the man-made atmosphere of Leoness.

"Blue?" Galen asked again.

"No," she replied with a girlish laugh. "Yellow. Brick. Road."

Cyan dove steeply, slightly canted to his starboard side.

Jade stood on the balls of his feet, calves tight, arms aching. His green shirt clung to his skin, soaked with blood. He kept his eyes closed.

There is a reason that I am the one here, he thought. *Not Scarlett, not Blue. This is not just chance. I don't believe it was chance that Scarlett was taken first and burned alive. I don't think Blue or I could have taken that. But Scarlett had the greatest will, the greatest determination of us three. She fulfilled a purpose in that role, and now it is my time to do the same. Now it's me. I am here for a reason.*

Jade swallowed but his throat was dry and it made a hollow, clicking sound in his throat. *But what it is it?* Jade searched his mind frantically, racking his brain for the reason why a backwoods little elf like him was the one hanging from shackles like a badly used pin cork.

Well, what makes me different from the others? For starters, and going for the obvious, I'm the only male Jordan for our Dragon. What purpose could that serve? If my captor was female that might give me an advantage, but that is obviously not the case at this juncture. I'm not seducing anyone here.

The thought of seduction sent his mind towards the reason he had chose to come to Leoness on his patrol. *Ana.* His face contorted as he realized that *he* was the one that had been seduced. Jade turned his thoughts from that path and set them back on their original course.

I am the oldest by far, he thought, letting out a careful sigh. *What purpose does that serve? I don't think I am any wiser because of it. Well, maybe less reactive. I think more logically than they do, and definitely with less emotion.*

So fucking what???

Jade's eyes slipped open and they watched from under heavy lids as Bjorn selected another tool from his kit and plucked it out as if it were an appetizer from a passing tray. Jade realized he was getting a little loopy. Bjorn nestled the handle of the tool into his palm, a slender cone of steel protruding through his fingers.

It looks like a wine stopper, Jade thought and then chuckled softly. *Why am I thinking about wine?* His head lolled to the side and rolled back. *Maybe I need a drink.* Another soft laugh. *Too thin, though,* he decided, looking at the tool. *Too slender for a wine stopper.* He shifted his weight slightly and his head fell forward again. He found out within a second what it *wasn't* too slender for – to fit between an elf's ribs. Barely.

With what looked like an uppercut to his body, Bjorn punched the conical blade into Jade's lower ribcage. Jade's head snapped back as he stifled a scream and it cracked sharply into the wall. He let out a yelp of pain and surprise and hot tears streamed from the corners of his green eyes.

Worse, Jade thought. *This is worse.* His head fogged and his breath started coming in ragged gasps. Or maybe he had been doing that already – he wasn't sure. All he knew was that agonizing had become excruciating. Not only did the latest instrument puncture his skin and rip through his flesh, but the wide base of the tool tore through his intercostals and pushed his ribs painfully apart.

The room echoed from above with Verdana's roar. Jade watched with watery eyes and a bit of detached satisfaction as everyone looked fearfully at the vibrating ceiling.

Why? Jade thought desperately. *Why me?*

There was no self-pity in it, only a frantic plea to know the purpose behind his circumstance. He was sure to his core that there had to be a reason.

But what is it? Why is it me?

Jade sighed so hard it was almost a sob. He sank down, letting the weight of his body rest on the small bones in his hands. It made his shoulders hurt terribly but he was past caring.

Bjorn pushed away from the table and walked to Jade. He stood over the sagging form of the Jordan and his eyes were not unkind.

"What the hell?" Jade whispered, panting shallowly. Each breath was a stab of pain that ripped through his body like jagged lightning. "What the hell *are* those things?"

Bjorn looked around, perplexed. "Oh!" he said at last, understanding. "The awls! Yes. They are tools for working leather and other heavy materials."

Jade gave a low, wet, chuckle. "And you thought you'd make a belt out of me?" Bjorn smiled and laid a broad hand on Jade's narrow shoulder. The Jordan winced.

"It is almost over, my little elf," he said softly.

Jade looked up at him, his green, almond-shaped eyes growing wide and round as his dark brows first drew together, then up in the middle.

"I won't make you suffer more than necessary," Bjorn assured him. "Despite the pain, it would take forever to die this way." He took a step back and cocked his head, looking at Jade's body. "I don't need the doctor to tell me that the first ones are already clotting. But the other Jordans are almost here. Once we have what we want, I will end this for you." Jade stared at him, his eyes full of gratitude.

"Thank you," he said softly. He let out a shaky breath that Bjorn thought was a sigh, but he was wrong. Jade chortled, feeling slightly crazed, and a bit of blood bubbled out from the corner of his mouth and ran down the side of his chin in a thin line.

Fucker must have got my lung on that last one. No matter. Not now.

Bjorn also thought that the gratitude was for the promise of the end but he was wrong about that, too. He had, unknowingly, given Jade his answer.

My little elf.

Jade chuckled again and more blood bubbled out of his mouth and thick droplets chased each other down his chin. Singularly, all his differences did not mean much.

Shit, Jade thought. *They don't mean anything. Put together, they mean everything.*

He saw his purpose. It was so clear. And it was so clear that he was the only one who could do it.

I have a purpose, Jade thought dreamily. His eyes were half closed and he waded through a consciousness that would have bordered on rapture if not for the burning and hurting and aching and throbbing that tried to consume him. There was no more panic. He was filled with a sense of calm. A sense of purpose. He let himself relax inside his shackles, sagging down, his aching arms in a far away place.

Jade.

The Jordan froze, shocked out of his peaceful reverie, half balanced on the ball of one foot. His name had come like a soft feather being trailed across his mind. He could feel it as much as hear it – a caress on his inner ear from one side to the other.

Verdana.

It was the Green Fledgling. The Emerald Fledgling. *His* Fledgling. She had spoken his name. She had never spoken to him before. All of their communication - for as long as they had been together - had been oral command and response, based upon a shared neural connection. Lately, though, they could feel what the other felt, and responded in kind.

If Jade was in a hurry, she pushed herself to the limit in speed without him having to say a word. If she was fearful, he reached out with the voice of his heart to make her feel safe and secure. Their bond was strong and always clear, but never verbal on her part. Until now.

Jade.

Her voice wrapped about him like a silken sheet.

Don't.

Jade looked about, uncertain.

The injured Jordan realized two things at once. First, that she had become as calm as he was. Second, was that she not only knew his feelings, but his intentions as well. His mind wanted to dwell on that fact, even explore it, but he pushed it away with a heavy sigh. He was running out of time.

V, it's the only way.

No.

I love you, he told her gently. He felt a deep, racking vibration in his chest and, though it hurt like hell, he knew it was the equivalent of a sob from his Fledgling. His bloody lips, pulled tight in a grimace of pain, smiled.

Please, Jade.

It's the only way.

Jade closed his eyes and pictured his body as objectively as he could. He saw it as a map of muscle, bones, veins and arteries. He could see the throbbing points of pain that were like beacons on the map.

Not the one in the ribs, he thought. *It feels like it is wedged in pretty tight and I might not have the strength.* His mental eye traveled over the map. *The next biggest one would be the one in my lower left side. It's my best shot.*

Jade opened his eyes. He could hear Verdana scream in fear and anticipation and horror, though it sounded far away because he was already cutting himself away from her. He was resigned. He was determined. He was filled with purpose. He would do this for her. For the other Fledglings. For Blue and Scarlett and Brogan. For the Dragon.

He felt for them and lifted his chin, wishing there was something he could do to ease their pain. They flew through his thoughts as he reached out to them. Blue, slim and sexy with her perfect-by-not-perfect face and deep eyes and deep heart. Scarlett, dark and angry. Her temper as fierce as her eyes and as blistering as her body. He thought of Brogan, who always counseled Jade as if he were a son.

The thought of Brogan tore at Jade the most because the very deep part of him, the part that knew he was going to die, also knew that he would be seeing Brogan again soon. Much sooner than the others.

Verdana's scream shook the room and he squeezed his eyes shut as the tears came forth hot and fresh as he thought of her. *Who would be chosen to take care of her? How would she handle his loss? How long would it take for her to overcome the grief?*

A scream of his own shot out suddenly from his throat. Jade looked down to see Bjorn towering over him with his fist against his ribcage. Jade watched, mesmerized, as blood oozed through Bjorn's fingers. Jade felt his shoulders drop once the surprise wilted away. With a sad sort of resignation he realized that he couldn't feel how long the blade was and didn't care.

He gathered his strength and his thoughts returned to his crewmates, his Dragonmates.

I love you, V. I love you, Blue. Scarlett, you too. Brogan, thank you. Thank you all so much, I love you all so much…

He knew his thumb would break and the flesh might rip but that was okay. His hand would come out. It would come out because the shackles were meant for a human and not an elf. Certainly not for a little elf.

The Jordan remembered back to a philosophy class long ago where the students had discussed the paradox of the unstoppable force. The young elves had gone round and round about what would happen if an immovable object met an unstoppable force. Jade realized, with a slightly bloody smile, that he was about to find out first hand.

First hand.

The small elf chuckled out another small mouthful of blood.

Jade sucked in his last breath and pulled on his right hand with all that he could. His forearm pulled taut but his hand was stopped short on the shackle by a small jut of bone in his thumb.

The circlet of steel was the immovable object; Jade's purpose was the unstoppable force.

The Jordan folded his thumb tight into his palm, pulling harder. His small bicep bulged under his shirt as he used it for all it was worth. He pulled harder, focusing all of his strength into a single part of his body. His effort caused his congealing wounds to open up again, forcing the blood out of his body in erratic pulses.

Finally, there was a loud snap from the joint at the bottom of his thumb as the obstinate knob of bone did not just give, but exploded inside his flesh. It was immediately followed by a tearing of skin as the steel manacle shaved his pinky finger near to the bone, but his hand came free.

Free! His mind screamed, though not for the ruined hand that now flapped about his chest. *Free!*

There was a collective noise from the Chimera, too short to be an actual gasp, more of a hitching of the breath. Bjorn whirled around in surprise, but without any trace of fear. For what would there be to fear from a little elf, injured and shackled and tied to nothing and no one except for an unshakable sense of purpose?

Though his shoulder joint felt like it was on fire and the rest of his arm was numb, Jade raised his bleeding hand and groped across his body, trying to find the handle of the awl that had been left inside the flesh just above and to the front of his left kidney.

Jade fumbled at the handle sticking out of his side with sickening dismay. His hand didn't want to work without the thumb. He had no idea that the thumb was the shepherd of the hand and without it the sheep were not only as useless as they looked, but terrified and insanely uncooperative.

"Bastards!" Jade shouted. "You dirty bastards!" The Chimera, of course, assumed he was cursing at them. No one suspected he was shouting at his wayward fingers.

Mustering all his effort and coordination, Jade thrust his hand down under the handle in his side, wedging the metal between his ring and middle finger. He curled his fingers around the handle, yanking it free. Fresh blood burbled out of the hole it left and, as it did, Bjorn was the only one in the room beside Jade himself that knew what was coming next.

"No!" he shouted, lunging for the elf. He moved too fast and his left foot caught on the back of his right heel, tripping himself and sending his body sprawling. He was up in an instant but it was an instant too late.

The other Chimera stared at the Jordan as Bjorn scrambled to his feet, the horror etched on their faces from what Jade had done, not from any fear of what he might do. He was just a small elf, still shackled to the wall, and he was grossly outnumbered.

After Jade yanked the awl free, letting loose a gush of blood from his side, without pause he thrust it deep into the side of his own neck. He pulled the tool out quickly. The awl dangled from his bleeding hand before it dropped with a lonely clatter to the concrete floor.

He could hear the Chimera shouting as they were galvanized into action. Metal tables and chairs scraped frantically across the concrete floor while others were knocked over. Jade felt hands on his body and thought dazedly that it must be the doctor. The sounds and the feelings became far away.

He tried his best to calm Verdana, though he could feel himself fading quickly. Reaching out with his heart, he told her that it was going to be okay. More important, that this was how everything was supposed to be. She screamed in anguish nonetheless. Jade heard the screams echo distantly in his head and realized it was not Verdana's screams reverberating, but those of the Dragon. The Jordan managed a feeble smile.

Gouts of hot blood pumped out of his neck, filling his collar and soaking down the chest of his flight suit. It was leaving him cold and numb. He felt as if he were shrinking. Shrinking into the cold. The cold of space and the cold of waiting for everything and everyone that he had ever loved but the spark of fulfillment warmed his heart. The knowledge of protecting those that he loved burned away the cold to the very edge.

I've filled my purpose, he thought, as a blinding white light enveloped his consciousness. *Thank you all so much for the unexpected and undeserved life you gave me. Thank you. I love you...*

Then everything went black forever.

TWO SEVEN

Blue dropped down into the bright dawn of the artificial atmosphere. She scanned the area on the holo screen, looking for a safe place to land, her hands gently guiding the Fledgling towards a four-story concrete structure. As she did, all hell broke loose in the Chimeran bunker at the airfield.

"Stop him!" someone shouted. Tables and chairs were knocked away but Bjorn was already lunging for Jade. The only one who remained calm was Welsner. With his massive body hunkered down into a plastic chair, he watched the scene before him with his emotionless, pale eyes.

"Put pressure on it!" Krista commanded and Bjorn clamped a palm over the pulsing red hole in the elf's neck. The blood that came out oozed between his fingers as the pulse quickly became slow and weak. It was too late. He tilted Jade's head so that he was looking right at the Chimeran Commander but the light had already gone out of his face. The eyes glazed over as Bjorn looked into them and he was filled with a feeling of dissonance that ran deep into his gut.

He stepped back from the body of the elf which now hung by one arm, shackled to the wall, and whose glassy green eyes stared dreamily at the floor. Bjorn's head, as well as his hand – a hand covered with the Jordan's blood - dropped slowly, as if defeated.

The Chimeran group waited for the fury to come exploding from the Commander, but none came. A loud crackle of static came from the coms. The seconds slipped by.

"Get him down," Bjorn finally murmured but no one moved. He looked up, angry, to see that everyone was listening to com sets; some of them sharing, holding the little earpiece between their heads. All eyes flicked up at Bjorn at the same moment. None were without trepidation.

"What?" he demanded, brow furrowed. Instead of answering, Krista held out her comset to him, forgetting he had his own.

"It's Stoj," she told him.

Bjorn noticed that the black com-strip on his wrist was crackling wildly. Someone on the other end had opened the link and was trying to get his attention. He motioned to the others. "Get him down!" he ordered. This time they moved quickly to take down the bloody figure that had once been the Jordan of the Green Fledgling.

Bjorn opened the link, holding his wrist closer to his face. "What?" he demanded again. Stojacovik's smooth voice spoke from the com.

"You need to get up here."

"I'm needed down here," Bjorn told him. He seriously doubted that was true, watching as Jade's left wrist was freed and his body lowered and laid on the floor, but he wanted time to collect himself before he had to deal with his Executive Officer. Bjorn turned his face away and saw the mercenary, crouched down in chair, watching him. There was a loud crackle as Stoj exhaled sharply, his impatience clear, even over the com.

"Well, I don't know what's going on down there, but it can't be worse that up here."

"Try me."

"For starters, the Fledgling is gone."

Bjorn pressed his lips together. The news wasn't good, but wasn't surprising either. They had known there was a chance it would be able to escape. It was part of the learning process. What they had to learn was how it would escape, so the next time it could be prevented.

"Did it go through the hangar door?" Bjorn asked. The door was steel, but unlike the rest of the hangar, the steel in the door wasn't reinforced.

"No."

Bjorn waited but Stoj didn't offer anything more. "And?" he prompted. He could feel the anger welling inside him, building into a nice sound fury.

"And nothing," Stoj told him. "It disappeared. The damn thing was there one second, screaming and charging, and then gone the next."

Bjorn took that in, his anger dampened by his puzzlement. "Well," he said finally, "that's not what we expected, but it's not worse than what happened here. Or it's about the same. Shit, I don't know."

"I'm not done."

Bjorn blew an angry breath through his teeth. "Well, don't make me start guessing."

"The first Fledgling is on approach. The Blue Fledgling."

Bjorn's eyes flickered. He wanted to ask about Scarlett, but knew better. Hopefully, she would be following the Blue Fledgling. Welsner had risen to his feet but Bjorn held up a hand to him and looked away. "Is she heading for the Research Facility?"

"No."

"Here?" Bjorn asked, his tone surprised but hopeful.

"No."

Bjorn looked around with mounting anger because there was only one other place she could be headed. And, of course, it was the only place they weren't waiting. "She's going for Residential?"

"Yup."

Bjorn roared in anger, cursing and ripping the comset off his wrist and throwing it against the wall where it shattered into fragments of plastic and pieces of bent wire. The other Chimera waited for the moment of fury to pass. They had seen it before. Krista's assistant stepped forward and offered Bjorn another comset, this one a headpiece. Bjorn's hands were shaking with rage but he took it and yanked it on over his ear.

"Godammit Stojacovik! If you don't stop giving me your one-word explanations I'm going to rip your balls out through your throat!"

"The Crimson Fledgling is only a few minutes behind."

Bjorn felt his heart jump. "What approach?"

"She's heading for Research. They'll shoot her down. At least we'll be able to take one by surprise..."

"No! Call Research and tell them to stand down. I'll go after her myself."

Welsner pushed a metal table aside with a massive thigh. It made a protesting squeal, like an animal being slaughtered.

"Commander?" he prompted. Bjorn's handsome face tightened, muscles shifting as he stood, indecisive. "You need to take me to the Blue Jordan," Welsner said. "That was our deal. My boss is the reason everyone in this facility stood down at your command, and why they are standing by right now."

Bjorn's right hand squeezed into a tight fist but he kept his composure. He nodded. "Fine. Let's go." He handed the com headset back to Krista's aide and strode from the room with the mercenary on his heels.

He hurried through long concrete passageways and up two flights of steel stairs. He entered the hangar control room and bodies moved aside to let him through. To the right was the bay where they had trapped the Emerald Fledgling and its Jordan.

Bjorn glanced through the window panels. Sure enough, the doors were still down and there was not sign of the Fledgling. Not that he doubted Stojacovik. He looked to his left where the next bay held the Chimeran fighter jets. Stoj was climbing up one. Bjorn ran into the bay, heading towards his own jet. Welsner kept right beside him.

"I'm taking him to Residential," he shouted at Stoj. "I'll meet you at Research. Keep the Crimson Fledgling contained."

"I'll do my best," Stojacovik shouted, throwing a leg into his cockpit. Bjorn stopped, his foot in the first rung of the ladder that had been pushed up against his jet. He could see the grin on Stoj's face.

"Dammit Stojacovik! I want her contained! Not killed!"

Stoj turned to him, angry. "I'm not going to junk this mission just because you want to bed the enemy!"

Bjorn laughed. "You're just pissed 'cause she stole your jet! Keep her contained, that's an order! I'll be right there."

Stojacovik sank down into his cockpit, fuming. If he could have slammed the hood shut, he would have. Instead, the pneumatic hinges brought it over with a slow, jerky motion and it sealed with a hiss as the air pressurized.

Bjorn pulled himself up and into the cockpit. He thought Welsner would be huffing by the time he got up the ladder but the human seemed to be as resilient as he was large. The man wedged his bulk into the narrow seat behind Bjorn without compliant. The Chimeran Commander was glad that the seats in the jet were one behind the other instead of one next to the other. He didn't want the human squished in by his side.

Bjorn dropped the hatch and ran his finger under the bottom line of switches on the dash. Flipping them up like a row of dominoes, he powered up all systems and started to roll. He guided the jet out of the bay door, pulling up the wheels as the thrust engaged. He switched on a double com-link so he could talk to both the control room and Stojacovik.

"You okay back there?" he asked Welsner as the jet took off from the surface of the moon and made its way north, gaining altitude.

"I'm fine," he huffed. "Just get me to the Blue Jordan. I have business I need to finish."

"Will you be okay if I just drop you off?" Bjorn asked, a smirk driving at the corner of his full lips. "Or will you need some assistance?"

Welsner barked laughter. "You can just drop me off. I'll be fine. Swing by on your way back, though. I'll need a ride home when I'm done." He laughed again and the sound of it made Bjorn want to cringe.

"Twenty on first target," Bjorn solicited over the com.

"Residential 235 by 30 by 877," the control room at the bunker answered. Bjorn followed the coordinates northeast towards the residential development. It ended at a square concrete parking structure next to the shopping mall. The Fledgling was nowhere to be seen.

It must be inside somewhere, Bjorn thought, his eyes searching the area as he set his craft down on the gravel road next to the building. He popped the hatch and Welsner was up in an instant.

"Are you sure you don't need any help?" Bjorn asked. Though he was anxious to get to Scarlett, he knew big money and big power had helped this particular operation go down. He knew better than to thumb his nose at any force willing to assist his own, even if it was for their own ends. "These Jordans can be..." he sighed looking for the right word, "unpredictable."

"I'll be fine," Welsner assured him, heaving his bulk out of the cockpit and placing a boot on the wing of the jet. He looked up the Chimeran as he steadied himself. "But thanks." He favored Bjorn with a jagged grin and then jumped from wing to gravel.

Bjorn winced at the sound and, as soon as he could see the mercenary running for cover, took off for the Research Center where the Crimson Jordan was already under fire.

Blue had just descended into the outskirts of the residential settlement that had been named Lion's Gate, when it happened. She had flown Cyan down and into a vast half-built parking structure. Four stories of reinforced steel and cement blocking made from the lime and gravel native to Leoness. She chose it purposely for its cover and concealment, and not just to the naked eye or aerial camera. The natural gravel of Leoness, and thus its cement, was full of pyrite. The concrete, full of the flecked metal, would also keep the Fledgling off any radar and, hopefully, safe.

The closer Blue had gotten, the more she could feel coming from Jade. By the time she had Cyan into the parking structure, she was practically writhing with the pain. She climbed out and down with a degree of difficulty. Galen was panting on her neck.

"Plan?" Galen asked.

"I'm going to slip through the mall and grab a small construction vehicle. I'm hoping to go for what they least expect." She took Galen's silence for disapproval and she sighed. "Surprise is the best chance I have," she explained, taking off at a slow run, crouching down as she crossed a cement bridge to the shopping structure. From the mall came the hiss of welding arcs and the grinding whirl of constructor droids. "And it's a good sign that they didn't have this place covered."

"I know," he admitted as she descended a block and brick stairway. She reached a landing and turned, heading for street level. Galen sighed. "I just feel, like something bad is coming."

Blue clucked her tongue at him, smiling. "Four doctorates..."

"Five."

"...and that's the best you can do? 'Something bad is coming?' You sound like a child."

"I feel like one," he whispered. Blue stopped.

"What do you mean?"

"I'm frightened."

Blue considered that for a moment. "I don't think I've ever heard you say that."

"I've never been so worried."

"I'll be fine," she reassured him and then, as she was taking the last few stairs, it happened - making her slip and fall the last three feet to the concrete floor. As her right foot reached out for the next stair it made her jerk and she fell, landing on her shoulder with a crunch and rolling instinctively to her knees.

There was a great sucking, from her body and her mind, as if a single filament from each cell in her nervous system was gathered up, pulled taut, and then torn away. It lasted only a second and then it was gone, leaving behind a rush of cold emptiness. She found herself on the gravel road, jagged rocks biting into knees, breathless.

"Are you all right?" Galen demanded.

"Yes," she breathed.

"What is it? What happened?"

"Jade," she whispered. Burning tears filled her eyes and spilled out down cheeks that now bore a fine layer of dust. "Oh my God." Blue hung her head, the saline from her eyes plopping down into the dusty road, leaving dark marks on the small, broken stones.

"What is it?" Galen whispered.

"He's gone." She choked on her words, unable to say any more. She realized that she was out in the open now, but didn't know what to do. Galen was speechless for only a moment.

"You have to get out of here," he told her.

Blue swallowed hard and nodded. Edged with grief and panic, without thinking, she dashed across the street. The road was wide - laid out to be four lanes someday with a wide median running down the center. The asphalt waited in the future, leaving the present thoroughfare as one of crushed gravel and chalked sight lines.

She made for the garage as she had first intended, where she knew there would be the construction vehicles needed for the numerous developments in the proximity. She bolted across the road and into the garage, looking around wildly, still not able to think, feeling like a cornered animal.

The place was huge and crowded with small and large vehicles armed with all sorts of scoops, hooks, and metal appendages for pushing dirt and hauling metal. It smelled of dirty rubber and diesel fuel. The only sounds were the rolling, sandy scrapings of droids as they went about their business with the vehicles.

"No, no, no!" Galen told her. "I mean *really* out of here! You need to get to Cyan."

"Of course," she agreed, looking around. "Of course." But she didn't move.

"Noel, there's nothing you can do. You have to get out of here."

"I know," she said. She blinked at her surroundings, not really seeing them.

"What are you looking for?" Galen asked.

"I don't know."

"Listen to me, Jordan. You need to get a hold of yourself," Galen said firmly. "And you need to do it now." Blue closed her eyes and took a deep breath and then another. She nodded.

"Okay. I'm Okay. Let's go." She was poised to flee back the way she had come when there was a roar of engines and a jet descended onto the half finished boulevard in front of her, raising a choking cloud of dust and spitting gravel in all directions. Blue ducked behind a huge rubber wheel the size of a small vehicle and peeked out through the glassless window of the garage.

The craft alit on the gravel for just a few seconds, long enough to let out a grossly muscled human who was armed to the teeth. He dropped to the ground, gave a few words to the pilot, and turned as the jet rose up, trotting through the rising plume of stone debris towards the garage.

The moon of Leoness was not the only place where hell broke loose. On Dragon 787, more commonly called the Opal Dragon, Captain Brogan was returning angrily to the bridge. He was completely furious. Furious at Blue for taking off, furious that he had been unable to stop even Scarlett from leaving, furious that she had taken the Engineer with her, and furious at himself for sending Jade alone on patrol.

He could feel the emotions welling and sloshing around his insides, like a silo on a seaship being filled with water as the ship itself was going down. He knew that many of these emotions were also coming from the Dragon. As he stalked into the bridge, Commander Blaylock, who had been talking to Dareus at the communication dash console, straightened and fell silent. He knew what had happened. The Executive Officer, however, had no idea what was about to happen.

Brogan might have known, just by the emotions boiling inside him, but if so, he never let on. Not even to himself. It was something that he did not want to think idly about, and so kept the thought pushed far from his mind and covered under darkness.

The Captain opened his mouth to instruct his crew on their next move, but nothing came out. His hands went to his neck, his fingers curling into his collar like claws. Everyone watched as Brogan's eyes filled with horror and anguish. And then anger.

The Captain fixed his eyes on each person, one by one. Dareus at the coms board, small and dark and quick. Chiara, folded into her chair like a great bird, her watchful eyes peering at him thorough the square black frames of her glasses. His orderly, Shawn, stood ready as always, a look of confusion on his young face.

Lastly, he looked at Blaylock. Their eyes met and the Executive Officer's blood ran cold. Brogan dipped his head in a short bow before he turned and strode for the pit and the circle of chairs. Before he sat down, the privacy wall went up, sealing him inside.

Commander Blaylock was shouting the Captain's name when the Dragon gave a great lurch, something the XO had never felt before. He had to grab the back of Chiara's chair to keep from falling.

"Sit down," he told Dareus as he hurried to his own chair. The Dragon gave another lurch as Blaylock reached his own seat and fell into it. "Call IGC command," he ordered. He turned to Chiara to give her the coordinates of an emergency safe-point but she was staring at her console, her hands raised away from it as it were hot and she was afraid to touch it.

"Sir?" Dareus whispered. Blaylock looked around at the Communication Officer and then at his console. What had formerly been a metal dashboard covered with controls, dials, readouts and three computer pads and a built-in acrylic system, was now smooth, silver, metal.

Dragonskin, Blaylock thought.

He glanced over at Chiara's console. Same thing. He turned to Shawn.

"Throw me a com set." The orderly turned and snagged a headset from a hook on the wall and tossed it to Blaylock. "Sit down," the XO told him as he pulled on the set and opened a broadband communication so he could address the entire ship.

"This is the Executive Officer," he said into the mike. "The Dragon is at OpCon Seven. Every crewmember is to secure themselves in their station."

Just then, Chiara gave a little yelp of surprise, staring down at her lap. Blaylock found out what it was without looking at her, for the same thing was happening to him.

Long silver tendrils were snaking up over both sides of his legs and around his waist. The ends met and fused together. Two more tendrils wrapped about his chest, meeting and fusing. They were snug, but not tight.

"What's happening?" Chiara asked, her voice taut with fear.

"I don't know," Blaylock said, imagining that it must be happening all over the ship. "But she's protecting us – which is a good sign. There's not a whole lot we can do right now," he said, but he knew there wasn't shit they could do. "We just have to wait and see what happens." They all looked up and through the eyes of the Dragon.

Blue, who had gotten accustomed to the feel of Galen as an almost constant heat on her back and her neck, felt her lover go cold to the bone. It sent a shiver down her spine.

The human ran to the front of the building with a laser rifle held across his body, not intent on going in, but simply to get under cover and get his bearings. He switched the rifle over to one hand and let it drop slightly as he pulled out a small acrylic and thumbed on an infrared locator. His head jerked up in surprise and he spotted Blue instantly through the open window.

"Run," Galen told her. "Run!"

The warning was too late. The human had flipped his rifle up to his shoulder with frightening speed and was already getting a bead on her. With equal speed, Blue pulled her pistol from its holster and fired at him. Laser fire and a plasma shot passed within a hair of each other. The human and the elf both ducked for cover at the last second.

Blue's shot went out into the street, trailing a shimmering wake of heated air. The laser fire from the mercenary disappeared with a hiss into the huge tire Blue was using for cover, filling the air with the stench of burning rubber.

"What now?" Blue asked Galen. "It's a stand-off. I can't get out and he can't get in."

"He can," Galen told her. "And he will." Blue was about to ask him how he knew when the mercenary jumped through the glassless window and came running at her, laying down his own covering fire with his rifle.

Blue jumped up, turned on her heel and bolted through the garage. Her speed and agility were astonishing, even to Galen. Like a gazelle from the lion she ran, darting between scrapers and haulers and diggers. The mercenary was terrifyingly quick for someone his size, and kept firing as he closed in on his prey. Each shot got closer as she dodged behind one machine after the other. The droids in the garage kept about their business – cleaning, repairing, refilling - as if no one was there and nothing going on.

Suddenly, Blue burst past a row of tractors and into a huge open bay, losing her cover. She sprinted for the vehicles waiting in rows on the other side but the mercenary reached the bay only a second later and led her with laser fire.

"Get down, get down!" Galen shouted.

The mercenary's fire would have effectively decapitated the Jordan had her foot not hit a patch of oil and sent her sprawling. She flailed wildly as her momentum carried her crashing down, rolling under the pulses of fire as she fell. A single pulse of laser fire caught her across her left shoulder, a searing cut through cloth and skin and muscle. Blue cried out in pain as she went down, and then again as she cracked her left elbow on the concrete floor.

The human came pounding after her, laying down a constant stream of laser fire until the charge ran dry. He hurled the weapon from him and pulled a long barreled light pistol from a holster on his chest. Blue rolled over her now useless left arm and smoking shoulder and came up to a recumbent position on her back, firing her own pistol between her knees.

The plasma fire caught the human on his right side as he was raising his gun, melting the flesh off the right side of his chin, neck, and shoulder. He screamed out in surprise and pain and bolted for cover to his left.

Blue rolled under the belly of a huge earth-mover and came up on her hands and knees, crawling frantically away. She threw glances over her burned shoulder as she ducked behind a small post-digger. Galen was near hysteria and she shushed him as quietly she could. She put her back to the digger and closed her eyes, quietly gasping for air and trying to ignore the pain in her back.

I can't let him drive me, she thought. *I have to come up on him and smoke him, or get the fuck back to Cyan.* Her blue eyes opened and darted about the collection of vehicles, scanning the floor underneath them, trying to pick up some movement on the other side. She saw nothing, not even a reflection.

She tried to guess where he could be, judging by the direction he ran when she shot him. She narrowed her eyes at the spot she thought he must have gone, behind the wheels of a huge tractor on the far side of the vehicles. She jumped as the air was cut by his laughter, gravely and derisive, and much closer than she had expected. His laugh was no more than a few meters away. She turned her head, craning her neck to see around the digger without getting her face shot off. She figured he had to be behind the very next row of machinery, just to her right.

Scarlett, too, was dodging laser fire. She spun Fledge through a rain of red pulses. Though the Fledgling didn't receive so much as a scorch, Calyph's face was decidedly green. Scarlett banked away from the reverse strafe that was coming from a small, isolated sector of the research facility.

"Don't worry," she told Calyph. "There's only a couple of guns down there, and they aren't very good."

"It's okay," Calyph said, swallowing. "This is a good thing. As much as I've worked with Dragons and Fledglings, this is the first combat run I've ever been on." He exhaled through barely parted lips. "I'm sure this will be very educational."

Scarlett grinned. "So positive!" she remarked. Calyph gave her a weak smile.

"Just make sure I live to use the education you are giving me."

Scarlett laughed as she spun away from the red beams that were shooting off at regular intervals from the surface of the moon. "You'll live," she assured him. She flew into the forest of the white towers, evading their flat, spinning blades with ease. The laser fire didn't follow. "Fixed cannons," she muttered.

"Where are Blue and Jade?" Calyph asked. Scarlett eyed the last holo she had called up onto the dash.

""It looks like they are holding Jade at the airfield." She clenched her teeth together. "I can't see Blue," she said tersely.

"Do you really think..." he started but Scarlett cut him off.

"I don't think," Scarlett said sharply, "I know."

Scarlett was pulling around for another dusting on the other side of the center when she cried out. Her right hand shot to her neck and groped about, trying to staunch the flow of blood - but there was no blood. There was rush of horrible pain followed by a great emptiness that left her cold inside. Her mouth fell open as if the hinges in her jaw were broken.

"Are you alright?" Calyph asked. Scarlett shook her head. "What's wrong?"

"Jade," she said, her voice breaking. "Gone."

"Dead?"

Scarlett nodded, her eyes welling and overflowing though they were now dazed and far away. They flew in silence, Calyph speechless and the Jordan in a state of shock.

Tears coursed down her cheeks. She flew blind, lost in the horror of everything. She didn't even notice that she had gone far past the research center. Fledge had taken over and was coasting low over the flat surface of the moon.

"I never knew I could feel him before," she finally said. "I knew he could feel me, and Blue too, but I thought it was an elfish thing and I never paid it any mind. Not until now." Her voice cracked on the last two words. "Oh God, now that he's gone, I know I must have been feeling him all along. I just didn't know."

The sense of loss was great that it was all she could feel. It immediately called to her mind the loss of her father - turning her already ragged breath into choked sobs. Her feeling of isolation was so great and the gulf in her life so wide that she yelped in surprise when Calyph reached over and took the hand that fallen useless in her lap.

"Why don't you take us down?" he said gently.

She looked at him for a moment, her dark eyes still overflowing with tears, though seeing him there seemed to make the well run dry. Having him there made her feel better. Stronger. It surprised her, but pleasantly.

She could feel Fledge as well - sending her waves of comfort through the ocean of sorrow that he felt as well.

Scarlett took a deep breath, and then another, and smiled. After a moment, having regained a few ounces of composure, she shook her head. She used the hand he was holding to brush the tears off her cheeks. She kissed the fingers on his hand before letting it go and finding the wheel again. She eased Fledge into a wide turn and headed back for the research center.

"I'm fine," she told him, taking a deep breath into her lungs in an effort to pull herself together. "Or at least I will be - when this is done." She reached out and grasped his hand again, squeezing it. "Thank you," she said. Calyph smiled.

"Of course."

As they drew back towards the center, Scarlett began to regain enough of her sense to formulate a plan.

The research center is no good, she thought. *They were already waiting for me. I could try Residential One, but if they already know I'm here and Jade is already gone, I might as well...*

Her thought was cut off as a jet came firing at them from the south. Scarlett dropped Calyph's hand and jerked the flywheel taking them past Research and into the maze of towers and blades. She flew between the spinning blades of one and low under the blades of another, frowning at the oncoming ship, trying to decipher who it was.

Calyph bit his lip, his eyes wide, but Scarlett didn't so much as flinch. She gave Fledge his throttle and pulled high, evading the fire coming from the belly of the other craft. Scarlett quickly pulled around to get behind the enemy and unleashed Dragonfire as she went. Calyph wished briefly that Fledge had been the first Fledgling he had been able to grow.

The other pilot pulled his craft around simultaneously, preventing Scarlett from following. There was an audible click from the coms console and Calyph and Scarlett both started, surprised. Only an IGC ship could open communications with a Fledgling. The click was followed by a melodious, if bitter, voice.

"It's not going to be that easy, bitch."

Calyph felt his own hand tighten into a fist as he awaited Scarlett's fury. To his surprise, she laughed.

"Well, well, well," she said, her voice more jovial than he had ever heard it. "Look what foul-mouthed play-thing stole themselves an IGC ship."

"You didn't leave me much choice."

Scarlett laughed heartily. "Stoj, is that you? I should have known that was your jet I took - it smelled like a dead Golgoth."

Stoj closed the distance and replied with a strafing of laser fire. Scarlett outmaneuvered him with ease, grinning and unleashing sulfur fire from the Crimson Fledgling. Scarlett took the high air as the jets screamed by one another and drops of sulfuric acid hit Stoj's right wing and began eating its way through.

As they passed, another fighter came barreling in from the south. Scarlett and Stojacovik doubled back as Bjorn joined them.

"Godammit Stoj! I gave you an order!" Bjorn shouted. To everyone's shock but his own, Bjorn hooked right and flew up alongside Scarlett. Scarlett stared, unbelieving, out her port window. She slowed as the Chimeran leaders closed the distance between their jets.

"You wouldn't dare!" Stoj hissed.

Moving deftly with a skill that Scarlett couldn't help but admire, Bjorn flipped his craft and shot at his Executive Officer. Belly to belly, he took out Stoj's guns without taking down his ship. Stojacovik realized what the Chimeran was doing only when it was too late to stop him. He spun off to the north, now unable to engage, screaming curses at his Commander and the Crimson Jordan.

Scarlett, barely able to believe what she had just seen, set her jaw and shot off to the south. She headed back toward the research facility with Bjorn in the heat of her wake.

"Scarlett?" he called over the com.

Scarlett reached out to the console and ran her thumb over the manual override on the communications system. Calyph looked at her and then looked forward again, closing his open mouth. Scarlett circled back over Research One and dove into the swarm of towers and blades. Bjorn followed.

Scarlett flew easily, dipping and rising between the flat thwap-thwap of the flat, massive arms. Bjorn flew in her wake, evading the rotors, though they came much closer to his ship. And with each pass Scarlett led him through, the giant blades got closer.

She slipped and spun while he dodged and swerved. Though he was a highly experienced pilot, the Chimeran Commander did not have Scarlett's grace as a fighter.

For the Jordan it looked a dance. For Bjorn it looked a dare.

Calyph gripped at the edge of his seat and waited. Seeing that the enemy would not fire on them, and that Scarlett was not going to fire on him, he knew it was going to be a game of patience and skill. The pilots watched and timed and dodged and flew, knowing that only the blades would mark the end of their silent battle.

Bjorn soon realized that Scarlett was timing each pass not just to keep her Fledgling from missing the blades, but in an attempt to lead *him* into one. He knew that a lesser pilot would have already gone down.

Scarlett took her Fledgling down through the hills, shooting out from the forest of towers and turning quickly, darting back into them on the southern side. They were pressed closer on the south face, and she dove carefully between the rotors.

She glanced at Calyph. "Don't worry," she told him, though he had remained silent for the dance through the blades. "I have the fastest reflexes of any of the Jordans and because of me, Fledge does too."

Calyph forced a smile. "That's not the reason you're smiling," he said, looking at the smug look set into her beautiful features. Her smirk was so far from contained that it was contagious. Scarlett nodded, the smirk widening as she darted between two spires and their spinning blades.

"I'm smiling because I can also feel what Fledge feels."

"And what is that?"

She grinned. "That the wind is picking up."

Scarlett pushed Fledge faster, dodging the blades that had begun to rotate with the speed of a snowball going downhill. Faster and faster they twirled – till the once lazy but massive arms now spun with fervor. Bjorn had to dip his wings with a quick jerk time and time again to keep them from being smashed by the flat blades and driven to the ground.

Though he trusted her completely, Calyph couldn't help the drops of perspiration that began to bead on his brow and upper lip. The seconds stretched and stretched like warping taffy, but Calyph knew that it had only been moments when it finally happened.

A sudden gust of wind blew from the west, sending the blades into a whirling frenzy. Scarlett glided through them with as much ease as ever, though perhaps a bit closer, but one was too close for Bjorn. As they passed a massive tower, a huge blade came whipping around too hard and too fast. It clipped the wing of Bjorn's jet almost midway through, smashing a chunk from his craft and sending him into a rolling spin towards the hills.

Scarlett, lips pressed tight and brows drawn down, looked almost angry at the outcome. She gave her head a small shake and pulled Fledge in a wide turn past the spinning forest and headed due south.

The Opal Dragon was aging, but far from old. Hundreds of years she had lived, flying through the cool vacuum of space and time. For a time she had flown with her sister and her cousins and the humans they had laughingly called Dragon-children. Long ago, they had fought together. Those times were glorious, full of excitement and victorious fire. But they were long ago and now she grew slowly and surrendered to the change.

Century after century, she had seen much come and go. She knew pain and loss. She had grown with her first Dragon-child only to see it eventually succumb to his age, despite the efforts of its human kin. The Opal Dragon had become one with her human, and she carried his essence within her.

She had known joy when she had manifested her eggs and exultation when all were borne and all were hatched. The Opal Dragon watched her Hatchlings become Fledglings and listened to the whispers of her sisters and their cousins from between the stars. She was more machine now than a creature of the heavens, and became more so every year. But still, she lived.

The Brogan-child had intertwined with her quickly. She did not know if it was to fill the void the first Dragon-child had left, or if was nature taking its calm and capricious course. The love for the Brogan-child grew and they began to know each other intimately. A courtship of over a hundred years and not yet blossomed. Why should it? She knew she had time.

Time stretched before her like the universe. Something to be worked or played, like black mud scooped from the primordial sea of an infant planet. Space was an equally malleable plaything.

She believed that her days of playing were over. Now she mostly slept, guided by Brogan's gentle hand and gentle heart, and kept a bemused but watchful eye over her Fledglings. She had thought that her days of fighting were behind her as well.

When she was young, she was filled with a great feeling of peace and knew that the humans and the elflings that cared for the Dragons were good creatures. She was naïve to think that all such creatures must be similar by nature. It wasn't until later years, towards the end of her growings, that she learned not all of the human-kin were good or peaceful. Some were destructive, greedy, and careless for the balance of the galaxies. Some were murderous, even to their own kind.

The war that she fought in when she was young, was won. The victory was great and the safety of the humans and elflings seemed assured. But Opal had watched speculatively over the last hundred years as the tides of the universe began to shift. She became wary. Another race had been born.

These were not the monsters of the Golgotha Galaxy, nor any of the other humanoid types that her kind had encountered throughout the universe. These beings were *new*. Opal and her kind referred to them as the Otherlings, not quite sure what they were, but assured in the fact that they were dangerous, and a threat. Just recently one of the Otherlings had invaded her body and had tried to take her life. The same race, so similar to the ones she cared for, had captured and tortured her Crimson Fledgling's Dragon-child.

At the time she had been tormented. What could she do? What would she do? The feeling was a volcanic turmoil. She could feel that the Brogan-child was racked with the same desperate indecision. Another of the Dragon-children had rescued the other, but the sweet relief had been short.

Now, another Dragon-child had been captured and lay dead upon a cold floor. The Emerald Fledgling had fled into The Black out of sorrow and despair. The Azure Fledgling remained frozen, silent and sequestered while its Dragon-child was chased and shot and injured. The Crimson Fledgling and child were *both* under fire.

There was no question now. No indecision.

The Opal Dragon stretched. She reached. She *remembered*.

Not all of the memories were hers, some were from those that came before, Dragon and human alike. She drew upon what she knew firsthand and what they remembered from long ago. Plans of defense and attack mingled with the echoes of Dragonfire and her knowledge of The Great Light. Of possibility. She stretched, pushing her living tissue deeper into the living metal that infused her body. The smooth outside of the ship wrinkled and puckered until the silver skin was shed, melting off in a thin flood of quicksilver - replaced by gleaming white Dragonscale.

The bottom of the Opal Dragon's head, topped by the semi-hollow area for the humankind to watch and lead, split apart as her jaw dropped open. Gleaming platinum fangs dripped with molten starfire.

The Dragon was awake, and she was drawn.

Drawn to her children and their Dragon-children. To their pain and to their need. Drawn to what was just and her explosive will to impose it.

The Dragon's deafening scream filled the empty void of space as she stretched her wings. Time and space were bent and pressed flat. They were creased. The Dragon crossed the solar systems of the galaxy like a shooting star of light, faster than thought and full of burning rage.

Jordan Blue froze. The mercenary was close. Too close. She wondered if he knew exactly how near he was to her, and then she thought wildly about how she was going to get away. The back of her shoulder hurt like hell.

"You elves surprise me with how much fight you have in you," he called out. His voice was loud and forceful.

He must not realize how close he is, she thought. She crept back, trying to get as much distance from him as she could without making any sound.

"Your boyfriend was the same way."

Blue stopped and straightened.

What? she almost called in surprise, before realizing that he was trying to get her to give away her position. She could hear him moving slowly. She could hear his heavy breath and smell his sweat. She shuddered and closed her eyes.

I have to get him to go the other way.

Her eyes searched the floor for something that she could throw. A tool, a dirt clod, anything. The concrete floor was clean of all debris and tools, polished clean except for a few lingering drips of oil that had been swiped but not completely removed by the cleaner droids.

She sidled up to a short backhoe, no more then six feet tall. She squatted down and looked at its tires. There were small gray pebbles stuck between the treads. She pried a few loose and then hurled them in a high arc to her left.

Blue heard the silence as the human froze, and then there was a soft whisping of fabric as he moved away. She backed up until she had the last row of machines in front of her and then stepped cautiously to her right and into the open bay. The human stepped out from the cover of the machines at the same time, only a few rows away, and leveled his gun at her. His smile was gruesome and cruel, and she knew instantly that she had been played.

Before the next electrical impulse could shoot through her brain, she was on the floor. The Jordan was thrown forward and down so fast she didn't know what hit her. Her bewildered mind tried to grasp at what had happened - if possibly an unseen accomplice had snuck up behind her or if she had been thrown down by some ricochet of force from his weapon.

Then there was a great ripping as her body was forced closer to the floor - the feeling of someone pushing her down while pulling the skin off of her back. Then she was shoved roughly away on her knees as her other plasma gun was jerked from its holster. The Jordan felt like a mashed heap thrown upon the floor.

"You!" The mercenary hissed. Blue looked up to see Galen standing protectively in front of her. He looked like a holo transmission and his form flickered with blue light. He had her second plasma pistol pointed at the mercenary. "Ohhhhh no!" The human accused, as if Galen's appearance at the party was in extremely poor taste. "You're dead!" The mercenary squinted as if unsure, and then nodded, sure. "I blew a hole you so big, you were practically in two pieces!"

Blue's eyes went wide at his remark and even wider as the mercenary, not wanting to take any chances, blasted Galen with a barrage of hot rounds. Blue ducked her head and the rounds went right through Galen as if he really were nothing more than a projection. The human shouted at him, reaching for another weapon. "I bagged and dragged your corpse all the way to Topeka..."

Galen cut him off with a flood of plasma fire from Blue's pistol. The human screamed and twisted away but Galen kept the gun trained on him, unrelenting. The plasma opened him up like a wax doll, melting him from the inside. His chest burst open, sizzling, and for one horrific moment Blue could hear his scream coming from inside his throat, as his trachea dissolved, as well as from out of his mouth. Then the midsection of the human burst into ash with a sickening belch.

Within only a few seconds, what was left of the mercenary sank to the floor in a stinking, smoldering heap. Galen lowered the gun and slowly turned. He looked at the Blue Jordan, his eyes full of fearful sorrow.

TWO EIGHT

Scarlett took Fledge down in a sweeping dive into the sector of land called Residential One. She flew over the hubs of half-built houses and made for the shopping district. Over the stores and markets that were mostly complete she dove, honing in on the large cement structure to on the east side of the shopping mall.

"How will you find them?" Calyph asked.

"I can feel them," Scarlett told him. "I guess I always could, I just never realized it. Kind of like how I never think of my toes, unless my boots are too tight. Then I am painfully aware of them. Otherwise, I have to think about them to feel them. Does that make any sense?"

"A little. What is that you feel?"

"Blue is hurt, but she is alright. She was in danger but now she is okay. She isn't with Cyan, but close to him."

She was amazed at her own sentience for the other Jordan and Fledgling. Now that she was conscious that she *could* feel them, she couldn't believe that she had never noticed it before.

Never under estimate the power of denial, she thought, shaking her head.

What she didn't tell Calyph was that she could also still feel Jade, like a phantom tingle in an amputated limb. There was a cold and numb feeling where there should have been none. She pushed the thought away. It made her heart ache too much.

"And you never noticed this before?"

Scarlett shook her head. "How much do you notice the bone in your ankle? Even though it sticks out from the bottom of your leg you probably never notice it all, unless something goes wrong with it."

Scarlett overshot the parking structure and circled back, looking for an entry point. She was pretty sure that Blue wasn't there, but was certain that her Fledgling was. She guided Fledge down into the wide, unfinished space and there was Cyan. The Crimson Jordan stared at the Blue Fledgling, amazed at the change that had taken place while she had been gone for such a short period of time. Scarlett set Fledge down on all four legs next to his brother, and smiled as she felt a wave of relief from them both.

Fledge opened and the two inside climbed out and down. Scarlett's eyes darted about the empty space and quickly spied the staircase. She jerked her chin in the direction of the stairs.

"There."

Calyph and Scarlett left the Fledglings and followed the same path that Blue had taken down the stairs and out into the unfinished boulevard. They had just crossed the first two lanes of crushed rock and were stepping onto the median curb when a jet dove from the brightening sky and came screaming down the street.

Its wings ripped apart at the tips as they drove through the tops of the restaurants and boutique shops, sending bits of brick and stone in all directions with the speed and sound of gunshots.

The hijacked IGC fighter craft tore a path of destruction along the gravel road and left a plume of spitting rocks in its wake. The firing weapons on the jet, along with its landing gear, had been blasted off. The fighter was being flown by a raving mad Chimeran officer. It was Ron Stojacovik.

He came barreling at the two in the street in a suicide dive and Scarlett thought she could hear his furious screams over the roar of his engines. Her hand went for her pistol, knowing it would be useless, but she also knew she would never make it to the other side. Her only instinct was to go down fighting.

Her gun was out and up but before she could pull the trigger the pistol went flying out of her hand as Calyph knocked her down fell over her body, protecting it with his own. Scarlett found herself on her hands and knees - her face inches from the crushed rock in the median lane.

Gravel. Jesus Christ why is it always gravel?

Scarlett turned her head, her cheeks brushing against the dusty jagged rocks, looking up as Stoj's jet came burning towards them. The wings shot off chips of brick and stucco like bullets from a semi-automatic. Calyph held Scarlett down with his right arm wrapped tightly around her body, and raised his left arm towards the oncoming jet, his left hand stretched out and his fingers splayed open wide.

Scarlett's eyes met those of the Chimeran Officer as her ears were deafened by the warbling scream of tearing metal.

The nose of the jet exploded against an unseen force, not twenty meters from where she crouched in the gravel road. Calyph kept one arm stretched out to stop the jet and the other held her close. The air was filled with a whining squeal as strips of metal peeled away from the imploding craft. Rivets and engine block flew apart and shot off in all directions except where the Jordan crouched, held tight by the Engineer. The fuselage split and melted and splintered into flying shrapnel and drops of molten metal.

The plexi of the cockpit hood shattered and Scarlett was now sure she could hear Stoj screaming as shards of plastique and bits of his instrument panel punctured his body before it was all gone in one final explosive burst

The entire ordeal was over in less than seven seconds. The Jordan and the Engineer were alone in the dusty street.

Wisps of blacked plastique wafted away over the buildings while smoldering bits of scrap metal plinked down into the gravel. The only piece intact was a remnant of the tail that had gone spinning off into the widow of a clothing store, breaking glass and half-built displays, sending all the worker droids in a scatter.

Stojacovik was nowhere to be seen.

Scarlett stared at the spot where he had been, dumfounded for near a minute. Then she shifted in Calyph's protective embrace, turning so she could see him. She stared, bewildered, into his placid face. His blue eyes were cool and calm.

"How in the fucking hell did you do that?"

Calyph shrugged. "I'm an Engineer," he said simply, as if it would explain everything.

She was still staring into his face as if she was seeing him for the first time, not just as a person but for who and what he really was, when the air was split by the scream of the Opal Dragon as it burst into the atmosphere of Leoness.

The two already crouched down in the street were thrown flat, the flesh of their faces smashed into the gravel with the force of the time pendulum crash. It was followed immediately by a sonic boom as the air exploded all around them.

Calyph and Scarlett stared, terrified and incredulous as the Dragon burst into the sky above them. Its great body was enormous, easily dwarfing the residential town, and covered with pearlescent scales that reflected the bright morning light in blinding prisms of color.

Sensing that the Dragon-children were now safe, she let out a deafening roar and wheeled south towards the airfield, spewing white-hot Dragonfire. There was still vengeance to be delivered.

Calyph helped Scarlett to her feet and slipped his arm around her waist. Together, they watched the Dragon turn and head for the airfield with frightening speed. Only a second later the sky to the south turned so white with the light of the explosion of starfire that they both had to shield their eyes.

They held onto each other like frightened children until Scarlett recovered herself and remembered what she was after. She took Calyph by the hand.

"Come on!" she urged as she led him across the street and into the garage. They stopped to let their eyes adjust to the darker interior and listened. Calyph could hear the hushed voices of two people. Scarlett could feel Blue immediately; she was like a soft breath of cool air on her cheek, though the air in the garage was still. She tugged on Calyph's hand. "This way!"

Noel hunkered down on the cement floor and swallowed at the terrible pain that rose in her throat, unable to speak. Galen, moving slowly, knelt down on the tarmac so that he was facing her. His blue, ghostly image flickered like a projection from a dirty holo. The gut wrenching sense of loss within her made her want to weep. The concern in his eyes made her want to die.

"Is it true?" she asked. "You're dead?"

Galen paused for a second, and then nodded. The wrenching in her gut twisted, driving deep through her. He was everything to her. *Had been* everything to her. The shock was too much, the pain too great.

Gone! She fell back, her rump dropping down on her heels. *Gone forever!* She bit back a sob and then shook her head.

"No," she said. "I can't accept that."

"Neither can I," Galen said softly. "I think that's the reason I am still here." Blue turned her face away.

We'll never be together again. We'll never have children, not that we ever wanted to, but still. I'll never go to sleep with my head on his chest or sneak up on him when he thinks he's alone. He can never hold...

As if to answer her thoughts, he caught her hand and held it between both of his. She gasped and tears spilled over the tops of her cheeks.

"We're together," he told her. "I know it's not the same, but I'm here."

Jordan Blue reached out with her other hand and touched his face with her fingertips. She could feel him.

Of course I can feel him, she thought. *I've been feeling him for…*

A sense of dread came over her like a cold and heavy cloak and she had to keep her body from shivering, from shaking.

"How long?" she asked, her voice barely above a whisper. Galen pressed his lips together as if he didn't want to tell her and then let out a sigh.

"Since the day after you left."

A strangled cry unwound from her throat and more tears spilled down her cheeks.

All this time. All this time!

Galen brought her hand up to his lips and kissed it, and then held her fingers against his cheek. "I'm still here. And I'll be here for as long as you need me."

"Galen," she whispered, not knowing what else to say. Her blue eyes searched the flickering blue image of his face. His black, now bluish-black, hair still hung in his eyes. His eyes were an even brighter blue. He was blue all over. His image shimmered. "How?"

Galen gently drew her hand to his face again, lightly drawing her smooth knuckles along the skin over his jaw.

"Life is a reflection of what is inside you," he said.

"How poetic," Noel said, her cheeks still wet but with the beginnings of a smile on her lips. Galen smiled back and arched a brow at her.

"member when I told you that classical physics always taught that there w   ly two realities – matter and energy, and quantum physics taught us that there is no matter - only energy, just in different forms?"

Blue nodded.

"Therefore everything, from actual objects to thoughts and emotions, are not determined things. They are energy, and that energy is composed of waves of possibility. On a subatomic level they are all just vibrating particles. At some point, our consciousness chooses a possibility and forms desire. At that point, all of the other possibilities collapse into one thing; our desire becomes our intent and our intent becomes our reality."

Blue closed her eyes, taking in what he said but still unable to grasp how he was *there*. Galen could see the struggle going on inside her.

Galen let go of her hand and sat back on his heels. "Do you remember what I told you about M Theory?" Blue opened her eyes and bobbed her head.

"The loaf of bread?"

Galen laughed and she was amazed at how real it was. "Yes," he told her, "the loaf of bread. There are many more dimensions than just space and time, and they are all held together, like slices in a loaf of bread. I had to move on when my body was destroyed, but I couldn't leave you. I'm just on one of the other dimensions – the slice closest to yours."

Blue smiled and was about to speak when they were interrupted by a sudden burst of sound. She jerked at the explosion outside in the street, and then cringed at the sound that followed. It sounded like a jet had flown into a recycler.

A silence followed but before she could ask Galen what he thought it was, the air around her warped and compressed, throwing her flat on the cement floor. Then the air was shattered by a sonic boom.

The new silence that followed seemed as deafening as the crashing air had been only moments before.

"Jesus!" Blue exclaimed. "What the hell was that?"

"You tell me."

Blue looked away, her eyes unfocused. "The Dragon," she said after a moment. "She's come for us."

"Holy shit."

Blue laughed nervously. "You ain't kidding."

Galen laughed and picked her hand back up. Blue smiled at him. "Just like old times?" she asked. Galen shook his head.

"Just like always," he told her. "We don't have old times. Just time."

Blue's eyes filled with tears again and he reached out a ghostly hand to wipe them away. The moment was broken by the skittering approach of running feet.

Galen dropped her hand and Blue snatched up her gun. She rose up on her knees, aiming across the open garage as two figures charged from between a dirt hauler and a tractor. They came to skidding halt just a few meters away. It was Scarlett and Calyph. Blue eased back down, sitting on her heels.

Scarlett had a look of grim determination on her face and her eyes focused immediately on Blue before glancing at the form next her. Then she did a double-take, her eyes going back to Blue before her face snapped back, her wide-eyed stare fixing on Galen. He looked at her and smiled.

"Hello, Scarlett," he said. He said it so easily. Like she had just come down for breakfast.

"You!" she whispered. Her eyes darted about, looking for what had to be projecting his image. "Where is he coming from?" she demanded. "A chip in your head?" Blue only looked her, nonplussed, lowering the hand that had picked up the pistol. It dangled against her knee like she was too tired to hold it.

Calyph held still by Scarlett's side but felt out with his metallurgic senses, feeling the machinery around them. He knew immediately that there was no machinery in their vicinity that could project a holo.

A ghost in the machine? He thought. *Is that really possible?*

His eyes flicked about, uncertain of what he was seeing. When Scarlett couldn't find where the image of Galen was coming from she shook her head, frustrated.

"We need to talk," she said, looking directly at the other Jordan.

"Not now, Scarlett," Blue told her. "Go to the Dragon." She sounded tired. Tired and sad. That, coupled with Galen's unexpected hologram, threw Scarlett off – but only for a second.

"Oh, I'll be going to the Dragon, alright. In my Fledgling. I'll be escorting you there. It will be the last time you fly Cyan." Blue looked at her like she was crazy.

"What the hell are you talking about?"

"You're never going to fly again. Not for the IGC, not for anyone." Blue only frowned at her, confused. Scarlett lifted her chin, bracing herself. "You're the enemy," she told Blue, her voice flat.

Blue barked laughter, short and harsh. "Jesus, Scarlett! You really started freaking me out there for a second. Quit fucking around. This isn't the time." She turned her face away but Scarlett stepped closer, undeterred.

"There are a lot of things about you that didn't add up, things that niggled at the back of my mind, but now they are making perfect sense. I always thought it was *you* that was so irritating, but it was all the things *about* you that didn't add up. *That's* what bothered me so much. Now I know that it's not your fault. You're just a victim."

"Victim? What are you talking about?" Blue demanded, but then sighed and shook her head. "Never mind. It doesn't matter. Scarlett, I don't have time for this. I'm...I'm more than a little *unsettled* right now and I just need some time to think, to come to terms with things."

Scarlett snorted. "Well, I'm so sorry to have come at such a bad time, but it's about to get a lot worse."

Calyph and Galen both watched the Jordans, silent.

Blue let out a deep sigh, resigned to the fact that Scarlett wasn't going to leave her alone until she said her piece. "Well, what is it?"

Scarlett tried to smirk but only managed weak grimace. She shook her hair away from her face, defiant. "You aren't real, Blue," she told her. "You're a construct." Blue looked at her in stunned silence for three seconds before she burst out laughing.

"Scarlett, I told you I don't have time for any crap right now, though if you are trying to cheer me up I appreciate it. Please just go away, I have a lot to..."

"I'm not kidding, Blue!" Scarlett said, her voice loud. *"You* are a construct!" She tossed her gaze at Galen. "He made you." Blue laughed and looked at Galen but his eyes were fixed on Scarlett. She stared right back at him. "He's with the Chimera." Blue's laughter cut off abruptly.

"That not funny, Scarlett."

"But it's true," she said. She looked from Galen to Blue. "Everything about you that made me crazy and didn't make sense makes perfect sense now." Blue was about to protest again but instead looked at Calyph.

What Scarlett was saying was totally absurd, so why wasn't he saying anything? What the hell was he even doing here?

"Your age," Scarlett continued, "the way you progressed, your knowledge of physics and starflight combined with your maddening simplicity and absolute lack of creativity - choosing Blue for both your name and your Fledgling."

"You named your Fledgling, Fledge!" Blue shouted, her temper drawn out. "That's not exactly the acme of creativity!" Scarlett shook her head.

"I tried to name him Fletch, after my Grandpa Fletcher. That dumb-ass S-4 simply heard Fledge and I never corrected him, not wanting to bother. I knew in my heart what it meant and that was good enough for me. In fact, I liked that it was just a little bit different."

"Heart!" Blue scoffed, her voice becoming low and dangerous. "If you only had a heart!" Scarlett only smiled.

"And if you only had a brain," she said. Blue's eyes widened. "Yes," Scarlett told her, "I know what all that bullshit is about now. All your silly references come from only one place. Do you know that? And I have a feeling that *that* tune is the only one you know. Can you whistle anything else? *The Starfighter's Ballad*, perhaps? Everyone knows that one, or maybe..."

"Enough Scarlett," Galen said suddenly. Blue felt a wash of relief from him stepping in, but she had already swallowed the bitter pill Scarlett had forced upon her. It stuck in her throat, slowly dissolving. Also, courtesy of the Crimson Jordan, she could now hear her favorite tune starting to bob and weave about inside her head. Scarlett and Galen began to exchange scathing words but Blue could only hear the song.

I could while away the hours, conferrin' with the flowers, consulting with the rain....

She shuddered violently.

"Enough! Go away Scarlett, I need to talk to Galen."

Scarlett ignored her request. "Do you know why it was so easy for you to get aboard the *Macedonian*? It wasn't because of any sort of skill you might think you possess. It's the same reason they let us get away!"

"It *wasn't* easy getting on the *Mace*. And they *didn't* let us get away! I had to sneak onboard in filthy clothes! Trust me, I was discreet."

"You aren't discreet! You have the most recognizable face in the universe!" Scarlett straightened and lifted her chin. "You even wear their insignia," she said with a look of disgust, throwing Blue the jacket she had mistakenly taken home with her. "The symbol for infinity."

Blue looked down at the double loop stitched onto the shiny Mylar sleeve of one of her flight jackets.

"It's an *eight* you crazy bitch!"

Scarlett shook her head, unfazed. "Why would you be eight? Cyan isn't the Eighth Dragon."

"I don't know. Why are you sixteen? The numbers obviously aren't in order - I'm sure it is just a coincidence!"

"Jade always said there were no coincidences."

"He said there were no accidents, there's a difference!"

"Why eight?"

"I don't know!"

"I do," Scarlett said, her voice smug. Calyph knew the meanings of their numbers, but was too stunned to speak. Jordan Blue started to shake with anger.

"Shut up, Scarlett! You don't know anything except that you hate me, you always have. Usually, I couldn't care less but right now you should just leave!" Scarlett shook her head.

"Not before I show you something."

"Leave her alone, Scarlett," Galen warned. He moved closer to Blue in an effort to protect her body with his own flickering form.

When Scarlett and Calyph had first burst in, Blue had immediately noted the gun in the Crimson Jordan's left hand. Her training and her instincts would not let a weapon go unchecked. But now she also saw that Scarlett was holding something in her other hand that her jacket had hidden. Small slips of paper were tucked carefully into her palm.

It wasn't the papers that gave Blue a moment of doubt, it was the way Scarlett was holding them. And the look on Scarlett's face certainly rang a bell for her. Though there were only two slips of paper, Scarlett held them like she would hold a hand of cards. They were held apart with her thumb and facing her thigh, concealing what they were. Her face had the same expression that Blue had seen so many times as she sat across the Omaha table from her – an inscrutable mask of smug distaste.

So the Queen of Spades is here to play a hand, Blue thought.

For the first time since Scarlett had started her tirade only moments ago, Blue felt a tremor of doubt. It had nothing to do with Scarlett's outrageously ridiculous claim. She was obviously playing games with her. It was the game Scarlett had chosen that made Blue nervous. She had never beaten Scarlett at Omaha. She also knew that Scarlett had only just played her first card - it was to get into Blue's head, even just a little. The seed of doubt did not even need to be planted; it just needed to be watered, for its existence to be *known*. Blue swallowed nervously, knowing two things; that the ploy had worked, and that Scarlett would always lead with her lowest card.

The song that had been playing in her mind had begun to ebb but now it came back, louder this time, as if someone were turning up the volume on a music system inside her skull.

My head I'd be scratchin' while my thoughts were busy hatching...

She felt hot tears behind her eyes as the song danced in her head. Blue shook her head hard enough to make it hurt.

"I don't care what you have! Just go!"

"Not before I give you this," Scarlett told her. She closed the distance between them with a few steps, pulling out one of the paper slips.

"Scarlett," Galen warned, as he stepped directly between the two Jordans, "don't." Scarlett ignored his warning and sidled around his image, careful not to brush against it, and pressed the slip into Blue's hand.

Blue shrank from her, but took the paper. She looked down at what Scarlett had given her and her face softened immediately with recognition and nostalgia.

It was a digi-photo on shiny photo paper, the kind that had been popular many years ago. It showed a strong, burly man holding up a little girl on his shoulder. The girl was obviously a much younger Scarlett, with dark hair, bright brown eyes, and cheeks still a bit chubby with childhood. The man's smiling face was full of joy and pride and the little girl was laughing, her hand holding a toy jet that the photo caught as she zoomed it through the air.

"My picture," Blue said softly. "Except..." She could see the difference in the photo, the difference in the two girls, right away. She frowned at it and then looked at Scarlett. "I don't understand."

"It's *my* picture," Scarlett said. "Galen took it when he moved out, god only knows why, or what else he took." She shot him an accusatory look but he shook his head.

"I didn't take it. I found it later, in a box with some of your other things that had gotten mixed in with mine. I simply didn't get rid of it."

Blue frowned at him, doubt growing like an evil weed poking its stem up through the soil. "What did you do?" she asked, her voice quiet. Galen met her eyes and then looked away. The doubt shot up and bloomed - a sickly flower that wrapped its leaves around her heart.

"The good doctor, doctored the picture," Scarlett said, her voice smug. Blue blinked at her.

"Why?"

"He was trying to give you a past! He doctored records, photos, even your pilot transcripts." She waited for Blue to make the connection but she just sat there, confused. Scarlett drew a deep breath. "You're not an anomaly Blue, you're a goddamned *construct.*"

"Shut up, Scarlett," Galen said, his voice flat. Blue tried to laugh but all that came from her throat was a sound like a wheeze.

"That can't be," she argued. "You're crazy! The whole idea is ridiculous!"

"Is it? How much of your past do you really remember?"

Blue stopped, taken aback. "Not much," she admitted. "But it's because of what I did. It's from smoking Lethe after my pilot graduation."

"Like hell it is," Scarlett told her. "The IGC would never license a pilot who used Lethe."

"You're insane!" Blue told her, but even as she said it she could see how it also made sense. And how it didn't make sense. Things were beginning to unravel. Worse, her mind was invaded by the image of the scarecrow in the movie, dancing around and singing about his damned brain.

I would not be just a nuffin'
My head all full of stuffin'
My heart all full of pain...

Pain. Her heart had been full of pain. That's why she had been using the Lethe. But why? She had graduated with honors, the youngest elf ever. She had applied to the Jordan Training Center and with her ability and scores she was practically guaranteed entrance. She had that picture that showed a happy childhood.

But if I were happy, why would I be using Lethe?

"That's why he put that scar on your face," Scarlett told her. "It gives you credibility – a bit of a past without having to say anything, and it lends a viable reason to why you can't wink your eye."

Blue shook her head. "No. He didn't put that there, I did. He just couldn't fix it." She didn't add that Galen thought the scar was a beautiful part of her.

"*He couldn't?*" Scarlett asked, her voice and expression full of mocking disbelief. "Blue, he is an astrophysicist *and a brilliant surgeon*. Look at the neural and optical work he did on your eye. Are you telling me he couldn't do a *simple skin graft?*"

"*Shut up, Scarlett!*" Galen hissed. He turned to Blue and tried to pick up her hand again but she pulled it away. Her blue eyes were wide and scared. "Noel," he said gently, it's not that I couldn't fix it, it's that I wouldn't fix it. You know why."

"He's lying," Scarlett insisted.

"Shut up, Scarlett!" Galen shouted. He looked back at Blue. All the color and life had drained from her face. Her scar stood out – bright pink and stark and ragged lines carved into a pale face that had gone two shades paler. "Jesus Christ, Noel!" he said, looking at her. "Don't listen to her!"

But the seed of doubt that Scarlett had watered had taken root in her mind.

"Galen," she whispered, "am I real?" He closed his eyes for a moment, sighing. He opened his eyes and looked at the frightened Jordan.

"Of course you are," he told her gently as he edged up next to her. Too gently. The gentle voice of a father when his daughter comes homes with a torn face and she asks him if she is still pretty.

Blue pushed him away and sank closer to the floor. She pulled away physically and mentally, pulling deep into her mind. *Yes, I have a mind, not just a mind but also a brain,*

If I only had a brain...

Remember! She demanded silently. *Remember.* She pulled back as hard as she could, making herself go back, something she never wanted to do. She remembered Galen, of course. Waking up in the white room. What was before that?

That night. Can I remember that night?

It was foggy, but it was there. She could feel it. A memory stored away in a dark attic.

The night he saved me. Had he saved me?

She dug deep and played the memory every way she could. What she couldn't see, she tried to feel. She turned the memory in imagined hands, because her mind's eye couldn't see.

Maybe you can't see because you didn't have eyes yet, she thought with growing horror. She pushed that thought from her mind as quickly as she could. She fought to keep the doubt from growing into an ugly and terrifying garden.

Had he been helping me up, or pushing me down? Was he taking the pipe out of my hand or putting it there? Was it a burning pipe he held in his hand, or a laser curette?

Blue shuddered and pressed her fists against her temples, squeezing her head.

If I only had brain...

Stop it, God Dammit, stop it! I can't wink but I can whistle. Can I? Or is it just the sound I am programmed to make when I purse my lips. No! That's crazy!

The scarecrow could whistle too, but he didn't have a brain.

If I only had a brain...

Memories. She dug for memories before Galen. There were some but they were so faded and far away. Was that from the drugs? Or was it because they didn't happen and were simply mnemonic leftovers on a high-grade chip? Or was it just that she was a young elf and never did remember much anyway because there were so few things she cared deeply about. Her sisters had all grown and were gone before she was born – of course she would hardly remember them. She remembered her parents, vaguely.

I am their daughter, aren't I? I am Noel de Rossi, aren't I? I have everything. I had everything. Then why the hell would I be smoking Lethe? The questions rose faster and faster like screams from a grave.

If I only had a grave...

Blue almost let out a feeble laugh at that but let out a scream instead as she felt a hand close over hers. It was Galen, sharper and truer than she had seen him in his new image.

"Stop it, Jordan, stop it. I can see what you are doing to yourself - just stop. If you were a construct, I wouldn't feel the need to protect you like I do." Blue sighed. His words calmed her, made her feel warm and whole.

"He's just protecting his investment," Scarlett scoffed. Galen threw her a scathing glare.

"Why the picture, then?" Blue asked. "Why did you change that picture and put it with my things? Why did you want me to think it was mine?"

"Because I wanted you to have at least one happy memory," Galen told her. His expression was pained. "You idolized your father, Noel, and he despised you. You and *all* of your sisters." Blue felt tears well up in her eyes. Something tore inside her heart. "He was an ace pilot and when his glory days were over all he had to look forward to was a son that would carry on where he left off. But your mother just kept having daughters. Being part human, your sisters matured quickly as well. But you learned and developed even faster. You were always pushing the envelope in an effort to please him. You wanted to show him that you were the child he had wished for, even if you were a girl. He never bought it."

Blue sank down, a sob escaping her lips. She looked up at Scarlett. "Why are you doing this?"

Scarlett knelt down by her side and laid a hand over her arm. "Because, you are a Jordan. And despite how crazy you make me, I could never hurt you because of the bond that we have. I don't know what the IGC will do to you, but I will try to protect you as much as I can, even if you aren't a real person. That's a lot, coming from me."

"But I am real," she told Scarlett. "I wasn't manufactured. I can't be a construct. I just can't. I have a *family*. Galen said they..."

"He knows your *family* alright," Scarlett sneered. "He's been working for them for a hundred years, or more."

"No," Blue told her. "I would know that."

"Didn't you ever see his lab coat? The initials monogrammed on the left side?"

Blue nodded. "There was a DR, for doctor."

Scarlett shook her head. "It stands for de Rossi." Blue looked as if she had been slapped. Her eyes sought Galen's.

"Is that true?" she asked. Galen hesitated and then nodded.

"Yes, but it has nothing to do with you or with GwenSeven! I was working on the Thermopylae for their space faring division, you know that."

Scarlett snorted. "It was a front."

"Don't listen to her," Galen said, his eyes boring into the Crimson Jordan. "She is just jealous. She has always been jealous of you and angry with me."

"That's not true!" Scarlett said. She took a shaky breath. "Not entirely." Galen turned his eyes from her to Jordan Blue, his expression softening.

"She is out to get you Noel. Don't let her. You are *real*." Blue looked at him, her eyes full of hope and fear and he pressed his lips together into a tight line. "Do you remember the rings of Saturn?" he asked. Blue shook her head, but slowly, as if she wasn't sure. Galen nodded. "You need to. You need to remember your family, even though you don't want to. You need to remember the rings of Saturn, it will prove what I am saying is true."

"I can't remember anything," she said, her voice cracking on the last word. She turned and faced Scarlett. "But I know," she told her, "that I am real." Scarlett shook her head.

"You are a construct, and his greatest work." Scarlett laughed softly. "Here, where a construct isn't even allowed aboard an IGC ship, he manufactured one that not only got through, and is not only in a current position of power, but might one day could have been Captaining one of the most powerful ships in the universe." She turned to Galen. "I've got to hand it to you, you really are a genius."

"You crazy fucking bitch," Galen hissed. "You'll stop at nothing to bring her down! What is this really about? Is it about not being able to live with the fact that she is a better pilot, a better *person* than you are?" Scarlett shook her head.

"She's not a person. And it's about stopping you."

"I'm not doing anything!"

"You are supporting the rebellion."

"What you are saying doesn't even make sense, do you realize that? How could I be working for both the Chimera and the de Rossi family? GwenSeven is the largest financial supporter to the IGC! They are openly anti-Chimera!"

"Not all of them," Scarlett said. The look Galen gave her was so caustic that she knew if they had been alone he would have killed her.

Blue sat and listened to them bicker, numb at first but after a while she felt a spark of anger growing within her. The spark blossomed into flame.

How dare they treat me like this! She thought. *I am a person! I have a brain, not some goddamned chip! I don't give a shit what either one of them has to say. I've had enough.*

"Shut up the both of you!" Blue shouted, rising to her feet. "This is insane!"

"What is insane," Scarlett shouted back, "is how long the two of you have gotten away with this charade!"

"Fuck you Scarlett!" Blue nearly screamed, struggling for breath. "Galen is right, you've always had it out for me. What's more, do you realize, that everything you have accused me of applies to you as well? Maybe *you're* the construct!"

Scarlett laughed. "Don't be ridiculous!"

"It's no more ridiculous than what you are throwing at me. After all, you were with Galen before I was. Who's to say he didn't make you?" She gave Scarlett a look heavy with contempt and disgust. "And then threw you away to do your dirty work once he was finished."

Now it was Scarlett's turn to look slapped. Galen grinned. Calyph looked terrified.

"And, since you brought it up, do you know any other tune besides *The Starfighter's Ballad*? As I recall, that was the first song on Galen's music chip. It always came on as soon as I started the podment sound system."

Scarlett's jaw clenched as the flickering form of Galen rose to its feet and Blue took a menacing step towards her.

"The reason we probably got away so easy on the *Mace* was because of *you*, and your obvious relationship with their Commander." Her last comment made Scarlett's clenched jaw drop open. Blue's smile became as malevolent as Scarlett's had been only moments ago. "I heard you two over the com-link," she whispered knowingly.

Scarlett, still speechless, shook her head from side.

"Was that your boyfriend that infiltrated the Ventricle on the Dragon?"

"Don't you call him that!"

"And we never found out how he got on board. He was probably safe within your quarters for weeks!"

"He was not!"

"Then why didn't you kill him when you had the chance? You obviously knew it was his jet! You could have put a Claymore in there, taking out who you *knew* was a leader in the rebellion! But, instead, you rig his fighter with tear gas! Like some high-schooler pulling a prank!"

"Stop it!" Scarlett shouted, fuming. "I don't have to explain myself to you!"

"Because you can't! You probably weren't even captured! You were just brought in to see how much we knew. Or to make sure your cover hadn't been blown."

Scarlett looked like a pressure cooker that was about to blow. Blue laughed. She had enough of Scarlett beating her down for every goddamned thing. It was time she got what was coming to her.

"Maybe they burned you just so it would look legit. Or maybe they were just destroying evidence. Did you have a rib-wire, perhaps?"

"They tortured me! They were trying to draw the Dragon!"

"Perhaps," Blue went on, "But perhaps you were in on that as well. I talked to Dr. Westerson. He said they put a Chimeran tissue ichor on you to heal your burns. What would you like to explain first – why they used it, or how it worked so well?"

"How, how dare he!" Scarlett stammered. "He's a doctor! That information is privileged and private!"

Blue's laugh was high and mocking. "You're IGC property. Nothing is privileged *or* private! And, being a Jordan, I outrank Doc Westerson. He answered every question I put to him." Scarlett was so angry she started to shake, which only made Blue laugh again. "Look at you Scarlett! *You* are the one with the terrible temper - you've had it for as long as I've known you. I think there is a name for that." Blue tapped her lip with one finger, pretending to think. "What is that phrase I'm thinking of? That colloquialism used to express that hotheaded rage you work yourself into...hmmm...oh yes! A Chimeran temper. That's what it's called."

"Stop it!" Scarlett shouted. "Stop it! How dare you try to make me question my own reality!"

"Why shouldn't I? You're making me question mine!"

Scarlett shook herself as if to rid herself of doubt and remember what she had come to do. To Blue, she looked like a wet dog shaking water from its fur. Galen now watched their exchange with mild amusement. Calyph had simply stood there the entire time, seemingly too shocked to move.

Blue took a deep breath, feeling more sure of herself by the second. The doubt within her soul had wilted.

I am real, she thought. *I am not a brainless scarecrow – though Scarlett is obviously as the heartless as the tin man. My god, where is the cowardly lion in this story?* She suppressed a lunatic giggle and took a deep breath. She faced Scarlett with her chin lifted.

"What you are trying to do here is pathetic, Scarlett. I am real. I am not manufactured."

"You think so?"

Blue nodded. "I *know* so." Her voice was firm, as was her conviction. "I am Noel de Rossi, the sixth daughter of Christa de Rossi and the bastard that she married."

Blue could remember him now, though the image of him in her mind was blurred. She could remember clearly how he had been – callous and mean. The picture had been a lie, but one Galen had given to her out of love. She was their daughter, their sixth daughter, even if she had been unwanted.

"Are you sure about that?" Scarlett asked, her voice even.

"Yes!"

Scarlett stepped forward once again and gave Blue the second piece of paper that she had been holding, her eyes never leaving Blue's. It was her last card, and Blue knew that it wasn't a bluff. Scarlett's smile told that much, at least. Whatever she now held, was Scarlett's winning hand.

Deflated, all the wind gone from her sails, Blue simply held the paper for a few seconds, staring at Scarlett. She knew that look. She knew that smile. She had played Omaha with Scarlett enough times at the JTC. It was the same look Scarlett had when she knew that she couldn't be beat.

It was her ace in the hole.

The ace of spades.

The doubt inside Noel, so recently wilted, pushed forth a thorny vine bearing a dirty flower. It rose up and wound around her throat.

Blue swallowed and looked down at the paper, already tasting defeat. Knowing she was beat. She let out a shaky breath and turned the paper over so she could read the words that were printed there in choppy, dot matrix.

It was biographical readout, printed on the flimsy, thin paper used by the trolls. She looked up at Calyph and suddenly knew the purpose of his presence. He was there to validate whatever Scarlett was going to claim. Or at least validate the source from which she had received the readout.

The decaying flower of doubt opened like a baleful eye.

"The King of Spades," Blue whispered, looking at Calyph, a small smile playing at the edge of her scarred lip. The Engineer felt a chill run up his spine. Blue looked back down at the paper. It was an abbreviated bio on her mother, dotted out in a few lines of scoot. It had her place of birth and date, names of parents, places of residence, religious background and so forth. Blue frowned as she read it, wondering what Scarlett's point was to all this. When she got to the bottom of the readout she knew.

I am Noel de Rossi, the sixth daughter of Christa de Rossi and the bastard that she married, she told herself like she had told Scarlett just seconds ago.

Everything began to spin inside her head. Feelings, memories, the past, the present, fears, love, hate, hope. They flew around like a scarecrow caught in a cyclone.

I am Noel de Rossi, the sixth daughter of Christa de Rossi and the bastard that she married.

Blue sank back down to her knees.

I am Noel de Rossi, the sixth daughter of Christa de Rossi and the bastard that she married.

It was a single line on a flimsy piece of paper. One line at the end of a bio that was public information. Just one simple line of only four words. The last line of scoot for the micro-bio on Christa de Rossi read:

Known Children: Daughters - Five.

Blue let the slip of paper fall from her lifeless fingers. Her eyes found Galen's, but she hardly saw him, her eyes were already very far away.

"Noel," he said. His voice was gentle but distant. "Stop this madness. Stop letting her get to you. You are real." Her vacant eyes looked into his. Looked through his.

"As real as you?" she asked. Galen sighed.

"No, not like me. You are *real*. You are..." He watched as she slowly reached for her right wrist. "No! Noel! What are you doing?" Galen's voice was low and barely controlled, knowing full well what she was after. "Don't do it, Noel! Stop! You have to listen to me! You have to believe me!"

Blue slipped her fingers under the platinum band around her left wrist, searching out the switch for the com-link.

"Noel, listen, you have to remember the rings of Saturn. *YOU HAVE TO FIND FAITH!*"

His final shout sounded far away and the image of Galen himself blinked out of existence as Noel cut the link.

Jordan Blue collapsed, feeling sick and angry and lost. She closed her eyes for a long time waiting for the feelings to pass but they only churned around inside her. She felt drained.

Fuck it, she finally thought. *I know who I am. At least I think I do.* She chuffed out soft laughter. She suddenly thought of something Galen had told her years ago. He had been quoting one of the great physicists of Earth.

As far as the laws of mathematics refer to reality, he had said, *they are not certain; and as far as they are certain, they do not refer to reality.*

She thought about what Galen had told her about love and intent, and about turning conscious thought into physical reality. *Is reality simply what we choose to create from the ether? Are any us of who we really think we are?*

She looked up at Scarlett who, along with Calyph, had remained silent and motionless for the last minute. Scarlett looked calm, but her hands were balled into fists and Blue could see that she was still shaking. She looked at Scarlett's face and let out another soft cackle of nervous laughter.

"What?" Scarlett demanded.

"You're bleeding,' Blue told her.

Scarlett's hand went up to her nose and came away bloody. Blue's cheek puckered as her smile widened into a gruesome grin.

"Your mouth, too."

Her soft laughter echoed throughout the hollow spaces of the hangar and echoed in Scarlett's left ear that, also, was beginning to trickle blood.

AUTHOR'S NOTE

Questions? Of course, there are always questions. The one I ask most often is, where the hell are my keys?

First, I want to say that I did not leave this book hanging with uncertainty just to sell a second book. In fact, I did not intend to answer any questions in the next book. But, for fear of reprisal and bodily harm from my closest friends, I might answer a few.

Second, I should warn you, I will ask a few more.

The questions most obvious here are: Is Blue real? Is Scarlett? Is anyone? My question is: Are you? Are you sure? Is anyone?

If so, how real are you? Are you living in a reality that you have created, or are you living in one created for you? Are you who you want to be, or who someone else wants you to be?

Like the troll, you have the answers; you just need to ask the right questions.

For me, right now, it isn't where are the keys, but what are the keys? Choice. And, of course, intention.